THIS SIDE
OF GONE

THIS SIDE OF GONE

A Novel

Saundra Mitchell

WILLIAM MORROW

An Imprint of HarperCollins*Publishers*

For Eden, who made me write this *book*

THIS SIDE
OF GONE

Prologue

*S**he was always going to be a victim.***

Her family guaranteed it—the way they huddled like vermin in their estate of trailers just outside town. Nearly every last one of them, they were all dirty blonds made dirtier by intermittent access to running water. Only one of them had electricity, for fuck's sake.

Extension cords wound from one trailer to the next, rat kings dishing out stolen electricity on bright orange tails. When the lights were on for one, they were on for all. And when the lights were on, the Adairs were probably up to something.

Half the girls were pregnant; half of them lived with their single mothers. The rest? With boyfriends and baby daddies or random friends with an extra room. Filthy toddlers ran around in dollar-store diapers and layers of grime. They still had pacifiers, and bottles full of Mountain Dew and water.

The boys were out shooting shit with anything from an air rifle to a shotgun, depending on the boy's age and list of priors. But as soon as they hit the late teens, they sprouted pedo goatees and an unusual knack for chemistry that wasn't reflected in their schoolwork. That was the hell of it. The Adairs were smart.

People who wanted something questionable knew they could ask an Adair. Drugs, yes. Guns, obviously. Rumor had it that one of the aunts (or "aunts," everybody out there was related by birth or choice) was the go-to for the abortion pill and under-the-table antibiotics.

The less industrious Adairs just made a business of stealing. Didn't matter what; they'd find a way to unload it. Long Paul Adair—six and a half feet tall in bare feet—did five years for car theft. Little Paul (five-two) was still at State for his Chocolate for Charity racket. The candy? Stolen. The charity? Little Paul Adair's vape fund.

Petty theft, grand theft, larceny, shoplifting (an Auntie Adair special), burglary, robbery—it didn't matter if it was nailed down, locked, or alarmed. The Adairs would find a way. If they had just used all that intelligence for something worthwhile . . .

And Avery Adair wasn't going to be that exception. She was seventeen, pretty, but not quiet. Not neat. She didn't work hard for her grades; she wasn't the singular. The one. The good apple in the rotten barrel. She had weed, for the right person. She didn't start fights at school, but she finished them, oh yes she did.

And last anybody saw, Avery left for school and never came back. It took a week for her mama to report her missing, and making the report wasn't even her idea. She figured Avery'd had enough, since her mother had just brought home a squalling newborn. When you haven't got anything going for you, running away seems like a reasonable escape.

To the disinterested police, it was pretty obvious she was dead. There wasn't a body yet, but the eighty-seven dollars she had in the bank hadn't moved, she hadn't called home, and there wasn't a tower in the whole county that could find her phone. The assumption: she'd jumped all in, into the family business, and paid for it with her life. Oh well. Another wasted Adair.

Her last digital signature was a single ping north of town, at a

McDonald's, where she bought two large fries and a soda. After that, Avery Adair dropped off the map.

Where she was, it wasn't snowing, or raining; the sun didn't shine, and the moon couldn't make a dent in the dark. The temperature didn't change much, and the wind didn't blow. She was just another statistic in a family full of them. Poor Avery Adair, trailer trash. Dumpster rat.

Nobody was ever going to miss her.

Chapter 1

Third store, and if Henk's General didn't have shutter hooks, then Vinnie Taylor was shit out of ideas.

She'd moved to Wills Harbor two months ago, and trying to find anything was an . . . adventure.

Wills Harbor clung to the Maryland shore, aggressively quaint with brick and brightly painted rowhouses all the way up to the water. Cafés and restaurants crowded between souvenir shops and historical markers. There was an ice-cream store on every corner, and a trolley, an honest-to-God trolley, that jangled up and down the narrow streets on a regular schedule. Every weekend was a festival—Blue Crab Festival, Blue Moon Festival, Pride, Juneteenth—she'd never seen so many different kinds of bunting.

The whole tourism bag meant no box stores, no Walmarts. Even the Starbucks was disguised as an olde timey nautical shop. The familiar green lady presided over a window full of anchors, net, and plastic marine life. Because of this dedication to aesthetic, Vinnie was still figuring out where to buy most anything.

She was used to the Midwest's 24/7 Meijer supercenters, where she could pick up air filters, white bread, and work shoes, all in the same two hundred fifty thousand square feet. Errands, the least favorite part of her week, used to take an hour or two on

Sunday. Now it was a trip all over hell's half acre. She had to buy milk at Ohland's Grocery, shop rags at Dollar Gala, toilet paper at the Red Stripe, and hopefully, shutter hooks at Henk's General.

An item, by the way, she'd had no idea existed until she rented the octagonal cottage in the woods. Real shutters, Rich Watts, the landlord, had pointed out on the walk-through. Hadn't bothered to mention that if she wanted them to stay open or closed or in any fixed state whatsoever, they needed *hooks*.

It was hard enough learning to sleep in the wilderness when she was used to the city. It was worse when rest finally came and the wind rattled the shutters like they had a warrant. (That was another novelty: wind. Wind all the time, from every direction. Wind, even when it wasn't due to storm.)

So. Hooks. Henk's General was a step in the right direction. It was the first store with nails and screws, so it was possible she was onto something. Vinnie stood in an aisle full of hardware, fingering one box, then another. But she wasn't reading the labels.

The voices in the next aisle held her attention. It didn't take her long to pin names on them either. They were young, high school age, if Vinnie had to guess.

"Hannah, for real?" the boy repeated, voice slightly raised. A touch nasal, somewhere between a whine and a warning.

"I'm not messing around, Tyler," Hannah replied. No fry, and no fear either. Solid as concrete, planted in the ground. "I'm working."

Tyler huffed a laugh. "It's your dad's store."

"I said no."

They shuffled, sneakers squeaking and rustling against linoleum. Then, suddenly, Tyler blurted, "Seriously, quit being a little—!"

"Get out," Hannah said.

The hair on Vinnie's arms prickled. This was none of her business, and it sounded like Hannah was doing just fine. But Tyler's tone, that dangerous edge of a golden boy who is shocked, *shocked*, to hear a *no* tossed in his general direction, prickled in Vinnie's ear. Grabbing a box at random, she walked to the end of her aisle.

Hannah came into view, backed up against a shelf. To Vinnie, she looked like a toddler in mascara and a shop apron. Tyler clocked only slightly older; like the mean kindergarten kid who liked to kick shit and smile while he did it.

Professionally, Vinnie guessed they were sixteen or seventeen. He was definitely shaving, and the first hint of cheekbones carved some of the baby softness from her face.

Despite the facts, these kids looked like *kids*.

They all did now. Going through a drive-thru at midnight, Vinnie did a double-take at the ten-year-old at the window. In reality, he was probably twenty, but youth looked very *young* to her anymore. Felt like it too. That was part of why she'd had to get out of that place.

"We reserve the right to refuse service to anyone," Hannah said. Her eyes darted toward Vinnie as she came around the corner. She had that tremble on, that weight of holding it together while trying to do her job at the same time.

Because Tyler was the kind of shit-heel who knew how to play the adults around him, he instantly softened. Put on a friendly—warming—smile. He had charisma that he could turn off and on, and right now, it was full-blast Eddie Haskell. He stepped gallantly out of the way so Vinnie could walk on by, no doubt ready to play the "crazy bitch" card on Hannah as soon as she left.

Cutting between them, Vinnie held up the box. "I just moved

here. Are these the right hooks for my shutters, or am I looking for something else?"

Hannah exhaled. Turning on her customer-service voice, she said, "Oh no, those are for hanging tomato baskets."

"I could show you," Tyler offered, still slick with insincerity. He wasn't tall enough to loom over her, the way he did Hannah. He bounced off Vinnie's personal space, recalibrated, tried again.

"I thought you were leaving."

"Yeah, no," he said with a laugh, and boy, he sounded genuine. He tried to catch Hannah's gaze. "We were just messing around. Right, Han?"

To her credit, Hannah shook her head. "Wrong. You should go."

His mask slipped, just a little. The corner of his lip curled in disgust. Puffing himself up to seem bigger, he said, "For real?"

It was a reflex. Out of instinct, Vinnie flicked open her jacket. Her Glock hung there in a shoulder holster, heavy but comfortable. Familiar, even. But as soon as she touched the holster, she felt two things. One, a sick sense of reckoning, and two, an acrid taste of fear. She had nothing to back up that hand but bullets, and she wasn't about to shoot a *child* in a small-town general store.

But *he* didn't know that.

With the blood draining from his face, Tyler puffed himself up a little more. He didn't look bigger. He just looked like a scared kid pretending to be brave. Flashing an even broader smile, a feral show of teeth and desperation, he said, "Whoa, lady, lighten up. Nothing like that is happening here."

Vinnie took a step closer, silent. She called bullshit with the cut of her gaze and her flat, unimpressed expression. Tyler hesitated, then took a step back when she pushed closer still. Lowering her voice, she murmured, just for him, "That's right. It's not. Bye,

Tyler." He made a sound, the threat of a response, and she repeated, "Bye, Tyler."

Torn between fight or flight, Tyler took one last look at Hannah, then tried to play it off. "What the fuck ever. Byeeeeee," he said, mocking with a feminine voice. Strolling out, he casually slapped at a Missing poster next to the door, tearing it down, then sidled away. As soon as the bell rang, the door closed, and the air slipped back into the room.

Hannah brushed herself off awkwardly. "Sorry about him, he's—"

"Nope," Vinnie said. "Don't apologize for him. You all right?"

A blush crawled Hannah's cheeks and she waved a hand without making eye contact. "Fine. Let me get you the shutter hooks," she said, and disappeared down the next aisle. Over the top of it, she called, "Can I ask you a question?"

"You bet," Vinnie said, tamping down on the nausea that always came after the burst of adrenaline. She needed to mind her own business, she told herself. She needed to quit carrying the gun. Just the prospect made her dizzy, numb panic masking her face, tightening her throat. Not yet. Maybe one day, but not yet.

"Are you a cop?"

Jesus. The question burned like a brand. She *really* should have stayed out of it. Hannah would have been fine if she'd just interrupted with a boring customer question. Tyler was a douchebag, but he wasn't out of control. He wasn't the kind of kid who acted out in front of adults. He counted on them to vouch for his character later. Vinnie had met a thousand Tylers in her life; she could have defused the whole situation without getting involved.

"Are you?" Hannah asked again, slightly plaintive.

"Not anymore," Vinnie finally said.

There was a long quiet. Then Hannah headed for the counter. She still made no eye contact; she quietly rang up the package but closed the register drawer when it opened for payment. She wrote the receipt, then dropped both in a paper bag with HENK's GENERAL printed on it in red. She put the package on the counter, right next to a flyer taped there. The same one Tyler had ripped off the wall.

AVERY ADAIR, AGE 17, MISSING—ENDANGERED.

Vinnie reached for the bag, then hesitated. What was this kid saying without saying? Was she afraid to be here alone? Afraid to end up like the kid on that poster? Vinnie studied her face, then asked, "You need me to stay?"

"My dad'll be back soon," Hannah said. It was abrupt. Like she was cutting off a thought, or a moment. With a plastic smile back in place, she said, "Thanks for shopping Henk's!"

Suddenly, Vinnie had a hundred questions for Hannah. But she swallowed them like dry aspirin. Questions weren't her job anymore; Hannah's silence and unspoken stress were none of her business. Vinnie opened the door to leave, the bell merry and oblivious, and she fought the temptation to look back. She failed. Hannah still stood at the counter, now folded into herself.

Vinnie said, "Thanks again."

"Welcome to Wills Harbor," Hannah said, then turned away.

Chapter 2

"We talked about this yesterday," Vinnie told her cell phone impatiently.

Hefting a toolbox onto the floor, Vinnie tapped it with her foot. The box was mostly red, with mangy patches of rust for variety. A look at its crusty hinges and broken lock promised that the thing probably housed fifty thousand spider babies. Perfect.

If Vinnie had realized that DIY came with the cozy cottage package, she wouldn't have sold her tools with the rest of her possessions.

"No, we didn't. How long are you planning on being gone?" Bev Taylor asked.

If Vinnie was impatient, Bev was irritated. That was her perpetual state of being, aside from the omnipresent confusion that only seemed to present itself when it came time for her to remember anything Vinnie had ever done right. "How much vacation can you possibly have?"

Rolling her eyes, Vinnie flipped open the toolbox. Oversized screwdrivers rested on a nest of Allen wrenches, bathing in flecks of iron oxide and metal shavings. "It's not a vacation, Ma. I *retired*."

"Well, la-di-da," Bev replied. "Paint a red rose on your ass. Must be nice; some of us work for a living."

It was all Vinnie could do to point out that Bev hadn't worked for a living for almost twenty-five years. She coasted on better-than-average looks and a personality that was charmingly quirky as long as you weren't related to her. The only thing that kept Vinnie silent was experience. Pointing out her mother's bullshittery never improved a conversation. So, instead Vinnie said, "I know."

Bev made a ticking sound at her. "Are you trying to get me off the phone?"

"No, Ma."

"Some people don't have mothers to talk to."

"I know, Ma."

And with that, Bev was off on a haunting but familiar refrain that Vinnie liked to call the Parade of Dead People. It started with the memories of grandparents that Vinnie no longer had, and how Bev would *kill* to have one more phone call with them. Then it progressed to great-aunts and uncles, cousins of unknown provenance, and every single friend Bev had ever lost in the "senior community" where she now lived.

All Vinnie had to do was nod along and input the right re-sponses: *I know, Ma. I'm sorry, Ma. Oh, I didn't know she died, Ma.* As long as she kept up, Vinnie was free to do just about anything she wanted—which, at the moment, was fishing for the right size Phillips head with a flathead the size of a sharpening steel.

"Fuck yes," she muttered to herself, claiming her prize.

"Excuse me?" Bev said.

"I said, fuck, that's sad."

Mournfully, Bev replied, "It really is. Seventy-four years old. So young. What are you doing? What is that racket?"

"I'm fixing the shutters."

"What do you know about shutters?" Bev demanded.

Nothing, Vinnie thought. But it didn't take a Rhodes scholar to figure out that an eye needed a hook. The clues were all there: the scuff marks on cedar shake siding; empty, blackened holes where something used to be; and a heavy-duty loop that dangled for want of a mate. No matter what she said, her mother would twist it, so Vinnie stuck with "It's not hard."

"But is it your responsibility?" Bev asked. "Don't you have a landlord?"

Before Vinnie could respond, she heard the crunch of tires on gravel. The unpaved drive was private; somebody was either lost or way the hell out of place. Abandoning the toolbox, Vinnie slowly walked around the cottage. There had been birds and squirrels chattering a minute ago. Now they'd gone quiet.

Sputtering into the phone, Bev demanded, "Did I lose you?"

"Ma, shhh," Vinnie said, then stuffed her phone in her back pocket. Her mother could bitch at her ass for the time being. Walking up to the porch, Vinnie stood in front of the forest-green door and waited. The wind rose up, and it carried a soft puff of dust with it.

After a moment, a soldier-blue Interceptor appeared. It rolled to a stop behind Vinnie's rental. The sun bounced off the tinted windows, but the spotlight and roof bar were familiar enough. Kerry County Sheriff's Department.

The engine cut, and the SUV's hidden driver sat in silence. They didn't open a window, a door. Nothing.

Her heart squeezed in two, then four, trying to compress itself into a stone. Her breath thinned, and she scrubbed the rising sweat off her palms and onto her jeans. Her lizard brain screamed at her to run. Where? Nowhere. Anywhere. Just run, runrunrun!

Instead, Vinnie sweated it for a minute, then started for the driver's side. Her stomach roiled, both sour and rising, but nobody could see that. What was visible was that *walk*, that heavy-gaited, carrying-a-lead-weighted-belt-on-her-hips kind of walk. She couldn't help it.

"You lost?" Vinnie asked, thumping the driver's-side window with her knuckles.

"Are you talking to me?" Bev mumbled from Vinnie's pocket.

The window glided down an inch. "Ma'am, step back, please."

Head full of screaming static, Vinnie did as he asked, then crossed her arms over her chest. Planted her feet so she wouldn't wobble when he got out. And secretly, she gave herself a little squeeze for comfort, because she had no idea where this was going.

It wouldn't have always unnerved her to see a cop in her driveway, but that was *before*. She wasn't part of his brotherhood anymore. Whatever professional courtesy she could have hoped for had burned to ashes with all the bridges behind her.

Her brain squirmed, protesting a vulnerability she hadn't felt in twenty-five years. That she didn't care to feel now, even though she'd put herself here on purpose.

The cop took his time, then finally stepped out. Dust dulled the black of his tactical boots, but his brown slacks were precision-perfect. It looked like his duty shirt, mostly hidden by a bullet-proof shirt-vest, had seen the business end of an iron recently. He even tucked his campaign hat against his chest as he stepped out.

He was handsome, in his own way. Like old Italian art, with dark, silver-streaked curls, heavy-lidded eyes brown as espresso, and full lips that dripped from his bronze, rounded face. Back in the day—hell, back last year—she might have been happy to invite him inside for a couple of hours just on looks alone. Somehow, that year ago felt like a lot longer as she fought her anxiety, and the flop sweat painting the back of her shirt.

As he closed the car door, he dropped the hat on his head, then rested his hand on his belt. Just above the holster snap, thumb ready to break, hand ready to pull. Instinct. Habit.

"Ma'am, I'm Sergeant Nathan Rosier with the Kerry County Sheriff's Department. Just to make sure we're on the same page here, your name is?"

Vinnie squinted at him. He sounded genial, but he wasn't here for coffee and cake. This was button-down procedure. She lifted her chin and said, "I assume since you're in my driveway, you already know. Vanetta Taylor."

Bev raised her voice, demanding, "Is that a man?"

Vinnie's pulse spiked, and she told Rosier, "I'm reaching for my back pocket. I need to hang up on my mother."

Chapter 3

Without amusement, Rosier nodded. "Go ahead."

With a quick "I gotta go, Ma," Vinnie ended the call without a goodbye. Then, she turned the phone to Do Not Disturb, because Bev would be calling back at least fourteen times until she got the hint they were done talking for the day. Vinnie waved the phone, then slid it back into her pocket. Now you see it, now you don't.

She squinted at Rosier again, sizing him up. Neat uniform could mean any number of things; the lack of smile when she told him she needed to hang up meant he was good at cop-face: hiding his humanity with a flat affect. The Joe Friday act meant they would not be stepping inside for this chat.

If they did, it would be worse than the panic attack she was currently staving off. He would mentally catalogue her possessions, rate them on a scale of normal to deviant, and keep in mind anything unusual to use against her later. That's how good warrants got written, and it wasn't something he could turn off even if this *had* been a social call.

Vinnie said, "So this is the welcome wagon, huh?"

"Could you tell me where you've been today, Ms. Taylor?" he asked, straight-up ignoring her question.

Her stomach coiled like a viper, and her mouth went sour. Yep. He was here for a reason, but Vinnie wasn't about to let him lead her in incriminating circles. With a shrug, she said, "I'm not under arrest; I don't have to answer that. And I'm not going to. You have a good day."

"Is this really how you want to introduce yourself?"

"Actually," Vinnie said, backing toward her front door, "yeah. I don't wanna make friends. I don't wanna make enemies. I just wanna be left alone."

Rosier didn't move—but he didn't leave either. His physical presence applied its own kind of pressure. Easily six-two, broad shoulders—then the body armor, it all added its own gravity to the situation. "If you don't want to make enemies, why are you threatening teenagers in hardware stores?"

Now Vinnie smiled. Somebody had run and tattled to his parents; said parents complained to Brooklyn Nine-Nine, and now Brooklyn Nine-Nine was waving his badge around like it mattered in this particular situation. Should she have put her hand on her holster as she moved that kid along? No. Was it a crime? Also no. She shook her head and said, "Uh-huh, you have a good day."

Before she could open the door, Rosier broke. Slightly. It was in his voice—frustration touched with determination. "If he did something to Hannah, I'm all ears. I hear the rumors, but nobody *talks*."

"What kind of rumors?" Vinnie asked. *Fuck, don't ask questions*, she told herself. *Don't get interested.*

"The kind you'd expect to hear about a star athlete in a small town."

The wind shifted. It felt a little darker out, as if a cloud had covered the sun. Of course small towns had rot. Everywhere has rot. It's how people treated it that mattered. But that wasn't Vinnie's job anymore. She'd made sure of that. With a hand on the doorknob, Vinnie said, "That doesn't surprise me one bit. But I'm sorry, I can't help."

"You scared him," Rosier said. Offered, really. He was coaxing her toward talking.

"Then he scares easy."

Rosier sighed. Letting his mask fall, he changed. Suddenly, his unreadable eyes held warmth and sympathy; the gentle lines on his face told his history. This was a man who cared about what he was doing, and Vinnie recognized that.

She'd stood in front of that mirror herself. If she had to guess, based on rank, based on the weathered softness of a jaw that didn't match the tight cut of his body, he was around her age—fifty, fifty-five. Young enough to stay fit; old enough to have to work at it. Firmly, she reminded herself, none of that was her concern.

"I'm going in now."

"Wait," he said. "Wait. We're on the same side, here."

"We're really not," Vinnie replied. "Go ahead and leave a card in the doorframe if you want. I won't be calling. Whatever shit Joe College gets up to on your watch is your responsibility, not mine."

"If you believed that, you wouldn't have stepped in at Henk's."

With an empty laugh, Vinnie said, "You don't know me well enough to know what I believe, Sergeant. Have a good day."

Closing her ears, she went inside and shut the door, firmly. She locked it, then pressed her brow against the wood. Every breath felt cut out of her, but slowly it softened. Quiet erased the numbness; her heart remembered how to beat.

It was over. She was fine. And Rosier seemed like a rulebook guy (with her, anyway. She was a grown-ass white woman—intellectually, she knew he wasn't going to burst through the door and demand answers). Now, if there really was something bigger going on with this kid, Rosier might keep hounding her. But he wasn't going to do it with blunt force.

She'd have to keep her head on a swivel when she went into town; she'd probably find him watching her and making notes in a chicken scrawl that was impossible for anyone but him to read.

Yeah, if Rosier decided to excavate her past, he'd have all kinds of shit to hold against her. And he *would*, because there was one simple rule in the police: with us, or against us. Leaving didn't erase the betrayal, not for the rank and file.

Anxiety came for her again, and she took a deep breath. Another. She reminded herself she didn't live in that world anymore. She lived in this one, where a big day was getting groceries and running errands. She was a private citizen—a private citizen who had some maintenance to do, if she hoped to get any sleep.

Listening for the sound of tires on gravel, she waited until he was good and gone. Then, she shook out the last of her nerves, turned, and looked around.

The cottage wasn't what she'd imagined, but that's what happened when you rented a place sight unseen. In her head, *cottage* meant something Hansel-and-Gretely: pitched roof, whitewashed walls. Maybe on the inside, a Hobbit hole, dark and cozy and full of nooks. Fireplaces were supposed to be involved.

Instead, what she got was an artist's interpretation—literally. According to the landlord, the place was built in the 1930s by a painter starving for different kinds of light. She'd plunked down a frame in the shape of an octagon, cutting the cottage into pie slices of illumination. Each exterior wall boasted tall double-hung windows, a different view through each one.

The middle of the octagon was wide open, furnished with IKEA sleekness in shades of grey. A couch, a chair, a bookshelf—and a few oversized poufs that could serve as decoration or seating on a case-by-case basis.

A curated selection of nonfiction, mostly history and biographies, lined the shelves—chosen more for their aesthetics than their content. For extra warmth, a black potbellied stove rested in a brick footprint between two windows.

Separated from the living room by nothing but a wood-and-paper divider was the eat-in kitchen. All the appliances in the kitchen came in miniature, as if the cottage were an oversized dollhouse. They were top of the line, gleaming in chrome next to the modern grey cabinets. To save space, the kitchen table folded flat against the wall like a Murphy bed, its two matching chairs hanging on pegs beside it.

A long wall on the north side of the house cut out private slices for the bathroom and bedroom.

Like the kitchen, the bathroom was brand-new and designed with spartan luxury in mind. The whole room was slate tile that drained in the middle. It had to, because the rainfall shower wasn't contained by a box. It hung in the center of the ceiling, ready to wash the whole place down once someone figured out how to use the digital panel that controlled it.

In addition, there was a Japanese soaking tub, and a dark granite sink just wide enough to wash one hand at a time. The only fully dry seat in the house was the commode, and that was a little cramped because of the minimalist linen shelves stacked above it. This window was covered with a stained-glass cling, crowded red roses with emerald vines. Probably, the bath had sold some people on this place. Vinnie thought it looked like a vampire's locker room.

The bedroom resembled the original artist's vision the most, Vinnie assumed. The walls were bare cedar, windows framed in each outside angle. The vaulted ceiling was definitely original, although the rustic, antlered chandelier was probably not. The bedroom boasted a wide sleigh bed and matching nightstand on one side, an armoire in place of a closet in the middle, and a writing desk with chair on the opposite.

A few tasteful throws and pillows decorated the space; pleasantly monochrome photos of the house itself, and its surroundings, hung on the walls. The place was beautiful, but that's not why Vinnie picked it off the rental website. No, what sold it for her was a drone shot, revealing the perfect isolation.

It was the mile-long private drive, back to a house set in the woods, above the water—isolated from the rest of the world. It was quiet, the closest neighbor easily another mile in either direction. No landscaping to maintain, just natural wildflowers and grasses that gave way to the trees. This place was sturdy enough to weather a nor'easter, and self-contained with its own well and generator.

Tossing her phone on the couch, Vinnie grabbed the bag from Henk's and popped the staple. This box of hooks had caused enough trouble for one day.

The light was fading, and she wanted to finish this odd job so she could take a load off. Maybe have a beer. Listen to some birds or to a podcast about rock music or ghost stories or funny people doing dumb shit just for kicks. You know, the kind of shit she'd planned to do in her retirement.

When she shook the box, the receipt fluttered down. That was trash, so she swooped down and crumpled it in her hand. But something caught in her brain, like a splinter. It tugged and insisted, an old instinct to look deeper rising to the surface. As she walked to the kitchen, Vinnie couldn't make herself throw the receipt away, not just yet.

She smoothed it against the fridge, then frowned. At the store, the handwritten receipt had just seemed quaint. Now it constricted her breath and wound a band around her chest. She had a heart, and it beat in anxious rhythms as she read and reread the girlish handwriting above the tally of four dollars, fifty cents.

Please help me. I think he killed Avery.
Hannah415@gmail.com

Chapter 4

"Fuck," Vinnie said. Then she thought, *fuck!*

She turned the receipt over. Nothing written on the other side, no additional information. To the front again, yep. Still there.

Please help me. I think he killed Avery.
Hannah415@gmail.com

Dammit! All she'd wanted was an escape. A brand-new place, full of strangers she never had to meet. A place to be alone and left alone and most importantly, to leave alone.

That last part, that was always going to be the hardest. It was like it was printed in her DNA and carved into her bones, an inability to stay out of shit. It had gotten her in trouble in the trailer park where she grew up, where she punched a boy for flipping girls' skirts up with a stick. Trouble in high school, for reporting the biology teacher who liked to trap girls between the lab tables to *Channel Six Investigates* when complaining to the principal hadn't worked.

Trouble when she went undercover for Internal Affairs, then testified against cops she'd worked with for years. In the words of any number of men in her history, Vinnie just couldn't leave shit alone. It was an irresistible force, one that felt like a constant pressure in her head. (Sometimes, when Vinnie thought about her death, she wondered if she'd have a stroke in that spot. Just a bright pinprick bleed, blooming into her brain and turning her off for good. The concept didn't scare her the way it used to; in her thoughts, it was almost peaceful.)

So the first question that came to mind was whether this was even real. Maybe Hannah was seeing things that weren't there. Imagining connections and crimes that didn't exist, motives made of make-believe. Teenagers weren't stupid, but they weren't experienced either. Everything was the biggest, the worst, the most tragic . . . a mundane truth like the fact Avery might have run away wouldn't sit right.

Next question: Why her? Why not Rosier? He had time to climb up her ass, he sure as hell had time to read a missing-persons report. Vinnie scratched at her memories—had she seen the poster all over town or just in Henk's?

Because maybe Rosier *had* read the report. Maybe there was nothing to this, maybe Hannah was blowing a runaway out of proportion. Or maybe this missing girl wasn't good enough, nice enough, bright enough to get the gift of case assignment. Both were possible and Vinnie didn't know enough about Wills Harbor to tell which.

Which led to the third question, the one that was going to get her into trouble: *Who was Avery Adair?*

Abandoning the shutters, Vinnie fired up her laptop at the little fold-down table in the kitchen. This way, she had a view of the driveway, just in case. With a few quick strokes, she pulled up an article from the local paper. Well, *article* was being generous.

What she found was more like a blurb or a snippet; a perfunctory acknowledgment that a thing had happened.

LOCAL TEEN REPORTED MISSING
Camila Vega, Staff Writer

Avery Adair, age 17, a junior at Liberty High School, was reported missing on October 12, in Wills Harbor by her mother, Kassadee Swain, 32, also of Wills Harbor. She was last seen leaving for school on Friday, October 6, and has not been in contact with family or friends since. The Kerry County Sheriff's Office has released a statement indicating they believe Adair is voluntarily missing and might be staying with relatives out of state.

Vinnie frowned. The spare paragraph about her disappearance was irritatingly short on details. And there was a lot of weaseling around in that paragraph. *They believe. She might be.* It still didn't tell Vinnie if someone had bothered to actually investigate. It was a fine line with missing people. Most of them who wanted to come home, did. Some of them who never returned were living their best lives elsewhere.

Sure, *Dateline* made it look like crazy serial killers lurked around every corner, but it just wasn't true. Dying in a car crash was more likely than a murder, and it was a big fucking leap from missing to dead. But it bothered Vinnie that the kid's friend thought she was dead. Even had a suspect. One that Rosier agreed could be dangerous.

Digging back into the search, Vinnie found plenty of Adairs in the news, including Avery. It was all written up in paragraphs and police blotters: narrow glimpses of a small-time, white-trash crime family. Most of the articles had the same perfunctory quality to them. Red Adair arrested for siphoning gas from a patrol car. "Big" Paul Adair hauled in for stripping copper off a construction site. "Little" Paul, public intoxication.

And then there was Avery: another little article from a few years back—two months in juvenile detention for public intoxication and violating a burn ban. Vinnie squinted at that, read between the lines. Sounded like the cops busted up a beer blast. Either Avery was the slowest runner out of the bunch, or she'd provided the beer.

Victimology was getting Vinnie nowhere. There were too many possibilities, and the internet wasn't helping her narrow them down. Avery Adair was a ghost online; didn't have a TikTok, an Instagram (maybe a Snapchat, but without knowing the girl, it would be impossible to guess what the username might be).

Vinnie banged around, data scraping until she figured out the local high school's email format. First initial, last name, graduation year. Unfortunately, the only thing attached to that were a few school projects posted behind a password, indexed but unavailable.

Once again, she was left with nothing solid, except for two dates: last seen, and reported missing. Vinnie *didn't* like the space between those numbers, but even that could be explained. Her mother wasn't worried (although her friend already was). The police weren't worried, and the paper wasn't exercised about it. Maybe she ran away all the time.

Or maybe they thought she wasn't worth the effort.

So Vinnie tried again. *Hannah Henk*, she typed. That pulled up a schoolteacher in another state, and a couple of LinkedIn profiles with women far too old to fit the description. *Hannah Henk Wills Harbor* did the trick.

Turned out she was actually Hannah Candlewood. According to another blurb in the paper—one that was two paragraphs longer than Avery's missing article—Hannah's grandparents bought Henk's from the original owner back in the '90s and never changed the name.

And Hannah Candlewood was all over the local news. She ran track and held a couple of school records. She led the high school's volunteer club. There she was, holding up an award with the mayor, and over here, helping build a house with Habitat for Humanity. The school newspaper had a couple of articles written by her—bright, idealistic stories, passionately arguing in defense of DREAMers and the LGBTQIA+ community.

On the official record, she was perfect.

But she was human, which meant Vinnie just hadn't found the rest of her yet. It wasn't hard, though.

Hannah's school email address led to an almost identical Google address, which led to an explosion of social media. It was a perfect reflection of the good girl in the newspapers, the same pictures from different angles. Awards, recognitions, performative citizenship. It all culminated in the most recent post: the Missing poster for Avery.

That wasn't giving her what she wanted, so Vinnie glanced at the receipt and typed in *hannah415@gmail.com*.

Jackpot.

The first thing that showed up was the finsta, a second Instagram meant for Hannah's friends, not her family. There Vinnie found an unsurprising array of party pictures. Beer-blast theory was looking good for Avery's JD record. This version of Hannah gathered in the woods with her friends. Three ruined rowhouses stood among the brambles, long shadows painted on them by a campfire in the foreground. Anonymous teenagers danced in silhouette, limber like reeds.

Then a jarring switch from forest to sea.

Another bonfire, this one on a rocky beach, where Hannah buried her face against a boy's shoulder. Was it Tyler? Impossible to tell; he kept his face studiously turned away from the camera. Still more of Hannah with her girlfriends, huddled together, each making that stupid *ahegao* face—eyes crossed, tongue sticking out. All of it a record of just being a teenager.

Vinnie clicked on a video post of Hannah and Avery together and enlarged it. It lasted a spare three seconds—in tandem, they leaned in, then kissed the air for the camera. The clip was short, but finally Vinnie could get a sense of Avery, the actual girl. Not the stiff, grainy school-picture version of her on the Xeroxed Missing poster.

Narrow, thin-lipped, Avery had two slightly crooked canines that gave her smile a mischievous tip. Too much eyeliner ringed her huge, waifish eyes, and freckles flecked the bridge of her nose. A delicate silver hoop decorated an eyebrow the same shade of chestnut as her hair. When she leaned in, cheek to cheek with Hannah, her chin sharpened and her lashes fell.

Repeat. Vinnie watched again.

Once more.

No, one more after that. With each replay, Avery felt more alive. More vital. More . . . fragile, because there she was, just a moment of her. A hint of her. Light and color and motion making her disappearance more than a footnote in a small-town paper. Dead or alive, Avery Adair was out there . . . somewhere.

Hanging her head, Vinnie closed her eyes. The video played on repeat in her thoughts until she sighed and opened her email.

TO: hannah415@gmail.com
FROM: vinnie.taylor91@gmail.com
Subject: Tell me more about Avery

Even as she typed, she berated herself. This was none of her business. This was not her problem. This was not her city. This was not her job. But unfortunately, one thing remained true:

Vinnie Taylor couldn't leave shit alone.

Chapter 5

The ride into the Hill felt like a memory.

Trailers clung to their spaces jealously, boasting tiny decks big enough for one lawn chair. The two-foot slices of grass in front and along the sides, the odd colors of aluminum siding on the oldest trailers competing with the austere greige of the newer ones.

It was like driving through her childhood. She almost expected to see her cousins playing in the street, only scattering when the rental car got close enough to bump. The asphalt was patchy on the road, and cracks spider-webbed along the concrete parking decks. The speed limit was five miles an hour and Vinnie would have bet cash money that the dips on this street had once been speed bumps.

In her mind she tasted the scent of oil and gasoline, remembered the night her father and his friends had set the new speed bumps in *their* trailer park on fire to soften them, then rolled over them with pickups until they were flat. They watered that victory with Budweiser, late into the night. She tucked that memory away, out of sight, but not entirely out of mind.

One more turn, and Vinnie found herself at a modest yellow double-wide. Trash cans sat nearly against the siding, but there was no deck. Just three wooden stairs leading to the front door. In the yard sat an old plastic playhouse, and a jumble of child-sized furniture. The sun had baked the color from it, leaving a forlorn garden in its wake.

A different kind of anxiety played through Vinnie's fingertips as she cut the engine. It was a touch of excitement, but a reminder to be careful. She had no business poking her nose in any of this. But she had a novel of an email from Hannah Candlewood, a biography written by a best friend, and Vinnie felt it burning like a new twenty in her pocket.

Hannah sent it shortly after midnight, with her phone number attached. There was no way in hell Vinnie was going to call a teenager in the middle of the night, but the whole exchange left her a little sleepless. She couldn't stop turning it over in her head. It didn't matter that she had absolutely nothing to work with, her brain itched to sort the scant facts into categories. Even when she took a swallow of Nyquil from the bottle and jammed the pillow over her head, her thoughts busied themselves with possibilities and procedures. She'd finally passed out around three thirty, and here she was, up at nine in the morning . . . parked in front of Avery Adair's home.

Still time to leave, she told herself. She had no power, and she had no desire to stir the police up either. This was none of her business. Then again, wouldn't a parent welcome an extra pair of eyes looking for their daughter? Stepping out of the car, Vinnie brushed off her jacket and her doubts. It was two steps to the deck, and she knocked on the storm door.

The mother's name and age in the newspaper hadn't told Vinnie much. But seeing her here, rubbing her hands dry on a worn dish towel and peering suspiciously from the other side of the door, told her a lot.

"I'm Vinnie Taylor," Vinnie said. "Are you Kassadee Swain?"

"Unless it's Girl Scout Cookies, I don't want it," Kassadee said, still locked behind the screen.

Last chance to stay out of this, and still Vinnie said, "I'm looking into Avery's case, and I have some questions."

Instantly on high alert, Kassadee narrowed her eyes. Tipped her head to one side. "Where's your badge?"

"Don't have one," Vinnie said, her tongue ashen. "I'm not a cop."

For a long moment, Kassadee considered her. Then she finally unlocked the door and walked away from it, an invitation to come inside. She walked straight back to the sink, throwing her towel over her shoulder.

Vinnie let herself in, drinking in the neat but worn details of the trailer. Faux wood paneling everywhere, toys erupting from a box in the middle of the living-room floor. Pictures all down the hallway, on every available wall. School pictures and snapshots and the kind of portraits you get in a bundle for thirty bucks from Walmart.

"I'd say, are you sure you're not a cop, but you know how I know you're not?"

Vinnie shook her head.

"You're *here*," she said pointedly, plunging her hands back into the sink. Baby bottles bobbed in soapy water, thumping emptily against each other. "Every time something goes wrong, here they come up the Hill, but when Avery goes missing, where are they, huh?"

Kassadee smoothed her hair back with wet hands. She wore her age like a thin shawl. Exhaustion and responsibility had bleached her like desert bones, and the cheap scrubs she wore home from work didn't flatter her angles. Old enough to have a high school junior, she also had a four-month-old snoozing in a car seat on the kitchen floor. She had more than earned the dark circles under her watery eyes.

"I'm sorry you're not having any luck with the police," Vinnie said gently. "But that's all right. I can do their job for them. Can I ask you a few questions about Avery?"

Almost imperceptibly, Kassadee's shoulders slumped. She fished the kitchen rag from the sink and stuffed it inside one of the bottles. Instead of a brush, she used the rag and the long handle of a wooden spoon to scrub the thing out. "I mean, what's to know? She went to school, and she didn't come home."

"Were you worried?"

"I wasn't, not at first." Kassadee turned to her, a brief wall flashing between them. "And I don't feel bad about that."

"You don't have to," Vinnie said, no judgment in her voice. She didn't know enough about mom or daughter to hold it against her. Not yet, anyway. "But can you tell me why?"

Kassadee rinsed the bottle and sat it in the dish strainer. "Because she's *grown*. She's doing better than I was when I was her age. She's been tutoring online since eighth grade! Figured out how to have a job without having to . . ." She gestured at herself, clad in navy polyester.

"I understand she had to spend two months in detention."

Irritation flashed across Kassadee's face. "It was an election year, and the sheriff was looking to be tough on crime. It was bullshit; it was her first charge, and they skipped right past warnings and community service—nope, right to detention with Avery because of her family name. The part that really pisses me off is that most of the time, Avery keeps to herself. She helps with Paisley if I need it, but she hibernates in her room. Comes and goes like a cat."

With that, she shooed a ginger feline off the counter, directing its fall to keep it from landing on the napping baby.

Vinnie's gaze trailed back to the pictures on the wall. She touched one of the frames, the one that held the picture from the Missing poster. It was obviously a school photo, a generic stormy backdrop and a standard three-quarter angle, but this Avery was younger. Before the brow piercing, before the eyeliner—that age where teeth look like giant Chiclets in a baby face. The freckles were even more pronounced in this photo, the smile wider and uncomplicated. "May I?"

"Go for it," Kassadee said.

"So even though she just spent time in lockup . . ."

"Oh, that was a bullshit charge and everybody knew it. Why would I hold that against her?"

There was no reason to point out that Kassadee had a legal obligation to keep track of her kids. All that would do was shut her up, and she was talking freely at the moment. The more Vinnie could soak in, the more she had to work with. She rubbed her thumb against the picture frame thoughtfully. "She's left home before?"

"Yeah, but no," Kassadee said. "Maybe for a couple of days at a time. Spending the night with her friends, you know? But even if she's not *here*, she still goes to school. Of course, I didn't find out she wasn't in school until that next week. That's when I *did* file a report."

"The school didn't call?"

A flash of anger. "No. They did not."

"And Avery hadn't texted or called during that time, either?"

With a snort, Kassadee shook her head. "I don't think she even knows how to make a phone call. But no. No texts, nothing. I'm telling you, though, that's normal for her. It was the school thing that got me worried. She wants to walk."

"Walk?"

"Yeah, walk, like"—Kassadee dug for the right words—"like at graduation. I dropped out and got my GED; her daddy dropped out and went to technical school. So she wants to graduate, for real. Cap and gown. Just to say she did. In fact, last time I saw her, she was talking about buying herself a laptop for school, 'cause she's tired of sharing mine."

Vinnie glanced around the trailer again—its worn furniture, its weary weight. She replaced the picture. "New laptop, that's not cheap."

"She was saving up from tutoring and her daddy told her he would pay half." Then she added under her breath, "Jackass."

"And the jackass is . . . ?"

"Keith Adair. He lives right down the road. Works construction in the summer, and HVAC in the winter. He could afford to buy her a whole brand-new one, if he wanted to. He just doesn't want to. I've had to chase him around her whole life trying to get child support out of him. He thinks the sun shines out of her ass, but he can't stand me, so . . ."

As if to punctuate her mother's irritation, the baby in the car seat let out a trembling proto-wail. Instantly, Kassadee scrubbed her hands dry on her uniform and picked the baby up. She held her close, smoothing a damp palm over the wild muss of dark hair. Smiling, she murmured, "Oh, no, no cries, Paisley, it's okay, baby girl."

So she was a good mother, Vinnie thought. Or at least, good with babies. There were plenty of people who loved babies but lost interest once the kids started having their own opinions and thoughts. But still, the way her eyes locked on the baby, the total change in her tone of voice, she seemed like a loving mother.

Likewise, the seeming disinterest in Avery made its own kind of sense.

Avery was the same age her mother was when she had her, and Kassadee had figured out how to be an adult. She'd even called her grown. In Kassadee's mind, seventeen was old enough to go missing for a couple of days. She had an internal clock for signs of danger that didn't match up to other people's, but it wasn't blind neglect.

Thoughtfully, Vinnie asked, "Did Avery take anything with her?"

"Just what goes to school every day. All her clothes are here, if that's what you're asking."

"All right, I'm about to get out of your hair, but one more thing. Could I take a look at the email coming in from the Missing poster?"

That's when Kassadee hesitated. Swaying with the baby, she turned to Vinnie and looked her over. "You know, you never did say what exactly brought you up here."

"To be honest, a little bit of curiosity, and . . ." Vinnie shrugged. "Somebody asked me to take a look. Off the record."

Instantly, Kassadee asked, "Was it Mr. Demers? I bet it was. He's a good teacher."

As a matter of fact, it wasn't, but now Vinnie had someone else to question.

Chapter 6

The tipline account was a bust.

Kassadee logged in on Vinnie's phone, and they scoured the messages together. It wasn't totally crickets, but it was pretty damned close. What tips were there had come mostly from psychics, none of whom agreed on a single thing except that Avery was missing.

A couple letters from locals claimed they'd seen her after the Friday she disappeared, so their names went on Vinnie's list. There was also a note from Hannah Candlewood. She'd called all the hospitals in a hundred-mile radius looking for Avery, but no luck.

And of course, it wouldn't be a public investigation without the four different dick pics attached to anonymous emails. Even if Vinnie graded on a curve, the offerings were C+ at best. Wills Harbor definitely hadn't sent its best and brightest.

After she left Kassadee, Vinnie took another slow roll through the ersatz trailer park dotting the Hill. The low-level, worn-down grime of the place didn't faze her. Bikes lay where kids had dumped them, and wind chimes sang softly in the breeze.

Some of the porches had vegetables growing in five-gallon buckets. She drove over an extension cord running from one trailer to another—something she'd helped her own father do when his sister couldn't afford to turn the power back on at her place.

Neighbors shared laundry lines and electricity; there was an honor table in front of one of the trailers. It had a couple rows of homemade bread in plastic wrap, and an old coffee can to collect the quarters. There was poverty, but also community. Just because the Adairs had concentrated on the Hill didn't mean the Hill was inherently *bad*.

That thought twitched in Vinnie's brain like the first blisters of poison ivy. She hadn't always seen the tomatoes and toys, not when she was growing up in Wheel Estates. And not twenty years ago, when she still walked a beat. She probably would have been one of the cops rattling the cages up here herself.

Back then, things were simpler, because back then, she didn't question whether she stood on the moral high ground or not. That was a *given*. In her mind, she was protecting the community the best she could. She was earnest and determined and had blazed her path from beat cop to detective without stopping to catch her breath. Everything she did, everything she was, had been contained in that badge and the strength she felt wearing it.

The first prickling of awareness came when the local Pride parade declined their services. At the time, it seemed ridiculous, even though she had heard more than one shitty comment in the locker room about the parade and the people in it. Easy to write off as a few bad apples, reasonable to write it off as a handful of Pride radicals. She took it personally, because she dated women, although she kept that quiet at work. At the time, it made sense.

But then Ferguson happened. BLM happened, and the talk in the station and the locker room and in the bars after long nights got more and more strident. Vinnie thought it was clear to anybody with eyes that George Floyd was murdered. But going to work was like falling into Wonderland, all-day, every day opposite day, listening to her colleagues, her *friends*, explain all the ways it wasn't a crime.

How many bad apples could there be until they were all rotten? She was surrounded by them; she started holding her tongue around them. It was dangerous to piss off somebody she might have to rely on for her life. And after years of being a good cop, or thinking she was, anyway, she started doubting herself.

Had she always been fair? What about objective? In retrospect, there was definitely shit she let slide with coworkers because they were on the same side. And there were things she did because everyone did them—printing out notes on the back of a rap sheet in case the defense wanted the notes to be put into evidence, for example. Faking lie-detector results with a photocopier to get somebody teetering on the edge of confession to fall off. The number of drunk drivers in her own division took two hands to count, easily. Had she ever pulled them over? Ticketed them? Hell no.

It nagged at her. The news bore into her, a parasite, constantly twisting. Instead of spending free time thinking about anything but work, Vinnie scoured her old cases. Reread her own notes until she nearly memorized them. She compared her investigative files to transcripts of her testimony, just to see if her memory of events got sculpted to fit a theory.

It wasn't a lightbulb moment. She didn't wake up one day completely transformed. It was a struggle, and a lonely one. She hit all the stages of grief, and doubled back on some of them as she learned more and examined herself more honestly. For a while, she thought she could leave it alone and live with being "one of the good ones."

It took more than a couple-three years before she realized she couldn't be a "good one" if she was ignoring the shit going on around her. Every day, she was steeping in it, and once a stink sets in, it lingers. She couldn't keep going the way she had been; something had to change. That was the fuse.

She lit it when she went undercover for Internal Affairs.

Deep down, she knew her career was over. There would be no going back to Homicide after snitching; there would be no other department willing to risk her.

But by then, she knew she couldn't do the job anymore either.

Every time she rested her hand on her holster, every time she looked twice at a Black kid, every time somebody handed out one of the Fraternal Order of Police business cards—basically a free pass out of a traffic ticket—guilt swallowed her whole.

Once upon a time, she had truly believed the police were the good guys *because* they were the police. Once upon a time, she had truly believed the mission was to serve and protect.

But *once upon a time* only opened fairy tales.

When the truth crashed down around her, Vinnie couldn't help but see it. She knew good cops, she did. But she was increasingly aware they were in the minority. *She* was in the minority.

When she left, the plan was to erase her past. The city and state she'd grown up in, the people she knew, the decorated dress uniform, everything. She ended up in a small town that may as well have been at the end of the world, in a geometric oddity of a cottage, and left no forwarding address. Her mother was the only one who knew where she was.

This was supposed to be a new beginning.

But it had taken all of two months to get ankle-deep in a new case. One that she had no resources to investigate properly, and one that she couldn't resolve without dipping right back into the law-enforcement well. She didn't even have a private investigator's license. (Didn't know how to get one either.)

As she turned out of the back loop on the Hill, she caught a glimpse of motion. Instinct told her it was male, and young. She couldn't go much slower, but she tapped the brakes anyway. Scanning the trailers around her, she looked for faces in windows, or shadows on the opposite sides, but nothing.

It was eerie, like realizing you weren't alone in an empty house. Nothing supernatural about it; just unnerving. Back in the day, she and her partner would have called it *hinky*, a mystical sensation in the gut and the hindbrain that told them something wasn't quite right.

Now she had to brush it off. That kind of thinking is what had made it easy to coast for so long without really examining her job in the first place. Plenty of people had probably taken a glance at her, her car, since she was a stranger. Her pseudo-psychic suspicions weren't facts. If somebody on the Hill had something they wanted to tell her, well.

They knew she had spent two hours in Kassadee Swain's trailer, so they could figure out how to find her.

Chapter 7

There was glass on the floor.

Vinnie had spent the rest of her afternoon on unfinished errands, and now she stopped at the first sight of glittering shards scattered across the living room. Her stomach churned, vision tunneling a little as she stood, unsteady, in the doorway. She threw away her first thought, that somebody from Indy had found her. No one was supposed to know where she was. *No,* she told herself firmly, *no one knows where you are.*

The second thought, that the shutters had finally broken one of the picture windows, died instantly. The windows were intact. The random knickknacks remained in place. Everything was whole and pristine, just the way she'd left it. When she didn't see a reason for the glass, her anxiety volunteered an explanation.

Fewer than three hours looking for Avery Adair, and somebody had already decided to threaten her.

Drawing her gun, Vinnie stepped into the cottage ready to sweep it. Her ears tuned up, straining for the slightest out of place sound as she stepped around the glass. Closer now, she recognized it as a drinking glass, one she'd left sitting on the coffee table last night. But as far as she was aware, Maryland didn't get a whole lot of earthquakes, the windows were closed, and she didn't believe in ghosts.

Maybe kids, she thought, except the door had been locked.

Maybe ghosts after all, she thought, because it only took a minute to clear this half of the house. That whole open-concept thing didn't leave a lot of places to hide.

Her heart rumbled; she sniffed the air as she headed for the bedroom door. Nothing smelled different. No telltale cologne, or body odor, or hint of "just different." Her mouth was a desert, and she swallowed against the knot in her throat. This wasn't the quiet isolation she'd expected when she signed the lease on this place.

Pushing the door open with her shoulder, Vinnie burst into the bedroom. Lights off but shutters open, the room glowed with late-day sunlight. It cast the world in oranges and reds; it felt like an autumnal music box.

She moved quietly but not silently, checking behind the door and inside the armoire. Tuned tight, she stopped at the edge of the bed. If the intruder was under there, he was well and truly trapped. And trapped people acted a lot like trapped animals. Reaching for the side of the mattress, Vinnie said, "Just come out and nobody gets hurt."

Silence.

So Vinnie counted off to the beat of her heart, one, two, three . . . She flipped the mattress up. Something black shot out. It streaked from the room. She couldn't even get a bead on it.

A cat. A goddamned cat.

With a slump, Vinnie dropped the mattress, then sat heavily. Her heart pounded away, even as the adrenaline faded. She was pretty damned sure Rich Watts would have mentioned a resident feline when he turned over the keys. He seemed more like a fussy dog type anyway.

Therefore, this stray had found a way inside. And that meant another damned DIY project. Just add it to the list!

But first, she had to find the thing and put it out.

Vinnie had never owned a pet, not even as a kid. She didn't dislike animals. In fact, she'd always kind of wanted one. A cat, a dog, even a hamster or goldfish. But her mother had refused while Vinnie still lived with her. And after that, it would have been cruel to bring a living creature into a home only to leave it alone for days at a time. Policework wasn't conducive to long-term relationships with living creatures of any kind. Near everybody in her department had been divorced at least once.

Holstering her weapon, Vinnie rolled to her feet. There was glass on the floor to clean up and notes to review.

After she put everything back in place, she double-checked for an open window or door (nope). Then, she pulled the kitchen table down. Arranging her notes carefully, she also laid out a cutting board to make a quick dinner. Her favorite poverty meal: fried potatoes and smoked sausage. There wasn't a lot of nutrition in it, but it was hot, and filling, and felt like comfort.

Her dad used to make the one-pan dinner when her mother worked late, because he didn't know how to cook much else. Of course, that was a memory with forty years of dust on it. She couldn't quite remember her father's face, but she shared a meal with him every time she skipped takeout with this one.

As she peeled and sliced, she read over her notes. Kassadee wasn't the strictest mother, but she still paid attention. That's why Vinnie knew that Avery had had a rough week at school before she disappeared. There had been some kind of incident, but that was as close to specifics as she had. Avery had explained it to her mother as an old beef, hoarding the details for herself.

Chances were, high school drama had nothing to do with this. But Vinnie had to rule everything out before she could rule anything in. Her mental list grew as she oiled the cast-iron pan that came with the cottage. The potatoes, dusted with flour, sizzled in the grease as Vinnie ordered her next thoughts.

She was going to have to talk to Hannah Candlewood again. Her email had painted a picture of Avery Adair that didn't match the reality of her. As far as Hannah was concerned, Avery was funny and generous and told it like it was, and everybody loved her for it. But there had to be a reason Hannah wrote down her suspicions instead of just speaking them aloud. Henk's was empty at that point. Tyler had already been sent off to nurse his bruised ego by then. There was no one to hear the accusation, so why the mystery?

At that, Vinnie dumped the sausage in her pan, but not before she left a few slices on a paper plate on the floor. The cat was around somewhere. She couldn't get it out if she couldn't find it. Sure, she had more time on her hands these days than she used to, but she wasn't looking for a roommate.

With one hand, she went ahead and texted as she stirred.

VTAYLOR: I talked to Avery's mom today.

HCANDLEWOOD: Oh good! What did she say?

VTAYLOR: Nothing new.

HCANDLEWOOD: Oh. 🙁

VTAYLOR: I don't know that I should be messing around with this. This is really for the police to handle.

HCANDLEWOOD: But they're not handling it!

VTAYLOR: Why not?

HCANDLEWOOD: They have a thing against her family, okay? Please do this. I'll pay you.

Suddenly, another text came in. Vinnie frowned and pulled the pan off the fire.

011502: Hi, CashMeApp, here! Awesome news, Hannah Candlewood just sent you twenty dollars! To get your cash fast, download the CashMeApp here!

Vinnie turned her phone over and put it down. A little too hard, actually; she winced and checked to make sure she hadn't cracked the screen. Nope. The offer of twenty dollars stared back at her accusingly. She neither needed, nor wanted, the money.

But the money changed things. This was more than a kid scribbling a rumor on a receipt. Hannah got Avery reported missing. Hannah made the Missing poster. Hannah set up the tipline email. And Hannah was serious enough to try to *hire* someone, serious enough to accuse a(n) ex-(boy)friend(?) . . . there was more to this. Even if it wasn't a homicide, it was *something*.

The pan of potatoes and sausage had stopped popping, so Vinnie grabbed a fork. There wasn't anybody else around, so she dug into her dinner directly from the pan. Sleek, salty grease coated her tongue. Browned, crispy potatoes scrubbed it clean. She went in for another bite and played out a what-if.

If this *were* an investigation, what would she do next? Who made the list of people to interview?

Bit by bit, Vinnie mapped out the next (hypothetical, she told herself) day.

Track down Keith Adair; catch up with Hannah Candlewood. Oh yeah, and the teacher. She could probably kill two birds with one stone if she could catch them at the school. Plans locked into place with a satisfying click. Three interviews, one day, that was easy. *If* she were going to do it, that is.

And if she were, she'd want to talk to as many people as she could before Rosier got wind of it. She wasn't stupid. She knew how small towns worked. Sooner or later, it would get back to him that she was asking questions. He'd make another "courtesy" call to the cottage, and she'd have to explain herself.

Could she explain herself? Probably not, but she could have a tight binder with all the facts to hand off. *If* she did it. *If* she got involved. *If* she clicked here to download CashMeApp, which she did. Right after she finished her dinner.

Chapter 8

Liberty High sat on a hill above town.

Unlike the rest of Wills Harbor, which went out of its way to look quaint and historical, the school was a concrete block with touches of tinted glass. Forbidding thorny bushes huddled beneath the windows, the only greenery on-site. A tall chain-link fence boxed the school off from the surrounding woods, and the requisite flagpole stood in the middle of the paved parking lot. The place looked like the '70s: drab, asymmetrical, and exhausted. Vinnie could practically smell the floor wax and industrial lunches from here.

Parked in the visitors' lot, Vinnie watched as students huddled outside the front doors, waiting for them to open.

They nestled together like sparrows, puffed up in their coats to conserve heat. A good half of them clutched cups of coffee in the chill just after dawn. Steam floated from their lips after each sip.

Vinnie checked her phone again, the pictures she'd saved the night before.

The first was a selfie of Hannah Candlewood. Vinnie was pretty sure she'd recognize her again, but she was taking no chances. The next picture, Tyler Purnell. She didn't necessarily want to talk to him yet, but she wanted to be able to clock him. And finally, a

yearbook snap of the teacher Kassadee mentioned, Mr. Christopher Demers.

He wore a beige jacket over a T-shirt that read EVERYTHING
I SAY WILL BE ON THE EXAM. Cute. His rounded shoulders in
the picture told Vinnie that he was tall, probably well over six
feet. The posture was a permanent, self-protective stoop. He was
young, maybe late twenties, with serious brown eyes behind wire-
rimmed glasses. Interestingly, less serious, he'd bleached his wavy
hair platinum blond. His dark roots were obvious, maybe even
deliberate. He taught history, according to the caption beneath
his photo.

Vinnie watched the teachers' parking lot, a steady trickle of
sedans and SUVs slowly filling the spaces. Then, a green Mini
Cooper rolled in. It glided past, quiet as a ghost. Electrics creeped
Vinnie out a little; it shouldn't be that easy for two tons to sneak
up on you. As it passed, Vinnie squinted through the windshield.
The driver bore a familiar haze of pale hair, and light reflected
right where a pair of glasses would have perched on a nose.

This was probably the guy, she decided. She got out of her car
and then watched him get out of his.

Demers was unmistakable as he unfolded himself from the
driver's seat. Long scarecrow legs, and a stoop that still couldn't
hide his height. He towered over his car, easily six-three, then
ducked back in (careful of his head) to grab his satchel. It was
leather, and beat to hell, like he'd bought it from a classic movie
about a beloved teacher and made it part of his personality. Another flavor of *gut feeling* hinted he might be gay. It was nothing
specific—the thinness of his belt, the sweet, self-conscious studying of his body language . . . To her, an elder queer, he read like
a closeted twink.

Approaching, Vinnie had a card ready. One of her old cards from the department, but she'd written her new number on the back of it. She'd doctored up a handful of them over breakfast, after tearing her luggage apart looking for them. This was a brand-new dirty trick, an appeal to authority she just didn't have anymore.

A persistent, anxious thought bothered her; she wondered if all the changing she'd done was a lie. A lie to herself, about herself. Something to make her feel like a decent human being, even when she wasn't. If she wasn't. Vinnie didn't know, and she shoved it out of her thoughts for the time being.

"Christopher Demers?" she asked, her voice steady and clear.

He hesitated, pushing up his glasses with the back of his hand. "Yes, can I help you?"

"Hi, yeah, my name is Vinnie Taylor. I'm looking into a missing-persons case. Avery Adair, one of your students?"

The uptalk let her ask a leading question without actually asking a question. It was like the essay on a test, open-ended, ready to be filled. It was a blank space, and the things people put in there could tell you a lot about them. Big talker? Shy? Whatever Demers said next would be useful, no matter what it was.

"I keep hoping today's the day I walk into class and she's back at her desk. Is there any news?"

His voice was warm and low, and *what* he said felt like it confirmed her gut. There was a soft accent to it that he worked hard to disguise. And then, just the words he said. Straight men, usually, when questioned by a woman, didn't tend to be verbose. And they didn't tend to answer at first—they demanded qualifications, and maybe a little more authority, before responding.

"Not yet," Vinnie said. Gently leading with the past tense, she asked, "She was in your history class?"

"World History, yes."

"Good student?"

He smiled. "When she wants to be. Engaged in class but doesn't turn in homework. Tons of ideas but refuses to write them down. Delightfully infuriating; what are you going to do?"

Present tense. Just like Mom. Vinnie fell in beside him, offering her card casually. "I heard something was up the week before she disappeared."

"Ah, that," Demers said.

Not an answer. Vinnie pressed him, trying to nudge him out of cagey and into honesty. "Big or little 'that'?"

With his keys fumbled into his satchel, Demers now had a chance to look at the card. He read the front, DET. VANETTA TAYLOR, INDIANAPOLIS METROPOLITAN POLICE DEPARTMENT, HOMICIDE BRANCH. His eyes lingered on the black streak of marker, obliterating her old phone number and email address. He raised his gaze to Vinnie's face before turning the card over. "Actually, ah . . . I don't know if I should be discussing a student with you."

Trying to be casual, Vinnie said, "I understand. She has rights. You have responsibilities. I talked to Ms. Swain about her daughter, and she seemed to think you might have some insight into her disappearance, that's all."

Demers' brows flickered slightly, dark shadows that slipped behind the curtain of blond bangs. "You talked to Kassadee."

"I did," Vinnie said. "And if you want to think about it, or talk to your union rep or whatever, before you talk to me, I get it. Believe me, I get it."

"I just don't know if I can help," Demers said finally. But he didn't return the card. That was a good sign. Whether he had anything useful to tell her or not, keeping the card meant he wasn't ready to cut her off completely. He finished locking up his car and took a half step toward the school. Yeah, he wanted to tell her something. He just didn't know if he should.

Instead of pushing, Vinnie gave him silence. Not a cold one, just a beat. Another blank space he could fill in with anything on his mind. And he took it, and another half step toward the school.

"I just . . . I've been thinking about it, and I don't know why she'd run away. There's not a lot out there for a girl like her."

"Like her?"

Uncomfortable, Demers shifted his satchel and keys again. "If you talked to her mother, you probably know about her family situation."

Vinnie offered, "I know the Adairs have a reputation."

"And they earned it," he said. "I've known a lot of Adairs in my day; feels like I've taught most of them. One of her cousins is in my American History section this year . . ." Demers trailed off guiltily. He glanced toward the school, then murmured, "I don't want to speak ill of any student. They all have their own needs, and a good teacher meets them where they are. So I'll say Avery could rise above, if she wanted to. I just don't think she wants to."

"Just to get a look at the whole picture, does she have a lot of family at the school?"

"Well. There's Red, he's in my class. The twins are freshmen, Lexi and . . . you know, I don't know her brother's name. He's in David's section. Jaylin, maybe?"

"Does Avery spend time with them at school?" Vinnie asked quickly.

"Maybe at lunch?" Demers shrugged, offering a sheepish laugh. "I'm pretty focused on my classroom."

"Any problems there?"

"Nothing unusual," he said emphatically. "Kids love each other one day, hate each other the next, rinse, repeat. High school is one percent learning and ninety-nine percent drama."

A roar rose up, and they both turned to look. Striding into the sea of people in front of the school, Tyler appeared. Today he wore a letter jacket, a living stereotype offering up fist bumps to his friends with his free hand.

"What's *his* name?" Vinnie asked, letting a little distaste slip into her voice.

"Tyler Purnell," Demers said with an edge. Even when he'd talked about the other Adairs, he hadn't sounded like this. It was like he'd forgotten himself for a moment; let the professionalism drop just long enough to reveal that teachers were human. A guy like Demers had probably had to deal with a lot of Tyler Purnells in his lifetime.

Vinnie murmured confidentially. "Bad news?"

"No, no, he's great if you love big egos and bullies." A shadow passed over Demers' features, a little dark, a little hateful. Then shame put his mask back on and he cleared his throat. "I shouldn't say that. He's just a kid."

"Kids can be assholes too," Vinnie offered.

Demers huffed a laugh. "Truer words."

"All right," Vinnie said, closing her mental notebook. "I'm going to get out of your hair. One last question before I go . . ."

"Yes?"

"What do you think happened to Avery?"

The faint, sick-sad smile reappeared. "I don't know. I just hope wherever she is, they appreciate her."

Chapter 9

Vinnie still hadn't seen Hannah by the first bell.

She must have slipped inside while Vinnie talked to Demers. That meant another trip to the hardware store after school, because Vinnie knew for a fact that she wouldn't get past a front-office receptionist.

Times had changed since Vinnie went to high school. Seniors didn't have a school-sanctioned spot to smoke cigarettes, and kids weren't allowed to leave campus for lunch. Most importantly, strangers couldn't waltz in and expect to be let past the first set of locked doors. Even when she still had the badge, there was no guarantee she'd get past the front desk.

All those things were meant to protect the kids from shit they shouldn't need protecting from, and they made her job—was this really her job?—a lot harder.

So Vinnie skipped down her list and found herself at Able Heating and Cooling. The building looked like it had been a gas station once, the front walls glass from the knee up, and a jaunty angle to the roof. Scars pocked the parking lot where an awning and pumps had once stood. A rush of sweet antifreeze and skunky pot washed over her, bells jingling as she opened the front door.

A couple of orange plastic chairs sat against the wall, but the front desk was unmanned. The walls went bare, and she saw little evidence of an actual business. It didn't escape her notice: there were no parts, no tools, no boxes as far as the eye could see. She heard conversation in the back, though, so she called out. Everything went quiet, but no one answered. So, Vinnie raised her voice and tried again.

"Anybody back there?"

"We're closed!"

A man, equal parts baffled and annoyed. Vinnie looked around—no Closed sign, and it wasn't like she'd jumped through the windows, here. With a mental shrug, she called out once more. "Door's open."

A moment later, someone emerged from the back. An unpleasant face, drawn with tight, narrow lines, came together under a shock of shaggy hair somewhere between blond and grey. His hands, she noted, were clean—even under the fingernails. Wiry and engulfed in blue coveralls, the man gave Vinnie a once-over, then settled on glaring at her in annoyance. "I said we're closed."

If Vinnie were the betting type, she'd wager her left leg that this place was a front. Probably laundering money, because there didn't seem to be enough space to chop stolen cars or to move bulk stolen property. And honestly? She didn't really give a shit. None of that was her problem anymore. She glanced at the name patch on the coveralls—Keith—and met his gaze.

"That's okay, my AC is fine. Are you Avery Adair's father?"

"Who's asking?"

This time, Vinnie didn't share her doctored business cards. She had a feeling Keith here would be more willing to talk to a private detective than a cop. She offered her hand, which he pointedly didn't take, and said, "I'm Vinnie Taylor, and I'm looking for your daughter."

He narrowed his eyes. "Why?"

"Because she's missing," Vinnie said. "You *are* aware she's missing?"

Rubbing a hand over his sharp chin, Keith scowled. "She's my kid. So yeah, I know. But I don't know *you*, and I don't like strangers getting up in my family's business."

I bet you don't, Vinnie thought. Because the family business, from the looks of things, was under the table and against the law. Nevertheless, if Keith had information she could use, Vinnie intended to prise it from him. She said, "I'm not interested in anything except bringing Avery home safe. The cops don't give a shit, but I do."

There was nothing soft about Keith Adair, but his eyes warmed a little. Not friendly, furious—but at least not at her now. "They didn't do an Amber Alert or nothing. Her little friend Hannah made the Missing poster and set up the email address for tips. We're the ones looking for her."

"Any idea why that might be?"

Keith hardened again. "They have a problem with me. But Avery's not me, and they should fucking care when a little girl goes missing. While we're searching for her, they sit around jacking each other off."

What a charmer. Vinnie asked, "Where are you looking?"

"Everywhere!" he exclaimed. "In town, the school, the woods . . . hell, some of the boys took a boat out to Little Pea to see if she was out there for some reason. I hired a guy who does searches for a living. He was here last week, gonna be here this week too."

Little Pea was a small island just past the harbor mouth. As far as Vinnie knew, it was uninhabited. Just a rock with some trees on it. Now that she thought about it, it was probably a good spot for teenagers to congregate in private. Something to dig into a little deeper, later on. Right now, she had Keith Adair talking and she didn't want to stop him. "Have you talked to her friends?"

Keith waved that off. "Kassadee says she called all'em. There ain't that many. Unlike her mama, she don't run around."

"And when's the last time you saw her?"

"That Wednesday. She came to get some money for her laptop. I gave it to her, and she left."

That sounded about right, but it didn't sound like the whole story. Vinnie pressed, "Did you hear from her after that?"

"No, I didn't."

"Where do you think she might have gone?"

Keith hesitated, but not with uncertainty. His face remained masked and stony; any doubt or fear he might have had, he kept locked beneath a layer of suspicion and anger. The greyish cast to his skin only made him seem more impenetrable. "Why are you asking me? You think her *family* had something to do with this?"

Interesting. He could have been telling on himself. Hinting at something he knew but didn't want to share. Or he could be a low-level criminal who was fed up with the cops blaming his family for everything that went wrong in Wills Harbor.

Soothingly, Vinnie said, "I think her father knows her better than I do."

"Look," Keith said. He drummed his fingers on the counter between them. Pent-up frustration turned to repetitive motion. If she was reading him right, he was pissed but not nervous. Not guilty. Anything he knew would have been helpful, but it was pretty clear he didn't want to share anything he knew. Not with somebody outside the family.

Vinnie stayed patient. She didn't have a time clock; she didn't have to pound this case out because another one could fall on her desk at any moment. For the first time, actually, she had all the time in the world. "I'm listening."

"She was supposed to do some running with Red that weekend, but she went missing. She was gonna ride up to Howard County. That's where she was getting the laptop; some guy up there refurbishes them."

"So Red never saw her?"

"Not so far as I know, and his little ass is hiding out right now, so I can't ask him. Didn't none of us know she was gone until the Candlewood kid talked to Kass. Nobody's heard from her. *Nobody*. So wherever Avery is, it's because somebody took her. She can raise some hell, but she loves her family."

Vinnie found that curious. Avery disappears, and then Red makes himself scarce. People don't fade out for no reason, so that gave Vinnie some direction. Talk to Red, talk to the laptop guy, if she could find him. Make sure Avery never left the county . . . or prove that she did.

So far, nobody could pinpoint the actual moment Avery went missing, and that was a big fucking point to resolve. Without that, it was still a huge leap from missing to murdered, no matter what Hannah Candlewood thought. But the jump was getting shorter with every witness.

"Now, I'm just asking out of an abundance of caution," Vinnie said, trying to forestall his temper. "But is there any reason somebody would want to hurt your daughter?"

"Except the usual reasons? She's a pretty girl. You and me both know there's plenty out there who ain't happy unless they're destroying something beautiful."

"Anybody in particular come to mind?"

Something made Keith stop and abruptly change the subject. "You a PI?"

"Something like that," Vinnie lied.

"Who hired you?"

In for a penny, in for a pound. "A family friend. I'm on your side, Keith. I just want to find Avery and get her home safe."

Something clattered in the back room, but Keith didn't turn toward the sound. Whatever was going on back there was business as usual. Slowly, he curled his arms on the counter and leaned forward. His brows shot up, and he lifted his chin, as if to say, *come closer*. Vinnie did, but braced her hands between them, just in case he popped off.

Instead, he lowered his voice. "I'm not saying he did anything to her. I'd break his fucking neck if he did. Find Red and shake his tree. I don't know for a fact there *was* a laptop she was after."

Oh really? came to her tongue, but aloud, she asked, "Why not?"

"Because she coulda bought a brand-new one right here in town. I was matching her dollar for dollar, and I gave her twelve hundred. What kind of used computer costs twenty-four hundred bucks, huh?"

"Then why did you give her the money?" Vinnie asked.

"She asked for it." Keith shrugged simply, then stood back up. He was obviously done sharing his suspicions about his own family. "Now I got work to do. And we're closed."

Ordinarily, Vinnie wouldn't let a guy like Keith Adair dismiss her. But she had nothing else *for* him, and he'd given up a lot by giving up his nephew. She liked to reward cooperation; made it easier to get more of it in the future. She didn't bother to leave her name or number. She just nodded and thanked him for his time.

She had a feeling if he wanted to find her, he would.

Chapter 10

Serpentine roads kept Vinnie's foot on the brakes.

For her, Kerry County was brand-new, in every single way—and Vinnie couldn't help but see it all as she drove back into town. Southern Indiana could be curvy, but where she came from, roads stretched for miles in straight lines. There were trees in town, but little ones, carefully caged and stunted by steel grates and concrete curbs.

Here, trees engulfed everything. They were changing colors fast, bright streaks of scarlet and gold mixed in with the deep, solid green of the firs. They flashed by the windows, fluttering past the hood of her car as she drove. This place took its nature seriously, forcing people to fit its shape instead of the other way around. Vinnie couldn't tell if she liked it yet.

For sure, the remoteness of the cottage was what she wanted.

But she wasn't used to the East Coast. How the storefronts were hidden away; how an eleven-mile drive meant spending a half an hour in the car, easy. She'd never had to navigate around a peninsula, where there was one road in, one road out. And then, slices of sky disoriented her. Impossibly blue, always framed by crepe myrtle and oaks and alders. Underlined by the occasional stretch of kudzu. There was no such thing as a wide-open plain here, at least, not that she'd seen.

Things she'd taken for granted turned out to be pretty regional to the Midwest. No subs here, just hoagies. Free parking garages instead of wide-open lots. No tornado sirens on Friday (or any other day, for that matter). That left Vinnie uneasy, that she couldn't tell when bad weather was coming until it was on her. Storms moved with their own will in this place, north or south, east or west, they formed a black, boiling sky. It rained like the movies: hard, straight down, the wind careening through to make the trees tremble.

Hell, even the squirrels were different. Grey streaks zipping around, instead of the red, bushy variety back home.

Home.

That was a funny word, *home*. Whenever Vinnie found herself frustrated at the wrong brands of bread, or circling what seemed like the entire town just to turn left, she compared this place to home. But Indianapolis didn't feel like a refuge to her. It wasn't a place to remember longingly.

She'd spent her entire adult life working, working overtime, and going through the motions of having friends from work. She'd seen the worst of the city, over and over. When she mapped it in her mind, the landmarks were grisly: That's the gas station where a fourteen-year-old gunned down his friend over a pack of Pop Rocks. There're the apartments where a divorced dad killed both his kids and himself, so he didn't have to lose custody to his ex-wife.

Blood stained every inch of her mental map of *home*. Homicide engulfed her days. What little she had outside of the job was a scrap of family. Some aging aunts. Distant cousins. Her mother.

Since Vinnie was an only child, she got the full brunt of her mother's perpetual dissatisfaction. Maybe Mom hadn't always been like that. Vinnie had vague memories of a brighter woman. One that sang in the kitchen and sewed clothes and curtains and dolls for fun. Vinnie had been a kid then, a little one. Young enough that her father had still been around.

But Wayne Taylor bailed on the family when Vinnie was eleven. Later, Vinnie found out he'd cheated on Bev with one of her cousins. By then, he was already a ghost. He fought paying child support, made it Vinnie's responsibility to come see him, and eventually, she just quit. He didn't want her, and she didn't need that. She had enough shit to worry about.

Nowadays, Vinnie had a vague idea of where he was, but that was it. His face was frozen in time; she wouldn't recognize the old man he'd become.

So there wasn't much to miss about Indiana, except its familiarity. Knowing the streets. Being able to navigate. Understanding the language, the unspoken tongues. A little part of her resented the need for GPS apps to get around, but sometimes, it came in handy. Like now, when the denuded map showed the outline of a building, with a label: *The Harbor Voice*.

That's the paper where Vinnie had found out very little about Avery, but everything about the Adairs. Out of curiosity, Vinnie pulled a hard right, then a harder left to maneuver into the narrow strip-mall parking lot. That was another thing to get used to. Everything from five-star restaurants to medical clinics to newspaper offices inhabited strip malls on the outer edges of Wills Harbor.

Pulling into a space in the back, Vinnie parked. When she stepped out, she scowled at the parking job. For some reason, she couldn't park a straight line here. Maybe it was the size of the lot; maybe it was the rental car. It was a slightly weary Chevy Volt;

it felt like a quarter the size of the Charger she used to drive for work. Put another thing on the to-do list, she thought, buy a car.

A woman backed out the front door, her arms laden with a bag and a Yeti bottle as big as a cocker spaniel. Wavy black hair haloed her long face, a face that was somehow approachable and forbidding at the same time. A touch of scarlet lipstick brightened her winter-gold skin while black, winged liner widened her dark eyes. She stood at the door, juggling keys beneath her bag to lock the place up.

Ignoring the electric sizzle in her chest, Vinnie took too-long strides to catch her. "Hey! Hey, hold on a second."

"Sorry," she replied, giving the door a tug to check the lock. "We're closed for lunch. Come back after two."

"One minute and I'll get out of your hair. I just need to find out who wrote . . ." Still moving, Vinnie produced her phone and skimmed the gallery. It didn't take long to find the screenshot she'd made of the missing-persons notice in the paper. She thrust the phone at the woman and said, "This. Do you know the reporter?"

She smiled wryly as she slung her purse over her shoulder. "I wrote that. Camila Vega, staff reporter. High school football games, grannies with prizewinning watermelons, little lost kittens—I write it all."

Stung by the low, brown-sugar buzz of her voice, Vinnie smiled and hoped the heat she felt on her skin wasn't visible. Offering a hand, she said, "Nice to meet you, Camila. I'm Vinnie Taylor; I'm new in town and I have a couple of questions, if you've got some time."

What a useless thing to say, Vinnie thought. The handshake was over before she could register the touch.

"Walk with me," Camila said, already taking the first step. "I've got a half an hour, and I'm starving."

Falling into step with her, Vinnie said, "Great, let me buy you lunch."

Camila laughed, a sound like silk and summer. "I love free food. You're on."

get paid to write the news, not to make it."

Camila broke a mozzarella stick in half, stretching the cheese thin, then dropping it on her tongue. They had settled at Donna Italia, a café-cum-pizzeria across the road from *The Harbor Voice*. The owners had crammed as many Italian clichés as they could into the small restaurant.

Pictures of gondolas splashed across the walls; red-and-white gingham tablecloths covered each table. "Funiculì, Funiculà" played from a hidden speaker, tinny like a phonograph in a nonna's attic. Notes of basil and garlic hung in the air, mingling with a slight undertone of grease.

Sitting across from Camila, Vinnie made sure her gaze didn't wander. This wasn't a social call; she wasn't here to flirt or make a friend, no matter the giddy lightness in her chest. In a way, Vinnie thought it was nice to know she could still feel that rush of attraction. She was fifty, not five hundred, and Camila Vega was a package. She just wasn't hers to unwrap.

"So *The Harbor Voice* doesn't do anything investigative?" Vinnie asked.

Camila shook her head and pushed the dish of red sauce toward Vinnie. "We're so close to Baltimore and D.C., we let them handle the big stories. Us, we keep it local. Mostly press releases. Comings and goings. That kind of stuff. Go ahead, dip it. Their marinara is fantastic."

With a glance at the fried ravioli in her hand, Vinnie did as she was told. The bite wasn't eye-rollingly good, but it warranted a surprised "Nice" from her.

"Right? I could drink it by the gallon," Camila said, bathing hers before taking another bite. "Anyway, the shop's only three people. Me, the editor, and the ad guy. I'm the only one who comes in every day."

Plowing through the crispy ravioli, Vinnie covered her mouth between bites so she could still talk. "The piece about Avery Adair, that was . . . ?"

"Sparked by a press release," Camila said. "They send them over on Tuesdays and Thursdays, usually. A whole bunch of them all at the same time. Me and Kingston—he's the editor—thumb through them and pick out the ones that seem important."

Vinnie arched a brow; heard herself saying with an edge, "Important?"

Suddenly, Camila sprawled back in her chair. She seemed disappointed as she shook her head. "Not like that. If I have space to print one story, I'm printing the one about a missing kid, not missing laundry from the coin-op. They show up in one batch together, but they're not the same."

Backing down, Vinnie nodded. "Fair."

"Thankyew," Camila said, diving back into her appetizer. "Anyway, we get the press releases, pick the important ones, and then I write them up. That one in particular, I called up her mother. That's how I found out about the time gaps. Avery was missing a week before her mother called it in. Which was a week before I got their press-release packet."

Vinnie sat a little straighter. "Did you call the department too?"

"Of course." Camila rolled a shoulder, her waterfall earrings glimmering. "I went to high school with Nathan Rosier; we go back. It's not his case, but he checked in with the guys on it. They said they had a reliable source, who insisted that the kid was at an aunt's house in Virginia."

A reliable source could have meant a lot of things. But when it came to missing persons, the only thing that actually mattered was clapping eyes on the victim. Emails, texts, voicemails—too easy to fake. But if they'd already actually found Avery, she could wrap this up before dinner. Vinnie said, "That's not in the article, though."

Camila huffed a breath. "No, it's not. Because all they got was a phone call at the station. Didn't follow up, didn't see her in person. They heard her voice, so, good enough, I guess."

"That's not how that works," Vinnie said instantly.

"Tell me about it."

The waiter glided over, cutting them off for a moment while he cleared their plates and put down new ones. These were heaped full of luscious pasta, stuffed to plumpness and gleaming with more of the red sauce. Camila had a fork in hers instantly. When a tortellini threatened to jump from the tines, she just balanced it with the side of her finger. A finger that she licked clean without shame.

No ring on that hand, Vinnie noted, then dragged her attention back to her own plate. Almost rhetorically, she said, "You don't need a press release when somebody's not missing. Why didn't they close the case?"

Amused, Camila leaned over the table. She met Vinnie's gaze, her nose crinkling, and teased like they'd known each other for years. "That's a very interesting question that somebody should answer."

Fuck. Fuck, fuck, fuck.

Vinnie had managed to live in this town for two months without getting to know anybody, and she liked that. She liked the anonymity, nobody knowing her name, having no reputation to precede her. She liked the quiet she'd cultivated around herself, and the fact that she could try out new things without anybody's eyes on her.

So what the fuck was wrong with her, that she threw herself headfirst at the first hint of something complicated? Not to mention interconnected, in a web of people who had known each other their entire lives. This was the opposite of the plan. And here she was, wading deeper every moment.

"All right, let me ask you this," Vinnie said, trying to wrestle the conversation back to facts and formality. "What do *you* think happened to Avery Adair?"

For the first time, Camila's expression darkened. "Nothing good. Nathan's tight-lipped when he wants to be, so I can't get him on record to say he's worried. But knowing him? He's the reason the case isn't closed."

Well, if she was doing this, she may as well do it right. Vinnie dug into her own plate. "What do you know about Tyler Purnell and Red Adair?"

"Mmm, not enough to help," Camila replied. "They're in high school; they're on the football team."

"Both of them?"

"Pretty sure, yeah." Now curiosity crept into Camila's voice.

"Red's related to her. Why? What do *you* know about the Purnell kid?"

Instinct and experience told Vinnie to shut up. It was important to ask the reporters your questions, and to dodge theirs when you could. It never helped to have your whole case vivisected in the news before you'd even finished working it. Her neck went tight, and her jaw clenched in reflex. Then she remembered one thing:

She was on her own side, now. And right now she could use the help of an experienced, *local* journalist with resources of her own.

So she gave Camila a thumbnail of everything she knew, including her read on the parents (probably not involved). It wasn't much; she could admit that. But she gave up Rosier's suspicion that Tyler was a little shit, and that the girl's best friend thought he'd outright killed her. For a kid without a record, that was a big accusation. And now that Vinnie knew someone claiming to be Avery Adair had called the police station to solve her own case, well . . . that made it interesting, didn't it?

"If it were up to me," Camila finally said, "I'd be up Rosier's tailpipe about that call."

"You could have asked; why didn't you?"

With a smile, Camila shrugged and said, "Like I told you, I don't get paid to make the news. It's a community rag. I'm lucky they pay me at all."

Vinnie took that in, folded it up, saved it for later. And since they were sharing shit, Vinnie pushed her plate to the side and asked, "Wanna split a tiramisu?"

Chapter 12

Lunch went longer than expected, so Vinnie's next stop was the hardware store, again.

The bell rang as she walked in, but instead of the teen she expected, she found a man in his forties at the front counter. His face was familiar, from the photos in the paper. Whenever Hannah appeared in the pages of *The Harbor Voice*, she was usually flanked by her parents. A proud, round father on one side, a delighted, streamlined mother on the other. This guy's nametag confirmed it, Robin Candlewood, Hannah's dad.

"Welcome to Henk's!" he said brightly. "Let me know if you need anything!"

"Thanks," she replied, then tried to blend into the aisles. She could talk to Robin, for sure. But she'd learned a long time ago that parents were completely oblivious to certain sides of their children. She had a feeling that Hannah's suspicions about Tyler lived in a space she didn't share with Mom and Dad. Why else write it out secretly, to hand to a stranger?

Unfortunately, Vinnie beat Hannah to Henk's, and doubling the misfortune, the store was marginally bigger than a bread box. There were only so many times she could walk the aisles before Robin left the counter to help her.

"New around here?" he asked as he came around the aisle. "What can I do you for?"

Oh yeah, he was definitely Hannah's father. They shared the same big eyes and heart-shaped face, although he angled his out with a close-cropped beard and mustache. Since it wasn't generally popular with parents to find out that a cop—not a cop, an investigator—was staking out their kid, Vinnie transformed into a perfectly nice customer.

"Well, I just rented a place for the winter, and a stray cat got in last night."

Robin nodded pleasantly. "Uh-huh, uh-huh, uh-huh, and are you wanting to catch the stray or keep him out, or both? Because I can help you with both. You just lead the way."

"I only need to catch the one, once, if I can keep him out."

With a clap of his hands, Robin waved for her to follow him. "Next question, what are you renting, one of those tiny houses out by the Severn?"

"No, it's a cottage," Vinnie said. She held her hands out, approximating the shape. "An octagon, up in the woods."

Lighting up, Robin bobbed his head. "Ahhhhhh, the Dooney Cottage! Beautiful place! Ha, Rich is doing everything he can to keep that place from ending up on the historic register, but that tells me exactly what I need to know about your little stray problem! Just a cat so far?"

That *so far* ran a shudder down Vinnie's spine. How many more animals should she expect? "Yep, just the cat."

"All righty, since I know Rich would lose his mind if you did anything permanent to the place, I know just what you need. Screen wire and blood spray!"

For a brief moment, Vinnie was wildly homesick for the little apartment she'd left behind. Sure, the neighbors could get rowdy on a Friday night, but then again, she hadn't been home most Friday nights. What mattered was that she'd never had to worry about needing something this guy gleefully called blood spray. "I don't know about all that . . ."

"Oh, it sounds worse than it is," Robin assured her, leading her around the store. He picked up a roll of screen, tucked that under his arm, then asked, "Do you have a staple gun out there?"

"Uh, no. Just a toolbox with the regular stuff."

With that, Robin plucked a bright-yellow staple gun from the shelf, added a box of staples to his armpit, and kept moving. "Now, what you're gonna wanna do is cut this about yea wide, and then staple it to the shakes, then the frame of the eave, and the overhang. Get it tight. Loose screen is an open door!"

Vinnie watched helplessly as Robin abandoned the screen pile on the counter, then ducked into the back. He returned almost instantly with a trapdoor cage. He said, "Since you're new, and it's just the one cat, I'll rent this to you instead of selling it outright. Unless you think you'll need it later . . . ?"

"Renting is great, thanks," Vinnie said, glancing toward the door. Hannah still hadn't arrived. Across the street, she saw a couple of teenage boys loping between the parked cars, so school had to be out. She just needed to stall until Hannah arrived. Rubbing her hands together, Vinnie approached the counter and asked slowly, "So what kind of blood is it?"

"In the spray? Oh, pig mostly. Animals don't like it; makes 'em think a big predator's close by. But the plants love it. Completely non-toxic, how about that?"

"Amazing," Vinnie said. Then, casually, after he showed her

how to bait and set the trap, she touched the Missing poster taped to the counter. "This is sad."

For the first time, Robin Candlewood looked less than ecstatic. His whole expression soured, though it was obvious he was trying to school it back to neutral. He nodded and said, "Sad, but not a surprise, really."

"Runs with a fast crowd, huh?"

Robin lowered his voice, as if there were anyone else to overhear. "More like she's the fast crowd everybody else runs with. Even went to juvie in middle school."

Vinnie wondered if he knew that fast crowd included his daughter. "So a runaway, you think?"

Robin scooted from behind the counter, back into the store. He didn't seem flustered; just uncomfortable. Maybe that was a grown man realizing it wasn't a good look to bad-mouth a missing kid, but it could have been something else. Vinnie watched him keenly as he picked out a white jug with a red spray nozzle. His face had gone pink, a color that shone through the thinning spot in his hair.

"Got to be," he finally said, returning to the counter. "Wills Harbor is a safe town. You can leave your doors unlocked around here. Your windows too. The worst thing that would happen is"— his smile returned, and he patted the cage—"the wildlife stopping by to say hi."

Nowhere is that safe, Vinnie thought. Bad things happened everywhere; quaint seaside villages included. Criminals *also* liked to work smarter, not harder. An open window was a door, and an unlocked door was practically an invitation.

A wave of light spilled from the back of the store, then a slam came before shuffling footsteps and something soft hitting the floor. It was like a reset button; Robin's flush faded, and his smile returned. He took a step back and called out, "Hey, Hanny-doodle, how was school?"

"Fine," Hannah said, then emerged. She had a plastic, pleasant expression on her face when she realized there was a customer there. Then it melted when she realized who the customer was. A quick shot of panic streaked across her features as she looked from Vinnie to her dad, then back. "Sorry, I didn't know you were busy."

"Your daughter, I take it?" Vinnie asked Robin, trying to smooth over Hannah's anxiety. "She's a good kid; she helped me out the last time I was here. It's why I came back."

Robin puffed up, patting Hannah's back. "That's what I like to hear. Good head on her shoulders, this one!"

"Are you checking out?" Hannah asked, pulling on the signature green smock with the store's logo plastered on the front. "I can get this, Daddy."

"It's all right—" Robin started, then looked up when the entry bells rang again.

A man stuck his head inside. "Rob-o, you got a minute? I keep throwing a chain and I don't know why."

Hannah shooed her father toward the door. "Go ahead. I can take care of this." She smiled and nodded him out the door, standing like a perfect employee at the register, ready to help. As soon as the door closed, Hannah turned to Vinnie and lowered her voice.

"You're taking the case."

"Yeah," Vinnie said, pulling out her wallet. "I'm taking the case."

Chapter 13

Vinnie let Hannah load the trap into her car because it gave them a chance to talk outside of the store. Fortunately, she'd parked at the café, so it was a jog from Henk's. That gave them a chance to talk privately.

"You didn't say anything to my dad, did you?" Hannah asked, the moment they crossed the street. The cage dangled from one hand, and the blood spray from the other.

Vinnie shifted the roll of screen over her shoulder. "I didn't. I figured you had a reason for the secrecy. And now would be a good time to let me in on it."

Even though they were well out of her father's earshot, Hannah still kept her voice low. Her gaze darted forward, back, like she was afraid somebody might be listening . . . following. "He doesn't like her. I mean, basically, it's the whole family. Their reputation. He tried really hard to keep us from being friends in middle school."

"But you're friends now. He gave in?"

Hannah made a face. "I got sneakier. He's nice to *everybody*, but he couldn't even fake it around her."

"Why not?"

A storm settled on Hannah's features. "I don't know."

With a gentle edge, Vinnie said, "Well, you partied together; could that be it? I know it was more than once. I've seen the pictures. Were you at the party that got her arrested in eighth grade?"

Hannah's cheeks turned pink. "Okay, yes. But it's not hardcore! And *he* used to do the same stuff when *he* was in high school. Go look at the dock on Little Pea. My dad carved his initials into the post. Like, they're still there."

Vinnie stopped at the trunk of her car. Freeing the keys from her pocket, she casually unlocked the trunk. She didn't want to spook Hannah, but she did want to corner her a little, so she changed the subject abruptly. "If you think Tyler killed her, why bother with a Missing poster?"

"Because I didn't know for sure. Not at first."

"So when *did* you know?" Vinnie asked. She dumped her purchases into the trunk, then leaned against the car. The sky stretched out above them, a shockingly pure blue against the oranges and reds of autumn leaves. A cool breeze teased down her collar and tugged at the hair that sprang free from her braid. She wasn't going to accuse or press; she was just going to ask questions until the answers made sense.

"Okay, here's the thing," Hannah said, flustered. "She didn't come to school that Friday, weird, but okay. Whatever. *Then* she wasn't answering texts, also weird. And the whole week, I kept waiting for her to show up—"

"What about the week before? 'Cause I heard something went down."

Hannah rolled her eyes instantly. "Oh God. We got into a stupid fight about Squidgey Mac."

Feeling herself take a step back, Vinnie tried to keep the bafflement on the inside. "Squidgey Mac?" The *what the fuck* was silent.

"You know, Squidgey Mac." When Vinnie rolled her shoulders, Hannah sighed, exasperated. Then she explained, as if talking to a particularly stupid Labrador retriever. "She's a BookTuber; she makes funny videos. And posts them to YouTube, it's a website where—"

"I know what YouTube is; go on."

Both embarrassed and annoyed, Hannah said, "Anyway, Avery said she was using her popularity to ho it up, because she hooked up with Bookcraft by Bex, then Zach from Dos Bros, *then* Aura; their channel is just called Aura Points. And I was like, you're not a ho just because you date people, and Avery said people said she was wilding at VidCon, which is a rumor, not a fact . . ."

Jesus, teenagers. With a wave of her hand, Vinnie brushed her off. "Okay, I get the gist. Back to the week she disappeared, you didn't stop by her house? Talk to her mom?"

Hannah dropped the cage and spray into the car, then stepped back. She crossed her arms over her chest, and damn, she looked so young. Just a little kid, trying to make the inexplicable make sense. "Not till Friday."

Mirroring her posture, Vinnie crossed her arms too. "You knew she was gone before anybody else. Why didn't you say anything?"

"Because I didn't know there was something wrong!"

"She was missing school."

Hannah's frustration led to furiously waving hands. "So?"

"So I'm trying to understand the timeline, Hannah. Help me make it make sense."

A car rumbled past, blocking out the sound of Hannah's sigh. It was visible, though. Her whole body rose and fell with it. "I didn't talk to her mom at first, because she was . . . God. Everything is so messed up right now."

"Just start at the beginning," Vinnie coaxed. "Avery wasn't at school on Friday. She stopped answering texts. You weren't worried—"

"I *was* worried," Hannah interrupted. "Because the last time I talked to her, on Thursday, she said she was going to do some 'errands' with Red."

"Right, she was buying a laptop."

Confused, Hannah squinted. "What laptop?"

Vinnie made a mental note right there: different stories for different people, never a good sign. Avery had told her parents she was buying a laptop. Kassadee believed it; Keith hadn't. And apparently, he was right not to, since Hannah knew nothing about it at all. Vinnie said, "Oh, that's what I thought I heard; guess not. So what kind of errands are we talking about?"

Squirming, Hannah looked past her. The wind pulled her hair into her face, and she made no move to push it away. So that was answer enough: Avery disappeared doing something illicit. But there were lots of kinds of illicit, and in this case, the truth might have made a difference.

Gently, but firmly, Vinnie said, "You said you wanted my help. I can't do that if you won't help *me*."

Almost whispering, Hannah said, "He deals; I thought he was cutting her in." Then, fiercely, she added, "I was like, why are you even doing this? And she's like, I need the money."

Another lie to the best friend. If Keith Adair's accounting held up, Avery had disappeared while in possession of the better part of three grand. Playing dumb, Vinnie asked, "For what?"

"I don't know. I mean, maybe just to have? Clothes and makeup and stuff? She didn't make that much tutoring, you know? So yes, I knew she was gone, but at first I thought she was with Red. And I figured she probably had her phone turned off because . . . ugh, this makes her sound like a criminal."

Yeah, a little bit, it does, Vinnie thought. Turning off a cell to hide from tower pings was premeditation. Avery wasn't innocently riding around with a cousin; she knew they were committing a crime, and she didn't want to get caught. "What kind of drugs? Pot's legal here."

"Not if you're in high school. But it's X mostly," Hannah mumbled. "Sometimes shrooms, stuff like that. Party drugs."

"Nothing harder? No meth? Heroin?"

Hannah shook her head furiously. "No. No. Avery would never."

"Okay, keep going. She didn't come back; she didn't text back. I'm still missing a huge piece of the puzzle here. Why do you think Tyler's involved?"

Glancing up the street, Hannah didn't quite meet Vinnie's eyes. "Because he was playing on her phone, pretending to be her."

"What makes you so sure?"

"Because Tyler doesn't text full sentences, and Avery does. Tyler's always like, *kk, cu, w* slash *e, sup.* He ignores autocorrect, and he just . . . look." Hannah pulled her phone out and started to scroll through it. "This is him texting me before we broke up."

Taking Hannah's phone, Vinnie skimmed.

Tyler: You defiantly coming fri?

Hannah: I can't, I have to study.

Tyler: Fr tho? You gotta come fr fr fr!

Hannah reached over to switch to a conversation with Avery. She scrolled past a handful of pictures, mirror selfies mostly, then stopped. "And this is how Avery texts."

> **Hannah:** I'm so super serious right now, if he shaved his head, I'm going to be maaaaad.

> **Avery:** LOL you can be mad, but you'll get glad again. You always do.

> **Hannah:** I know, I'm a CoolGirl™!

> **Avery:** No, you're a real one! And anyway, hair grows back.

With a frown, Vinnie looked up at Hannah. "Connect the dots for me."

Scrolling again, Hannah abruptly stopped. "This is the text I finally got the Friday after she disappeared."

> **Hannah:** Okay if you don't text me back by tonight, I'm going to your mom's. Or the police. Or both. I'll do both, Avery! Where are you????

> **Avery:** Your being fr rn? Bitch I'm good!

Chapter 14

"When I got that text, I went to see her mom," Hannah said. Tears hung heavy in her eyes. Rather than let them fall, she tipped her head back, blinking into the sunny sky. Her hands fluttered helplessly now, pressing fingers beneath her eyes, then palms against her cheeks, before starting over again.

"She didn't even know Avery was out of school! I didn't tell her about the texts, because I didn't want to scare her when I didn't know what, exactly, was going on. But she called 911. I was there when the police came. The deputy was nice, I guess, but he didn't . . . like, he wasn't concerned, you know?"

Oh, Vinnie knew. There was nothing wrong with being polite but reserved when taking a call like that. The deputy, whoever he was, wasn't in a position to actually help.

His job was mainly clerical, kicking that paperwork into gear. The most he would get to do is emphasize whether something seemed terribly wrong in the residence. And even then, he wouldn't have been the one working the case. That was a detective's job.

Vinnie asked, "Did you ever talk to an investigator? A detective?"

Hannah laughed bitterly. "Yeah. They came to the store the next day. *They* just wanted to hear about how bad she was. They kept saying she was probably in the family business, and I told them no! She's not like that!"

"Wait," Vinnie said, stopping her. "Did you lie to the police about her delivering drugs?"

Ashamed, Hannah dropped her head to stare at the ground. "Not exactly. I said I thought she might have been with Red, which is *true*."

"But not what she was doing with him," Vinnie supplied.

Nothing exploded quite like a teenage girl. Everything that had been bubbling inside her, restrained by social graces and expectations, burst out. She threw her arms out and fixed her feet to the ground. She took up twice the space she did a moment before. Red-faced and furious, she fought to keep her voice down, but that battle was lost the moment she opened her mouth.

"Because I wasn't sure! And I knew what they were thinking! That she's got a record and she's trashy and they were looking for an excuse to write her off. And I was right! Because after I showed them the texts, they were like, oh, so she *has* been in contact with you, case closed! I tried to tell them about Tyler, and that it wasn't *her*, but they blew me off."

"But why do you think Tyler killed her?"

"I mean," Hannah sputtered, "she's not in his back pocket! She didn't come home!"

Pushing off the car, Vinnie stepped a little closer. She felt for the kid, she really did. Because Hannah wasn't entirely wrong. The only person who should have had Avery's phone was Avery. And there was no good reason for Tyler to impersonate her while she was missing. It was still a big jump to murder, but just a skip to foul play.

Unfortunately, she couldn't comfort Hannah. She couldn't

pat her and tell her it was okay, and it was all going to be all right. Honestly, it didn't sound like a happy ending in the making, so Vinnie did the one thing she could: she took the kid seriously.

Vinnie asked, "Why would Tyler want to hurt Avery? You liked him enough to go out with him. Did he hurt you?"

Slightly deflated, Hannah shook her head. "It's complicated. He doesn't seem mean at first, but he really is. Like, he'd say my shirt was cute. Then he'd point out somebody really pretty and say, 'I wonder what *she* would look like in it.' Stuff like that. 'Have you ever thought about dyeing *your* hair blonde?' 'She's so skinny, I bet I could pick *her* up, no problem.'"

"I see," Vinnie said. Then, she asked, "And did Avery ever date Tyler?"

"She talked *the most* shit about him when we were still dating. She literally made me a cake when we broke up."

"How did he feel about her?"

"He didn't. He ignored her; it was like she wasn't even there."

Maybe Hannah didn't hear it when she said it, but Vinnie did. The disparity between Avery's reaction to Tyler, and his reaction in return, that felt significant. It was a shred, the tiniest hint of a possible motive. Because Tyler didn't strike Vinnie as the kind of guy who liked being disliked. Nor, evidenced by the way he behaved in Henk's, did he like being ignored.

"Do me a favor," Vinnie said. "Give me a copy of those texts."

She wished she could just take Hannah's whole fucking phone. That's what she would have done back when she had a badge. Preservation of evidence, chain of custody, all that. But for now, screenshots would have to do. She needed them for the next conversation she needed to have.

They stood behind her car as they traded numbers, and Hannah sent over the screenshots. Vinnie kept an eye on Henk's. They hadn't been talking long, but they were pushing it. It only took a few minutes to load a car.

Robin was bound to peep out the door anytime now looking for his daughter; the last thing Vinnie needed was parental suspicion. Especially when he'd reacted so viscerally when she asked about the Missing poster.

People were entitled to their feelings. He didn't like the Adairs, made sense he didn't want his promising daughter mixing with them. The memory of his pink face slotted a little too easily into suspicious to her. And if she wanted to keep Hannah talking, it was better to keep that to herself.

"Okay, sent," Hannah said, returning Vinnie's phone. "Now what?"

"Now," Vinnie told her, firmly, "you let me handle it from here. If Avery's in trouble, I don't want you following her into it. If I need more information, I'll reach out. You just keep your head down."

"But I know people here and you don't. I can help."

Vinnie remembered long-closed cases, where families had tried to "help" her investigation. They never realized that talking to people could taint what they had to say. It wasn't intentional; it was even a good instinct. But the questions they asked, the way they asked them, could subtly weight the reply.

Self-preservation alone prompted people to carefully cultivate their answers. Some people didn't want to get involved. If they thought the truth would land them on a witness stand, they might leave out something important. If they thought it might make them look bad, they'd sculpt their answers—even the truth—to make themselves look better.

Anxious witnesses were afraid to look guilty. Depressed witnesses often felt guilty even when they weren't. And sometimes, people just fucking lied.

They wanted to be involved when they knew nothing. They wanted to be involved because they knew too much. They were afraid of the police or felt like sticking it to them. Vinnie's old partner called them case gremlins. They wrote themselves into and out of stories that weren't theirs and left disasters in their wakes.

Vinnie didn't want Hannah seeding the potential witness pool with her own suspicions. Vinnie needed to talk to them clean. Or as clean as possible; there was no telling how many people the sheriff's department had already questioned. Although, based on everything she'd heard so far, probably not that many.

Gesturing toward the road, Vinnie gently shooed Hannah back to the safety of Henk's. "If there's somebody I should talk to, tell *me*. If you hear something, tell *me*. If you *think* of something, tell *me*."

"And if the police come back?"

"Tell your dad. Tell the truth. Then tell me."

Chapter 15

She'd been avoiding the obvious next step, even trying to hide it in her thoughts.

Sitting in her car, she clutched the wheel with white knuckles, staring at the entrance to the Kerry County Sheriff's Office. The knot in her throat made her feel like a python swallowing a rat. The humidity rose in the car, her fear and her sweat souring the air by the moment.

Worry threw up sparks in her brain, little sizzling spots that throbbed as she tried to mentally walk through her plan. Get out of the car. Go inside. Ask to talk to Nathan Rosier. Talk to him. Leave. It was exactly the kind of plan her therapist had urged her to try when it came to triggers.

The problem was, Vinnie quit going to the therapist after a couple months. Every session felt like exposure. Like being dumped in a bucket of ants that squirmed and skittered and bit her everywhere. After a handful of sessions, she'd bailed. She figured she could get through everything but the nightmares on her own.

Unfortunately, she never got to the part where this stuff was easy. Visualizing herself doing this hard thing did nothing to stop the hummingbird beat of her heart. But it *did* make her feel like she might vomit in the parking lot. So she took a quick swig of water and forced herself to get out of the car.

Take the steps.

Open the goddamn door.

Breathe.

The scent of burnt coffee, bodies, and industrial floor cleaner transported Vinnie. She stood there now, waiting to talk to the receptionist, but her brain and body stood in Indianapolis, frozen in time. The last time she'd clocked in as a homicide detective; the last case she'd closed before going undercover.

It was a sad, stupid, senseless murder. They all were, but this case circled that truth in red.

A couple of kids skipping school had found the nude body of a woman in a cornfield. It had taken less than twenty-four hours to track the woman back to Jordan's Fish & Chips, where she worked. The victim had clocked out at midnight and started walking home. She never made it, but it wasn't a deep-down whodunnit.

The autopsy revealed the last of the woman's mysteries on a cold steel table. She was pregnant, only a couple of months along. When Vinnie spoke to the boyfriend, he pretended to be shocked. Had no idea she was pregnant. Always wanted a son with her. Loved her more than any woman he'd ever known.

Funny, though, he ground the heels of his hands against his eyes, and broke his voice into pieces, but he couldn't summon a single tear.

And he didn't pay his debts. Which is why his cousin gave him up two days later. She told Vinnie everything, about how he never wanted the baby. How he'd been trying to get his girlfriend to have an abortion. How he accidentally-on-purpose knocked her down the stairs trying to get her to miscarry. When none of that did the trick, he picked her up halfway home from work and put a bullet in her head.

Then he stripped her body and dumped her in a cornfield. It was just about harvest time. He figured the tractor would destroy any evidence he might have left behind. He didn't count on rain delaying the harvest, or two kids finding a cornfield more interesting than calculus.

Renée Williams. Twenty-four.

Vinnie couldn't remember the boyfriend's name. He'd only inhabited her thoughts long enough for her to testify against him. That was how she used to keep going, one foot in front of the other. Remembering the victims, erasing the perpetrators.

Once she'd started to doubt, it was that trick that left her awake studying old notes in the middle of the night. Searching them, to see if she had done good, or done damage.

"Ma'am," the receptionist said, her voice raised. The nameplate on her desk read LORRINE WHITE, and the expression on her face read professionally annoyed. Vinnie must have missed the first time she had addressed her.

"Sorry," Vinnie said reflexively. "I'm here to see Nathan Rosier. Is he in?"

She could have asked for the detectives working the Adair case, but . . . well, she didn't want to. One cop had already penetrated her bubble, and that was enough. If she had to deal with law enforcement, she wanted to keep it to a bare minimum. Rosier could answer questions just as easy as anybody else.

Without a glance back into the bullpen, Lorrine asked, "Do you have an appointment?"

"No, but I think he's expecting me. Could you tell him Vinnie Taylor's here?"

Without a reply, Lorrine pushed her chair back, then walked away. She moved slowly, her knees stiff and a hand on the small of her back. She left a desk full of knickknacks and family pictures. If Vinnie had to guess, she'd have said Lorrine had been the receptionist there for as long as anyone could remember.

While she waited, she studied the pictures on the walls to keep from thinking too much. The sheriff and undersheriff, the chief deputy and captains, all the way down to the deputies. Out of them all, there was one woman, a captain, and five deputies of color out of fifteen. The Homicide unit in Indy had been a little less homogenous, but not by a lot.

That clawing in her stomach came back. It was a chronic, acid grind full of shame that she hadn't noticed things like that before, tainted with frustration that her ideals fell far short of her actions. It swirled together with a kind of homesickness for a place that never really existed. Bringing it all together was a mocking harlequin, *There goes the white guilt, cry those white woman tears!*

What Vinnie wanted to be was *good*, but the best she could manage was *good enough*. And she compressed all of that into a hard, dark seed inside her chest when she saw Lorrine return. She took her time, stopping to chat with one of the deputies at his desk before coming back to her own.

"He'll be out in a minute," she said, taking her seat again.

Vinnie nodded and took a step back to wait. An uncomfortable tickle of realization gnawed in her. She should have emailed him or called. After all, he *had* left his card in her doorframe, just the way she'd told him to. There were easier, less face-to-face ways to share information.

When he came out of the back, he had his hat against his chest while he worked his way into his jacket. He was already on his way out; Vinnie suspected she'd have his attention for the length of time it took to walk from here to his car. Immediately, she started sorting her evidence into important and not as important. If she didn't have much time, she'd have to make it worth her while.

Rosier came around the counter and said, "Let's go for a ride."

He didn't even break his stride; he just kept on walking right out the door. She followed him outside. A hot flush speckled her throat, climbing her face. Sounds warbled, both too faint and too loud at the same time. Nevertheless, she walked with him, and said, "I can't get in a car with you."

"I'm not gonna force you to do anything," he said with a shrug. "But this is my lunch hour; you can tag along, or you can make an appointment with Lorrine. I'm probably free next Thursday around eight."

They reached his cruiser and he got in. She stood at the passenger side, ignoring the grey wraith of her reflection in the glass. Rubbing her fingers together, she pressed her lips flat and dared herself to reach for the handle. The door unlocked with a *chunk*, and now she had to do *something*. In or out. Stay or go. It felt like she was breathing through a straw, but she forced herself again.

Take the steps.

Open the goddamn door.

Breathe.

Chapter 16

Y ou know I can't tell you anything about an open investigation," Rosier said, taking the scenic route out of town.

The SUV was overwarm, and it smelled like, well, *him*. An inescapable combination of soap and musk that perfectly matched
his soft but serious exterior. Also, he was talking shit and Vinnie
wasn't going to let him get away with it. It had taken a few minutes to find her voice again, but not much more than that. She
wasn't *comfortable*, but she wasn't about to fall out either.

She nodded and said, "Uh-huh, that's why we're in a car alone,
getting the hell out of Dodge so we can talk in private."

Rosier didn't sigh, exactly. Nor did he shrug. There was just
something about his body language that murmured, quietly but
insistently, that she wasn't wrong. They came around a tight curve,
framed by trees and privacy walls, and merged into bridge traffic.

Suddenly, the sky was impossibly wide, and the water below it
seemed to spill out forever.

The shortest glow of happiness filled Vinnie. There weren't a lot
of sights like this in Indiana. The closest was coming up on Lake
Michigan, but that was a three-hour drive away from Indianapolis. Not exactly a trip to take every day. The water soothed Vinnie;
it felt like peace.

There was no explaining it. She'd grown up in a city that jutted out of farmland. The White River ran through it, but it was carefully tamed by concrete boardwalks in town, and once out of town, it hosted camps for the displaced and unhoused. She'd never driven past its shores and felt free.

But somehow, the Chesapeake Bay did it for her, and all the thick rivers and tributaries that ran to it, through the confusing landscape. That's why she'd picked the cottage she had: woods all around like home, but out the back windows, the water. It was her favorite thing about moving, so far.

Rosier turned onto a crooked, tree-lined road barely big enough for traffic to pass on the other side. Sunlight streaked through the canopy, light dancing all around them. The shoulder of the road disappeared, and a Deer Crossing sign appeared.

Suddenly, it felt like the middle of nowhere.

Vinnie's chest clenched, breath thinned. Alarm sent flares up her spine while her brain careened on irrational winds. *Jump out*, it told her. *Just grab the handle and pull it.* The wilderness sprang up around them, somehow completely desolate just a mile from civilization.

Old instinct said she was safe because he was a cop; new instinct begged to disagree. She couldn't reconcile either of them. Her hands trembled, and she knotted them together furiously. Her voice barely wavered when she asked, "How far do we have to go for this conversation?"

"We're almost there," Rosier said. The little side road widened a bit. A brown sign appeared, declaring the entrance to a state park. Rosier slowed at the gatehouse, traded a quick nod with the ranger there, then drove on. Once the gatehouse was well and truly in the rearview, Rosier finally asked, "What are we talking about?"

Trying to relax, Vinnie leaned against the door window, fingers flickering against each other in her lap. "Avery Adair. And Tyler Purnell. And for fun, why two of your deputies closed her case based on a voicemail that could have come from anybody. Let's start there."

Rosier set his jaw, then said, "The case isn't closed. Let's get that straight."

"Really? Nobody's looking for her but family." A beat, then pointedly, "And me."

"I'm not going to lose my temper, if that's what you're aiming for." Rosier turned onto another side road, one with a PARK EMPLOYEES ONLY sign posted. The asphalt gave way to gravel, and the forest pressed in from either side.

Shocks of scarlet and gold robed the trees, broken up by the heavy, green boughs of firs. The stripe of sky bared by the roadcut was so blue, it almost burned. Then suddenly, the road opened up to a cedar cottage and the pearl grey expanse of the bay.

There was no beach; just a long, thin strip of land studded with loaves of stone and marked off by slate boulders. Rosier threw the car into park. Then, deliberately, he keyed the mic on his shoulder. "Dispatch, Unit 202, 10-7, six-zero," he said.

Out of service, sixty minutes, Vinnie mentally translated as Rosier switched off the radio completely, then the dash cam, then opened his door. He stepped out, then ducked back when she didn't immediately follow.

"I thought you wanted to talk."

It probably wasn't against the rules for him to turn off the camera and the radio on his lunch break, but it definitely made Rosier feel less like a rules guy. The isolation tasted like cinders on Vinnie's tongue, but she opened her door anyway.

Her holster's weight reassured her; if shit went down, at least she had a fighting chance. Mutually assured destruction wasn't *ideal*, but it made it easier to get out of the car.

With a vague wave at the cottage, Rosier said, "Used to be a summer house, back in the twenties. Mostly storage for the Parks Department now."

"Fascinating," Vinnie said. She walked to the front of the SUV, and when he sat back against it, so did she. The warmth of the engine bled through her jeans, heat in contrast to the cool wind coming off the bay. "Nobody can hear us now. Speak, mouth."

Rosier pulled a hand through his salt-and-pepper curls, his eyes cast out toward distant flecks of white on the water. Responsibility hung heavy on his brows and pulled at the corners of his lips. He took a moment, hesitated, then finally said, "The case is still assigned to them, but I'm looking into it. This is a small town, and things are complicated."

"Things are complicated all over," Vinnie said.

"Dixon caught the case; he was best friends with Mike Adair in high school. All the way up until Mike got his sister pregnant and ran out on her."

"Are you fucking kidding me?" Vinnie asked.

Rosier went on. "And his partner, Reed, he had a run-in with Big Paul his first year on the force. Left a scar, right there." He gestured at his chin.

"Let me guess, Keith kicked somebody's puppy too."

"No, actually, I get along fine with Keith, and he doesn't hold it against me when I have to haul him in. We played high school ball together." Rosier finally turned to look at her. "Everybody has a conflict of interest around here, because it's a small town.

"No matter who picked up the call, it was gonna be complicated. Everybody's arrested an Adair, everybody went to school with an Adair, everybody's friends or enemies with an Adair, everybody. I review all the cases in my unit, but there's only one of me. I can only do so much, so fast."

Vinnie frowned. "It shouldn't be down to just you, Rosier. Hannah Candlewood told . . . who was it, Reed or Dixon . . . about the text she got from Avery's phone. She knows that message was from Tyler, but your guy blew her off."

"But *I* didn't," Rosier told her, still talking with his hands. "And when I found out you had stepped in because he was harassing Hannah, what did I do? I came to you. Because you were there. You heard something. You saw something." He tapped his temple, returning her sarcasm with a volley of his own. "But it seems to me like *somebody* told me she didn't want to get involved."

Direct hit. "I assumed a kid like Tyler, his parents put a bug in your ear."

"Oh, they did," Rosier said, for the first time sounding almost light. "I used to run with Tyler's dad in high school too. But I listened to the words coming out of his mouth *and* the implication, because I already knew about the texts. You're not stupid; you obviously know how this works."

A little embarrassed, Vinnie nodded and played it off. "What about the voicemail? When did that come in?"

"End of last week, somewhere around there."

"And you just went with that?"

"I don't think you're going to like this," Rosier said. "I've heard it, and I'm pretty sure it was her. I know the kid; I'd bet money it was her voice. She said she was fine, she was visiting her mama's people, and she'd be back soon."

"You can make people say a lot of things under duress."

"I'm well aware. I followed up, Vinnie. I made calls, asked the locals in Fredericksburg to check up, and nobody there has seen Avery since last Christmas. So now I know a couple of things." Rosier held up a single finger. "Nobody noticed her slipping away."

Vinnie held up two fingers. "Tyler Purnell has her phone."

With a frown, Rosier raised a third. "She was still alive when she made that call. But I have no idea how long that's going to be true. If you know about the text, that means Hannah talked to you."

"Yeah, she did," Vinnie admitted. She didn't like the sudden click between them, that subtle shift from negative to positive. It was like flipping a pair of magnets, and just as fast. A thread of adrenaline snaked through her veins, and she was homesick for it. *Ravenous* for it, the good part of investigation—the inspiration, the drive—the collaboration. The words fell from her lips without a second thought. "Are you aware she was possibly running drugs with Red Adair that first weekend she was missing?"

Surprise raised Rosier's brows, and he tipped his head. "No, that's all new."

"Hannah was afraid that would keep you guys from looking for her."

"Huh, because when I came by Henk's to follow up on the texts, her parents wouldn't let me talk to her." He stopped, then pushed off the car, taking a few steps before turning back. "But they let her talk to you."

Instantly, Vinnie shook her head. "No, actually . . . she wrote me a note on a receipt. Then she asked to hire me, to look into it. All on the down-low."

"Did you tell her yes?"

Vinnie shrugged. "I'm here; what do you think?"

"Then *Hannah's* willing, and you can get close to her," Rosier said. There was a different light to his dark eyes, potential flickering there—possibility. "Will you keep talking to her? Did she say anything else? Does she know where Avery and Red went that weekend? What were they selling? Who were they selling it to?"

Vinnie shook her head, Rosier pressed. "But you could find out."

This time, the hesitation was hers. But he knew the same interrogation tricks she did, and he just watched her, silently. Letting the quiet stretch out until it begged to be broken. She *wanted* to help. She wanted to bring Avery home.

Finally, she said, "Who I need to talk to is Red."

"That would be nice, but nobody knows where he is," Rosier said. "He got IDed stealing a Jet Ski a couple of days ago. We've got him on a BOLO, but he dropped out of sight. He's probably hiding up in the city."

Vinnie sighed. "Well, fuck."

"So . . . you'll talk to Hannah?"

She was definitely going to talk to her. But there was strange tension, twisting inside her, when she looked at Rosier again. He had a kind face. A warm gravitas that felt like caring. But what was the difference between being a cop and working with the cops? Was there a difference at all?

She was pissed because all her philosophical wrestling was supposed to be over. Done. Decided. Even her body was mixing up its signals—terrified of a sheriff's parking lot but halfway to comfortable with a sheriff. What the hell was that about? Dammit, this missing girl and this insistent man were dredging it all up.

Vinnie hated walking this line again, and she suspected if Rosier knew a little bit more about her, he wouldn't walk it with her anyway. So she did the only thing she could do.

She offered a compromise.

Chapter 17

She didn't like the way Rosier lingered in her thoughts.

And she didn't like the fact that the stray had made itself at home in the middle of the table. His green eyes barely glanced her way as she came in, banging the cage against the door, sliding the blood spray onto the counter. Vinnie put the pointless cage down, then leaned in to stare into the intruder's black-whiskered face.

"You don't live here."

The cat yawned and stretched its front paws. All ten claws popped out, then retracted as the creature rolled back into the beam of sunlight it had claimed as its own.

Well, at least now she knew it was a tom. A tom who was going to the vet first thing in the morning to get neutered and find a new home. For now, he could get off the table. Vinnie picked him up and deposited him gently on the floor. He purred and strolled into the living room, unbothered.

Vinnie could admit he was handsome, despite the slight crook in his tail, but she refused to *enjoy* him. She'd narrowly avoided one railroading today. She wasn't going to get tangled up in another one in her own house.

The compromise sat heavily in her stomach. She wasn't going to work *with* Rosier. She'd stumbled into this case; she had nothing like jurisdiction on her side, but she couldn't get Avery out of her head. Vinnie had grown up with people like the Adairs; hell, to be fair, *she* basically was one of them too.

She didn't know enough about Avery to know if they were alike. But she recognized Avery's world all too well. Driving through the Hill was like driving around the trailer park of her childhood. It was a place that lived on a strange precipice, like home and hopelessness all at the same time. And it was way too easy for her to imagine her own face hanging with the family's mugshots.

And this was happening, now, in real time, in Kerry County. Exactly the kind of shit that had shattered a twenty-five-year illusion that Vinnie'd believed in with her whole soul. An illusion she'd shored up by letting things slip, even when they stirred the acid in her belly.

Because what woman didn't swallow shit down just to live and breathe in the world? And double the ration if she was brave or crazy enough to walk into a boys' club and expect respect. That wasn't specific to the force; that was just existing.

But somehow, in deflecting the guys who called her *honey-sweetie-baby*, and scoured her T-shirts for a hint of nipple, and decorated her desk with pads and tampons, Vinnie'd also learned to ignore the way they talked about everybody else.

She choked down the slurs, even the ones that drew a target on her. She'd steeped in the disdain for fucking everybody and hadn't even noticed the *us-versus-them* that embedded itself in her.

Realizing that had broken her.

Rationalizing it prolonged the sickness.

Trying to fix it had nearly killed her. Even now, she double-checked the locks when she closed herself in for the night, because she never knew when the past might come back to bite her in the ass.

Maybe it was paranoia. Or maybe it was pragmatism. Either way, she knew for a fact: She didn't want to be the old Vinnie Taylor again. And there were people who didn't want the new Vinnie Taylor walking around six feet above.

As if a mere thought could taunt the universe, her phone flashed. When she saw the call was coming from her mother, she declined it instantly. She'd have to talk to Bev eventually, but that was the beauty of eventually. It wasn't *right now*.

Vinnie dug through the bag from Henk's to find the staple gun. Loading that up, she set it on top of the fridge for later. The sun had already dipped beneath the trees. It was too late for DIY, thank God.

Unfortunately, without a project to occupy her brain, Rosier swam to the surface again. The way she'd just gotten in his car—that bothered her. She knew better than anybody that people lied; cops lied. That men with warmth in their eyes could turn deathly cold, even men whose kids called you Auntie Vin.

Rosier's invitation had set off an alarm beneath her skin. Stirred embers she thought she'd doused, and left her nerves burning. Sitting on the hood of his car, looking at the water, talking the case—it felt good. He felt *comfortable*, for lack of a better word. Like he fit into her life somehow.

And that wasn't going to happen.

Because no matter how right it felt to put pieces together, no matter how high the rush had been when the lightbulb started going off for both of them, they weren't partners. They couldn't be, because Vinnie wasn't about to go back. It was impossible for one person to fix a system that didn't want to be fixed. And as far as she knew, Rosier didn't even think it needed fixing.

So Rosier had to swallow the compromise: He had his case. She had hers. And she'd share what she could, but she wasn't gonna wait around, take his lead, follow his orders. She was her own detective now, and he'd either die of it or get over it. She wanted to be able to look her younger self in the eye and feel good about it.

Heading back out to the rental car, Vinnie stopped to look out at the water. The bay at dusk gathered the fading sunlight on the waves and washed it into a darkened distance. A chill rose like mist toward a sky that reached for star-studded royal. Her phone buzzed again, reminding her to move. With a shiver, Vinnie grabbed the extra bags that filled the trunk.

Working outside the law meant giving up some advantages. But not all. And lucky for her, Baltimore was close enough to throw a stick at. She'd found everything she'd needed there, and more. Locking up behind herself, she hip-checked the door, just to make sure, then headed into the kitchen.

There, she unpacked a police radio, centering it on the table where the cat had staked his claim for the afternoon. Making a mental checklist, she unpacked the rest of her all-new new-life gear.

Night-capable binoculars. Digital voice recorder. Wireless mics. AirTags. Zip ties. Flashlight. First responder's kit. Ammunition—two boxes. And exactly two cans of Fancy Feast for the furball, just in case.

It felt like dropping a winter coat at the first sight of spring. The weight hit the floor and left her senses sharp and fast . . . and hungry. Maybe there had been a point where Avery Adair's case could have been an interesting article in the paper and nothing more.

But Hannah wrote a note.

Keith and Kassadee held a search party.

The school didn't call; the assigned detectives had turned their backs.

And Vinnie, as different as she was now, hadn't retired her conscience. Her sense of justice. In fact, those were sharper than ever, and she was just arrogant enough to think she was the one who could make a difference for Avery Adair. So yeah, Rosier had to live with a compromise.

Vinnie Taylor was taking this case.

Chapter 18

"We're searching for Avery today, will you come?"

Vinnie answered Kassadee's text with an absolute *yes*, then tried to roll over in bed. There was a ten-pound, black-furred problem weighing down her legs. He had the audacity to peep at her with narrowed eyes, annoyed that his regal slumber had been broken.

"Yep, time for you to go to the vet, buddy," she told him. He purred until she threw the covers over him and hopped to her feet. The blanket didn't seem to bother him, so hey, one thing down. She didn't have to hunt for him to put him in the humane trap.

She took a quick shower, then braided her greying hair in a single taut plait. She'd always worn it that way, but lately she noticed her hairline seemed a little thin. The texture had already started changing when the color had. What was once thick, dark, and wavy gave way to white in some places and wiry. She wondered if it was time to cut it all off. Was she *of a certain age* yet?

Fifty wasn't bad, really. But it was different. She didn't think she'd ever been one of those sylphlike twenty-year-olds, the ones who floated down the street effortlessly graceful and made out of beauty. She'd always had wide hips and wide shoulders; she was five-seven—not wildly tall, but taller than most of the women around her. Vinnie had always thought of herself as solid.

Her mother, on the other hand, told Vinnie she looked like a rawboned washerwoman. Thanks, Ma.

Work and exercise, gravity and time, all had a hand in shaping her rounded edges. There were scars she wore proudly and others she didn't even remember getting. And when she stood with her feet on the ground, she felt rooted in a way she hadn't when she was young. And it wasn't just her body.

Something had started creeping in, in her forties. The slow, delightful inability to give a fuck about what people thought of her. It revealed an inner strength she'd always had, but not always used. In fact, she remembered the first time her give-a-fuck had run completely out.

She'd been watching a couple of trash cans with her partner, Kyle Stewart, for hours. They were waiting for their suspect to throw something away so they could grab it and test for DNA.

She'd always enjoyed working with Kyle. He wasn't as unfinished as most of the guys in the department. Rarely raised his voice, always played good cop in the interrogation room, never trapped her in a surveillance car with chili cheese dogs and the unfortunate results. He didn't throw slurs around, in the bullpen or in private. But he didn't have to.

"I don't get it, I don't get what the gays want," he'd said, conversationally. "First they want us at the parade for protection. Now they *don't* want us at the parade for their protection. Make up your fucking mind."

They'd had these circular, endless conversations for years. And for years, when the subject of *the gays* had come up, Vinnie swerved. Or nodded. Let him think she agreed, because it was just easier that way. There were out cops in the department, and they suffered for it. Few of them had managed to break the patrol-to-detective barrier; the ones that had were subtly chained to a desk for the rest of their career. So Vinnie had surprised herself when she said, "Maybe they remember us busting up their heads when we raided the 501."

The 501 was a gay leather bar downtown, disguised as a package liquor store. It had been on the department's hit list for decades.

"Fuck, Vin." Kyle glanced up from his sandwich. "That was the '70s. Shit, you were barely a glimmer, and I was in diapers. That shit stopped happening a long time ago."

"Maybe, if you were white."

At that, Kyle frowned and turned to her. "What are you saying here?"

"I'm saying, there are Black, gay people in that parade who wanna feel safe too." The rest slid right out. "And for the record, you *are* aware I'm one of 'the gays'?"

"Since when?" He scoffed.

"Since always, dumbass," she replied. "I'm bi; always have been."

Jesus, she'd said all of it and hadn't even flinched. She could have taken it back, told him she was bullshitting him; they would have laughed and moved on. Probably, he even would have avoided the subject for the rest of the night, just in case.

But for the first time, Vinnie just let it hang there. Her heart didn't even race. It was perfectly content with the confession. All the years of hiding and obfuscating, blanking out over the casual homophobia, the not-so-casual racism, that permeated the profession, it fell away like scales. One minute, she was someone who kept her secrets to keep her position, and the next, suddenly, she had no fucks to give.

"Well, go on and be a gay if you want to," Kyle finally replied magnanimously.

She grinned and settled back in her seat. "Thanks, I will."

She stayed high off her own supply that night. It was a new feeling, an imperviousness she'd never known before. A certainty that she was who she was, and if that came with one out-of-control eyebrow, a thicker waist, thinner hair, well, so be it.

Looking at it in the rearview, she realized that was probably the moment when everything changed. Because at the time, it was one little confession to one guy she considered family. How could she have possibly known where it would end?

Anyway. Fuck it. Enough introspection. Lotion on the face, lotion on the elbows, and then dressed for a day tromping through the woods in a search grid. Boots, jeans, a Nirvana T-shirt, and a black hoodie instead of her leather jacket. Couldn't take off her leather and tie it around her waist when the work got hot.

"C'mon, goofus," she told the lump in the bed. She scooped him up with every intention of putting him in the humane trap. He purred against her neck and curled in against her, warm and soft. She rubbed her cheek against his head as she carried him into the kitchen.

The cage sat where she'd left it, on the kitchen floor. She hadn't remembered it being so . . . spare. It was nothing but bent wire. It didn't even have a floor in it, and she'd have to shove him through the trap front to get him inside. He stretched and pressed a paw against her chin, and she melted.

What could it hurt to just carry him to the car? He was about to have a real bad day; the least she could do was comfort him until she handed him off to the vet. But that was as far as it would go, she told herself sternly as she headed out. She absolutely was not going to keep this cat.

Period.

Chapter 19

When Vinnie left the vet's office, she found another stray waiting behind her car.

"I'm not stalking you," Hannah said, shifty. She kept her hood up and her head down, her eyes darting all around. "I need a ride to the search; you're going, right?"

Warily, Vinnie took a long, slow look around. Nothing seemed out of place for a Saturday morning. Cars glided by; people in sweaters and flannels walked from shop to shop, hands wrapped around smartphones and coffees.

Halloween garlands rustled in the wind; oversized pumpkins sat in stacks of hay, each carved with elaborate designs. There was a sign with a QR code next to each one: VOTE FOR YOUR FAVORITE, WIN A GIFT BASKET FROM LOCAL VENDORS!

All this competed with the Pumpkin Spice Crawl, hosted by the town's coffee shops. If it were any more wholesome out here, it would be some Norman Rockwell fever dream. But all that busyness meant nobody noticed Hannah standing with her, right out in the open.

"I was planning on it, yes. Where's *your* car?"

Hannah ducked her head again, furtive. "My mom has it. I

get to drive it when she doesn't need it. Can you please give me a ride?"

This was probably a bad idea. She didn't have kids, but she knew Robin Candlewood didn't want Hannah mixed up in this. He would no doubt be *thrilled* to find out his daughter was begging rides from a virtual stranger. Nevertheless, Vinnie slid behind the steering wheel, unlocked the doors, and waited for Hannah to get in.

"I don't know how comfortable I am with this, Hannah. It would be one thing if your parents gave you permission—"

"That's never gonna happen," Hannah told her, pulling on the seat belt. She turned to Vinnie, shadows in her eyes, weighed down by sincerity. "I can't not help. She's my best friend."

For a moment, Vinnie said nothing. Instead, she started the car and backed out, waiting until they were on the road to speak again. "For the record, it's a bad idea to get in a stranger's car."

"You used to be a cop," Hannah scoffed. She was sixteen and still invulnerable, apparently.

Vinnie kept her eyes on the road. "That doesn't make me safe, kid."

"I know about you." Hannah crossed her arms, pressing her feet against the floor of the car and leaning back into her seat. "I looked you up. There aren't that many Vanetta Taylors in the world; you weren't that hard to googlestalk."

A scorching flash of heat slapped against Vinnie's chest and face. Her chest tightened, lungs drawing in thin breaths. She tried to brush it away; it was irrational. Of course anybody could find out who she used to be. It had been in the papers, and the internet never forgets. Shit, Rosier was probably doing the same thing—she would have, in his place.

Still, there was a stark gulf between what happened in court and what really happened. Leveling her voice, Vinnie said, "Then you should *definitely* get that being a cop doesn't mean being safe."

"Were they your friends?" Hannah asked softly.

Old, familiar faces flashed across her gaze—not when they met, when they ended. Their grim satisfaction starkly lit by street-lights, echoed against brick alley walls. It was a hook in the gut, wrenching and turning, realizing that they could have gone farther than they did. That they'd *wanted* to go farther, and would have, left to their own devices.

She couldn't think about that. She couldn't go there. Quietly struggling, Vinnie stuffed it down inside. She waved a hand in front of her face as if she could banish memories with a gesture. "Not in the end, no."

Hannah melted a little. She started to reach out but then took her hand back self-consciously. "I'm really sorry."

The way she said it knocked something loose inside Vinnie. Her throat closed up, and thankfully she felt the spark of tears but they never coalesced.

All Hannah knew about was the trial; that was enough. Vinnie had sat in the witness stand, explaining how men she'd worked with, some for a decade or more, were using their authority to rape vulnerable women. How they traded one woman back and forth, as if she were some empty vessel for them to fill. Disgust wormed in loops inside her, and Vinnie shoved it down again. "I appreciate that."

Trying to lighten the mood, Hannah said, "ACAB, right?"

In spite of herself, Vinnie laughed, a little. Part of her still wanted to argue *Not all cops*, but today, another part of her couldn't help but agree. How could she not, when she was driving to a search party for a missing kid, organized not by the police but in spite of them? Rosier's extra eye out didn't put boots on the ground.

As they turned up the road toward the Hill, Vinnie said, "I'm gonna change the subject on you, okay?"

Hannah nodded, bracing herself. "Okay."

"And I need you to be honest with me."

More wary, Hannah nodded.

"Was this the first time Avery ran drugs for the family?"

"*Yes.*" Hannah exhaled, leaning her whole body into the word. "She always said she was smarter than that. And that she wasn't going back to juvie."

"Was she doing anything else to make money? It doesn't seem like tutoring would bring in much."

Hannah rolled a shoulder and looked into the woods. "As far as I know, it was just tutoring. It's not like she had a job-job."

"What's the relationship with Red Adair?" Vinnie quickly added, "I know they're cousins, but are they friends? Are you friends?"

Questioning teenagers was like chasing otters. They were slick and fast, and changed direction without notice. Hannah was no different. "You don't think he did something to her, do you? He wouldn't. They were like this—" She crossed her fingers and held them up. "Red's not the one who texted me from her phone."

Vinnie gave her a moment to settle. Then gently, she told her, "Nine times out of ten, it's the people we know who hurt us. You think it's Tyler. I think that's possible. But I have to rule people out if I'm gonna rule Tyler in."

"I get it. I do. I'm just . . . we've been searching the woods like we're trying to find a body and it's a lot. It's really a lot." A tear rolled down her face; she swiped it away angrily. "Why can't you just go and talk to *him*?"

That's exactly what Vinnie would do if she still had a badge. She hoped that's what Rosier was going to do. But she was just an adult, a stranger, who'd already threatened him once. Enough that the family called their old pal Sergeant Nate to come have a talk with her about him.

They weren't the kind of people to let their kid talk to the authorities without a lawyer. Rosier had the badge to get in the door; *she* would have to engineer her moment carefully.

"I'm working on it," Vinnie said, helpfully vague. She followed the GPS into a park just past the Hill and raised her eyebrows in surprise.

The parking lot was *packed*. Every spot filled, people clutched in groups, people with armbands and clipboards directing them. Somebody had erected a white information tent, and people stood in line anxiously. The whole scene was spattered with pink— T-shirts and headbands and ribbons.

Before Vinnie could get out of the car, Kassadee was already at the window, tapping on the glass. Her expression brightened when she saw two passengers instead of one.

"Vinnie! I'm so glad you're here! And you brought Hanny!"

She stuffed one T-shirt into Vinnie's hands. Then she straightened and pulled the hem on her own to give them a look. Screenprinted on the fabric was the same picture of Avery that was plastered all over town. Kassadee turned to show off the back. It read COME HOME AVERY, WE LOVE YOU.

"Keith got them made," she said, her expression a mixture of wonder and distress. "I sure wish we didn't need them. Come on. We'll get you one, Hannah, and get you guys in a group. I know exactly where I'm gonna put you, too."

Vinnie climbed out of the car warily. "Do you, now?"

"Damn right." Kassadee lowered her voice. "Tyler Purnell showed up with half his boys from the football team. Interesting, 'cause they ain't friends of hers."

Most of the time, Vinnie had to wait for a moment. For once, the moment was waiting on her.

Chapter 20

Vinnie had to give the Adairs credit: they put together a hell of a search party.

There were easily a hundred people who'd shown up to help, and there were search captains ready to organize them. They'd already gridded out the previous efforts and printed maps to point out landscape features that needed special attention. Dogs strained at their leashes, led by handlers in tactical gear.

The search boss, a reedy-looking man in his sixties, made sure everybody downloaded FamGPS on their phones.

Hannah's thumbs zipped across her screen to get the app up and running. "Why, though?"

"Tells us where the searchers have been," Vinnie replied. "Makes sure we're not leaving holes in the grid."

Just then, a mechanical *zizz* cut through the air. Vinnie tipped her head back, squinting under a hand to see a drone streak into the sky. She couldn't tell if it was a professional model or someone's toy, but it didn't matter. The Adairs weren't fucking around with this search. They wanted their girl home.

The problem was, it felt like they were searching in the wrong place. Sure, this patch of land was adjacent to the Hill—between home and Liberty High, and near where Kassadee had seen her last. And according to Hannah, Avery had disappeared before school. She hadn't even gotten to the part of her day where she was due to ride north with her cousin, either buying a computer or selling drugs.

The missing Red Adair probably had better information. At the very least, he could have told them if she'd made it to Howard County. Too bad he was in the wind instead of standing around here, paying a dollar fifty for one of the pink awareness ribbons with the rest of them.

Despite the money, time, and effort the Adairs had poured into this, Vinnie had a gut feeling that it was a waste of time. Howard County was easily twenty miles north of here; so far from Wills Harbor that this search was probably going to be a pointless walk in the park.

For them, anyway. It gave Vinnie a chance to talk to Hannah's number one suspect.

Soon, groups were assigned and Vinnie started for her rally point. She rolled the handle of her walking stick as she walked, getting used to the weight of it. Good for keeping balance, the pole had another function that she was glad they wouldn't need. It was great for testing the difference between earth and flesh.

Coming over a rise, Vinnie caught sight of her group. A couple of Adair cousins, she guessed, based on the family resemblance, and Tyler Purnell. His teammates had been distributed to other groups. That way they could spread the wealth of strong young men, especially given how many middle-aged, middle-shaped people were on hand. But Kassadee had whispered the other reason to Vinnie during the search captain's speech.

"If they're gonna be here, they're gonna work!"

When Tyler saw Vinnie, his face curled into an uncomfortable mask. Around other adults, he pasted on a gleaming smile that screamed All-American-Boy. Around peers, his expressions were more mobile and seemed to be graced with a case of Untouchable Asshole. But with Vinnie, he was out of his element. She already knew he was an asshole, junior-grade, and she'd already out-alphaed him. What a conundrum.

"Vinnie Taylor," she said, offering her hand and taking in the others' names, one by one. Jaylin Adair, one-half of the twin pair that also attended Liberty High; Dustin Dominguez, another Adair cousin, this one hovering in that indistinguishable place between high school senior and college freshman; Kira Lee, possibly an aunt, midtwenties, with the worn-in exhaustion of a much older woman, and of course—

Vinnie offered her hand to Tyler. "We've met. Good to see you."

A restrained anger flickered in his eyes. She could feel the tension in his handshake, how he longed to squeeze her hand as hard as he could. But there were teachers and friends' parents scattered around, and he had to keep his mask on for them. "Yeah, same." Then, taking credit for something he plainly had nothing to do with, he released her grip with a "Thanks for coming out today."

"Absolutely," she replied. "Here, let me get y'all into formation."

She arranged everybody an arm's length apart and made sure that Tyler would be by her side for the entire grid search. They waited for the search captain to blow an air horn, then started their slow walk into the forest.

"What do I do when I get to a tree?" Kira asked, hesitating.

"It's okay to go around. Just keep your eyes on the ground," Vinnie told her.

There were plenty of civilian questions to answer. After all, how many people had actually taken part in a search-and-rescue operation? Not that damned many. Most never would, if they were lucky.

It had been easy to poke fun at the civvies back in the day. Their questions were the low-hanging fruit Vinnie and her colleagues could trade in the locker room or in the cars during long shifts. It was easy to see now that they were only "stupid" if you already knew the answers.

The underbrush turned into a tangle as soon as the canopy closed over them. Most of the trees still had their autumn leaves, enough to cast a shadow. The temperature dropped almost instantly; Vinnie was grateful now for the extra T-shirt.

She kept her eyes forward, using the stick to dip through the underbrush before taking a step. She heard the drones sweeping overhead, though she couldn't see them. Voices occasionally rang out to stop a search line. They each had a bundle of pink vinyl ribbons to use, in case they found anything unusual. Someone with more experience would come along behind them to decide if it warranted further examination.

"How do you know Avery?" Tyler asked. He'd finally recovered, back on his feet and ready to needle Vinnie if he could. That was fine by her; the more he talked, the more she learned.

"Kassadee asked me to be here," she said. "How about you?"

His plastic smile never faltered as he joked, "Well, we went to the same kindergarten."

Jaylin laughed, leaning forward to look down the line. "Same here. And the same birthday parties."

"That's sweet, are you guys close?" Vinnie asked.

Rolling his ropey shoulders, Jaylin said, "She's family."

"And family's *everything*," Kira added.

"I imagine you're all pretty upset," Vinnie said, fishing a little.

Talking to a victim's parents, their best friends, well, that told you one thing about them. But talking to the family that knew the dirt but didn't care about hiding it, that added a whole new dimension to the profile.

Dustin said, "Yeah, you know, she's a real one." Somehow, in the last ten feet, he'd picked up a stick of his own. Just a long branch that towered two feet over his head when he held it like Gandalf. When he spoke, he thumped the stick on the ground in time with the words.

"Sorry," Vinnie said with a self-deprecating smile, "I'm old, what does that mean?"

"She was real with you," Kira supplied. "She wasn't fake. If you know her, you *know* her. You know what I mean?"

Tyler snorted a laugh, which he disguised as a cough. His reactions told her as much as, if not more than, his words did. He wore insincerity like a letter jacket and smiled around a core of unkindness.

Keeping him in her peripheral vision, Vinnie addressed Kira. "I get it. Kind of like, what you see is what you get?"

"But chill," Jaylin said. "Like, if you smoke, she's not going to snitch or anything."

"She stays in her lane," Dustin said. *Thump.*

Scribbling mental notes, Vinnie held up a hand to stop the line. A downed tree stretched in front of them, and she wanted to check under it before they moved on. She wedged her hiking stick under one side and encouraged Dustin to do the same on the other. "Now, just give it a heave, good, there you go."

As the log rolled, up rose the sweet, loamy scent of decaying earth. There was nothing there except rotten leaves and a blue-striped skink startled from its cozy hidey-hole. Bits of rot flecked off the log, exposing the ornate tunnels some beetle had left behind. All perfectly ordinary, absolutely unremarkable. Satisfied, Vinnie dropped her hand to leave it, and they kept walking.

The hill took a sudden, steep dip that threatened to throw them all off their feet. Kira and Jaylin hesitated, taking in the embankment with anxious glances. Tyler kept tromping forward until gravity snatched him, and he almost planted his face in the moldering undergrowth.

"Here, like this," Dustin said, and demonstrated. Turning perpendicular to the hill, he stepped down like the ground was a staircase. First foot, step, bring the other next to it, repeat. Everyone followed his example, except Tyler.

Even though he'd already tripped once, he insisted on big, ropey steps, wobbling with arms akimbo. He looked like an idiot, and he was probably going to hurt himself doing it, but that was his problem. Vinnie followed Dustin's lead, occasionally stopping to run her stick through the underbrush.

Out of breath, Kira asked, "You've done this before, huh?"

"A couple times," Vinnie answered.

Tyler chose that moment to strike. With a sheen of victory, he asked, "Was that before or after you got fired for snitching to the cops?"

Chapter 21

A barbed-wire fist squeezed Vinnie tight, and a slap of heat stung on her face.

That's not what happened. She could argue it, but the damage was already done. The rest of the party pulled back into themselves, suddenly suspicious. Until now, she had been a random acquaintance of Kassadee's. Now she was something else in their eyes—and something they weren't sure they wanted to trust.

Vinnie rolled her shoulders, summoning a faint smile. "Yeah, but I was also snitching *on* the cops, so . . ."

She let her sentence trail off. Between that and the casual response, the rest of the search party relaxed. A little. That's really all she needed, for them to be comfortable enough to talk around her. They weren't making friends here; just working. And Vinnie knew how to work with all kinds of personalities.

Curious, Kira clutched a tree to brace herself, stepping down over a huge rock jutting from the hillside. "For what?"

Now dead serious, Vinnie said, "Messing around with little girls."

"Sounds like they had it coming," Kira said. She rubbed a pile of leaves away with the tip of her sneaker. Nothing under the boulder except more rocks and dirt. "Guys like that, they shouldn't even get a trial. Just put a bullet in their heads."

"That's the real shit, right there," Dustin said, thumping his stick.

Now that sentiment toward her had softened, Vinnie had to resist the temptation to needle Tyler. A little "What do you think, Tyler, should old men be diddling teenagers on the clock, or nah?" She wanted to, but she refrained. One, he was a dick, but he was still a kid, and two, she didn't want him defensive. His attempt to fuck with her had fallen flat. That was the only prize she needed.

Two years ago, she would have rubbed his face in it, over and over, until he lost his cool. Because two years ago, that would have been useful. Getting a perp to take a swing was the quickest way to lock him up, just long enough to get the judge to sign off on a search warrant for something more serious. Those little extra charges added up, and they were useful. Used to be useful, that was.

Now she was "just" a woman in the eyes of the law. If Tyler hauled off and coldcocked her, Dustin and Jaylin would probably pull him off . . . probably. Pretty much everybody would agree she'd had it coming, and that's where it would end. So antagonism had to be chucked out of Vinnie's toolbox. That kind of plausible deniability didn't work in the real world—it shouldn't have worked in law enforcement, but it *did*.

"Let's keep moving," she said. "We got a lot of ground to cover."

They searched on, most of them occasionally shivering. The day never warmed past sixty—not in the woods. Vinnie still had Indiana skin, and back home, sixty was *pleasant*. Windows-open, air-out-the-house, head-to-the-orchard, do-your-errands-without-a-coat-on weather. Maryland would probably be back in the eighties tomorrow.

"I hope she's not out here," Dustin volunteered after a while.

"Same," Jaylin said. "'Cause we're not looking for *her*, are we?"

"What do you mean?"

Jaylin held out a hand for Kira, to help her step over a pile of rocks jutting up from the earth. "She's not *lost*, right? Like a hiker or whatever? Like, she didn't go out into the woods to party and get turned around. So if she's out here, somebody . . ."

"Hurt her." Kira's voice broke.

Vinnie watched Tyler's reaction, though he was doing his best to make it hard. He kept his lips pressed together in a grim line and his focus on an imaginary point in the distance. It was like he was completely outside the conversation instead of in the middle of it.

"It's been too long," Dustin said. "I always heard you gotta get them back in forty-eight hours, or they're not coming back."

Technically, sort of true. But that was mostly for murders. Right now, this was still a missing-persons case. Without evidence to the contrary, Vinnie preferred to assume she was still looking for a live girl she could bring home safe. After all, Avery had been able (forced?) to make a phone call to the police—that counted for something.

But this was a conversation with an opening, finally. Both reassuring the family, and poking at Tyler, Vinnie said, "I heard she texted her best friend. They're taking their time, but the cops can trace that cell signal. They'll figure out where her phone is and go from there."

"Ohhhhh," Kira said, like Vinnie had just explained a magic trick.

Instantly, Tyler said, "Not if she turned it off."

"Nah," Vinnie said, with all the sincerity she could manage. "Even when a phone is off, there's a chip in there that pings off the towers every couple minutes. Kinda like a black box on a plane. They started adding them to phones a couple years ago."

Which was a huge fucking lie, but Tyler didn't know that. He bit at his chapped lip but kept walking.

With a thoughtful frown, Dustin said, "I hope her phone is with her, then."

"You and me both," Vinnie said agreeably.

"Yeah, but if she left it somewhere," Tyler said suddenly, "somebody else could pick it up and just use it."

"Still helpful," Vinnie said. "Because then you have somebody to talk to, who can tell you where they found it, right?"

Tyler's reply was a shrug. He wasn't exactly wearing a light-up sign that said I HAVE A SECRET, but he may as well have been. The lazy ease he usually wore was replaced with telltale twitches. He shoved his hands into his pockets, then pulled them out. Back in; out again.

It wasn't a revelation—after all, Vinnie already knew he was the one who sent the text to Hannah.

No, it was a seed, planted in fertile ground, and left to sprout. Now Vinnie just had to wait for the bloom.

Pointing to the top of the opposite ridge, Jaylin squinted curiously. "Hey, is that the Red Stripe up there?"

Vinnie followed Jaylin's finger, and sure enough, it was the back of a local grocery store. It felt like they were impossibly deep in the woods, and yet . . .

Vinnie wondered how far they'd gotten. She had a suspicion they weren't in Wills Harbor anymore, not technically. The town itself clung to the water, just like Kerry County, and with each step she took she hiked farther from the bay. Out here, towns stacked on towns stacked on towns, a matryoshka of communities up and down the coast. She couldn't help but think this case was destined to be a jurisdictional nightmare, once they found Avery.

But upside for Vinnie, jurisdiction didn't concern her at all. She got to go where the evidence took her, no barriers, no borders.

As her team reached the gulley at the bottom of their embankment, the wind shifted. Dogs that had been silent all day suddenly bayed. The drones appeared, all of them heading toward the dogs. A moment later, a helicopter flew over—way too low to be simply passing by. Pressing her tongue behind her teeth, Vinnie pulled out her phone. Yeah, they seemed deep in the woods, but there was her signal, three bars lit up.

She hesitated over the contacts, then finally touched Rosier's number in the scroll. With her thumb, she pecked out a quick text.

Somebody found something out here.

There was hardly a beat before he replied.

I know.

Chapter 22

A body lay in the woods, unnamed but not unsexed.

Visually, it was a young woman, but that's where the agreement ended. Whispers burning through the search party claimed she was alternately a teenager or an adult, possibly an old woman, but maybe a middle schooler. The remaining rumors were fucking horrifying.

Whoever it was, they'd allegedly stumbled over an ersatz coffin and instead of flagging it, decided to open it. The body was in pieces, jumbled in a steamer trunk—or possibly a hard-sided suitcase. The head may or may not have been in the same case; possibly it was in a backpack next to it. Found perhaps by one of the Boy Scout Explorers or by one of the guys from the football team.

What was certain was that someone had called the police. Now the woods were taped off, a crime scene. Deputies pushed the searchers out, back to the rally point in the parking lot. Their stone faces couldn't soften with sympathy. They had a job to do—they had to make room for the investigators, the crime-scene techs, the coroner, the fire department. Flashing lights filled the parking lot as the entire search team was displaced by law enforcement.

While the officials could make the searchers leave the woods, the park was open to the public. A steady stream of cars flowed out, but the family refused to leave.

The mood settled to bleak, beneath skies that agreed. Dark clouds pushed in, so low they seemed to skim the treetops. Knots of people clung to each other. Crying or praying, for news they never wanted to get. There weren't any other missing girls around Wills Harbor. There was one logical conclusion: they'd found Avery Adair.

Hannah stood by the car, waiting for Vinnie to unlock the doors. Her face was smudged, and eyes rimmed with red from crying. She'd wrapped her arms around her chest, tight, as if she desperately needed a hug. She moved like she knew her best friend was never coming home—slow, weighted with shock that would part for sudden bouts of grief.

It *was* a logical conclusion, a reasonable assumption, but the only thing Vinnie felt was a demanding, burning desire to get as far from the uniforms as possible, and that had nothing to do with Avery or the body. Her reaction wasn't cold detachment; she just knew that weird shit happened, and she couldn't know if they'd found Avery until an autopsy confirmed it. The search grid still didn't make sense based on her last, true known position.

Vinnie's attention fell on Tyler. Something had drained out of him when the news rippled through the woods. What was interesting was that he looked shifty, not guilty. Like he suddenly had ants in his pants but also didn't want to draw any attention. But the one thing he wasn't was sorry. The news crashed against him and fell to pieces, like he was some impenetrable wall.

"I'm gonna pay for your Lyft home," Vinnie told Hannah,

watching as Tyler backed out of the huddle he shared with his teammates.

Vinnie had tickled his line, bringing up Avery's phone and its imaginary black box. Now she needed to follow him. Find out what he did with that information.

"Can't you take me?" She trembled, either on the verge of sobbing or losing her shit.

"Hannah, I'm sorry, but I can't."

Ticking her tongue, Vinnie shook her head, trying not to lose sight of Tyler as he slipped between the cars to get to his truck. She pulled up CashMeApp, sent Hannah fifty bucks for the Lyft, then opened the driver's-side door. "That should be enough to get you home."

Hannah's trembling turned to buzzing, fury twisting her face. "Seriously? They just found my best friend's body and you're going to bail on me?"

Vinnie wanted to comfort her. She really did. But she couldn't tell her it was okay when it definitely fucking wasn't. She also couldn't expect Hannah to understand that nobody could know whose corpse that was yet, not for certain. All Vinnie could do, right now, was chase down a kid who might have had something to do with it.

"Who are you looking at?" Hannah demanded, twisting to get a look. Her hair floated in the wind, a slap flush staining her face. Welp. She was a teenager, but she wasn't stupid.

Vinnie led with the truth; it was the only reassurance she had to give. "I have a lead," Vinnie told her. "I have to go, Hannah. Just tell me you can find a ride home here."

"No, take me with you! I want to go."

"Absolutely not."

"You're only here because of me!"

It wasn't the first time Vinnie had dealt with an angry loved one; it probably wouldn't be the last. With a firm, gentle tone, Vinnie said, "No, I'm here because of Avery. And I have to go now. I'm sorry."

Then she slid into the driver's seat and locked the doors before Hannah had a chance to throw the passenger side open. Vinnie tried not to look at the anger and betrayal in Hannah's eyes; just because she had to handle her didn't mean she enjoyed it.

It was part of the hardening every cop went through, walling things off and cramming them into boxes, separating the soft, compassionate, human part of your mind from a job that served horror for breakfast. Instinct wanted to stay and comfort Hannah; experience demanded she follow Tyler. There was exactly one possible piece of physical evidence in this case outside the remains, and she couldn't let this kid get rid of it.

Tyler's truck rumbled by, a pair of shocking-pink Truck Nutz dangling from the rear bumper. Inwardly, Vinnie rolled her eyes. At least they would make him easy to tail.

Flicking the new dashcam on, Vinnie pulled out slowly, then stayed on Tyler's tail. It was all perfectly normal, with all the traffic flooding out at the same time. She felt a little pop of relief now that all the flashing overheads on the cruisers were in her rearview.

They turned onto the main road, which twisted and doubled back on itself before spitting them onto a short stretch of highway. That was Maryland for you; two lanes of mystery splitting in every direction, usually at three different speed limits.

Of course, speed limits meant nothing to Tyler. As soon as he broke free of the loop, he gunned it. Vinnie followed, one lane over, close enough to surveil. All she needed to keep up was a flash of pink rubber genitals. Yep, she was following the bouncing pink balls. This was her life now.

And it wasn't even the strangest day of it.

Chapter 23

Tyler Purnell had swallowed Vinnie's bullshit in a single gulp, and now he was sick with it.

The truth was, cell phones and flight recorders had nothing in common. Unlike a distress beacon, phones didn't ping satellites when they were turned off. No signal, nothing to track. The evidence of absence didn't mean absence of evidence—the last known location before the phone went dark could still be extremely useful.

But Tyler didn't know that. That's why he floored it, sometimes veering onto the shoulder to pass. If the phone wasn't already in his truck, he'd stop to get it—but if he had it on him, he might chuck it out the window at any moment.

Adrenaline and tension played like overtuned guitar strings, tight in Vinnie's chest and threatening to snap. The hamster wheel in charge of her rental resented the heavy foot on the gas pedal; the poor thing was a four-cylinder. It would have to break the laws of physics to actually catch up.

The distance had advantages—Tyler probably wouldn't notice her. It had disadvantages too. If he threw the phone out the window, she might not see it. If he hit one of the many hidden exits, he might be swallowed by the tree line and lose her entirely. This wasn't home, where Vinnie knew the roads and shortcuts like old friends. She could get around in Maryland, but she was keenly aware that getting around might not be enough.

An idea suddenly bloomed in her brain. It was light with clarity, the spark of inspiration. She jabbed the Voice Search button on her steering wheel and gunned it. "Call Camila Vega," she ordered it as she whipped into the other lane to make up ground. Ringing filled the car, then suddenly, a crackly quiet replaced it.

"What can you tell me about the body?" Camila asked by way of greeting.

Vinnie didn't have time to enjoy the sound of Camila's butterscotch voice. *Later*, Vinnie told herself. *Something to mull over later*. Right now, she needed Camila Vega the journalist. She was the only resource she had.

"I'm currently on—what the hell highway is this? Whatever, it doesn't matter. I'm following Tyler Purnell and I might lose him. Can you do me a favor?"

Something rustled in the background. "Name it."

"The family hired a search expert, I think his name is Fitzpatrick. He had everybody download FamGPS, have you heard of it?"

"Yeah, it's a creepy little spy on your phone. Mostly used by helicopter parents to keep track of their kids."

"That's the one. Can you get me that guy, or get me the search data?"

One of the blind on-ramps disgorged a giant delivery truck. Vinnie cut hard into the left lane. Horns of protest sounded behind her. She ducked slightly; she doubted Tyler knew she was behind him, but better safe than sorry. Except, now she was boxed in. The traffic thickened, pushing Vinnie and Tyler farther apart.

"Absolutely," Camila said. "Now, what can you do for me?"

Vinnie almost grinned. She expected nothing less; favors were never free. Still, she enjoyed the certainty that talking to this reporter wasn't going to land her ass in a knot with her captain. The beauty of self-employment, baby. "Right now, I can confirm they found a female body in the woods. You might hit up the Explorers; it's possible they're the ones who found her. No ID yet; it's gonna take DNA or dental records."

Red lights lit up like flares, and Vinnie hit the brakes. One of the pass-through towns was slowing things down. Fingers drumming on the steering wheel, Vinnie strained to search for Tyler's truck. Her belly fluttered, anticipating the worst. Warm relief softened her shoulders when she finally sighted him again.

"Question I already know the answer to," Camila said. "Any police presence at the search?"

"Nope."

"What about the family?"

"A *lot* of family."

"Hey, where'd you say you were again?"

Vinnie leaned forward as traffic started to move. Tyler was still in the left lane. Good; that meant he didn't plan to exit just yet. She glanced at her GPS and said, "177, still in Pasadena. If he gets to Ritchie, he's gonna be gone."

Tapping came through the line and Camila said, "You might have a bigger problem. His family owns a boat, the *Julie Bird*. It's moored on Veall Creek, just north of Annapolis. He'd have to get a ride out to it, but . . ."

Vinnie's stomach sank. There was a big difference between an Indiana creek and a Maryland creek. In Indiana, you waded in them and caught crawdads and minnows in pickle jars. In Maryland, it's where you took ten of your closest friends and five cases of beer on your twenty-eight-foot cabin cruiser. And all of the creeks around here spilled directly into the Chesapeake.

If Tyler dumped the phone in the bay, it would probably be lost forever. It wasn't a pond that could be drained; dredging could pull up fifty phones or none at all, depending on the depth, the wind, the tides. As Vinnie swallowed the sour taste in the back of her mouth, her mind raced. What to do, what to do, how to keep that phone out of a hundred feet of water.

That's when Vinnie realized she'd left her best tool back at the parking lot. Fuming, as a matter of fact, and furious with her. But since Vinnie couldn't pull Tyler over, let alone search his truck legally, she had to use every tool at her disposal.

"I'll loop back around with you," Vinnie told Camila, getting ready to hang up.

"Hey," Camila said. "Dinner tonight?"

This wasn't the time or place to focus on the brief thrill that ran beneath her skin. Later. Feelings needed to stay in their boxes while she was working. "Yes. Text me. Bye," Vinnie said, then hung up. She took advantage of crawling traffic to turn on call recording on her phone, then dialed probably the last person who wanted to hear from her. It was stupid how grateful she was when Hannah picked up.

"What?" she said flatly.

Yep, still angry, still hurt. Vinnie didn't have time to coddle her, so she got to the point. "I need your help. I think Tyler's getting ready to dump Avery's phone, and I'm afraid he's heading to his family's boat."

There was a sharp breath, then Hannah said, "Oh shit."

The noise around Hannah made it sound like she was still outside. Other voices greyed out the background, nothing clear but definitely present. If Vinnie had to guess, she'd say Hannah was still at the park. She'd be safe there if Tyler came back. Whatever creepy bullshit he'd been on at the hardware store, he wouldn't pull it in front of adults.

Vinnie wedged into the right lane, forcing a sedan to let her over. "Can you reach out to him? Pretend you're upset about Avery, ask him to come meet you. I need to turn him around, and I have to do it fast."

"I can't make him . . ." Hannah said. Then she steeled herself. "But I can try."

"Keep me on the call with him," Vinnie told her. "I'm recording."

"Okay, but you know nobody calls anymore, right? He might think it's weird."

Seriously? Vinnie said, "Then text him and send me a screenshot. And don't ask him to come to your house. Stay where you are, make sure there are plenty of people around you."

Hannah made a sound that stood in for *okay*, then hung up. Vinnie sat up higher in her seat, practically leaning against the steering wheel. She stared at Tyler's truck until her eyes burned. How long did it take to send a text? How long to consider an answer and reply?

Ten seconds? Twenty seconds?

Thirty?

Chapter 24

Two minutes later, Hannah called back.

"He's on his way," she said, practically breathless. "What do I say when he gets here?"

"Nothing," Vinnie said, watching Tyler veer off on an exit without signaling. She drove up the shoulder to follow, gravel grinding beneath her tires. "I want you to take that money I gave you and get a ride home right now. I don't want you to be there when he gets there."

"I can help," Hannah insisted.

"You *did* help," Vinnie told her. "But you're not bait. Please promise me you'll get a ride home right now. Tell Tyler your dad showed up and made you go home. Just, leave, okay? I'd never forgive myself if something happened to you."

She could tell Hannah wanted to argue. She heard the hitch and hesitation in her voice. But just as Tyler flipped a bitch at the next intersection, Hannah capitulated.

"Okay. I will."

"Thank you, talk soon," Vinnie said, then hung up. She needed to pay attention; she couldn't afford to have her mind split between cosseting a teenager and tailing another. Every muscle in her body tensed; it felt like her knuckles were grinding to dust as she gripped the wheel with all her strength.

Unlike Vinnie, Tyler knew the back roads. He sped past her, then turned onto a tiny tributary without a name. She had to be careful now, because it was a long stretch with no traffic. It would be abundantly obvious that the car behind him was matching him, turn for turn.

Dropping below the speed limit, she let him get ahead a ways. It was no high-speed pursuit, that was for sure. And that was for the best. Chasing a kid who'd only been driving a couple years at most was a good way to get people killed.

A long blind curve separated the two of them. It was a dance of acceleration and braking until the truck came back into sight. Brake lights flashed, a stuttering morse code of indecision. Vinnie was sure of it; he was looking for the right place to stop. He was probably measuring how deep the woods looked from the road.

There was a clear choice. On the east side, there were houses studding the hills, long driveways barely cutting through the brush. Mailboxes stood sentinel, sometimes along with elaborate brick and wrought-iron gates, sometimes next to garden-center concrete lions. Throw the phone there, somebody could find it while picking up their mail, letting themselves onto their own property, taking the trash down at the end of the week.

The west side was the only choice. It was wooded, with hints of water behind the spindly black gum and bushy chokeberries. The ground sloped away from the road on that side, and autumn had denuded the raspberry brambles and greyed the grasses. Roadside litter flapped in the breeze or nestled down in low spots full of time-bleached aluminum cans and a glitter of broken glass.

"C'mon, c'mon," Vinnie murmured under her breath. He hit the brakes again and she tensed her jaw. It looked like he was rolling down the driver's-side window, but it was hard to tell at this angle. Then suddenly, his arm emerged, a brown paper bag clutched in his fist. He took a couple of practice swings, then flung the bag into the woods. As soon as it landed, he peeled out and sped up the road, eraser-pink Nutz wobbling in his wake.

Vinnie parked on the east side of the road and grabbed her phone. She needed to make a record of everything. If this phone, and who disposed of it, became evidence in a crime, she needed to be able to demonstrate a clean chain of custody. It had to be impeccable, because she was inserting herself into a police matter.

In her experience, prosecutors loved to ignore the most obvious evidence and seemed incapable of connecting the dots when things got complicated. So Vinnie left the dashcam running, then turned on the camera on her phone as she darted across the road. For the second time today, she found herself goat-footing it down an embankment. *Thanks for the lesson, Dustin*, she thought.

Sliding to a stop, Vinnie caught her balance and trained her camera on the fast-food bag nestled on top of the underbrush. For good measure, she took pictures from every angle and included a dollar bill for scale since she didn't have a ruler. Then she did something that would have pissed off Detective Vinnie Taylor: she picked the bag up and opened it.

There, among crumpled Big Mac wrappers, a phone lay. Her heart buzzed, but she made herself wrap the package back up and carry it to her car. As much as she wanted to turn the thing on and start digging, she knew she couldn't without gloves.

The visual trail she'd created was strong, but she needed to preserve Tyler's fingerprints. It would be the only way to prove *he* hadn't just thrown a bag away for a friend, completely innocent of what was inside.

Back in the car, Vinnie checked for traffic, then pulled back onto the road. She needed the map app to get herself back home. Probably, eventually, one day, she'd know this place as well as she knew Indianapolis, but until then, she leaned on the technology crutch. Especially since the roads here looped and curved and twisted, probably following old game or Native people's trails. It wasn't intuitive; the straight lines back home were a thing of the past.

Once again, she told the digital assistant to call Hannah. She wanted to check and make sure that she had vacated the park before Tyler arrived. This time, it rang until it went to voicemail.

The recorded message startled Vinnie: the voice was obviously Hannah's, but much younger. She'd probably set the message years ago, when she got her first phone. She sounded like a baby; it was a stark reminder that these kids really were *kids*. Vinnie hung up without leaving a message. Hopefully, Hannah was already headed to the safety of home. Once she got there, she'd see the missed call and reply on her own.

Then, as the map app led her out of the woods and onto a major interstate, Vinnie pressed the button again and said, "Call Camila."

They were going to have a lot more to talk about than dinner.

Chapter 25

If you have to put on gloves to do it, is it really legal?" Camila asked.

Vinnie grinned as she snapped on the second latex glove. Picking up the McDonald's bag, she unrolled it gingerly, then reached inside. "What? It's not illegal to innocently find a phone. Not illegal to *innocently* try to find the owner, either. This is straight-up Good Samaritan shit."

Swirling a pair of chopsticks through her carton of lo mein, Camila watched, countering with amusement, "Yeah, I see your halo from here. Tampering with evidence is definitely a crime."

"It's not evidence yet," Vinnie pointed out.

Even though she needed to be scrupulously careful handling the phone, she realized she'd have rather been looking at Camila.

Camila had twisted her black hair into a messy at-home bun and worn a scarlet, silky-soft V-neck sweater. The combination made her golden neck seem impossibly long, shaping her like art. Gorgeous, casual art who didn't haggle when it came to food. She'd turned up with a massive bag of Chinese, told Vinnie she owed her nineteen dollars, and settled in.

At this point, Vinnie didn't know if tonight was work or a date.

She was surprised to find she wasn't anxious, either way. Part of that *Fuck it, I'm fifty* evolution. Whatever happened, happened, and she was okay with that. It didn't mean she didn't still feel that familiar sting on her skin at the prospect. After all, Camila's lips were full and glossed from the noodles; her laughter hung in the air like incense.

But Vinnie had only so much time with this phone before she ruined its evidentiary value. So flirting, maybe, yes, but figuring out if there was anything more? Not this minute. Still distracted by the rich scent of ginger and garlic, and the warm buzz of Camila's voice, she got to work on the phone.

First, she took a picture of it lying on a clean white towel, front and back. Though she was handling it as little as possible, the cops would be pissed and the judge would probably frown upon it, but the DA would be thrilled. All that documentation, turned in by a law-abiding citizen? Good luck calling this the fruit of the poisonous tree.

Camila stood and stretched. "Beer in the fridge?" she asked, already walking that way. She didn't need an answer; she opened the door and retrieved two, her fingers strangling the necks as she carried them back one-handed. She opened them for both, then sat down closer to Vinnie. She ran hot; warmth radiated from her and Vinnie savored the way it made her toes curl.

"Ready to see what's on this thing?" Vinnie asked her.

"Dazzle me," Camila said, raising her drink to her.

Under her breath, Vinnie laughed, and she plugged the phone into her laptop. With a couple of clicks, she opened DroidCreep—a shitty name for software usually used by shitty people. It bypassed the root on any Android phone; passwords became irrelevant. Hidden files sprang into the light, ready to expose their secrets.

She cloned everything on the phone, re-creating it on her computer. That way, she could dig through it without damaging or corrupting the data. It took a few minutes, a countdown bar in bloody red, measuring out the secrets in dollops until it filled completely.

Carefully, Vinnie ejected the phone digitally, then unplugged it from the computer. Back into the fast-food bag whence it came, and then into a clean paper bag for safekeeping.

"Would you mind taping that off and dating it?" Vinnie asked, pulling off her gloves. It didn't break her heart that Camila had to reach past her to grab the masking tape. A hint of soap and clean, new winter teased her, the scent of Camila's skin as she brushed against Vinnie's wrist.

With the bag secured, literally, Camila twisted toward Vinnie. "I'm gonna plug in and charge mine, okay?"

"Go for it," Vinnie said, giving up one of the USB ports on the laptop.

With a wide grin, Camila nudged her, and said, "Let's get to the good stuff."

"We can't; you didn't find the GPS guy," Vinnie teased.

"Shut up."

"Yes ma'am," Vinnie said, still smiling. "It's not important now anyway."

She turned the laptop so they could both see it, then activated the cloned copy of the phone. The screen flickered, then brightened. An animated version of the phone sat in the center. The first thing that came up was a lock screen. The mood in the cottage took a darker shift.

A picture of a girl graced the monitor. She stood on a pier, washed with sunlight, tugging a Ravens hat down over her eyes.

Even though her face lay in shadow, it was still clearly Avery Adair.

She looked young, wearing the kind of thin that couldn't last past the teens. Her blue jean shorts gapped at the back, but the purple tank top clung to her figure jealously. It was a good picture. The lighting, the angle, the everything—it captured a perfect summer moment for a girl whose days were counting down to an autumn disappearance.

"Jesus, she's a baby," Camila said, speaking for both of them.

"Like what the fuck, right?"

Vinnie clicked the toolbar, and the program drew Avery's pass pattern, lighting up each stroke on the monitor. Then the phone opened to the home screen, all its apps and icons exactly where they were on the real thing. DroidCreep also had a sidebar, listing all the files and folders inside, the contents normally tucked out of view behind the UI—the user interface.

Because Avery was a teen, and Vinnie had so recently been reminded that nobody calls anymore, Vinnie started with the text messages. There were thousands, literally thousands, but Avery had helpfully pinned the most important conversations to the top. Vinnie chose *Han* first, assuming it was a discussion with Hannah.

> **Han:** Okay if you don't text me back by tonight, I'm going to your mom's. Or the police. Or both. I'll do both, Avery! Where are you????

> **Avery:** Your being fr rn? Bitch I'm good!

"Right, so that's the message Hannah says came from Tyler." Camila reached into her bag and pulled out a pair of readers.

They were bright red and magnified her brown eyes beautifully. "Yeah, that doesn't sound like any of the rest of these at all. Keep scrolling."

There was the conversation where Avery told her best friend that she'd be doing "errands" with Red that weekend, and she was turning off her phone. A handful of texts that linked into celebrity Instagram pages with snarky commentary intact. Threaded in there were a few need-a-ride/want-a-ride queries. Absolutely nothing extraordinary, so they kept scrolling.

It wasn't natural to read text messages backward, but it had its benefits. Instead of getting caught up in the conversations, they homed in on aberrations. The parts that weren't like the others. Like the explosion of exclamation points that happened about two weeks before Avery's disappearance. It picked up in the middle of a conversation, probably one they'd started in person.

Han: I thought we didn't lie to each other!

Avery: Yeah well I thought we didn't fight, either.

Han: I said I was sorry but omg I have SEEN you sneaking around and you're never around when you're supposed to be. I deserve an explanation!

Avery: Whatever.

Chapter 26

So much for a fight over Schrödinger's ho.

To Vinnie's surprise, it hurt to find out Hannah had lied to her.

It wasn't the first time, and probably wouldn't be the last. But she'd somehow expected the truth from the girl who'd all but forced her to take this case. Hannah hadn't mentioned tension between her and Avery. Nor any sneaking around or suspicious behavior. She hadn't even hinted at it.

According to Hannah's version of events, things were perfectly fine until suddenly they weren't, and now Vinnie knew that wasn't true. Pressing two fingers against her temple, Vinnie shook her head and kept scrolling. Camila scribbled in her notebook, her left-handed scrawl leaving smudges on the pages.

They got a couple of months deep, back to a time where none of the conversations were strained. They went on at length, for what had probably been hours, talking about everything and nothing, the way best friends did. It was a stark contrast to the end of the text exchange, but eventually they realized there was nothing new to learn from the past.

Closing that thread, Vinnie clicked on the next one, between Avery and her mother. Thank God, there was nothing unexpected in there. A litany of *good mornings* and *good nights*, *I love yous*, and *can you pick me up some Huggies and wipes?* It was sweet; briefly, Vinnie wondered what having that kind of mother was like. The thought wisped away as soon as it came. She was old enough that her mommy issues were well contained in a lockbox in the back of her mind.

"Can we see deleted texts with this thing?" Camila asked, after they'd looked over the rest of the pinned threads without anything useful rising to the surface.

"Absolutely."

Vinnie scrolled the sidebar, then opened the Trash folder. Although she knew how to use DroidCreep, there was plenty of stuff under the hood she didn't understand. Scraps of files that did nothing when she clicked on them, fragments of images that made no sense. Under her breath, she muttered, "Huh," because the folder was packed.

"There, there, click on that," Camila said, reaching for the keyboard but then drawing her hands back.

"Be my guest," Vinnie said, turning the laptop toward her.

"Yeah, this is where the gold is," Camila said, and razor-quick, she resurrected a conversation from the digital crypt, between Avery and contact name Asswipe. It was juvenile, but then again, Avery *was* a juvenile.

Asswipe: tick tick tick

Avery: Fuck you. I paid you. Now fuck off.

Asswipe: I still know things that I might oops slip and tell

Avery: You cocksucker, we had a deal.

Asswipe: Yeah but your still a whore and I need
new tires lol

"Hot damn," Camila said.

"Fuck," Vinnie said at the same time. The same things that made this a juicy story for Camila turned this case into a nightmare for law enforcement. And, well, Vinnie. She had a hunch, and she picked up her own phone to text Hannah. She spoke the text out loud for Camila's benefit. "What is Tyler's cell number?"

Instantly, Hannah replied, "Why, did you find something?"

Still aloud, Vinnie replied as she typed with her thumbs, "I'll let you know."

Two seconds later, confirmation lit up her screen. She showed it to Camila, shaking her head. "Asswipe is officially Tyler Purnell."

"It ain't looking good for the handsome young quarterback," Camila said. "I'm seeing the headlines already: 'Secrets and Lies in Small-Town America.'" Echoes of the article to go with that headline sounded in her voice.

"Too bad your paper's not that kind of paper."

Camila shrugged. "It'll get covered in *WaPo* or the *Sun*."

"Tough shit for TyTy," Vinnie said with a slight smile.

Before this moment, Tyler had a questionable reputation, and a penchant for cornering girls in hardware stores—nothing to hang a byline on, that's for sure. Now he was in possession of a missing girl's phone and had been blackmailing said girl before she went missing. Talk about a trove in twelve-point type.

The story of it didn't concern Vinnie. What she needed to

know was what he had on Avery. She bounced a knee, nervous energy burning off with each thump.

"But what the fuck did he know?" she asked rhetorically.

She hopped up to refresh their beers, stretching and popping her shoulders as she walked into the kitchen. She had maps in her head, ways to proceed spidering out from that moment. One for a dead girl deserving justice; one for a live girl desperate for rescue.

Grabbing the last two longnecks from the fridge, Vinnie popped the caps on both and carried them to the living room. Camila held her notebook in one hand and scrolled with the other. Vinnie thought the red reading glasses were cute; it was like live-action Lois Lane working the case right in front of her.

As Vinnie settled next to her again, Camila said, "She deleted a bunch of apps two days ago. And when I say she, I mean giant air quotes *she*." She took the beer with a thank-you and a salute, but she couldn't drag her eyes away from the computer.

"So he shows up at the search to find out what the family knows, *and* he was already destroying evidence of his existence on her phone."

"The answer's gotta be in here," Vinnie said. Camila dug into the phone's trashed files again, but a file name caught Vinnie's eye. She clapped a hand over Camila's. "Go back. Instagram."

When Camila didn't respond quickly enough, Vinnie pressed Camila's finger to the trackpad and scrolled back to that folder. Vinnie explained, "First thing I did was look for her socials. Found *nothing*. But up in those texts with Hannah, they're talking about stuff they saw there. And voilà, there it is. She *had* one, but *he* deleted it."

"Mmm maybe not," Camila pointed out. "Look at the date, August twelfth. Tyler didn't have her phone yet."

Vinnie's brows rose curiously, and together, they clicked. The app itself was gone. When Vinnie tried to pull it up on *her* phone, the corresponding account was gone too—it would have to be recovered with a warrant. That didn't mean the pictures were gone though.

Circling back to the deleted folders, Vinnie found the DCIM—the digital camera images—folder; every Android phone had one. It contained subfolders galore, both videos and pictures. For images, it separated pictures into types: screenshots, taken by the phone's camera, pictures that had been downloaded. And . . . those altered for social media. Avery's social media folder had two subdirectories. One labeled "Instagram/Aaaavery," the other "Fans/Crush Baby."

A sharp spark caught in Vinnie's chest; next to her, Camila pressed closer. *Fans?* But with fingers tangled, Vinnie and Camila opened the Instagram folder first, just to be thorough. Normal, ordinary photos spilled out. Holding her baby sister, standing in cutoffs and a bikini top on a pier. In one, Avery plastered her cheek, in stark shadow, against Hannah's. It was a companion to the pictures on Hannah's Instagram—the party at the rowhouses.

"Boring," Camila said, then clicked back to the other profile.

Neat, square thumbnails filled the screen. Vinnie braced herself as they loaded—if this turned out to be Child Sexual Abuse Material, she would have to turn her whole damned computer over to preserve the evidence and to keep her own ass out of a sling. But what appeared, as all the pictures filled in, was something that walked a curious line.

Feet. There were easily fifty pictures of, presumably, Avery's feet. Always perfectly manicured, toes painted a whole rainbow of colors from pic to pic. The feet were in exquisite focus as they dipped into a bowl of pasta and sauce, as they bathed in a drizzle of Hershey's syrup. But mostly as they stepped on stuffed animals, or multicolored balloons, eggs and peas and apples. There was even a long series of her stepping on stress toys—the kind with the eyes that bulged out comically.

"What the fuck?" Camila said, eyes glued to the screen.

"Fetish pics," Vinnie told her, weirdly mesmerized. "Foot-fetish stuff, but it looks like she was concentrating on crush porn. These guys, they like looking at women stepping on stuff. We're lucky she's not crushing anything living. Or anything that belongs in somebody's pants."

Camila reclaimed her hand. It went directly to the back of her neck, which she squeezed as she took it all in. "Kingston told me once, if you can think of it, there's porn of it on the Internet. He wasn't kidding. How did she get mixed up in this?"

"If I had to guess, creeps leaving messages on her regular posts gave her the idea. And sex work pays a hell of a lot better than tutoring."

"Am I grateful it's just foot stuff?" Camila asked, incredulous.

"That's all we've found so far," Vinnie said. She opened a text search. "But now we know about Fans4U for sure." She clicked the magnifying glass to search, then leaned in to type in the name of the amateur sex-work site. It hesitated, so Vinnie added *Crush Baby* to go with it. Two seconds later, the Fans4U app opened in DroidCreep, autofilling the login and password to give them direct, instant access to the profile.

Vinnie was sickly grateful that the pictures they found there were more of the same, along with some videos that connected the dots between photo shoots. If they wanted to, they could watch six whole minutes of Avery pouring different food on her feet.

The teen had been careful to make sure her body and face never appeared onscreen. In fact, even her voice sounded slightly digital, like it had been autotuned.

Looking a little green, Camila reached over and muted it instantly. "I can't listen to a kid trying to talk dirty."

"Yeah, not great," Vinnie agreed, and backed out of the video.

She pulled up the profile page for Crush Baby. There, at the bottom, was a link to "Subs & Tips." Vinnie asked Camila, "You know how Fans4U works?"

"I barely know how my voice memos work," Camila said flippantly.

"Okay, so usually, people buy subscriptions to specific sex workers, to see exclusive content. Members get access to a suggestion box where they can send the performer ideas for new pictures or videos. And then, they can reply. Sometimes they do live shows; there's a chat stream at the bottom of the page. And some of them do shoots, or private videos."

Reaching past Vinnie to use the trackpad again, Camila scrolled. As she did, she asked, almost offhandedly: "Does shit like this ever make you wonder what you might have done at that age if you'd had this on your phone?"

Chapter 27

The question caught Vinnie off guard.

She'd grown up poverty-adjacent. Not so poor that she ever went hungry, but they never had AC in the summer. Or in their used cars. Thrift stores and hand-me-downs were the brands she wore to school.

Thinking about it now, there had been a lot of meals at Grandma's house when she was a kid, and more than once she'd stood in line for free groceries. The rubbery heft of government cheese was a memory made of scent and taste; it squeeged between the teeth and lingered yellowly in the back of her nose. Not bad, but not great.

What *would* she have done as a teenager? If she could have afforded things like new boots, or a steak dinner, or a trip to King's Island, an amusement park the next state over. She wondered who she would have become. The money would have seemed so easy; having plenty was a drug that few could resist.

Kept locked with her other secrets, Vinnie had spent most of junior high perfecting her shoplifting skills at the Village Pantry down the street. The only reason she never graduated to bigger or better venues was lack of access. No car, and she couldn't afford to sit on a bus for an hour to get to greener shoplifting fields.

So yeah, a couple of pictures in exchange for a lot of dollars sounded like a good trade.

Finally, Vinnie said, "I can see it, yeah. Way too easily too."

Rubbing a hand down her throat, Camila remembered aloud, "I wanted a Firebird so bad when I was sixteen. One of the ones with the slick black body and gold phoenix on the hood?"

"That was the dream, huh?"

Camila's face was soft with the memory, and it was a pleasant distraction from reality. Her teenage self lingered there, a brightness in her eyes as she remembered, a smile both rueful and sweet in the wake of a fantasy that still felt real to her after all these years.

Finally, Camila waved it off, slipping back into herself *now*. Older, wiser, and still a feast for the eyes. "That was the dream. Now it's a good night's sleep and always remembering what I came into the room for."

With a snort, Vinnie said, "Tell me about it."

"Anyway, where were we?"

Attention on the laptop again, Vinnie started putting links together. She wished she'd found a cell phone for every victim, every suspect, when she still worked in the department. People's whole lives unfolded on the damned things, more than they even realized.

So far, Vinnie and Camila had looked at the easy stuff. The GPS data showed every step Avery had taken until she disappeared—and Vinnie's gut paid off on that. The phone *had* made it to Howard County the day Avery disappeared, putting her forty minutes from Wills Harbor.

After that, someone—presumably Tyler—had switched it on and off a couple times in town. He put in different passkeys, locking himself out until he finally got the right code. Then, the phone was switched on long enough to text Hannah from what appeared to be Tyler's driveway. After that, it was dead again until today.

People complained about surveillance in the streets and on the internet, but every day they freely walked around with a little box that recorded every move they made. Was a surveillance state good for the public? The answer to that was well above Vinnie's pay grade, but she had to admit, for an investigator, it was a gold mine.

Vinnie cleared her throat and said, "The day before Avery disappeared, she had two hundred thirteen subscribers and transferred five hundred dollars from her Fans4U account to an online bank called Cheeky. And that's not the same account her mother made for her. That one hasn't been touched, and it has maybe a hundred bucks in it, as I recall."

"Therefore," Camila said, clicking around and digging into the guts of this app, "it's a hop, skip, and a jump to paying off Asswipe and disappearing on the same day."

Staring at the screen, Vinnie frowned. Hannah had lied about the argument—about Avery keeping things from her. Did she have an inkling? Was she aware of this shadow life? Was she the reason Tyler knew?

Vinnie watched Camila jump from the Fans4U account and into the other files revealed by DroidCreep. In a few keystrokes, she found the app for Cheeky, the online bank where Avery kept her cam money.

There was still a balance of eighteen hundred dollars—and a paper trail for the cash transferred the day Avery went missing. Five hundred dollars went in from F4U, then immediately went out through an ATM north of Wills Harbor, in Howard County.

Then came a single purchase at a McDonald's less than a mile away. There were no more transactions after that.

"She was supposed to be going up there with her cousin Red," Vinnie said. "Dammit, I need to talk to him."

"Then do it and come running back to me."

"Camila, I'd love to," Vinnie said with a rueful smile, "but he's in the wind."

Camila scrunched her face. "Shit."

"Yeah."

Vinnie slowly rolled her head to look at Camila. There was color in her cheeks, and she moved with her own kind of nervous energy. They were both excited in their own ways, and Camila's was just a little prettier and happier. She said, "You know I kinda have to write about this."

Wincing, Vinnie shoved down the dark excitement building in her chest. She had leads now, good, solid leads, and shit. She had to figure out what to share with Rosier and how to ask Camila her next question without pissing her off.

"Are you willing to sit on this until I get some more answers? There's gonna be encrypted messages on this thing that we haven't even begun to look at," she said, pulling off the Band-Aid.

Instantly, Camila's expression sharpened. She put her notebook aside, her phone tucked beneath it. "How much of it?"

"The sex work, and Tyler's name," Vinnie said, ready to negotiate.

With a curl of her arm, Camila pulled her notebook closer and scanned her own handwriting as if divining the answers. "But *yes* to anonymous blackmail?"

"If you do that reporter thing where you hem and haw about it," Vinnie said. Then she did her best to give an example, but writing was not her strong suit. "Sources say they thought she might maybe could be being blackmailed."

Camila threw her head back and laughed. "Seriously, that's what you think the news sounds like?"

Heat streaked across Vinnie's cheeks. "You know what I mean."

"Do I?"

"Yes, you do," Vinnie said with a faint smile. "Do we have a deal?"

A quiet beat filled the cottage, with nothing but the wind outside to fill it. The temperature was dropping, and the cold pushed in against the octagon at every angle. Those big picture windows were great for light and scenery but did little to hold back the taste of winter nudging fall into the background.

Finally, Camila said, "I'll vaguebook it, for now. But I'm not going to sit on it forever. Not even for you."

Good enough. Vinnie just needed time to spring her newfound knowledge on a couple of people, before the rest of the world found out about it. With that settled, Vinnie closed the laptop lid. Everything she'd learned weighed her down and crept through her body, tightening and tensioning her from the jaw down.

She wasn't going to sleep; instead, she'd probably make lists and think about how to approach Tyler—she'd have to corner him, and it was going to end badly no matter what. Hannah could be boxed in, but she didn't want to scare her or shut her up. She just wanted the actual truth out of her.

All of that was work. All of that was going into their compartments in her brain so she could have peace for a little while. With a mental door snapping closed, she trailed a hand across the table, the back of her fingers skimming against Camila's. If something happened, it wasn't going to be tonight. But that, she didn't want to lock up, just yet.

"You wanna do this again sometime," Camila asked, nodding vaguely at the laptop. "When we're not on the clock?"

Vinnie shifted like a luxury car. She turned all her attention to Camila, savoring the lazy, dark-molasses smile tugging at her full lips. Burning the space away between them, she hooked a finger in Camila's and stroked the back of her hand with her thumb. Things could get complicated, mixing business with pleasure. But that familiar sting of first contact, the heat waves washing around them—it felt worth it. Vinnie's voice fell, low and lingering just between the two of them. The wind howled, but it wasn't loud enough to drown out her reply.

"I could be convinced."

Chapter 28

After the discovery, Keith Adair didn't want to talk.
He wanted to sit on a milk crate in front of the HVAC shop and let cigarettes burn down to the filter before starting again. He had a thousand-yard stare, one Vinnie had seen on countless faces before. That was a man looking into his own soul and coming up empty. A man who'd had to find out how to get his child's dental records for a coroner. And a man without answers. The coroner still hadn't made an ID yet.

"I'm not gonna keep you, Keith. I'm sorry for what you're going through, and I'm hoping for a miracle too."

With a long drag, Keith let the smoke leak from his nose and lips as he spoke. "I've got nothing for you."

Vinnie held up her hands. "I just want you to get a message to Red."

At the mention of Red's name, Keith's head snapped up. "If there was something there, don't you think I'd take care of it? Who the fuck do you think you are?"

"I'm the one still looking for Avery," Vinnie said. "And I'm the one who doesn't give a shit if Red stole a thousand Jet Skis. I just need to talk to him."

"I never should have talked to you in the first place. Go on and get the fuck out of here. I don't know where he is."

A lie. A big, lazy, obvious lie, told to detectives all over the world, every minute of every single day. Fortunately, Vinnie had two things going for her at the moment: she wasn't the police, and Keith hadn't moved from the milk crate. He looked and sounded like a junkyard dog, menacing just past a fence. But she could tell he was still listening, in his own way. If she played this just right, this might actually work.

With a step back, Vinnie said, "I have proof Avery made it to Howard County. Everybody agrees it was probably with him. So. I want to find out when he saw her last. If she never came back to Kerry County, what got found? Wouldn't be her."

Keith dragged the butt of his cigarette across the ground, then flicked it in Vinnie's direction. At her shoes, not her clothes, and then he pushed up. He wasn't a big guy, but he wore intensity like a favorite coat.

Eye to eye with Vinnie for a moment, Keith simply stared into her. He was trying hard to believe his daughter's life hadn't ended in a steamer trunk just a few miles from home. A moment passed, and then he headed inside, waving a dismissive hand. The door slammed, the glass all but rattling in the frame.

It was a gesture that said Keith would get word to his nephew, and after that she should fuck off. He'd do it because he desperately needed to control something in the midst of the most uncontrollable situation of his life. And she'd leave him alone if she could, because she wasn't stupid. Junkyard dogs didn't play when they got past the fence.

Vinnie hopped back into her rental and got out of the parking space before her phone rang. The stray thought, *nobody calls anybody anymore*, tickled across her brain. She was angry at Hannah, but she wasn't about to confront her. Not yet. Because now she needed to come at her like she was a suspect instead of a bystander. Vinnie needed facts to build fences around the kid. Maybe then she could get to the truth.

Anyway. The miracle of technology meant that Vinnie could punch a button on her steering wheel and answer the call. "Vinnie Taylor," she said.

"Ms. Taylor," a crisp voice on the other end said, "this is Ashley at the Bay Clinic. Your cat is ready for pickup."

"I'm sorry, what?"

"Your cat," Ashley repeated briskly. "Goofus Taylor."

That statement derailed her thoughts. She was in the middle of a case, and it took her a second to understand those words in that order. When she did, her pulse raced faintly.

"No, no, no, he's a stray. I just brought him in to get fixed. 'Only you can prevent kitten season' and all that," she said, idiotically repeating a slogan that the Humane Society had used back home, years ago. No idea where her brain had been storing that bit of cruft.

Undeterred, Ashley said, "You're the pet parent of record for Goofus, so we need to ask you to come pick him up. We have very limited space, and our only alternative is to transfer him to the county shelter."

"You should probably do that," Vinnie said with a stray twist of guilt.

Ashley made a sound that layered judgment and professionalism into a single *tch*. "Ma'am, we can transfer Goofus with the other unclaimed pets, but it's a particularly bad time of year for the shelter. They have limited space, and they can only keep the animals with the best chance of adoption."

Another twist. "What happens if he's not one of them?"

"Gentle euthanasia is, unfortunately, the answer. There are simply too many animals to care for and not enough resources."

Which was why Vinnie had taken the cat in to the vet in the first place, to prevent more strays! There she was, trying to be a good citizen, do her part, and look what it got her: a sleek, green-eyed hobo who'd already proved he would come and go as he pleased.

She wasn't a monster. Or maybe she was, but not the kind that sentenced a perfectly good cat to death. So that meant Vinnie made an unscheduled run home to drop off her new responsibility. Said responsibility blinked at her slowly, then went back to sleep.

"I hope you're happy," Vinnie told the brand-new cat carrier she had to buy from the vet, since they wouldn't release Goofus to open arms. Vinnie was surprised they hadn't followed her out to the car to make sure she put him in a seat belt. She put the carrier on the floor and opened the door. She expected Goofus to streak out and disappear for parts unknown. Instead, he gazed at her drunkenly before drifting back to sleep.

Yeah, he had an angle, most cons did. His was being adorable to keep her from being annoyed. With a sigh, she opened a can that smelled like day-old summer dumpster and topped off the bowl of water.

Hopefully he could wait until she got home with a litter box, or, you know, go outside since he obviously knew the way. She gave his dopey head a gentle pet, then grabbed her keys.

The phone rang again, and Vinnie answered it automatically.

"Oh, so I'm finally special enough to get an audience with the great Vanetta Taylor," her mother said, already tuned to a pitch audible to rodents in a five-mile radius.

Swallowing a groan, Vinnie headed back to the car. "Sorry, I've been busy. Are you all right?"

That was always a dangerous question to ask Bev. Still, Vinnie felt like she had to ask—she'd been dodging her calls, so now she had to repent and listen to her mother's rambling litany of petty discontents. She had fifteen minutes for her, the amount of time it would take her to drive to Liberty High.

Bev's sour expression came through clearly. "I've certainly been better. Dr. Paivanas said that I'm going to have to have a knee replacement. I've been telling him for *years* that it wasn't right! And your stepfather is useless; I'm going to have to spend three weeks in a nursing home because I won't be able to drive!"

During that short stint in therapy, the counselor had taught Vinnie how to be a grey rock with her mother. To simply exist, to stop pushing against her complaints. To take them in, then let them drain out without trying to solve the unspoken problems in her monologues.

There was no way she'd be going back to Indianapolis to nurse her mother back to health. It sounded cold, but Bev had a way of chipping her out until she was hollow. She did it to everyone; she was acid rain on limestone, constantly etching the happiness out of everything. She also always managed to land on her feet when she had to.

"I'm sorry to hear that," Vinnie said.

"Barb said she got bedbugs when she had to go to rehab for her hip," Bev added. Barb was her mother's best friend. She lived two doors down, but there may as well have been a tunnel between the houses, as much time as she spent in Bev's kitchen. They could bitch to each other for hours, so they were a perfect match.

Vinnie nodded to the rhythm of Bev's discontent. "Yeah, I heard that can happen."

Her mother's voice faded into white noise as Vinnie drove. She knew she didn't have to actually participate. All she had to do was acknowledge what Bev was saying whenever she stopped to catch a breath.

Instead, Vinnie focused on the road—the curving, intricate road bound by trees and hills. The leaves were starting to fall, flashes of color fluttering to the ground, leaving behind their shivering skeletal homes. It was funny; the last few weeks had felt like early summer. In the eighties, off and on, still humid. Autumn hadn't cracked the way it did in Indianapolis, but the trees were doing their parts.

Already, the long drive up to the school looked more barren than it had a few days ago. She could make out the football and baseball fields through the trees now, and the building appeared much sooner than before. Everything had started to look a little distressed, especially beneath heavy skies. It was like a magician explaining his own tricks, enlightening but disappointing at the same time.

Bev's voice cut through the haze again. "And I gave your address to your cousin Tammy; she wanted to send a Christmas card."

The problem with grey rocking is that it only worked when the target wasn't trying to get you killed. Vinnie drew a shallow breath, her face hot with anger. "Ma. I told you not to give my address to anybody."

"Tammy's not just anybody!" Bev argued.

"Anybody is anybody!"

And there it was. Nobody could push Vinnie's buttons like her mother. She was like a living Self-Destruct button, constantly flashing. Vinnie's throat closed as she built a quick mental map.

How many degrees of separation was her cousin Tammy from anybody in the police department? Was she close enough for them to follow, to engineer the information out of her? Would they bother to dig through her trash, looking for clues to Vinnie's whereabouts?

And oblivious to it all, perhaps intentionally, Bev whined, "I guess I can't do anything right!"

"Do not," Vinnie said sharply, parking as close to the football field as she could, "give it to anybody else. And tell Tammy not to share it either."

The mewling gave way to staccato annoyance, her mother's stock-in-trade. She could almost anticipate what Bev would say next; she'd said it hundreds of times, mostly when Vinnie refused to play along with the emotional terrorism.

"You're so dramatic, Vanetta. I don't know where you get it from."

Chapter 29

The temptation to tell her she'd learned it from a crazy bitch named Bev was close to irresistible.

But resist she did, because she needed to get off the phone. Driving at a speed just north of idle, she passed a long row of yellow buses, then the teachers' lot.

Her eyes landed on Demers' dark-green Mini, simply because it was familiar. And Tyler's truck was easy to pick out in the student lot, considering the flamingo-pink scrotum still dangling from the hitch. She looked for Hannah's car but didn't know it well enough to identify.

Vinnie finally made it to the back lot, the one closest to the sports fields, with moments to spare. Even this far from the building, she could still hear the last bell ring. Students eager to get home would fly out of the building, and the football team would stream into the elements for practice.

A woman dressed in a patriotic tracksuit and ball cap was already on the field. She harassed a tackling dummy into place as Vinnie extricated herself from her mother's phone call.

"Just don't, all right? I have to go."

"Already?! We haven't talked in *months*!"

"Mother, it hasn't been months," she said. "I'm working, I have to go."

Then she hung up before her mother could interrogate her about *that*. They didn't have the kind of relationship where Vinnie would catch up with her over a cup of tea on Sundays or whatever. It was always the Bev Show, with Vinnie the incompetent stagehand who ruined everything. The less her mother knew about her, the better.

Finally parked, Vinnie slid out of the car and leaned against the door. Kids started trickling past, some heading onto the field, others out to their cars or walking well-worn paths through the trees to their homes. Their faces were soft and unformed to Vinnie, just so young. They looked like little kids playing dress-up, pretending to be adults. Then they got into cars and drove away on their own; mind-boggling.

It took forever for Tyler Purnell to finally appear. He walked with a couple of friends, caught in animated conversation. The boys bounced off each other, hands thumping against arms and chests and backs. Lollygagging, that's what they were doing, and they were all startled when Vinnie called Tyler's name.

He stopped with an uncertain smile. His boys orbited him, planets to his star. Flipping his blond hair back out of his face, Tyler solidified and chucked his chin up when he realized who it was. With a brazen smile, he said, "You're supposed to check in at the office if you want to visit campus."

"I mean, if you don't want to talk to me, I can always talk to the cops instead." She didn't have to tell him she'd be turning the phone over to the cops anyway. This was more a courtesy call than anything else. She wanted to see his reaction in person. "You have a thousand reasons and a Happy Meal to pick me."

It took Tyler a minute to get the implication. But when he did, his face turned grey. She couldn't hear what he told his friends to get them to buzz off, but they peeled away slowly, watching the two of them until they had to mount the steps up to the field. When they turned away, that's when Tyler came down to the car.

He wanted to be threatening. He had on his pads, which bulked him up, but he was still a quarterback, not a defensive lineman. Just a few inches taller than her, he stepped into her space, puffed up like an angry parakeet. "Lady, I don't know what your problem is, but—"

"Should I go ahead and tell the cops you killed Avery Adair?"

The grey in Tyler's face turned ashen. "She's actually dead?"

The surprise seemed genuine, but then again, Vinnie had seen him turn different parts of his personality on and off like a switch. Maybe it meant something, maybe not. Either way, Vinnie tucked his reaction away for now and pushed on.

"I don't know how you're gonna explain how you ended up with Avery's phone in your possession. Your grubby little finger-prints all over it . . . doesn't look good, my friend. Does not look good."

There was a stutter between his brain and his mouth, like it was spinning in a desperate attempt to come up with an explanation. When the reel finally settled, he said, "You're fucking crazy. What phone?"

"*For real*, dawg?" Vinnie couldn't help herself, just this once, mocking his texts right to his face. Proof that she'd read them. Proof that he might not be bright enough to understand. "The one you threw out of your truck. You wanna see the pictures? I have pictures, I have prints . . . I apologize, the prints you'll have to take my word for."

"What does that even prove?" he asked, telling on himself.

Since he just essentially agreed that he'd had the phone, and thrown it away, Vinnie kept the pressure steady. "That thing is a treasure trove, Tyler. Avery paid you five hundred bucks in August, then again, this month. I have the transaction records from her bank, and I have the texts. By this time tomorrow, I'll have copies of *your* bank records too. How are you gonna explain that?"

"I was tutoring her," he blustered.

"At a McDonald's in another county? No, you were blackmailing her. She went to meet you and ended up dead, why? Did she tell you that she was cutting you off? She didn't care anymore if you told everybody about her Fans4U?"

Furiously, Tyler jabbed a finger in the air, close to her head. He trembled with rage; he wanted to hit her. It radiated off of him and got caught in the teeth he clenched as he spoke. "I didn't do shit to her."

Expansively, Vinnie shrugged. "Hate to say it, but that's not what it looks like, TyTy. She's dead and you had her phone. She's dead and you were bleeding her dry. I don't know much, kid, but I know how to add. Motive, plus means, plus opportunity equals first-degree murder, and you're seventeen. You're not going to juvie, buddy. You're going to Jessup."

Fear crept into Tyler's fury. Now he trembled with both, stealing quick looks toward the football field. He wanted a coach to come save him. An adult to come be on his side, because he was supposed to be their golden boy. Unfortunately for him, he was pretty much alone. The single coach on the field had walked out of sight.

Even so, he didn't break, not like some kids did, crying and begging and explaining. No. He was too certain of himself to melt down like that. But his voice was full of poison as he stepped into her space. His nose nearly touched hers, and she could feel the heat of his breath on her skin.

"You think you're so smart," he said, going for menacing but landing on shrill. "She left her phone in the booth at the Mc-Donald's. I found it and held on to it for her. I was gonna give it back when I saw her at school."

One eyebrow rising, Vinnie said, "And that's why you broke into it and deleted everything that connected you to her, huh? Then you just couldn't resist fucking with your ex-girlfriend, could you? You knew she was worried about her friend, so you thought you'd be funny—"

"Who, Hannah?" Tyler barked a laugh. "They weren't friends. Not anymore."

"What makes you say that?"

Now Tyler shrugged broadly. "My eyes. I'm not fucking blind. They weren't talking. I don't know why, and I don't give a fuck either." He found his second wind, confidence bringing the color back to his face. "And I didn't touch that chick. She gave me that money because she wanted to; she was alive the last time I saw her, so . . . I don't know what to tell you, lady."

"Who'd you get to call the police, pretending to be her?"

The question threw Tyler. Bafflement crossed his face briefly. "The fuck are you talking about?"

Unfortunately, he sounded sincere, and that one truth amidst the lies broke the flow. It had given him just enough time to re-cover, back to his swaggering, untouchable self. She was pretty sure he was done talking, but Vinnie tossed in one more question, just to test it. "How'd you find Avery's Fans4U account in the first place?"

An ugly smile crept to his lips. "Who says I did?"

Chapter 30

In a preemptive strike, Vinnie called Rosier before Tyler had a chance to run crying to Mom and Dad.

"I put the screws to the Purnell kid, and I have something you're gonna wanna see," she told Rosier.

She was already heading north, to Howard County. She wanted to see if she could sweet-talk some security footage out of the McDonald's, maybe shake a witness or two loose. "He chucked Avery's phone out of his truck right after the search stopped yesterday."

"You have it in your possession?" Rosier asked, each word clipped. Vinnie could imagine the thoughts running through his head. The last thing you wanted was compromised evidence, but compromised or not, you still wanted it. There would just be a lot of praying to the judicial gods that it wouldn't get thrown out.

Merging into traffic, Vinnie nodded. "Yep. Bagged, not tagged."

"Can you get it to me now?" he asked.

Though he couldn't see it, she shook her head. Hitting the interstate at rush hour was a stop-and-go demolition derby if you weren't careful. It reminded her, again, that she needed to get out of this rental and into a real car, real soon. "Sorry, I'm following up on a lead. I can leave it at the station when I get back."

"Let me guess," Rosier said, already resigned. "You've already looked at it. I thought we were going to share information."

"Is there an ID on the body yet?" she asked, testing that theory.

"It's too early to say."

Vinnie slammed on her brakes. Time for some of the stop instead of the go. "Uh-huh, that's what I thought. But I'm doing you a favor by holding off."

"This. This is a favor to me," he said, incredulous.

Slowly wedging her way into the next lane, Vinnie said, "Yep. I'm giving you the gift of plausible deniability when Tyler Purnell's dad calls to bitch about me. You're gonna be able to honestly tell him you have no idea what the fuck I'm doing. And it'll be the truth when you say you'll take care of it. Because you will. Just not the way he's hoping."

"I can't say that I particularly care for this cloak-and-dagger shit, Vinnie."

"See?" Vinnie said brightly. "You hate this. Plausible deniability."

After a few more non-pleasantries, they hung up. That left Vinnie to concentrate on the road. She didn't miss much about Indianapolis, but she did miss the wide-open straightaways on the city loop. The highways that branched off the loop were nice too, and straight, all the way to the next state.

Here? That was a different story. Heading north or south out of Wills Harbor spat her directly into traffic for Baltimore or D.C., and that was a lot like getting thrown into a blender. Hell, half the time, a perfectly normal road would turn into highway without warning. And the exits? Well, who didn't enjoy dropping from sixty-five to fifteen miles an hour on a dime? Jesus, this place.

Once she knew the streets better, she told herself, it would be easier. Having to rely on GPS instead of instinct was an added layer of difficulty. It was bad enough she didn't know the quickest way to the pharmacy or the grocery store. She couldn't begin to outwit local traffic until she'd learned some shortcuts and back roads.

By the time she made it to the McDonald's Tyler had placed both himself and Avery at, the sky had surrendered to a gradient sunset. Scarlet still hung at the horizon, with rippling purples pushing it from sight. It would be nightfall before she got back to Wills Harbor.

Everybody and God had come to McDonald's for dinner. The drive-thru line wrapped all the way around the building. Pulling a jacket over her holster, Vinnie walked into the fast-food restaurant and straight to the counter. There were lines at the registers, too, and she collected a handful of shitty looks at her bypass, but that was nothing new.

She pulled out one of her business cards and flattened it on the counter when the manager finally came over to see what she wanted. The manager didn't look *as* young as the rest of the kids working away in the back, but he wasn't old either. Vinnie guessed late twenties at best, because he still had little patches of acne on his forehead.

"Hi, Todd," she said, blustering forward instantly so he wouldn't look at her business card too closely. She wasn't exactly impersonating the police, but she was definitely encouraging him to make the erroneous assumption. "I'm Vanetta Taylor, and I'm looking into the disappearance of Avery Adair. I have evidence that she was at this restaurant earlier this month. I wanted to talk to your employees if I could, or look at the security footage. I have an exact time of day, if that will help."

It was pretty obvious Todd was an anxious guy. He had a flop sweat on before he'd even walked up to the counter. He tried to pick the business card off the counter a couple of times but failed. His nails were bitten down to the quick, so he had to sweep the card into his hand. Once he did that, he glanced at it but also glanced at the evening rush that was backing up his dining room.

"Come on," he said, opening the pass-through for her. "She was definitely here? You know for a fact?"

Vinnie produced her phone and showed him the screenshot of Avery's bank account, the final transaction of $9.87 at this address. It was enough to convince him to invite her into the manager's office. He sat at the computer, jabbing at the keys one by one. He typed like an old man, but Vinnie stood there and let him explain the system in excruciating detail. She already had a good idea how it worked, but she let him finish his spiel. People liked to cooperate with pleasant people, so Vinnie kept the neutral smile on her face and nodded a *lot*.

"Todd!" somebody yelled from the kitchen, panicked.

Plain as milk, Vinnie asked, "Do you need to go see what that's about?"

Todd hesitated, probably like his job depended on it. When multiple people started yelling for him, he gave up the seat. "I'll be right back," he told Vinnie, and hurried out. Sliding into the rolling chair, she queued up the inside footage, starting an hour before the time stamp in Avery's Cheeky account.

She recorded the security footage with her own camera, so she'd have a copy to study later. Every time something banged next to the office, she startled. Todd would show back up eventually, and she wanted to get as much as she could before he tossed her. Once he really *read* the business card, she'd be out on her ass.

She started with the front-counter view, simply because she knew somebody used Avery's account to order food. Either it was her, or it was Tyler, but it would key her into the right time.

Seven minutes before the time stamp, Avery Adair walked into view. Vinnie caught her breath. Knowing what came next, it was unnerving to see Avery alive and well, in motion, in color. She wore an oversized sweater and skintight leggings that disappeared into boots. She looked a little older here in person, but that was probably the makeup and hair. And she looked tense, her arms crossed tightly over her chest.

A young man stood at her shoulder—Red, no doubt, based on how easily they talked. There was a slight family resemblance, but that might have been a mirage. Vinnie knew they were cousins, so she could have imagined the similarities. Avery walked off-screen, leaving Red to wait for their order.

Switching views to the dining room, Vinnie found Avery easily. She studied her every move, trying to read her—trying to reach her—somehow across distance and time. But all she had was a window into the past, a moment in time she could only observe.

In the back corner, Avery sat in a booth. Her face was tight, her lips folded into a grim line. First she glanced at her phone, then she looked blackly out the window. She kept her phone in her hand, raising it, dropping it. Then, her already-unpleasant expression soured more, and she put her phone face-down on the table.

A rolling wave of smug appeared, Tyler Purnell swaggering into view and taking the seat across from her. The video had no sound, and only a questionable touch of color. Still, they were unmistakable. *She* was furious, and *he* reveled in it. He reached across the table toward her, and she slapped his hand away without hesitation.

Then Red walked into the frame, carrying a tray with two large fries and a soda with casual ease. He slid the tray down, knocking Tyler's hand away. From this angle, Vinnie saw Avery's phone slide toward Tyler's side of the table. Neither Avery nor Red noticed, because Avery was too busy digging in her purse, and Red was too busy glaring holes in Tyler's face.

Quickly, she switched camera views. Dining room. Front counter. Hallway. Drive-thru. Parking Lot 1 and 2. Tyler's truck was there—unmistakable. The rest were a blur of compacts and SUVs trying not to flatten each other. She wanted to get a survey of everybody in the restaurant; it could be handy later for digging up witnesses. Then she switched back to the dining room view, tight on Avery, Red, and Tyler.

Vinnie wished she could hear what they were saying. Red took a bundle of fries and shoved them into his mouth, talking around them. His gaze never left Tyler's, and Vinnie wondered if he knew why Avery passed a fat bank envelope across the booth to him.

It was an interesting trio. Somebody had told Vinnie, she couldn't remember who now, that Red and Tyler were both on the football team. Whether Red knew *why* the payoff was happening or not, it looked like there was no love lost between the teammates.

On the screen, Tyler tossed his hair out of his face, then moved to count the bills. At that point, Red slammed a hand down on top of Tyler's and leaned over the table. Vinnie didn't know how to read lips, but she read the body language just fine. *Quit being a fucking dick and get the fuck out of here*, she surmised.

Tyler decided to stay put a little longer. He slowly put the envelope on the table—right on top of Avery's phone. He looked like he was spitting bullshit, playing off the theft with slow, casual motions. Avery looked sharpish but said nothing; apparently

Red was there to do the talking. She fed herself fries, one by one, deliberately looking past Tyler as she did. The color wasn't good enough to tell Vinnie if Avery's cheeks darkened with a flush. From this vantage, she looked like stone.

Deliberately, with slow precision, Red sprawled back and put an arm across the back of the booth. He didn't fold Avery into it, and the move was apparently more than getting comfortable. Because suddenly, Tyler stared at Red, mid-chest, the smile knocked off his face.

"Shit," Vinnie said, clicking around to try to find another angle.

It took a second, but there it was. Red splayed across the booth with his jacket gaping open, a pistol tucked into the waistband of his jeans. The video quality wasn't great; there was no way to identify what *kind* of gun it was, but that didn't really matter. Since Tyler was alive and well, Red obviously hadn't capped him.

And then, just like that, Tyler took Avery's phone—disguised under the envelope of cash—and slid from the booth. Shoving both into his back pocket, he stood at the table long enough to say something else—something no doubt meant to be witty—then he backed away.

Vinnie could tell the exact moment Tyler left the store. Avery collapsed, abandoning the fries and burying her head in her hands. Straightening up, Red patted her in the middle of the back, the awkward kind of *there, there* that teenage boys excelled at with sisters and cousins. Any unexpected show of emotion could confuse them, but for the most part, they tried. It might have been awkward comfort, but at least he made the attempt.

She switched to the parking lot, to see if Tyler actually left. He did, pulling abruptly out of his parking space and cutting through the drive-thru line. It was pretty clear he was speeding, a perfectly appropriate response to someone bringing a gun to a shakedown. When she pulled up the restaurant view again, Red was sliding out of the booth. Avery waved him away with several insistent nods.

Huh. Red was her ride, so where was *he* going? Vinnie tracked him all the way out to a beater in the lot. She watched until he left, then flicked back to Avery. It made a kind of teenage sense, to pay off a blackmailer out of town. No witnesses, nobody from school ear-hustling long enough to learn her secrets. But why wouldn't she leave with her cousin?

The video stuttered slightly. Avery ate her fries and watched the door. Fast-forward. Again. Suddenly, she looked up. Confusion colored her expression; she leaned back in the booth as if stunned. Someone in her eyeline approached. But before Vinnie could switch views, Todd appeared in the doorway.

He stood there with her card in one hand, and the store phone in the other, and Todd? Todd did not look happy.

"Ma'am, are you with the police department?"

Chapter 31

O f course she told him no, and of course he threw her out. She wondered if he'd put her face on the wall in the back, like they used to do with people who bounced checks. Only for her, the sign would read, DO NOT SERVE THIS WOMAN; ILLICIT SECURITY FOOTAGE VOYEUR.

At least she'd gotten what she'd come for. She felt like she could rule Tyler out—at least as a murderer. He was well and truly gone in the video—Vinnie had watched him pull out of the parking lot. Avery had shooed her cousin away—that told Vinnie *she* knew she wasn't leaving with Red. There was a third person in play here; that's who Vinnie needed to find.

All Tyler had done was shake down a classmate, then get the shits when he realized his ex-girlfriend was about to report Avery missing. He deleted himself from the phone, badly tried to convince Hannah not to go to authorities, and then dumped the thing entirely when a body turned up.

Now. Could Vinnie whang the facts around to make Tyler look good for a murder?

Sure.

He was still blackmailing Avery; he'd stolen her phone. There was solid, direct evidence of that. Solid, direct evidence that he saw her alive much later than he'd previously admitted. Add to that, Red's threat.

It wouldn't be hard to spin it out, weave it like Greek myth in a tapestry—*Well, Tyler didn't take that threat too kindly. He got Avery alone, killed her, dumped her body somewhere out of the way. Tried to make it seem like she was fine by sending demonstrably real texts from her phone. Hell, Red was missing too; add another potential murder to the pile.*

By the time the second search came around, Tyler, budding sociopath and junior serial killer, knew the vultures were circling. Joined in the search to enjoy people finding Avery's body, maybe to see how close they were to finding Red's. Then he deleted as much evidence as he could and dumped the phone.

Vinnie could wrap Tyler up with a bow if she wanted to, hand him to Rosier, and go on her merry way. After all, Red wasn't around to contradict her. The circumstances made sense, the motive made sense, and the means were there with a little creative embroidering.

It would all fall apart if it turned out they had a different girl in the morgue, but that was a problem for another day. And that was the kind of shit that had pushed Vinnie further and further out of step with her partner and her colleagues in Indy.

She'd never put a case together that she hadn't believed in. That being said, there were definitely times she'd stitched the evidence together with gossamer thread. Once she started questioning, started paying attention, she noticed all her ragged edges; she saw her colleagues do it like it was breathing.

Suddenly it was everywhere: manufactured, institutional bullshit that separated citizens from their freedom, even if only for a night in the county lockup. It made her sick. It gave her nightmares.

So yeah. She could make this case disappear, except for one salient detail.

That wouldn't bring Avery back.

And worse, whatever had happened to her, framing Tyler wouldn't do shit to stop the bad guy from doing it again. Vinnie had no timer from the DA, no press screaming at her for a solution. As a matter of fact, she was doing this investigation out of the biggest part of her heart, because she sure as shit wasn't getting paid. And even though the kid that had ostensibly "hired" her had turned out to be a liar, Vinnie was in this. Not until the arrest, but till the truth.

And the truth was, whatever happened to Avery after she left McDonald's, Tyler hadn't done it. It was time to move on to other suspects.

She did have to wonder if Red had done something to his cousin. He could have left and come back to find Avery with a Mystery Guy and it pissed him off. He could have dragged her out of there, lost his temper . . . It seemed like a long shot, but a lot of men got funny when the women they knew and loved got mixed up in sex work. Sometimes they reacted violently . . . and sometimes, they decided they wanted to be cut in.

Everyone agreed on one thing about the Adairs: they were all criminals. But in general, the rumors also agreed that they mostly sold drugs and stole shit. Not a lot of pimping on the menu, to her understanding. No homicides that she was aware of. Still, it wouldn't have been the first time a nepo-criminal struck out on his own to make his bones on the big stage. She couldn't rule Red out, not yet.

The highway was still a nightmare, which gave Vinnie plenty of time to call Rosier. This time, it went through to his voicemail.

She rambled after the beep, filling him in on her trip to Howard County, and the fact that Red Adair was running around with a gun in his pants the day Avery disappeared. She wondered aloud if the kid knew how many guys had shot a ball off that way. She was guessing not.

It was pitch-black when she got back to Wills Harbor. Dialing Camila, Vinnie got voicemail there too. She hung up without a message. Looked like she was going home alone. Well, not completely alone. Goofus was probably waiting next to an empty food dish, or shitting in her bed, furious that the luxe life hadn't panned out for him so far.

Somehow guilted by a cat she never wanted to own, Vinnie swung into the Red Stripe parking lot. She needed a pan and some gravel, and more of that nasty canned food he'd seemed to like. The grocery store was surprisingly quiet, and a little dingy. Vinnie navigated the narrow aisles, occasionally flattening herself against a shelf to let a shopper with a cart pass by.

Once she found the food and litter, she grabbed a couple bags of pork rinds and a bottle of Barq's for herself. The bananas looked okay; she grabbed a bunch of those and then went back for a quart of milk. She should have gotten a cart, but she dumped it all in the future litter pan to wrestle her shit to the checkout line.

The problem with clearing one suspect was that now she had to reorder her investigation. Red was in play, but who the fuck was guy number three? Hell, for that matter, was it even a guy? She didn't want to bother Kassadee at the moment. The woman had a job, a new baby, and she was living in hell, waiting for an ID on the body.

If that body *was* Avery's, then somebody had dragged her back to Wills Harbor just to dump her in her own backyard. That didn't seem very likely to Vinnie. But if it *wasn't* Avery, a whole new Pandora's box opened. Were the girls' cases related somehow? Was there a predator passing through, chewing up high school girls as he went?

Vinnie paid for her groceries, then threw a reusable bag onto the belt when she realized there was no plastic to be had. New law, no disposable bags in Kerry County. Vinnie had a feeling she was going to end up with sixty-seven store-brand bags littering her car, and sadly, used just the once. She didn't hate the environment; it was just one more thing to learn about living in Maryland.

Taking her purchases, Vinnie walked back to her car. The Dark Sky lights in the parking lot glowed with a low, blue tint. True to their name, they let her pick out a few stars above, but they didn't do much to illuminate her way. She unlocked the rental with the fob and tossed the groceries in the backseat. She slid into the driver's seat, keys in the ignition, when the passenger door suddenly opened.

A dark figure in a ski mask got in, just in time to meet Vinnie's Glock 19.

Chapter 32

S he held the gun steady even as her heart raced.

"Out," she barked, her thumb resting on the safety. She didn't want to shoot anybody, let alone in a rental car. Her whole body was a trap, ready to snap. Unfazed, the unwanted passenger closed the door and turned to her. He didn't quail at the sight of the gun.

Instead, he pulled off his ski mask and said, "I heard you were looking for me."

Red Adair, in the flesh.

Vinnie choked down her adrenaline. Slowly, she replaced her gun in its holster. She was sorely tempted to deck the kid for scaring her, but the rational part of her brain intervened. The introduction was shit, but she was the one who'd asked Keith to get him a message. Looked like the message had been received. Now she needed to hide the tremor in her hands and calm the panic in her mind.

"You're gonna get shot, fucking around like that."

Slumping down in the seat, Red shrugged. "We all gotta die sometime."

The bravado helped break Vinnie's anxiety. Red Adair was still in high school. He couldn't have been more than eighteen; he had no idea how stupid he sounded saying shit like that. She put the key in the ignition and told him, "Yeah, yeah, yeah, whatever. Put on your seat belt, Clint Eastwood."

"Who's that?" he asked, and Vinnie ignored the creak of her rocker.

"Just do it," she said, and started the car. It didn't take long to merge back onto the main road; the traffic lights, for once, were on her side. Except now she had a fugitive in her car, which sounded a little too dramatic for a two-bit Jet Ski thief, but nevertheless. She was okay with bumping up against the law, but she didn't want to outright break it. "Where have you been?"

Red ignored her question, and asked, "Can you take me to Baltimore?" He pulled the ski mask onto his forehead. It rested just above strawberry-blond eyebrows and watery blue eyes rimmed with red. Based on the blown-out pupils and the pallor in his face, Vinnie guessed he was on something. Hopefully it wasn't something that made him dangerous and unpredictable.

Nobody knew where she was. Nobody knew who she was with. She should have said no. Instead, Vinnie changed lanes and informed him, "That depends on what you can tell me."

"Is my cousin really dead?" he asked. When they stopped at a light, he slumped deeper into the seat. Vinnie didn't know where Red had been hiding, but it was obvious he didn't want to get caught. Ironically, that fact helped her relax a little. He'd come back into a town where all the cops were looking for him, just to talk to her about Avery. At the very least, he cared about *her*.

Vinnie kept watch in her mirrors and headed for the highway again. "They don't have confirmation yet," she told him. He slumped a little more, and she decided to go with honest. "Look,

I know she went with you to meet Tyler. What happened after he left?"

The knobby little Adam's apple in his throat bobbed as he swallowed. "She was supposed to meet a friend, so I left her there."

"What friend?"

"You got a cigarette?" he asked, then shook his head when she said no. Rubbing his palms on his jeans, again and again, he licked dry lips, then said, "Some guy. I don't know. She wouldn't tell me who he was."

The kid was tweaking; it was hard to tell if that was making him more honest or a better liar. She asked, "That didn't worry you? Make you feel a little protective? You flashed your piece at Tyler."

Exhaling all his breath in a rush, Red said, "Yeah, but I didn't get in her business. She asked me to come to talk to Tyler. She didn't ask me—you didn't say. You never said. Is it her? Is she dead?"

Vinnie thought about it a moment, then said, "According to her mom, she didn't come back. According to her best friend, she didn't come back. Now according to you, she didn't come back from up *there*. So, in my professional opinion, whatever that's worth, she went missing *there*, not *here*. Is it fucked up that we found a body during that search? Absolutely. Is it your cousin? In theory, it could be. But it doesn't make sense to me for somebody in Howard County to hurt her and then dump her here."

"She's alive?" Red asked plaintively.

"I think I'd rather believe that and keep looking," Vinnie said. "Did you know what was going on between Tyler and Avery?"

The soft, almost little-boyness to Red burned away in a furious instant. "Not till that day. If I had, I woulda broke his fucking face. I *wanted* to break his fucking face at the McDonald's, but Avery told me not to. She didn't want me getting in more trouble; I'm on probation."

Curious, Vinnie glanced at him. "For what?"

"Well, *technically*, stealing a car," Red said. "But we were just joyriding."

It was almost funny how many times she'd heard versions of that sentence in her life. To teenagers, the only thing that mattered was their intent. They intended to steal a car and sell it for parts, that was a crime, and they all knew it. But if they *intended* to go for a high-speed jaunt in a car that didn't belong to them? That was just having a good time.

As Vinnie drove toward the glow in the distance, she kept Red talking. One, so he didn't have time to think, which would make it more obvious if he lied, but two, because she had a novel's worth of questions to ask him and only about twenty-eight minutes to ask them, according to her GPS.

"So you didn't know in August," she said, trying to sound off-hand. "But you definitely knew this month. What did she tell you?"

"That he found out about her side hustle, and he was blackmailing her. I didn't want her paying him again. In fact, I wanted to—"

"Break his face," Vinnie supplied.

"Damn straight, and get the money back he already took from her. He doesn't even fucking need it. He just wanted to be a dick."

Vinnie asked, "What makes you think he didn't need it?"

"His parents shit money for breakfast; his dad's a lawyer and his mom . . . I don't think she has a job. She just does rich-lady shit. And fucking Tyler, he's got a fucking card, a black card, he's allowed to charge anything he wants. Food. Games. He wrecked his truck and got it fixed, and his mom and dad didn't even know. They just pay the bill."

"Must be nice."

"No shit," Red said. "He didn't need to go and take Avery's money. He just wanted to, because she didn't fuck with him."

"Hannah mentioned she wasn't fond," Vinnie said.

"She fucking haaaaated him," Red said, rolling the window down. He leaned against the door like a puppy, his gaze off in the distance. His skin looked clammy; pale and damp as he sucked at the outside air. "It made him fucking crazy, because *all* the girls wanted to fuck with him."

There was a shock. A thin-skinned rich kid acted out when he didn't get everything he wanted, tale as old as time. Vinnie punched the window button, rolling hers down to even out the pressure. Well, that and the scent of cigarette smoke that clung to Red's clothes. She'd quit some ten years ago, but every so often the smell awakened a little lizard in her brain that desperately wanted a drag.

"Maybe I'm reading into it too much," Vinnie said, "but you seem to know a lot about Tyler Purnell."

"We used to be *tight*, like *tight*, you know? But he was in the car we borrowed too; he got hauled in with me. His parents bailed him out, because rich is gonna rich. I wasn't even mad I had to spend the weekend in until Uncle Keith could bond me out. That's just the way it goes. But you know what that fuckface did?"

Vinnie had a guess, but Red was on a roll, so she just waited for him to finish his sentence.

"His dad's a lawyer, right? Well, he got Tyler to roll on me, so *he* could get into one of those classes, like, 'Crime is bad, kids, don't do a crime.' The worst part? Tyler was the one driving! The whole thing was his fucking idea!"

Another shock, that a rich kid had avoided the system entirely with the right connections. Diversion programs made a difference, especially for teens who had simply fucked up and things spiraled out of their control. As long as they hadn't hurt anybody, trying to teach them to be better people seemed like the right move. There was no point ruining a fifteen-year-old's life with a felony conviction if they could be saved.

Unfortunately, the kids who got into these programs were usually the ones whose parents could afford to hire an attorney. So of course the programs were full of the haves, while juvie was full of the have-nots. Hell, that was evident from the two months Avery had spent in detention for getting caught at a party.

"How long ago was that?" she asked.

"Sophomore year. I didn't have to do time, but I'm on probation until I'm eighteen. My caseworker calls every week. She was supposed to get me into job training, but all she wanted me to do was volunteer to pick up trash on the side of the road. No, thank you; fuck that."

Vinnie didn't mention the stolen Jet Ski. She had a feeling Red knew he was only buying time, hiding from the police. There was even a chance they would quit actively looking for him and hold on to his bench warrant for the next time. If he waited too long, he wouldn't be a minor by the time he got caught.

All he was doing was saving a juvenile offense for an adult rainy day; if he kept fucking around, he'd spend his twenties in prison. Vinnie had a weird sympathy for him. His deck had been stacked since birth, and not in his favor. He reminded her of the boys in her trailer park, the ones with sweat-stained jean jackets and mullets that licked at the back of their collars. She didn't remember their names anymore, but she remembered too many of their faces as they were escorted into the back of a patrol car.

"So, you and Avery, you're real close?" Vinnie asked.

Proudly, Red said, "Our birthdays are two days apart. We always celebrated together."

"Do anything else together?" When Red shot her a look, she clarified, "I heard she was running small-time drugs with you."

Abrupt, Red sat up. He glared at Vinnie. His hand didn't stray toward his waistband, and as long as it didn't, they wouldn't have any problems. He glowered as he said, "There's some seedy motherfuckers out there buying my shit. I don't want her around that!"

"It was a cover story, then," Vinnie said calmly.

Still twitchy, Red pulled out an empty pack of Marlboro Lights. He peered into it, hoping for a smoke to appear. When none did, he crumpled the packet, squeezing it into a smaller and smaller ball in his hand. The plastic crinkled, playing like static on the radio. "Who'd she tell, Hannah? Pfff. She was probably just fucking with her."

Vinnie plucked the packet right out of his hand; the crackling was making her crazy. The sound of it made her mouth water. It was hard enough driving I-97 in a Matchbox car, she didn't need to be distracted by old demons. She said, "I thought they were friends."

"They *were*, until Hannah called her a whore."

Chapter 33

What Vinnie loved more than anything else in the world was being lied to.

Which was good, because her childhood was a minefield of lies, most of her relationships crashed and burned over lies, and for extra-special fun, she'd chosen a career where she could enjoy a truly diverse field of lies every single day of her life. But at this point, she was fucking furious with Hannah.

Keeping her temper just under boiling, Vinnie took the exit that would lead them into Baltimore proper. The trees had already fallen away to highway walls, cracked with occasional ivy, or maybe kudzu. She didn't know; she hadn't lived here long enough to know. The city cast an orange glow on low-hanging clouds, and she could already see lights from the stadium piercing the sky.

She had to pick and choose which emotions got to the surface, but she couldn't keep the irritation entirely hidden when she asked, "So Hannah knew about Crush Baby."

With a manic laugh, Red shook his head. "Oh, hell no. I knew because I helped her take the pictures, but I was the only one. Avery kept that shit tight."

"You're *sure*."

"Positive."

"Then how did Tyler find out?"

A slow, knowing smirk touched his lips. "How do you think?" And when Vinnie didn't immediately reply, Red jerked off the air to explain for her. A classic story, teenage boy, with unfettered access to the internet and a bottle of Jergens, in search of a new thrill . . . yeah, okay, she got it. But everything Vinnie had seen was carefully disguised, down to her voice, so that still wasn't an answer. She clarified, "Yeah, I get that, but how did Tyler know it was *her*?"

Red rolled his eyes and sighed. "She fucked up. See, she'd do private requests from a burner, and she showed her face in those pictures. Those pervs pay more for young girls, you know? And one time, she updated the public gallery but accidentally uploaded one from the privates. She didn't even realize it was there until Tyler called her out."

A deep, unsettled well ached in Vinnie's chest. Tale as old as time, but it still made her sick. "Was Avery planning on being done with Crush Baby, after she paid off Tyler?"

Serious again, Red nodded. "Yeah. Once he came at her, she started shutting it down."

"Started?"

"She had a couple clients she was still sending pictures to, off F4U. But once Tyler found her, she shut the profile down, got rid of the Instagram, all that."

Circling back like a shark, Vinnie asked, "Any idea who the clients are? Could that be who she was meeting?"

Red hesitated—not like he was hiding something, more like contemplating something for the first time. He offered a weak "Maybe? I don't know. I don't think she'd do that. Pictures were easy money, I don't see why she would . . . you know."

Unfortunately, Vinnie did. She didn't see the point in sharing that with Red; he was already distressed, coming down from God knew what, and jonesing for a hit of *something* to take the edge off. He didn't seem volatile, but she didn't want to push her luck. Besides, the phone still held valuable information she could farm, and now she knew better what to look for. It was pretty clear Red was tapped out as far as Crush Baby was concerned, so Vinnie changed the subject.

"So, you said she got in a fight with Hannah. Tell me about that," Vinnie said, keeping her eyes on the road. "Because Hannah's the one who brought me in, right? If they aren't friends, then why paint a target on herself by hiring a private detective?"

"Guilty conscience," Red told her, looking out toward the city. "That's my guess. Because Hannah was getting back with Tyler, right? And she kept seeing him and Avery talking; that pissed her off. They got into it in homeroom; that's when she called her a ho."

Vinnie frowned. "That's an argument; that's not a fight."

"Nah," Red said, "Hannah slapped her. Right there in front of everybody. Miss Goody Two Shoes, wannabe teacher's pet, queen of the brownnosers, yeah, she did. Avery just kept her hands up, 'cause that's the only way you don't get suspended for fighting too."

Her whole mouth sour, Vinnie hit the brakes a little too hard coming into the city. Red ricocheted forward, bouncing off the dash, then back into his seat. "The fuck?" he asked.

The fuck, indeed.

Flailing for the right question, Vinnie hit the long straightaway in front of the stadium and had to remind herself to slow down. "I don't get it. I've seen Tyler and Hannah together. She couldn't get away from him fast enough."

"I don't know what to tell you," he said. "Because Hannah really thought Avery was sweating Tyler. Called her a ho, slapped her, pow. And then somebody posted a video of the fight online and everything. Rob—that's her dad—hired Tyler's dad to get them to take it down. Didn't want to ruin her scholarship chances and shit, you know? She was still trying to get with him, last I heard."

"And the only relationship Avery had with Tyler was—"

"Him ripping her off. Yeah." When they slowed to a stop, he sat up a little straighter. "Turn right up here. You know where the Inner Harbor is? Yeah, just go right up here, I'll show you."

A dark thought flickered to the surface. Avery had seemed surprised, confused, at whoever showed up at the McDonald's after Red left. Whoever showed up wasn't who she'd expected to see. Vinnie asked slowly, "You're sure Hannah didn't know about Crush Baby."

"I told you. Fucking positive."

Yeah, well, Vinnie wasn't. Not anymore. But that didn't concern Red. Vinnie changed the subject as she navigated a road that curved deeper into the city. "All right, let me ask you this: what do you think happened to Avery?" Other people's ideas never hurt, especially not when they came from somebody who knew the victim, or the perp, well. And in this case, Red might have known both.

"I dunno, but if I find out somebody did something to her—"

"Don't say it," Vinnie told him. "I don't wanna be a witness, Red."

Red said, "Smart. Oh, okay, you see that light? Turn there."

Following Red's directions, they slid into downtown Baltimore. Buildings sprang up, lit even in the night. She couldn't see the actual Inner Harbor from the street, but the masts on the USS *Constellation* peeked through. This was nowhere near the police and security supply house she'd visited, and the mix of dilapidated and brand-new made it hard to get a bead on the neighborhood. She didn't want to roll him out somewhere he was going to get in more trouble.

Nevertheless, she pulled up where he told her to, beside a street of rowhouses. Their brick uniformity, their matching white marble steps, looked almost like a movie set to her. Underneath sodium streetlights, she felt exposed and invisible at the same time. Before he got out, she held an open hand in front of Red. She squared up with him. In her best cajoling, but could possibly turn into threatening voice, she said, "Gimme the gun."

"Fuck no," he said, laughing.

Vinnie told him, "Look, don't fuck with me. I promised your uncle I wouldn't turn you in, and I'm not gonna. But I'm also not gonna turn you loose with a heater. We both know you'll find another one if you're really motivated, but it's after dark. Cops are looking for a reason to stop you. If they find it, there goes your probation."

Even though he was reckless, Red wasn't stupid. After posturing for a minute, he pulled the gun from his waistband and put it in her palm. It was an old Heritage revolver. He blustered as she unloaded the .22 shells into her hand. "It's a piece of shit anyway."

"There's fifty bucks in the glove box," Vinnie told him, dumping the bullets in the cupholder and the gun beneath the seat. "Get something to eat and get wherever the hell it is you're going. Have one good, quiet night, will ya?"

Summoning the speed force or something, Red snatched the fifty and was halfway out the door before he stopped.

The dome light illuminated his face, still soft but a lot older in the eyes than the rest of the kids she'd talked to recently. He was a perfect example of the kind of guys she'd grown up with—the white-trash kid who knew the only future he had was the one he could beg, borrow, or steal. Vinnie didn't take Red for the begging type.

But he also offered up the kind of contradiction most people didn't want to acknowledge when they drove by the Hill. Red Adair loved his cousin, his birthday twin, a friend made by happenstance of biology but bonded against all weather. He asked, probably with the only bit of softness he dared to express, "What are you gonna do about Avery?"

Normally, Vinnie didn't make promises. But a lot had changed in the last twenty-four hours. Hell, a lot had changed in the last twenty-four minutes. She had a newfound drive to solve this case, one hardened by anger and honed by sympathy. She didn't try to comfort Red; it wouldn't have landed right. But in the half-smudged shadows, she swore to him.

"I'm gonna bring her home."

Chapter 34

As Vinnie left Baltimore, the highway seemed to leap from the ground.

It knotted with other elevated roads, seemingly dangled over dark waters that felt like a choppy void. It wasn't rush hour, but traffic still felt too fast. The unnatural voice of the GPS filled the car, reminding her to maintain her lane for the next three miles. Lights flashed, above and below her, headlights and taillights all peeling off in their own directions. It felt like a carnival ride gone very, very wrong.

Now that she was alone, her stomach twisted, acid rising up in the back of her throat. Hands tight on the wheel, she tried to revive the version of herself who'd placed in the top ten on the tactical course back home. Unfortunately, *that* Vinnie couldn't be summoned, because her brain was hurtling down a black, one-way track. Hannah Candlewood hadn't just lied to her, over and over.

There was a better-than-average chance that she'd *played* her.

Why hadn't Vinnie seen it? It wasn't the first time a suspect had inserted themselves into a case. But shit, Hannah had done it like a pro—making herself seem like a broken baby bird, when the whole time she might have been mining Vinnie for information.

Hannah's voice rang in her ears, asking what she knew, what had she found out, what did Kassadee say to her? Hannah had kept Vinnie from talking to her own parents. Hell, she'd conned her into covering for her *and* driving her to the search. She'd given her just enough bait—*this bad boy hurt my friend*—and Vinnie had swallowed it, hook and all.

Now the hook dragged through her gut, and tension twisted her muscles. Her fingers clenched into talons, and it felt like her jaw might actually snap. A teenage honor student had duped her, twisted her with a sob story and a sweet-as-pie offer of twenty dollars to make it seem legit. Vinnie felt like a rube.

But shit, why drag Vinnie into it at all? Hannah had reached out to *her*. Hannah had insisted that somebody look deeper. If she'd met up with her own best friend, to kill her over a walking turd like Tyler, why ask Vinnie to investigate at all? Was it some kind of preemptive alibi? Was she just trying to figure out if she'd covered her own tracks?

Thoughts ricocheted in the other direction: If Hannah wasn't involved, then why all the lying? She'd lied about them being on good terms. She'd lied about their argument. She lied about her own jealousy . . . it didn't make sense. Possibilities flicked back and forth: guilty, not guilty, mastermind, innocent.

Burning pinpricks raced from her face to her chest, frustration that set off a hot flash. Leave it to perimenopause to sense an opportunity and leap on it with full-throated glee. In this one instance, Vinnie had to admit, Bev hadn't exaggerated this kind of inferno. Already pouring sweat, Vinnie jabbed around in the dark until she got all the windows to go down at the same time.

The rush and roar of the wind came in with a shock. It was louder than the noise in her head, and insistent against the furnace burning beneath her flesh. Grabbing the front of her shirt, Vinnie fanned it as waves of sweat and sear battled across her body. She considered unsnapping her bra; hell, she considered peeling off her skin.

This particular gift from fifty pissed her off. There were plenty of body surprises at this age, and hot flashes were bad enough when they came on for no reason. It wasn't fucking fair that they could stop by for a boil when she was already upset. Worse, there was no telling how long this shit would last. Might last a minute or an hour. Who knew? Hormones did what they wanted.

Distracted, wind blasting straight at her head, Vinnie took a curve too fast. The tires ground on the rough shoulder, the chassis rattling like dice in a cup. With a hard yank, she jerked the rental back into its lane. Swerving into the next lane briefly, she pulled it back again, heart racing. The burn deepened, and her brain helpfully imagined careening over the guardrail into the black water below.

That's when red-and-blue lights burst to life right behind her.

"Motherfuck," Vinnie growled. She watched the rearview for a minute, to see if the lights were for her. And yep, the cruiser stayed on her tail. The officer even *blooped* his siren at her when she didn't pull over fast enough. Now her throat tied itself in a knot. She didn't want to be pulled over. She didn't want to be stopped. Who did, really? Except it felt like a heart attack. It felt like being hunted. All she wanted to do was floor it, flee, but this goddamned car couldn't outrun a bike cop, let alone a cruiser.

She pulled over in a puddle of light from a streetlamp and cut the engine. With a quick flip, she turned on the dome light, then put her hands on the wheel. Sweat gathered between her fingers;

trickled down her chest. The windows were already open. All she had to do was wait. Sounded simple; felt like dying.

Vinnie chewed on her lip, a taste of pain to clear her mind. The first time she'd been pulled over, she was nineteen and speeding on a road trip to Chicago. Back then, she waited for the officer to come to her window, ready to argue her case even though she didn't have one. That felt like a lifetime ago. This felt like a lifetime. Waiting. So much waiting.

Finally, the cruiser's door opened. A young officer stepped out, a block of gym muscles and oversized shoulders. He took a long, slow walk up to the passenger-side door. Vinnie knew he was checking her demeanor, her hands, looking for weapons.

He was also looking for excuses and extras—violations he could tack on if she gave him a hard time. Unfortunately for him, the rental was in perfect condition, her hands were fully visible, and the most interesting thing in the backseat was her groceries. Well, as long as he didn't notice that she was red as a lobster and soaked to the skin.

"Evening," he said, finally leaning down to look at her. He had a smooth, unlined baby face, and a whisper of a mustache trimmed within an inch of its follicles.

Ignoring the jumbled, painful beat of her heart, Vinnie said, "Hi there. You can see my hands; you need to know I have a licensed firearm in a shoulder holster, and another one under the seat."

His expression narrowed. "I want you to go ahead and reach outside your window and open your door. Slowly."

Why couldn't she just burst into flames? Incinerate right here, interaction over, laid to rest. Vinnie forced herself to follow his instructions, stepping out into the chill of night. The dark pressed all around her, only cut by the heat of exhaust as other cars passed. She had to fight her own body to walk to the front of the car. To put her hands on the searing hood.

She bit back a whimper, but nodded when he asked if he could reach into her jacket. Squeezing her eyes closed, she tried not to feel his touch, smell his aftershave. Too much. Too close. Her head swam; her breath failed. It felt like forever before he took the Glock from her holster and secured it. It didn't matter that she knew it was protocol. Her body believed something else.

"Why so many guns?" he asked.

"Personal safety," she told him. She couldn't stop the waver in her voice.

A truck blew past, throwing up grit and a diesel-stained blast of air. Another, deeper well of heat burned through her, and her stomach rolled. It threatened to bring back the takeaway leftovers she'd had for breakfast, and the root beer she'd gulped on the way back from Howard County.

The officer said, "I'm going to pat you down, all right?"

Her composure failed her; she croaked, "That's fine. My license is in my wallet, in my front pocket."

She was fine. She was fine. She was *fine*, until he touched her. Her thoughts screamed, trying to shove themselves back into the dark places. Instead, they burst out to engulf her. Time twisted, her body standing on the side of the highway as an officer rifled through her wallet, but her mind—

VINNIE CAN'T ENJOY the samosas at India Garden tonight.

She keeps watching the clock; she's due in court at eight a.m. There's been a lot of back-and-forth in the DA's office about when to deploy her testimony. There's been a bunch of wrangling at the bench to keep her identity as down-low as possible. Obviously, her name is buried in the prosecution's witness list, but nobody knows what she's going to say.

The defense assumption is she'll draw a thin, blue line around herself and the defendants, like the rest of the cops being called to the stand. After all, Vinnie's also a cop, and her brothers in blue are the ones charged this time. Family sticks together; it wears a uniform; it takes care of its own.

Sure, the guys charged with rape, kidnapping, and sex trafficking aren't her **partners***, but they work the same shift, same unit, scraping up bodies and speaking for the dead.*

Some reporter from Baltimore had summed it up, once, in a book he wrote after following the Homicide Unit for a year. Impossible to corrupt a murder police; all the money in the world can't bring back the dead. That's what the book says, that's what detectives repeat in interviews, in solemn tones, halos polished, and cheap shoes proof they're just lowly servants of the people.

The people never hear them joke about the way the dead lay akimbo in the streets. The judgments they cast on victims wearing short skirts; the nicknames they give family members—Bitchface, Dipshit, Dumbfuck—who have the audacity to ask for updates a little too often. The public doesn't know that lunch on third-shift Fridays is, traditionally, whatever the coroner says their latest vic's last meal was.

It's been bothering her, though, that she hasn't heard from her partner, Kyle, since she took her "leave of absence." It bothers her, but it doesn't surprise her.

Sometime in the past couple of years, they stopped being . . . not friends, not that they were friends before, exactly. Partners are something beyond that. It's a strange marriage, where you're literally ready to take a bullet for them, but Jesus Christ, you do **not** want to see each other naked.

At least, that's how it is with her and Kyle. He's only eight months older than her, but he wears his age like an anchor. Prematurely grey, both in hair and skin, he complains about his knees like he's ninety. And he's one of the few guys at work who's managed to hold on to his first wife. Has kids, two of them, who call her Auntie Vin.

So the thing that changed was ineffable; inexplicable. It was like a piano slowly going out of tune. It sounds fine, except also not. That's where she and Kyle are, after their one and only argument about Breonna Taylor a few years ago, the young Black woman from Louisville, shot to death in her sleep when cops executed an erroneous warrant.

Vinnie had called the excuses bullshit—even if you raid the wrong house, you don't go in guns blazing. Even if one person in the house brandishes a weapon, you don't rampage through, shooting indiscriminately. That seemed obvious to her, that these guys weren't good cops. They were power-tripping assholes who'd played too much Call of Duty, and they deserved to be punished.

As reasonable, or at least equanimous, as Kyle could be, he wouldn't go there. He looped around, again and again, to the fact that it was all an accident. Wrong house number, accident, law-abiding citizen acts like a perp, have to subdue him somehow, shooting a sleeping woman in her bed, in the middle of the night? Collateral damage.

That's not what Kyle had called it, but that's where his argument landed. She thought he was better than that, and he thought she was getting a little too woke for the job. He and Vinnie ended that shift screaming at each other in an unmarked car. The next day, they climbed into that same car, exchanged pleasantries, and got back to the grind. But it wasn't the same. It hasn't been the same since.

The stated reason for her leave of absence was her mother's heart-valve replacement surgery. Kyle hasn't called, hasn't asked about Bev, hasn't sent flowers.

Their work marriage had hit a rocky patch; that had made it easier to lie to his face about who she was. As far as he was concerned, she was still Homicide through and through, even if she had some "fruity" ideas. Still partners, more or less.

But as soon as he finds out she's been undercover for IAD, that she's the reason two fellow detectives and a detective sergeant are on trial . . . it's over.

Irretrievably, permanently severed, and that's the part that makes this hard. Everything is about to end; she's about to bring it down like a high-rise demolition. She won't be going back to work. She won't have anything left but a pension. Every friend she has is about to cut her off. So she wants to hold on to Kyle, just a little longer. If he's still her partner, the world hasn't ended yet.

Peeling flaky pastry and popping it in her mouth, she looks toward the obscured front windows again. She should be in her apartment like a good little girl, ordering in and eating in front of her laptop. But she's sick of breathing her own air and listening to her neighbors fight. Even sicker of the slim pickings DoorDash has to offer: pizza and tacos and Chinese.

She wanted biryani from her favorite place downtown, India Garden, a restaurant crammed into a deep but narrow building— the outside, beige brick, a promise of a hole-in-the-wall place. Inside, everything was dark wood and pale-green arches, deep-gold touches. The front windows are blocked by a massive sign on one side, and curtains on the other.

It's almost ten o'clock; the rest of the city is rolling up the sidewalks.

Still, it felt too much like breaking the rules (keep your head down, keep to yourself) to drive anywhere, so tonight she'd walked. India Garden's only a couple of blocks from her apartment; it's early enough in the summer that the heat breaks at sunset.

While she dissects her appetizer, she watches the window. Lights glare off the glass in the thin slices it affords her. Brightly colored flyers fill the bottom third, all for local events, further blocking the view. She eats, forking the aloo from the samosa into her mouth; she watches.

She's not sure what she's worried about.

It's nothing, *she tells herself, that hinky wariness that keeps her staring at the door.* It's nothing, *she tells herself again, leaning back as the waitress brings her meal. Because she wasn't raised in a barn, she thanks the waitress, puts the cloth napkin back in her own lap. She spoons fragrant meat and rice onto her plate rather than diving directly into the heaping silver dish. It's really meant for two people, but she's not going to share.*

She gets three bites in when the bells over the front door jingle. The owner slowly comes out of the kitchen, already saying, "We're closing. Only to-go."

Then, there's murmuring. Low voices, men. Two, maybe three. Vinnie takes another uneasy bite; it falls through her stomach when Mark Blaese steps into view.

Detective Mark Blaese, that is; he works first shift and shares a desk with Vinnie. She doesn't eat his strawberry hard candies, and he doesn't move her Happy Meal toys. Oh, and he's on trial for trafficking because of her. He just doesn't know it yet.

Probably.

Vinnie pulls the hood up on her sweatshirt and sinks into the chair. Maybe he's picking up a last-minute order. Maybe he, too, felt the call of naan after dark.

But when a uniform in plainclothes, that Vinnie recognizes but doesn't know, steps in after Blaese, her throat closes and refuses another bite.

The two of them, it's a weird combination. Blaese is up too late; and investigators don't usually mingle with the beat cops unless they came up with them. This uniform is gazing at thirty; Blaese is easily fifteen years older.

Vinnie's hindbrain decides it's time to flee. There's no specific reason; it's all instinct.

Fishing a couple of bills from her wallet, Vinnie drops them on her table and subtly backs toward the kitchen. The bathrooms are back there; they give her cover. When she walks into the blast furnace of a kitchen instead of the ladies', she shows the confused line cook her badge and asks, "Back door?"

He points the way, then turns to watch her leave. It's a little bit of excitement in the middle of breaking down the kitchen for the nightly clean. Vinnie pushes the door open, cool night air grabbing her breath as she steps into the night. The alley smells like rank cooking oil and overfull dumpsters, but it'll get her where she's going.

Head down, Vinnie walks away briskly, her stomach protesting the whole way. She's mapping the city in her head, calculating the fastest way back to her place, with the least amount of exposure. There isn't much of a back-alley system to downtown Indy. She's going to have to step into the open and—

A blinding flash fills her head. For two insensible seconds, Vinnie has no idea what's happening. Then the pain arrives. It's like a bomb, shattering agony in every direction. The snot, the burning, leaking eyes, they don't register yet. They don't register because the baton swings again. Without a whisper. A ghost in the night.

Vinnie's nose explodes.

Bones splinter. Blood sprays, a blue-black fountain in the weak glow of the streetlight. From behind, another crack. Her eyes bulge as her brain crashes forward. Nothing makes sense, not up, not down. She can't think, and her body flails helplessly. Where's her gun? Did she bring her—is she reaching for—

Another crack, her wrist shatters. Her ears are too full of blood pounding. She tries to get an ID at least. The guy in front of her. Can't be Blaese, hasn't been long enough for him to catch up, right? Clutching her wrist, red spattered down her mouth and chest, Vinnie staggers. She just needs one good look at the guy. The guys?

Suddenly, she flies forward. Someone kicked her from behind. Right in the kidneys. Lightning pain shears across her back; she struggles to catch her balance. It's ugly. Gravity fights her. She spins in place, almost falls over. Eyes wide open, but useless. They take in random flashes of buildings, the sky, the ground.

It's been six seconds since the first strike.

It turns into a frenzy. Laughter echoes in the alley; there's shouting. It doesn't make sense; she's going down. She covers the back of her head with her arms.

Knees crack into the uneven concrete. Blows like drumbeats blaze wildly across her back. Her mouth is full of bile and blood. It vomits out when a boot breaks against her jaw.

The voices start to sharpen. They punctuate the beating. Fucking rat, a crack to the head. Lying cunt, a kick that knocks her on her side. The ground is cold, maybe wet. The sky is a scarlet glaze. She smells blood and piss; the hailstorm of batons may as well be fists. The kicks flop her onto her back. Then, the weight.

The weight.

It doesn't make sense; she can't breathe because of the weight. She chokes on the slime of blood down her throat. Why can't she breathe? Why are there sparklers in her brain? Sparks flare across her gaze.

For a second, the weight fades. Relief, a breath—

It comes down hard. One of her lungs pops like a balloon. A thousand needles pierce her chest, and then, relief again. No weight. Then, crush. The realization feels weirdly celebratory, like congratulations, you put the clues together. Somebody stepped on her. Somebody jumped on her.

She vomits again; can't turn her head. The foul acid goes up the back of her nose. Down her throat. Every thin breath shatters into a cough that just spews it everywhere.

She's going to die in this alley, her gun trapped inside her jacket. She's going to be the case somebody catches first thing in the morning.

It might even be Blaese that takes it. Perfect crime, with big sympathy for the police department, holy shit, somebody took out one of our own, wear ribbons, support us, forget we have predators crawling through our ranks! And it would be a cold case to go. Wrapped up in a neat little bow. The guys on trial could attend her funeral in dress blues and laugh into their drinks after they're acquitted.

Up feels like the concrete digging into her shoulders. There's no down. Maybe sideways. Everything's fading now, except the pain. One voice shocks her back. For a moment. For a capsule of time that both flashes by and lasts forever. There's a voice. The voice.

"That's enough," he says.

Kyle stands at the mouth of the alley. His hands are clean. His clothes are clean. He is clean. Vinnie gets another baton to the head, another steel-toed boot to the hip. Then Kyle says, again, so loud it feels like a thunderstorm, "I said that's enough. She won't talk."

Oh.

Ohhh.

The last thing Vinnie says before consciousness fades is, "You fuck."

Chapter 35

Vinnie made it back to Wills Harbor but she didn't remember the drive at all.

As soon as she hit the first quasi-familiar exit, the numb shock dropped. It left her shaking, so hard her teeth chattered. All her wires were tangled. With one heaving breath, she wanted to burst into tears, another, she wanted to slap herself for losing it over a routine traffic stop.

Because it had been, completely routine. The officer checked her paperwork, gave her a quick orientation exam, then sent her on her way with a warning to watch out for those curves.

Nothing had happened. *Nothing* had happened, but her thoughts threatened her with flashes of the past. The attack looped behind her eyes, and by the time she pulled off the highway, she was a nervous wreck.

And for the first time in a long time, she didn't want to be alone. Most of her life, she'd been satisfied with her solitude. Even when she'd dated, she'd never moved in with anybody—never got close to it. Her schedule had had a lot to do with that, but mostly she didn't *want* to.

She *liked* a whole bed to herself. She liked leaving leftovers in the fridge, knowing they'd be there in the morning. If there was a mess, she'd made it. And if she wanted to spend all day Sunday watching TV and eating reheated taquitos, there was no one to complain about it.

But tonight felt different; scoured raw, inside and out, Vinnie Taylor needed a friend. Unfortunately, her new phone offered a sparse contact list. Her mother—hell no. Hannah—absofuckinglutely not, even if things had been fine. Rich Watts, the landlord? Nope, and that left her with two starkly different choices.

Camila or Rosier.

Her stomach threatened to rebel at the sight of Rosier's name. Not a cop. She absolutely could not, would not call a cop. That left Camila, who hadn't answered her phone earlier, and probably deserved better than the text Vinnie sent her when she reached her first red light off the highway:

You awake?

Vinnie was halfway down the next mile when Camila replied, What's up?

It was too much to explain. And Vinnie didn't even know if she wanted to—hell, if she *could*. But the trembling refused to settle, so she skipped past the etiquette and asked, Can I come over?

Camila responded with her address, which Vinnie immediately punched into her GPS. For some reason, she'd expected Camila to live outside of town, back in the trees and hills. Maybe in an apartment, maybe a townhouse. The price for a ticket to single-family homes around here started at four hundred thousand dollars, so that wasn't in the equation at all.

But instead of heading out of Wills Harbor, Vinnie found herself parking outside one of the downtown rowhouses, the ones with historical markers. Even from Camila's porch, she could hear the bar scene less than a hundred yards away, as it started to spill into the streets.

A silver lobster knocker gleamed on a door painted the glossiest black Vinnie had ever seen. The wooden shutters matched, and the rest of the place was pristine white. Fake poppies filled the flower boxes, still red even though October was almost gone.

Once again, Vinnie couldn't get a bead on it—was Camila this rich, or did small-town papers pay this well in Maryland? Those thoughts were intrusive and inescapable. When you grow up without money, you spend the rest of your life calculating it.

The door swung open after a single knock. A light from inside outlined Camila's body in her thin T-shirt and shorts. Her thick hips swung heavily to one side, her waist carved out beneath the low curve of her breasts. She'd tied her hair up again, and she stood there wearing a T-shirt with the collar cut out. It slipped off her shoulder, a look that had never gone out of style, as far as Vinnie was concerned. If it worked in the '80s, it worked in the '20s. Or at least, it worked for her.

"I have had a shit day," Vinnie told her, then stepped inside. She sat on the bench by the door and unlaced her boots, leaving them in the rack next to Camila's sneakers.

Genially, Camila said, "I haven't, but I'm sorry you did. Want a little nightcap?"

"Sure," Vinnie said, and declined Camila's offer to take off her jacket. She still wore her shoulder holster, and her frazzled insides demanded she keep it close. She followed Camila into the gauzy living room and hesitated to sit. Everything was just so *nice*.

Dimmed lamps warmed the living room and let the little fireplace add depth and shadows. The scent of burning wood soothed Vinnie. She wasn't particularly outdoorsy, but she did love a fire.

When she was a kid, her father's side of the family used to bring out their store-bought fire pits and burn them well past midnight. The whole trailer park joined in, cooking hot dogs and roasting marshmallows until the bags ran empty. Vinnie used to lie on her dad's driveway and watch the sparks float toward the stars; sometimes she fell asleep out there.

Of course, Camila's rowhouse was a long way from a trailer park in Indiana. Nothing but fawn-pale hardwood floors and furniture in shades of cream and white. Unlit candles stood in proud little thickets on end tables and windowsills. Ships sailed across canvases on the walls, mostly in dun, hazy shades, but occasionally a bright blue popped out.

As if reading her mind, Camila said, "Just *sit*. It's *fine*."

Still, Vinnie couldn't bring herself to settle on the couch. She took advantage of a beige pouf on the floor and sat there instead.

Satisfied with that, Camila left her there to go make drinks. She had work spread out on the coffee table, notes and phone, laptop open but screensaver floating through a hazy kelp field.

Vinnie leaned back against the couch and admired the fire passively, raising her voice just enough to be heard in the kitchen.

"I talked to Tyler Purnell," she said.

Now that she was warm, and safe, thirty miles from Baltimore and six hundred from Indianapolis, she slumped. Exhaustion leaked out, lead pooling in her extremities. She closed her eyes briefly, taking in the scent of the fireplace, with the soft sandalwood-and-spice note beneath it. That part was pure Camila, an incense that belonged to her alone.

Amused, Camila said, "Oh yeah? How'd that go?"

"He surprised me," Vinnie told her, tipping her head back and watching Camila return with two glasses and an ornate gold pen.

"One for you," Camila said, handing Vinnie a glass, a third full of something amber, on the rocks. "And one for me."

After a quick salute, Vinnie took a deeper swallow than she probably should have. It was her first decent drink in six months, and it burned pleasantly on the way down. The rocks made it a less generous pour than it appeared, but when Camila settled next to her, she found out why.

With a twist, Camila put the pen to her lips and inhaled. A light blinked on, and she exhaled. Compared to the discount vapes for sale at the gas station, Camila's was elegant. It even had calligraphic swirls etched onto it. As she exhaled sweet, citrusy steam, she offered the pen to Vinnie. "Five milligrams, mixed with CBD," she explained. "Just a nice chill."

At first, Vinnie raised a hand to refuse. It was a reflex, habit borne from a job that drug-tested on the regular in a state too stubborn to reap the benefits of a cannabis tax. Not to mention, she'd kicked that two-pack-a-day habit and intended to stay quit.

A strange, faint wind blew through her, though. She still tasted oil from the side of the road, and blood from memories that refused to fade. Her bones rattled in frustration, reminding her that she'd been beaten into paste fairly recently, and she couldn't heal like a teenager anymore. The lingering trill of anxiety vibrated through her; it nudged, just a little.

Fuck it, she thought. She took the pen and fuck, it burned. Sweet humidity seared through her protesting lungs, and she had to fight back a coughing jag. The vapor tasted like grapefruit and weed, somehow pleasantly unpleasant. It took a while for the fire in her chest to subside. Once she was no longer in danger of coughing up a lung, she passed the pen back. With a wry smile, she rasped to Camila, "Smooth."

"Uh-huh." Camila's laughter sweetened the air and teased along Vinnie's skin.

Leaning back against the couch, Vinnie propped her head in her hand and waited for something to happen. Lazily, she said, "You've been busy."

With a snort, Camila closed the laptop and stacked everything on the corner of the end table. "Not really. I was trying to be busy, but I ended up playing Minecraft instead."

Teasing, Vinnie asked, "The game? Where little kids push around blocks?"

"It's a *sandbox* game," Camila replied with a grin. "You can do whatever you want in it. Build stuff. Fight zombies. Battle a dragon."

"And what were you doing?" Vinnie asked. Coaxed, really, with a faint brush of fingers against Camila's shoulder and a liquid smile that came easily. Camila didn't shy away. In fact, she leaned in and ignited a spark. Pleasant heat twined up Vinnie's hand as she came into contact with skin, the curve of Camila's shoulder exposed by the T-shirt.

Camila glanced at her through her dark lashes and whispered, "Digging a big hole."

They both laughed, leaning toward each other. The subject had changed, all on its own and Vinnie let it go. There would be twenty-four hours in the next day, and the day after that—more than enough time to talk about the fucked-up underbelly of teenage crime she'd uncovered.

Instead, now felt like a good time to give up limbs to whiskey and THC and give in to the restless electricity between them. That was another beauty in fifty: the fire was still there, and the gawky uncertainty had long burned away. Two decades ago, they could have sat next to each other for months, searching for the nerve to hold hands. Now that mad twist of attraction unspooled into easy action.

Vinnie brushed her knuckles against Camila's cheek and slipped in for a kiss. Lush lips parted, and Vinnie stole a taste of her, traces of whiskey dancing on their tongues. It traced all the way down. Skin tight, getting tighter at the sound of Camila's ragged breath; Vinnie let her touch glaze the long line of her neck, then whisper across the bare skin of her collarbone. Too many clothes, Vinnie thought, hooking a finger gently in Camila's necklace to tug her in again.

Camila sparked like the fire, her scent spiraling with the smoke. Later, Vinnie would be able catch hints of her on her collar, between her fingers. All she wanted was more. Everything under her skin roared, hungry and feral. Camila was made to touch; all her curves soft and full, her mouth hot and her hair coiling jealously to capture her.

Pushing the coffee table out of the way, Vinnie smiled against Camila's lips as she pulled her in to fill the space between them. When Vinnie's hand fell on the curve of her waist, Camila rose up easily. She threw a leg over Vinnie's with a smooth, practiced glide, then sank down on her lap. Bathed in Camila's heat and weight, Vinnie chased the high of her kiss; noses nudging, pulses ragged and wild.

Then suddenly, a sting. It knocked both of them out of the haze. Another sting; Vinnie's phone vibrated insistently from her pocket. Both of them hesitated, and fuck, Camila was gorgeous. Dusky lips full and slick, her pupils blown wide and hair wild. The firelight glowed behind her, her chest full on a captured breath. The phone buzzed twice more, then stilled. The question hung in the air.

Why not forget everything? Why not try being *normal*? Nice, normal people almost never talked about corpses, and missing children, and sex work, and death threats over drinks. Why not let that phone go to voicemail, a recording she could listen to another time? A better time.

Vinnie didn't have to answer it; she wasn't on call anymore. But Rosier followed up the call with a text, because it turned out, he was thorough like that, and the moment was gone. Apologizing under her breath, Vinnie dug out her phone and ruined their night. At least she read the text out loud.

"Where's AA's phone?" she said, her voice rising. "Talked to the coroner. It's not her body."

Chapter 36

Camila inhaled sharply.

"Then whose is it?" She slid off Vinnie's lap instantly. Brow newly furrowed, she reached for a notebook and pencil. Expectation flickered in her dark eyes—she took the moment and waited.

The air cooled to cordial between them, and Vinnie had herself to blame. She could have ignored the phone entirely. Should have, even. Old, bad habits just felt so natural. There was a reason Vinnie was fifty and alone. Sex, she liked, but investigation, she loved. She'd been that way her whole life, and she had no idea how to throttle that.

"That's all he said," Vinnie said, texting Rosier back at the same time. I still have the phone but I can't drive atm.

Already theorizing, Camila said, "So is this related? Do we have a serial killer?"

"No," Vinnie said abruptly. "We don't."

"I mean, we could."

"This isn't a podcast," Vinnie said, then softened her tone. "It's almost never a serial killer. And anyway, we don't know anything about the deceased except she's dead and she's not Avery Adair.

We don't know if they're connected. We don't even know for a fact that it's a homicide."

Camila said, "Unless you can die of natural causes, dismember yourself, then pack yourself in a trunk. I'm thinking it's pretty good for a murder."

That sounded awfully specific. Vinnie almost made a smart remark about Camila being psychic when it hit her. Of course, *Of course* Camila hadn't been sitting in stasis, just waiting for Vinnie to show back up. She was a journalist, and even though she claimed she wasn't investigative, it sure sounded like she'd been out canvassing witnesses from the search party. Still, Vinnie had to ask.

"Where'd you hear that from?"

"Confidential source."

Vinnie swallowed a sigh and looked away. "Who am I gonna tell, myself? The cops already know."

Nonchalant, Camila leaned past Vinnie to pick up her own phone. With a few casual flicks, she pulled up a text chain and handed it to Vinnie. Leaning in to look with her, she said, "No, literally. It came from a burner. I already ran it down; the number doesn't exist."

> **Blocked Number:** Think we found AA. Def. found a body.

> **Camila Vega:** Pix?

To Vinnie's horror, but not shock, Blocked Number sent six pictures through immediately after the request. A black trunk lay on its side in a pile of fallen leaves. A Caucasian arm spilled out beside it. Literally just the arm, which had a strange shade to it—fully bloodless, but not decomposed.

Another angle. This time, a shot inside the trunk. It looked like a jumble of mannequin pieces, all the same off shade of beige. Vinnie couldn't help but remember how many times witnesses had told her, "I thought it was a mannequin." "I thought it was a doll." The human brain was funny; it knew that people didn't belong in dumpsters or trunks or the catchment of a canal. It tried to make sense of the senseless.

Vinnie scrolled down, and suddenly the rumor about the head in a bowling bag made sense. It actually lay separate from the trunk, in a depression in the ground. It peeked out of a fabric grocery bag, one from Ohland's Grocery. The remaining skin was waxy, but the dominant color was yellow: the color of fat exposed by carrion-eaters.

Kerry County was chock-full of vultures and coyotes, fishers and foxes—not to mention strays. They had nibbled away the soft parts: eyes and nose, lips and cheeks, little tastes of earlobe. All they'd left behind were empty sockets, open nasal cavities, and a fleshless grin showcasing immaculate teeth.

The last picture in the set gave Vinnie the whole scene. Now she could see that the trunk was broken—collapsed at the corners, every surface battered. The lid lay in the foreground, completely separated from the box, and the head completed the golden ratio, being slightly offset from the body and forward of it.

Thinking aloud, Vinnie said, "It was too heavy to carry by himself. He must have pushed it down the hill and it broke open at the bottom. The head either rolled out, or something dragged it out. But it doesn't make sense."

Intensely focused, Camila asked, "What doesn't?"

"Usually, bugs and animals and shit, they go for the juicy parts. The innards, the muscle, you know? They'll scavenge a head but compare that"—she pulled up the photo of the arm, then slid to the photo of the head again—"to that. Where are the bug bites? Why are they eating the worst parts first?"

Camila hazarded a guess. "Easier to get to?"

"Sure, to some extent. But there's something up with that body. Something we can't see, but scavengers can."

A low buzz interrupted Vinnie's train of thought. It was Rosier again, answering her question. Ruled out AA, no ID yet. Doesn't match any missing in Maryland. Checking NCMEC, VA, DC, DE.

Vinnie replied, Can you tell me more abt autopsy? Heard she was dismembered.

Rosier: You heard where?

She glanced at Camila, then typed, All kinds of rumors going around after the search.

There was a long pause. Camila's brows slowly rose in anticipation, and Vinnie rubbed her lips together. Normally, her thoughts would be racing with possibilities, but right now, they flowed in a slow, lazy stream instead. An idea occurred to her, then drifted out of reach. Shit, was that the whiskey or the vape? The near miss with Camila's immaculate body? Vinnie had no idea. They both jumped when the phone rang.

"Yeah," Vinnie answered.

"I really need that phone," Rosier said without greeting. "I can come to you."

"I'm not at home."

"Like I said, I can come to you. You have something I want; I bet I have something you want."

What she wanted to say was, *Yeah, but I'm not done with it yet.* Even though handing over the physical phone wouldn't erase the copy she had at home. It was that built-in possessiveness about a case, but it slipped away like a languorous unfurling. Her brain wasn't in the best place to work this case, but cases generally didn't give a shit about conveniences. If they had, Homicide would have been a nine-to-five job, closed on weekends and national holidays. A drifting current in the back of her thoughts wanted to stay. Stay here, with Camila. Stoke that fire again. Find out what kind of sheets she had.

But the case had heated up, and a case didn't wait. She believed, maybe more fervently than she should have, that Rosier had something good to share, and she wanted it. Could practically taste the sharpness of her own teeth over it. Funny how the chemicals tracing through her washed the anxiety away. At the moment, Rosier didn't seem dangerous at all.

With an apologetic look at Camila, Vinnie said, "I'm downtown, near Hix Tavern. Give me fifteen."

Sinking back against the couch, Camila put a subtle distance between them. She didn't seem angry. More resigned than anything. A bad place to be in the middle of a twenty-year marriage; probably a death knell on a second not-quite date. Camila traced her graceful fingers against her own cheek, waiting for Vinnie to hang up. As soon as she did, Camila said, "Didn't want to tell him you were here?"

"Didn't think you'd want him to know I'm sharing evidence with you," Vinnie replied.

It took a little too much effort to stand up. She wasn't wobbly, just weighted differently. Like gravity pooled in her feet and the rest of her body wanted to float away. Yeah, there was no way she was driving tonight. Everything seemed too fast and too slow at the same time. Then she frowned, a little well of guilt opening in the middle of her belly. "Oh shit, I need to feed the cat again."

"I thought it was a stray," Camila said. Vinnie could no longer tell if she was amused or engaged or even in the same orbit.

"Me too," Vinnie replied. She checked her pockets, wallet, keys, holster, Glock, safety still on, okay all good. She swayed toward the door but didn't actually take a step. The lights had turned warm and caramel, and Camila's skin glowed beneath them. Her dark eyes gleamed with endless depths, and in spite of it all, Vinnie still didn't sit back down. She didn't have an excuse to offer her, only an apology. "I'll call you tomorrow?"

Unbothered, Camila shrugged. "Okay."

She didn't see Vinnie out. Instead, she mated the two whiskey glasses and watched her leave as she sipped the remains.

Chapter 37

The sky was high and wide and black, a halo cradling the moon.

Vinnie sat on the hood of Rosier's cruiser in her driveway, downing a sub—no, no, a *hoagie*—from Wawa, and taking in the night. It was quieter now than when she'd moved in, wind just a breath through trees going bare. The weather had broken like a favorite vase; autumn raced toward winter headlong. The woods used to block the bay view in most directions, but now, she was almost surrounded by glimpses of grey water.

Wired and exhausted at the same time, Vinnie savored the snap in the air. It scrubbed her clean, cutting Camila's scent and the lingering desire with criminal precision. Gesturing up, Vinnie told Rosier, "That ring around the moon? That usually means it's going to snow."

Fortifying himself with convenience-store coffee, Rosier turned his gaze upward too. "Hate to break it to you, but if it snows here, everything shuts down. We get rain and fog. Why do you think Santa needed Rudolph?"

"Because of whiteout conditions," Vinnie said, the *obviously* implied.

"No. Fog. It's right there in the song."

"Whatever." She took another bite of what was possibly the best sandwich she'd ever had. Also, possibly, it was just a case of the munchies. It was a mystery, and she wasn't about to ask law enforcement to solve it for her. She'd copped to the whiskey, to explain leaving her rental downtown. The toke and the near miss she kept to herself.

It was cold outside, just on the edge of uncomfortable. Even so, she appreciated he hadn't even asked to come inside. They weren't friends. They were two professionals, working parallel cases, nothing personal to it. Knowing that made it easier to hand over Avery's phone, and to share the teenager's secrets with him. Everything seemed exceptionally sharp tonight; Vinnie felt like she could read Rosier's thoughts as they crossed his face.

Tyler probably felt like he was in the clear—it was a good thing he didn't get paid for thinking. Vinnie had a feeling that Tyler's lawyer daddy was going to be ponying up for a lawyer of his own after Rosier followed the digital blackmail trail. He didn't need Avery to prove that; just her phone, his phone, her bank records, Tyler's bank records, and the GPS off his tacky-ass truck.

Oh, and the video from McDonald's, which would actually tell them both the last person to see Avery Adair. Unfortunately, it would also break Red's probation, but he knew it was coming down the pike. With any luck, they'd both spend some time in juvie, soak up some rehabilitation, and turn their lives around. It was a fairy tale, and for now Vinnie chose to believe it.

Though he didn't know it, Rosier was operating on a little bit of a fairy tale too. Vinnie had kept Hannah's lies to herself. Since the body in the box wasn't Avery's, Rosier's investigation was going to get back-burnered. That was just the life cycle of crime investigation. Shit happened, and it didn't stop happening. Rosier had caught a body, and that took precedence. In a county with maybe ten homicides a year, this was a big deal.

It felt like it was on Vinnie alone to find Avery now. And it was a lot more personal. The fucking-around portion of her association with Hannah had concluded; now commenced the finding out, and the kid wasn't gonna like it.

Still, a murder in the middle of a missing-persons case— even though it looked unrelated, Vinnie was curious. It wasn't a normal homicide, what with the dismemberment and the odd disposal down a ravine, and suddenly she remembered she had questions for Rosier.

"Lemme ask you something," she said, folding up the paper from her sandwich into increasingly tiny squares. "What's up with the body? Those parts looked *clean*. Like, clean-clean, no fluids, no bloating. And nothing eating on that arm?"

"How do you know what they look like?"

Without shame, Vinnie said, "Well, either somebody at the search has a real good camera, or you got a leak, Rosier. I've seen the pictures."

"That fucking figures." With a swirl of his cup, Rosier mixed the dregs of his coffee thoughtfully. "All right. This is between us. I mean it."

"On my honor."

"She was frozen." Rosier drained his cup, then set it aside. His breath hung briefly in the air, but the haze faded once the warmth slipped from his mouth. "Solid. And once Doc put her back together, what little lividity there was didn't match the way we found her."

Vinnie's eyes widened. "So they cut her up, *froze her solid*, then put her in the trunk and dumped her. What the fuck?"

"Yeah. I've got guys talking to every refrigeration outlet in a fifty-mile radius; find out if somebody's put in a ticket for a walk-in freezer on the blink lately."

"Could be a chest freezer that went out; I'd check the dump too."

"Good idea."

Suddenly, Vinnie straightened. "Anybody talked to Keith Adair? That's his whole front, isn't it? Heating and cooling?"

Balancing a hand between them, as if to say, *Eh*, Rosier shook his head. "We'll take a look, but we've been through his shop before. He doesn't even keep freon; he's mostly a central air/central heat guy. Converts oil and coal boilers to electric."

Incredulous, Vinnie repeated, "Oil and coal? Are you shitting me?"

"Maryland's a lot older than Indiana," he pointed out, and she had to concede the point. Instantly, she veered to the next step in the investigation: how to ID the girl, how to do it fast.

"Anything special about the trunk she was in?"

Rosier shook his head. "Not really. We're thinking it came from Target or Walmart. It's not real luggage. The thing was glued together."

"Dorm decoration," Vinnie said. Kyle's eldest daughter had a trunk in teal that sat at the foot of her bed. She used it as a toy box when she was little and took it with her when she went to college. It was strange how clear that memory felt. Just an odd, random bit of trivia about a child she used to know.

Even though it was empty, Rosier picked up his coffee cup again. "So, that's got some possibilities. Lab's working on the DNA. Doc says she's sixteen to twenty-four, no signs of drug use, a little underweight but nothing crazy . . . no reason for her to have a profile in CODIS. Then again, you can fit a lot of rough living in without looking it."

"True, that," Vinnie said. The pictures from the Crush Baby profile were proof—sanitary, digital, and distanced. Sex work wasn't just walking streets or meeting johns in hotels anymore. Avery had tried to walk a fine line. Just the feet shit, that was weird but probably legal. Meeting special clients? That was illegal six ways to Sunday for everybody involved. More than a couple of kids had been prosecuted for taking pictures of themselves and sharing them, and that was just naïve experimentation. What Avery was doing was illegal *and* dangerous.

Vinnie was full of murders—her cases, other people's, the ones presented in all the classes she'd taken: forensic entomology, blood-spatter analysis, crime-scene management . . . she couldn't remember how many. But she remembered the victims and couldn't help but try to make connections. "He had to have room to take her apart, and then to store her, but he dumped her basically in the middle of town. He's gotta live around here."

"Or work," Rosier said.

Vinnie squinted at him. "He dismembered her and froze her; he doesn't strike me as a risk-taker. Would you pack up a body to dump on the way to work?"

"Then again, don't shit where you live," Rosier countered.

"Also fair." Vinnie rubbed her fingers together idly; she did that when she was thinking. "What was the COD?"

"Blunt-force trauma to the head. Curved and wide; we don't know what exactly."

An old sound echoed through her, the sound of a baton against the head—from the inside.

She snapped her teeth closed and shut up. Jesus Christ. Old, bad habits again. It was too easy to talk about this shit with Rosier. His gentle-giant personality was the perfect smokescreen for a cop. People mistook kindness and gentility for friendship— but for the record, no cop asking questions was trying to make friends. They were trying to make arrests.

Maybe it was the long day catching up, maybe she was sobering up, Vinnie didn't know. But she did know this had to stop. It didn't matter that it happened naturally, that he somehow slipped past the tightly woven net of her trauma. In fact, that was all the more reason to shut the fuck up and get inside to her new cat.

"Think I'm gonna crash," she told him. She pushed off the hood and stretched her arms behind herself until her shoulders popped. As cold air streaked into her jacket, she picked up the jumble of cat supplies she'd dragged out of her rental to carry home. "Thanks for the ride."

"Thanks for the phone," Rosier said. He stood, too, fishing in his pockets for his keys. Moonlight softened his features; civilian clothes disguised him perfectly. His brown sweater accentuated his shoulders, and his faded blue jeans were just the right amount of laissez-faire. In another life, he could have owned a country inn or built clocks by hand or something.

That absurd thought gave Vinnie the last push to head inside. *What the fuck does that even mean?* she wondered. Backing toward the door, Vinnie gave him a nod. "I'm not giving up on bringing Avery home."

"Me either," he told her.

As she slipped into the cottage, Vinnie wondered if she was a fool for believing him.

Chapter 38

After what was possibly the best night of sleep she'd had in twenty years, Vinnie woke up with sunlight dripping through the uncovered windows, and a sleek black cat curled on her chest.

His weight and warmth were unfamiliar, but she had to admit, it was kind of nice. His purr vibrated through her. He'd tucked his sleek head between his paws, an irresistible flick of ears tempting her to touch. Gingerly, she stroked his head, and he blinked up at her. For a moment, it felt like she knew him, and he knew her. Something warm and homey bubbled up inside her.

Then he shot off the bed, propelled by the devil and what felt like forty tiny knives in her skin.

"Thanks, asshole," she said, and rolled out of bed to start her day.

After a shower and some breakfast, which she was generous enough to serve to Goofus as well, she dressed for the day but left the gun in the drawer and the holster hanging in the closet. She took a Lyft to retrieve her rental, which gave her time to think. She needed to reorganize the case from the bottom up.

She had no contacts in Howard County, and Todd the Manager had thrown her out of the McDonald's. Like it or not, she was going to have to wait for Rosier to get around to getting a warrant. In the meantime she could get to cracking the rest of the encrypted messages on Avery's phone.

Tyler wasn't a suspect anymore; Red wasn't either, not really. The dead girl was probably unrelated, so Vinnie had two threads to pull: Hannah and her lies, and the mystery friend who was supposed to meet Avery the day she went missing.

She could start with both of those at home, with the phone she already had cloned on her laptop. Red had mentioned a burner, but Vinnie hoped like hell there was enough information left on this one to give her a lead. It would be the encrypted shit, and the encrypted shit was a lot harder to access. She knew her way around the internet and DroidCreep, but there were dark recesses there, out of her reach and beyond her ken.

She cursed under her breath as she clicked through the interface a file at a time. She knew she wanted to start with the remains of Avery's F4U account. If she was meeting somebody *from* there, then she must have made the contact there first. But without the obvious chat logs, Vinnie didn't know what to search for exactly. Was it a contact file that had been deleted? An email sent from an unknown address? Or something so totally obscure, she wouldn't recognize it if she saw it?

This was the kind of stuff she used to hand over to the experts. They would dig through computers and tablets and phones like eager rabbits, burrowing into the depths and returning to the surface with preciously subterranean caches of evidence.

Vinnie didn't have the first clue how the deep searches worked, and she wondered now if she had thanked the lab coats enough. Every day that Vinnie worked outside the police department was a good day, but damn, she missed the structural support.

As she opened file after file, Goofus leapt up and made himself at home on her lap. He didn't act like a cat recently out of surgery. His shaved white belly looked ridiculous against his black fur, but he had a burning goal and all the energy to pursue it. Said goal was standing in Vinnie's lap, blocking the computer, and licking her face. Of all the times Vinnie had considered a pet, this was not a scenario she'd imagined.

"Dammit, Goofus," she said, putting a hand over his face to gently push him away.

Denial made him more ardent; he rumbled with a purr and ducked around her hand to land a lick on her ear. She shuddered and pulled up the hood on her hoodie, grateful when he decided he was more interested in her sweatshirt's pull strings than exfoliating her entire head. His tail curled under her nose as she returned to the remains of the Fans4U account.

There were chat transcripts from Avery's live shows. Vinnie couldn't access the videos—they'd never been recorded client-side. It didn't matter. Anything important would be in the chat box, where Avery's audience begged for her attention and demanded their money's worth. When she deigned to answer their intrusive questions on video, her words showed up, transcribed in bold letters. Everything else was a chaotic mash of salivating men demanding more, more, more. The mystery friend should be somewhere in the chat. He'd want to set himself apart somehow, so Vinnie steeled herself to wade through.

It was vile reading. Page after page of suggestive emojis, and requests that ranged from innocuous to nauseating. These guys treated Avery like a toy. A cheap toy, to break and toss aside. They wanted to play with her and pose her, and what she chose to give them was never enough. Vinnie found donation records; some jackhat would toss her a dollar and demand to see her pussy, even though the room description was very clear: FOOT PLAY ONLY, NO NUDES. As if a dollar was all her body was worth.

Then there were the boyfriend guys, the ones who didn't understand that the girl on the other side of the glass didn't like them. They tried to make normal conversation in the middle of an abnormal video stream. Spankme86 spammed the chat with step on the grapes! step on the grapes! while alphatonic asked what she'd had for dinner, where she would go on a dream vacation, if she'd seen *Fight Club*, and if so, did she have an opinion on it?

It didn't make Vinnie's skin crawl. She'd met too many pervs in her career to spare a shudder for them. Instead, it weighed in her chest, an actual ache in her heart for Avery. Seventeen-year-olds should be running around with their friends, skipping school, dancing in the waves at the shore. They should be soaring, stealing away to the movies or taking their brand-new driver's licenses and following long roads just to see where they'd go.

They shouldn't have to sell parts of themselves to get by or get ahead. Life wasn't fair, never had been, never would be. That didn't mean unfair didn't hurt. Didn't scar. Didn't bend the path to the future in unexpected and ugly ways.

Vinnie rubbed her temple as she opened another chat log. Just then, her phone buzzed. In response, Goofus dug his claws into her thighs and stood on his hind legs. It was like he was trying to read the screen, the one with BEV plastered all over it. Vinnie sent the call to voicemail. Then she blocked her mother's number. *Not today, Satan.*

"You need to sit," she told Goofus, wrapping one arm around him. He stopped purring, but he obeyed, and Vinnie went back to work. As she read, he relaxed, melting into a puddle of kitten in her lap. His warmth soothed her as she raked through this garbage, pixel by pixel.

It took forever, but she finally compiled a list of all the screen names that appeared regularly. Then she compared it to subscribers and donations. After all, if Avery was willing to abandon the safety of her digital studio, it wouldn't have been for the nickel-and-dime guys. It had to have been for a big spender.

And in the end, there were two.

Chapter 39

Both of them boyfriend guys, of course.

Their real names never appeared anywhere. Instead, they chose to call themselves alphatonic and generalgentleman69. According to their Fan IDs, they were both single, with generic white-guy avatars provided by the site for privacy. Naturally, there were private chats with both of them, so Vinnie gingerly opened one from generalgentleman69—his bio claimed he lived in California.

> **generalgentleman69:** Hi honey. *gives you four dozen roses and a kiss on the lips*
>
> **Crush Baby:** That's so sweet. Thank you.
>
> **generalgentleman69:** Did you miss me while I was at work? I missed you. *shy because my erection is so hard right now* I hope you can't see it through my pants!
>
> **Crush Baby:** I missed you. I always miss you when you go to work.

> **generalgentleman69:** *trying not to rub against you but it's so hard* I missed you too. But Daddy has to bring home the bacon for his wifey, right?

> **Crush Baby:** That's right. You work so hard.

The conversation seemed endless, getting more graphic by the line, at least on his end. Avery was always careful to respond—always positive, always agreeing, but never giving anything up. She was smart, and she was street-smart. This was a job to her; whether she loved it or hated it, it was work and she did it diligently.

Vinnie wondered if generalgentleman69 saw that—if he realized that Crush Baby was playing a part, crafting a wifey for him who would keep him talking, keep him paying, without ever giving him a glimpse of her true personality.

After skimming through all six conversations with him, Vinnie couldn't square Avery meeting up with this guy. He would have had to fly in from California for one, but there was nothing in the transcripts that looked remotely like planning to meet up, not in Maryland, not even in another app. It was all just clumsy, repetitive roleplay.

Which left alphatonic. His Fan ID said he was from Pennsylvania and his bio, like the general's, was bare.

Vinnie rocked back in her chair, staring at this profile. Goofus tucked his head beneath her hand, demanding mindless scritches as she stared at the screen. Something about this guy's name bugged her. It just didn't make sense on a site where tags like *demtitties* and *chokemeout* were the norm.

With the cat settled on her chest like a baby, her nose itched, and her brain was starting to ache from too much screen time.

And annoyingly, so did her hip. All that goat-walking was catching up to her. Four hours ago, the prospect of staying home, staying in one place, had sounded like luxury. Well, her body was
done luxuriating. It wanted action.

Unfortunately, it was going to have to wait. She needed to
finish raking through this shit. She was sure something on this
phone was going to lead her back to Avery. So she opened the first
file with alphatonic, skimming it, then slowed down and read it.
Because these conversations were nothing like the general's sad
panting. In fact, they felt like conversations continued from another time and place, with half the words missing.

> **alphatonic:** I'm just worried about you. Are you doing this
> for the money? Because I can help with money. Tell me
> what you need.

> **Crush Baby:** Ha ha, I don't need anything. I'm having a
> good time. Don't you want to have a good time?

> **alphatonic:** Yes, but not like this. Can we watch a movie
> together and talk about it afterwards?

> **Crush Baby:** That depends on the movie. No more
> documentaries!

> **alphatonic:** You can pick. I'll even accept superheroes
> if you find one that follows Joseph Campbell to the
> letter.

> **Crush Baby:** You're so weird, ha ha.

alphatonic: You liked the book though, didn't you?

Crush Baby: It was interesting. But I read enough for my college classes. I want to have fun when I have time off!

alphatonic: It just gives us more to talk about. I love talking to you.

Crush Baby: That's sweet. I like talking to you, too.

alphatonic: If I tip you 500 dollars will you sign off of here for the day?

Crush Baby: I'll think about it.

alphatonic: Sent.

The chat ended there. Interesting that Avery seemed to have formed a connection with this guy—enough to read books he'd suggested anyway. (Or to lie about reading them, to be fair.) But this conversation was give-and-take, not like the one-sided fap wall with the general. This guy was a lot more open about giving her money; maybe that was the difference.

Only one way to find out. Vinnie moved to open another chat, but Goofus suddenly jerked his head up. He stared toward the door, his ears flicking. His muscles flickered from tip to tail, a reminder that he was still an apex predator. With a frown, Vinnie turned to look too. At first, silence, but then she heard tires on the gravel in her driveway.

"Who the fuck is that?" she asked the cat.

She scooped him out of her lap and carefully placed him on the floor, then walked to the front window. Even though the leaves had thinned considerably, she couldn't make out the front of the drive from the house. And close to the house? Nothing. No one. The only car in her drive was the rental. She waited a moment, but when nothing came rolling up, she relaxed.

It was a high, clear day, the kind that carried sound for miles. Somebody up at the main road could have turned around at the mouth of the drive. Hell, she could be hearing traffic from across the water, depending on the direction of the wind. Just to be safe, she checked the locks on the door, then checked them again.

Rubbing at her neck, she considered the screen still full of nauseating evidence, and then the cold, clear day beckoning outside the window.

The therapist who had taught her to grey rock her mother had also taught her to ground herself. It seemed a little whackadoodle at the time, but Vinnie did it anyway. That was always the push and pull, between her skeptical Gen X thoughts and the squishy meatbox where they lived. The therapist's suggestions felt dumb, but they worked, goddammit.

Taking inventory of her body, all right. Her vision was bleary, her spine tense and tight. When she closed her eyes, she felt her molars clenched together and stiffness in her fingers. She was on a case, true, but she didn't have to suffer for it. A walk down to the water, just to feel the wind on her face, take in the last of autumn before the trees stood fully bare would hurt nothing. In fact, it would help. She'd been at this for hours.

Throwing on her shoulder holster, then her leather jacket, Vinnie slipped her feet into boots and walked her ass outside. Instantly, the air peeled away the fug clinging to her clothes. It wasn't so much that she physically needed a shower, but after spending most of the day in Avery's sad, sorry transcripts, her brain needed it.

She walked to the edge of the tree line, stopping at the rickety wooden steps that led down to the water. Although she'd been promised they were sound, Vinnie wasn't so sure. The wood had weathered grey and some of the slats bore wide cracks. Nails had turned black, and some had disappeared. Vinnie made her way down gingerly. The weather-bitten rails nipped at her hands, and she cringed at each creak beneath her feet.

Sometimes, she wondered who she was now. Twenty-five years ago, she would have taken these steps two or three at a time. It wouldn't have occurred to her then that she might miss one and fall down the rest. She was pretty sure she'd never worried about tetanus back then, or unfamiliar roads at night; strange sounds in the dark or eating Italian after five p.m.

The world had changed; her mind had changed; her body was still changing. The Vinnie Taylor on the other side of the beat-down seemed foreign to her. Somebody who'd gone through a lot of trauma, a little bit of therapy, and came out the other side not better—just *different*.

She reached the dock at the bottom of the stairs and walked onto it. The water felt alive beneath the boards; it beckoned her to walk out as far as she could, till nothing stood between her and the water but the wind and her own willpower. It was colder down here, little flecks of spray biting her skin. Even though the sky was pure blue and bright, the sun was low enough that shadows fell across this bank.

The question Camila had asked, when they'd gone through Avery's phone together, floated into Vinnie's thoughts again.

Who would Vinnie be if she'd had a computer in her pocket at sixteen? A hypothetical: an impossible Vinnie, but it led to possibilities and paths not taken.

It made her wonder who she would have been if she'd kept walking lockstep with the police department. If she'd never had those doubts about whether she was doing right or wrong. Was there ever a version of her who could have let it go and kept going the way she always had, all the way to old age? The worst question kept poking, insistent, almost like a needle to the brain, until she swallowed the knot in her throat and faced it.

Was she any better now than she had been then?

Ugh, this case—that was the problem; she shouldn't have a case. Not anymore.

But she did. And it had never been this hard to be alone with an investigation, *or* with her own thoughts. Was there some version of her who had chosen differently at sixteen, lived a different life, made different mistakes—was she out there in the universe, wondering the same things from her side of the mirror?

Shaking her head, Vinnie muttered to herself, "You watch too much fucking *Star Trek*."

Then the air shattered.

Chapter 40

O ut of reflex, Vinnie ducked.

The sound shocked across the water. It danced on her skin, vibrated in her lungs.

Another blast.

Her brain kicked in; she sank lower. The water made for strange echoes. She couldn't tell if it was above her or along the shore, but it sounded close. Shotgun, she thought. Most handguns popped; rifles cracked. Only shotguns and hand cannons boomed.

Vinnie kept low, taking the steps one at a time. Her mind whirled with possibilities. Errant hunter? Too close to town for that, legally anyway. Fireworks? Unlikely; it was broad daylight. No, that sound was exactly what she thought it was. And probably exactly *where* she thought it was. At the cottage. At her home.

The back of her neck prickled and sweat rose on her skin. The quiet unnerved her, the silence of the birds like a warning. She crept up the stairs, intensely aware she was in the open if the shooter was on the other side of the water.

She had almost reached the top of the stairs when *boom!* Another shot, and now she knew for sure. Somebody was shooting up the cottage. She knew because, in the wavering quiet after the report, she heard glass. Delicate, silvery tings as it fell and hit the ground. All those windows, made to let in the light.

Vinnie reached for her gun, then stopped. Head-to-head, nine-millimeter versus shotgun, she'd lose every time. She was out-gunned, vulnerable. No more Kevlar, no more handcuffs either. If she popped her head over the ridge, she'd be nothing but a target. Helpless wasn't a good look on her. Her muscles tensed, her body expecting her to sprint now, toward the danger. But her brain held her back, made her sit. Made her hide.

All she could do was wait, listen. Her phone was in the house, and her next neighbor was a mile down by water, longer by land. A hot splash of humiliated tears stung her cheeks. Black, tremulous fear filled her, absorbing time and reason, ruining her instincts with anxiety. She should know what to do. She should have been able to evaluate and take control of the situation. But instead she was head-down and frozen.

She hid for what felt like hours. Hours that burned with tears, hours that spilled salt down her throat. But sirens, in the distance, broke the spell. Somebody had called 911; somebody had been dispatched to investigate the sound of gunfire. It happened all the time; it usually turned out to be something mundane. A cable snapped on a winch. The less-than-gentle delivery of a dumpster.

All the patrol would do was drive around in the area where the "gunshot" had been reported. Sometimes they'd stumble on the real reason. Other times, they'd just drive away, satisfied that the noise had stopped, and nobody seemed to be hurt. If somebody *had* been fucking around, the presence of police would chase them off.

As the sirens approached, Vinnie stood slowly. She made her

way toward the cottage, hyperaware of her surroundings. She had barely stepped out of the trees when she saw the damage. Three of the cottage's windows had been blown out—the two in her bedroom and one in the living room.

Fuck. Fuck, fuck, fuck.

It took forever to clear her way to the front door. As soon as she let herself inside, Goofus streaked from the bedroom to twine himself around her ankles. Relief burst open inside her when she saw him, scared shitless but unharmed.

She scooped him up in one arm, grabbed her phone and laptop, and walked right back out. It was a crime scene now and she didn't want to disturb it. She got in the rental car, releasing Goofus to make himself at home as best as he could. Then, she stared at the keypad on her phone, her mind tracing the numbers over and over, 9-1-1. But she couldn't bring herself to dial.

Rubbing her face on her shoulder, she wiped away new tears and took a deep breath. She had to call somebody, and there was one obvious choice. She wondered if he'd looked her up yet; if he'd already figured out that she was on the wrong side of the line. It didn't matter, really. She didn't have a choice. With trembling hands, she thumbed through her recents and touched his name to dial.

"Rosier," he answered.

Swallowing at a sudden knot in her throat, Vinnie said, "Somebody just shot up my place, and I need help."

"Are you hurt? Did you call 911?"

Frustrated, Vinnie said, "I'm not calling the cops, I'm calling *you.*"

"I'm on my way," he said, sounding equally frustrated.

Of course he was going to have to file a report. It wasn't her house; the landlord would probably have to make an insurance claim. But she didn't want it on the radio. Police calls were public record, and she didn't want her name floating out there. She was going to have to personally ask Camila not to write about it. Considering she'd left her hanging the night before, that was going to be a very exciting conversation.

Still. She was hiding for a reason. A good goddamned reason, and she wanted to keep it that way.

After she'd come to in the alley behind India Garden, with no other choice she called her mother to come get her. Bev screeched all the way to Methodist Hospital, screeched in the examination room, screeched when she wasn't allowed to go back while Vinnie got her CT scan and X-rays and MRI.

Four broken ribs, a broken nose, a punctured lung, and a fractured wrist. They stuck a needle in her lung, set her nose, and splinted her wrist. They offered to call the police for her, but when she showed them her badge and assured them it was fine, they backed off.

Because she was a cop, they loaded her up with good painkillers and a shitload of aftercare instructions.

They wanted her to stay, but they let her leave first thing in the morning anyway. Her mother screeched about that, too, but Vinnie had to be in court. And by God, she was going to be in court, even if she had to crawl.

The beatdown was a message, one that she got, loud and clear. What Blaese didn't understand about her, well, it would fill an encyclopedia. But what Kyle *should* have known was that sometimes, Vinnie was a contrary bitch. And contrary bitches lived on spite.

Vinnie *loved* spite. It made her work harder, work longer, work better—nothing made her happier at the end of the day than proving some fuckstick wrong.

So, in this case, they wanted to shut her up? Well, they should have fucking killed her. Because cameras were allowed in the courtroom now, and *The Indianapolis Star* had a photographer and reporter in the galley every single day.

Mark Blaese's ghostly face at the defendants' table told the story when she limped in and took the stand. The jury watched her, intensely interested *because* of the way she looked. Cameras don't click like they do in the movies, but everybody could see the photojournalist lining up his shots as soon as Vinnie came into view.

The bruises had bloomed and one of her eyes was swollen partially shut. She had to speak carefully to keep from breaking her lip open again, and her head throbbed. Every part of her screamed as she sat there. The painkillers were just enough to take the edge off.

She spent hours on the stand, through the prosecution's case, and then the defendants' cross. Through it all, she kept her composure and answered as if this were any other day, any other of the hundreds of times she'd testified.

On her redirect, the prosecutor added a couple extra questions before Vinnie was dismissed. The woman stood solemnly, her fingers steepled in front of her. With care, with concern, she asked Vinnie, "Were you afraid to testify today?"

"Objection!"

The judge weighed it for a moment, then said, "I'll allow it."

Slowly, Vinnie shook her head. "Not until last night, no."

"Are you afraid to go home?"

"Objection!"

"Sustained," the judge said, but the point had been made. She hadn't been in a car accident or a bar fight. She wasn't secretly a bare-knuckled boxer, and she didn't wrestle alligators for fun. Something happened last night to make her afraid to testify; something made her afraid to go home. Something, or somebody, sitting next to the defense attorney—who was spitting mad at that point.

The jury got it. Everybody got it. And boy howdy, the news at five and eleven got it. So did the paper—the front page of the *Star* bore a full-color, above-the-fold, half-the-page story about it. Detective Vanetta Taylor testifies in cop sex-trafficking case, and she looked like this while she did it.

That's why Vinnie spent her last months in Indiana in hiding, in an out-of-town apartment usually reserved for witness protection. She had to heal; she had to get her retirement in order. And she'd decided to say fuck it and take the prosecutor's office up on some free therapy. Once she was officially dismissed, she packed what little she owned and got the hell out. Left her car for her mother to sell, rented a weird little coupe, and headed east until she hit water. That's how she'd ended up in Wills Harbor, Maryland.

Where somebody had just shot the windows out of her cottage. She couldn't call the police, because she couldn't guarantee somebody with a badge hadn't been the shooter in the first place. She didn't even know if she could trust Rosier. But she'd run as far from home as she could already.

She couldn't run anymore.

Chapter 41

The question was inevitable, but he didn't ask it.

Who would want to hurt you?

Vinnie stood in the middle of the living room, alone with Rosier. Alone with him in her space. Now that he was enclosed, beneath a roof, in a familiar place, his size was evident. Well over six feet, broad, broad shoulders unfolded like wings. His voice caught in the ribs of the exposed cedar ceiling, sonorous and low.

She should have been terrified, but she wasn't.

He hadn't arrived with sirens, or with other deputies. Just him, alone, with the camera on his phone to take pictures. And he hadn't asked the most obvious question of all. *Who would want to hurt you?* He knew. He had to. She hadn't ever taken him for stupid, and her past wasn't hard to find. At least, not the newspaper version of it.

But she owed him an explanation, a couple of the pieces of the puzzle that hadn't made it to newsprint. She told him she'd taken a beatdown after turning state's evidence. Not who, just why and how. The facts. A summary. Just by looking at her, he could probably tell she was curating this story. He didn't know what she was leaving out. That real life had opened her eyes, that she'd stopped believing in the mission a long time before she ended up on that stand. That she was on her way out of law enforcement anyway. How she'd ended up recruited into IAD in the first place; that her partner had betrayed her—no, he couldn't be sure, but he had to know it wasn't everything.

And he didn't ask. Vinnie didn't know what to make of that.

"So, uh, yeah," she said, her gaze trained away from him. She wasn't embarrassed of her history. She'd chosen every bit of it. But now that she'd spelled it out, she worried it would change things between them. She sighed and said, "I have to think they're still gunning for me, even from prison."

He stood there, typing notes into his phone, then said, "I'll keep it in mind, but I think you're underestimating the Adairs here."

She blinked. What did the Adairs have to do with anything? "I've done nothing but help them."

Brows rising, Rosier said, "I take it you haven't seen the papers today."

Her stomach fell away, and she pursed her lips. She'd been elbow-deep in Avery's phone all day; what had she missed? Schooling herself to even out her response, she said, "No, I haven't."

"Take a look." He pulled up *The Baltimore Sun* on his phone and handed it to her.

Shock stung down her spine as she read the headline, DISAPPEARANCE OF MD TEEN TAKES DARK TURN.

Okay, not great. But she and Camila had an agreement. Some of those secrets were always going to come out and if it was just the blackmail, it would be fine. That would go a long way toward holding Tyler responsible for what he did. As long as it was *just* the blackmail . . .

Vinnie glanced at Rosier and kept reading. The article unfolded, and horror bloomed around Vinnie, poisonous as oleander.

Seventeen-year-old Avery Adair is still missing, but there's new evidence that sends her case in an unexpected direction. As the search for her continues, it no longer appears that Adair left of her own accord, as indicated by the Kerry County Sheriff's Department in their last briefing.

Instead, evidence obtained exclusively by The Baltimore Sun suggests the troubled teen's disappearance could be related to a secret life she lived on the internet. A source close to the investigation recently revealed that Adair had turned to sex work on Fans4U, a popular online site for amateur pornography.

Because of this, Adair had a serious problem in the days leading up to her disappearance. Text and financial records indicate a fellow classmate, Tyler Purnell, may have been extorting the missing girl. Purnell, also 17, is the son of Michael "Trey" Purnell, a prominent attorney and District 9 school board candidate.

Reading that was a punch in the gut. "That wasn't supposed to be in here," Vinnie said. "We had an agreement."

"I don't know what to tell you," Rosier said. His tone told the rest: she was a naïve idiot if she'd thought she could trust a reporter. Small-town journalists were still journalists, and it was never their job to make an investigation easier.

Something nagged at Vinnie as she read on. It felt like a match waiting to snap on sandpaper and burst into flame. The article spared no detail, laying bare the Crush Baby account, how long

Avery had been at it, how much she'd made doing it, and then—turning the page—three thumbnails from the account. Two of feet, one a blurry screen capture of Avery's face.

What the fuck? With a pop, the match in her head lighted. The fire burned away the haze, both painful and clarifying. She hadn't told Camila what Red had said, not in this much detail. And she and Camila had looked at some of this stuff together, but not all of it. Some of the story had obviously come from Camila's own research. But some of it Vinnie recognized from the files she'd opened *this morning*. The realization was a brand beneath Vinnie's skin:

Camila had a copy of the phone.

And then Vinnie saw it, right before her eyes, Camila asking for a charge and plugging into Vinnie's laptop. She'd made her own copy, right in the open, and Vinnie hadn't even clocked it at the time. Furious, she shook Rosier's own phone at him.

"She duped Avery's data!"

"So did you," Rosier said mildly. He reclaimed his phone and pocketed it. "Either way, she fucked you both. Since she made sure nobody thought the police were looking for Avery, everybody knows you're the source close to the investigation. I've got guys sitting at her place now too."

"Mo-ther fuck!"

Vinnie turned and paced away from Rosier, but only a few steps. Broken glass still littered the floor all around. She itched to sweep up the mess, but Rich Watts, the landlord, had told her to leave everything the way she found it. He needed his own photos for insurance.

The radio on Rosier's shoulder crackled, and he stepped outside to respond. Vinnie sank to sit on the edge of the couch. She stared at the glimmering mess, closing her jacket against the wind that streamed through the broken windows. Her stomach turned, acid and threatening.

When had she turned into such a fucking idiot? If it had just been Hannah, fine. She was out of practice and the kid was an especially good liar. But Camila was a reporter; Vinnie should have known better. Maybe Blaese had stomped the smart out of her in the alley. Maybe she'd never been as good at this as she thought.

Time was draining out, fast. If Avery wasn't a runaway, at this point, it was getting less and less likely she was alive. This drive to find her, to bring her home, Vinnie still felt it in her bones. But her bones felt a little more brittle now, her mind a lot more fallible.

It didn't seem like she was accomplishing anything, except ruining a kid's reputation and her family's memories of her. Maybe it was time to tell Kassadee Swain that there was nothing more she could do. Maybe it was time to pack her shit, and her cat, and find another little town to hide in.

Tears weren't gonna come again; instead, Vinnie slumped. Forearms on her thighs, head hanging low, she stared at the floor without really seeing it. Exhaustion hung like a yoke around her neck; she felt all fifty of her years, lead in her veins, granite in her feet. She only glanced up when Rosier knocked on the doorframe and walked back inside.

"They just picked up Little Paul Adair, Keith's nephew. He had a shotgun in the truck," Rosier informed her. "And he already lawyered up, so I expect this is a local problem."

Vinnie exhaled; gravity still pulled, but she said, "Thanks."

Rosier stood there, his hat tucked under his arm. A long, uncomfortable silence spread between them. He shuffled his feet softly, and she turned her hands over to stare at her palms. Quiet filled the cottage again, nothing stirring except the bare branches of the trees outside. Then Rosier cleared his throat.

"I can keep a guy at the end of the driveway, if you think somebody's still gunning for you."

She shook her head. "No. If your guys know why they're here, they might look the other way. All things considered."

"We're not all like that."

"But I can't tell by looking who is," Vinnie said.

Now the chill in the room wasn't just coming from the windows. Vinnie hadn't realized how open Rosier was until he shut it all down.

A cool, professional mask fell over his features; he subtly pulled his shoulders back and raised his chin. Already-dark eyes darkened, his lips downturned now in the faintest way. He hadn't taken a step but now he felt miles away. Now he really felt like police.

"Have Rich call me, and I'll get him a copy of the report. And if I were you, I'd consider sleeping somewhere else tonight."

Vinnie slumped as he shut the door behind himself. Everything was fucked. Everything; her case, her life, her head. Worse, she had no idea how to unfuck it. And there was still a teenage girl missing, while another one lay anonymously on the coroner's slab.

Fuck.

Chapter 42

When the landlord finally arrived he brought his husband with him.

"This is David," Rich said, ushering him inside.

"Deej," the other man said, shaking her hand. Rich moved like casual old money while Deej boyishly bounded from place to place. They worked in tandem, taking pictures of the damage—in the living room it was just the window. In the bedroom, however, the headboard was shattered, and the pillows had exploded in a shower of goose down. While Rich documented that, Deej came back to make conversation.

"You doing all right?" he asked. "I can make some coffee. If you have coffee."

"No, I appreciate it, but no."

"We're going to board the windows up and hopefully get somebody out soon to replace them. Do you feel comfortable staying here until then?"

What a question. And the honest answer was she had no fucking idea. If the nephew the cops had picked up with a shotgun really was the shooter, then she was probably fine. She wouldn't be welcome on the Hill, but they were unlikely to send wave after wave of gunmen at her.

She'd briefly met Little Paul at the search, one of dozens. He hadn't been that old, as she recalled—maybe early twenties. A young dumbfuck, willing to listen to the big man of the family bitch about meddling private investigators. Now he was in county lockup and it was pretty clear Keith didn't want to get his hands dirty. They probably wouldn't try it again.

There was still a yawning crevasse in her chest, though, the infinitesimally small but realistic possibility that Indiana had followed her here. That Little Paul had been in the wrong place at the wrong time and looked good for something he hadn't done. And it was that doubt, that possibility, that made Vinnie hesitate.

"We've got a place just north of here; we're in the middle of renovating, but the bedroom and kitchen are done, at least," Deej offered.

Finally, Vinnie shoved down her trepidation. If she was done running, that started now. Even though Deej had kind eyes and wore sincerity like an old band T-shirt, she didn't want to take advantage. She'd already done enough damage to one of his properties. The last thing she wanted to do was spread it around.

"I think I'm good here," Vinnie told him. "You want help bringing up the plywood?"

He accepted, and she cleared her mind ducking out into the cold and manhandling sheets of wood as tall as herself. The boards bit at her hands and set her off balance. It gave her something to concentrate on. Something concrete, to get herself out of her head. Sure, it was more exciting DIY, but that's what retirement was supposed to be for.

She set the board next to the open window frame. Then she started collecting her work. The laptop was still open, windows arranged in tiles. As she hefted it out of the way, she caught Deej glancing toward the screen. He wasn't staring; just curious. And she supposed he was allowed to be, given that one of his husband's properties was now the scene of a related crime.

"That's our yearbook," he said as she closed the lid. She'd had it open in one of her tabs, cross-referencing DMs on the phone to their real-life counterparts, while she waited for DroidCreep to finish decrypting the F4U account.

Curious, she asked, "Our?"

He nodded genially and grabbed the broom. As he scraped shards of glass from the corners and under the furniture, he said, "Yeah; I teach up at the school. Real estate is Rich's thing; I'm just a warm body."

Tipping back the couch, a thought popped into being. The question was out of her mouth before she'd even formed the words. "David . . . do you teach history?"

Squinting but amused, Deej said, "Got it in one. How'd you know?"

"I just talked to Christopher Demers; he mentioned a David in the department," Vinnie said. And then, because she couldn't fucking control herself, she asked, "Hey, can you tell me how absences work up there? Kassadee Swain says she never got a robocall about Avery being out that week."

Brushing glass into a pile at his feet, Deej tipped his head to the side curiously. "That's weird. It's hard to avoid the robocall. We do attendance in homeroom, on our Chromebook. That goes to the front office automatically, and then the computer starts calling. We've had calls go out for kids who were present, just late. It's that fast."

"So somebody had to mark her present, even though she wasn't there."

Deej considered it for a long moment, then nodded. "Yeah. That occasionally happens. You get a sub who doesn't know how the system works, or—say I talk to a kid before homeroom, and then they have to go to the bathroom or whatever. I know they're there, so I go ahead and mark them present, even if they're not in class."

"Any idea who Avery Adair's homeroom teacher is? I'd like to talk to them."

"Mmm, you'd have to check with the office," Deej said apologetically. "We had a couple teachers retire last year, and they had to redistribute the kids."

Well, that wasn't helpful. She offered Deej the dustpan and took over the broom. As she brushed up the glass, she took care to catch every last glittering spark. She didn't want Goofus walking around in bare paws if the floor wasn't safe. And even though she was in the middle of cleaning up the aftermath of getting involved in this case, her questions wouldn't stop coming. "And what happens if a kid gets into a fight? Straight to the principal?"

"Guidance counselor, but yeah." Deej looked up at her. "The dean signs off on the suspension. First offense is usually in-school suspension."

"Who runs that?"

"We all do." Deej shrugged. "There's a schedule, but it's just the teachers."

Vinnie took a step back so Deej could dump the pan into the trash. He still had gold in his hair, the hint of silver at the temples failing to scrub the boyishness from his face. He had an easy smile and interested eyes; he felt like a teacher who was probably close to his students. Like one of the ones who actually gave a shit beyond standardized tests and the student handbook.

Out of pure curiosity, she asked, "Did you grow up here too?

I feel like everybody did. And played on the football team, seriously. Mr. Demers, Sergeant Rosier, Keith Adair . . . Different classes, obviously."

He burst out laughing, an infectious sound that drew Rich's attention from the bedroom. Rich stepped into the doorway, phone to his ear, but black brows lifted curiously. He muted the phone to await an explanation. Deej repeated Vinnie's question, his grin broadening when Rich made a face.

"*Deej* went to State with the *baseball* team," Rich said with the patience of a spouse who's heard a story one too many times. "They don't mix with the *football* team, God forbid."

Putting the broom aside, Deej brushed off his hands and sized up the window. "And Chris didn't grow up here. He's from out of state. Georgia, maybe? Or maybe that's Kris Whitney?"

"Mm, no, Kris is from North Carolina," Rich said. This devolved into a conversation between the two of them. They sorted people they knew into regions, even as Rich continued his discussion with the insurance adjuster on the phone, and Deej started putting up the plywood. Vinnie helped carry the compressor in; it rumbled to a furious start in the living room.

As Deej loaded up the nail gun, he said, "You have that three-o'-clock stare that my students get. Body present; mind? Already gone for the day."

"I guess I do," Vinnie admitted. He wasn't wrong; she needed to talk to Kassadee, to help her understand what Avery was really doing—to reassure her that the news reports weren't giving people the whole picture about her child. There was no chance she'd get anywhere near Keith Adair again; of that, Vinnie was certain.

But even as she held plyboard in place, flinching each time the nail gun went off, she was summoning up the bones, deciding how to throw them down in front of Hannah Candlewood.

If the teen *wasn't* involved, she knew more than she was telling. And next round, Vinnie wasn't going to nod and eat whatever bullshit Hannah fed her.

It had felt wrong to give Hannah a ride to the search, to let her fill in the blanks, hell, to let her lure Tyler away from the water with Avery's phone—and it had been wrong for *a reason*. A lot of reasons, actually. Witnesses needed to be witnesses. They shouldn't be allowed to drive a case. Or to infiltrate it, because nine times out of ten, if somebody ended up dead—somebody they knew did the crime.

As soon as the cottage was boarded up and Goofus was safe inside, Vinnie had some visiting to do. And nobody, she was certain, would be happy to see her.

Chapter 43

Vinnie didn't have to shake the door—knocking hard with her keys on the frame, a pounding sound that would raise the dead. Instead, first, she rang the bell. A blue light came on—a camera taking a look at her, the same way she peered into it. Vinnie heard the scramble from outside, feet thumping down the hall; Hannah was trying to intercept the door before her parents got curious. Her flushed cheeks but pale face told the story when she flung open the door.

"Is it her?" she asked desperately.

The body. Of course. "No. It's not her, but that's not why I'm here. Your dad home? We need to talk."

"No, are you crazy?" Hannah asked, all but twitching out of her skin. Her eyes darted; she even hunched, as if she could make herself small and hide this all away. Unfortunately for Hannah, she wasn't the only one who could see the doorbell cam, and Robin Candlewood walked into the front hall with a brow furrowed.

Polite but confused, he squinted as he tried to place Vinnie. "I know you. You came in for a humane trap."

Hannah had taken on a slightly green hue, and she clutched the bottom banister for support. No doubt she was hoping the floor would open up beneath her, but unfortunately for her, this was the real world. She was going to have to stand there and let this happen.

Vinnie kept her attention on Robin and said, "Yessir, I did. I'm also investigating the disappearance of Avery Adair."

"That has nothing to do with us," Robin said, all warmth turned to frost in a second.

Don't, don't, don't, Hannah's expression screamed.

The bitch of it all was that the kid still seemed genuine. Genuinely afraid, genuinely desperate. Vinnie hadn't really noticed her charisma; before, it snuck up on her. Influenced her. Now she stood there with eyes wide open, and part of her brain still wanted to protect Hannah. But only a part.

"Actually, it does."

The moment Vinnie said it, Hannah's face twisted. She scurried toward her father, huddling close to him.

"Do you have a warrant?" Robin asked, puffing up his chest. He reached for his pocket, then his fingers flickered anxiously—as if he'd been reaching for a phone that he realized too late wasn't there.

Standing her ground, Vinnie shook her head. "No sir, I don't. But it's in Hannah's best interest if you talk to me, before I take my evidence to the police."

Incredulous, Robin said, "Are you *blackmailing* us?"

With a sigh, Vinnie pulled something up on her phone. Something she'd found in Avery's deleted files and saved for this specific moment. With her thumb, she loaded the video and started it. Then she turned it toward the Candlewoods, still clutching together in the hallway.

Hannah's voice echoed down the hall, tinny from the phone's speaker, but still clear in all its ferocity. *I'm so sick of you lying to me!*

Then Avery, her voice in Vinnie's ears for the first time, her voice finally heard during this case, screamed back, *Not everything is about you, Hannah!*

The fight video. The one Red clued her into; the one that definitively proved that Hannah had been lying about her perfect friendship with Avery. The one that the Candlewoods seemed to have successfully scrubbed from the internet. At some point, Avery had downloaded it—everything online lived forever.

On the screen, Avery tried to push past, silent. Hannah grabbed her awkwardly—she was not a girl to the boxing ring born, for sure. Avery had the opportunity to haul off and deck her, but instead, she stepped back, *stepped out of her coat*, leaving it in Hannah's grasp.

Then she ducked around Hannah again, throwing her hands over her head. Just like Red had said, protecting herself from the school, even though it left her open to attack. Hannah shoved the coat at her and then swung a hand wildly.

It connected, the *smack* accompanied by the hoots and laughter of their classmates.

Then, a man's voice rang out, *Enough!* And the camera shook violently before the video went black.

"You told me," Vinnie said, clearing the screen, "that you were *best* friends. That you couldn't think of *anything* unusual that happened before she disappeared. That everything was fine between the two of you, but Hannah, I don't think that video is *fine.*"

Robin put an arm around Hannah's shoulder; his face hardened. "It's not against the law to have a fight in school. We already dealt with this, as a family, so if you'd like to—"

"Mr. Candlewood, I'd like you to understand what's really happening here." Vinnie put her hands on her hips, watching as Hannah's furious, embarrassed face turned a darker shade of scarlet. As tears started to fall; as the girl clutched herself, like she might fall to pieces. All Vinnie could think was, *Good.*

But what she said was, "Hannah hired me to find Avery. She got a message after the girl went missing—and your daughter's smart. She realized that message wasn't from Avery Adair; she even identified who sent it. But the thing is, she lied to me. She told me she thought Tyler Purnell had killed her—"

"What?" Robin exclaimed, then looked incredulously at his child.

"I didn't lie," Hannah sobbed.

Vinnie continued. "Although she didn't know why. The Purnell kid is a POS, but he didn't have anything to do with Avery going missing. Hannah also pointed a finger at Avery's cousin Red and told me that they were dealing drugs together. That wasn't true either. Based on conversations I've had with other people, Hannah *knew* that wasn't true."

"I thought that's what she meant," Hannah insisted.

With a sigh, Vinnie said, "I have her phone, Hannah. I've read her email. I've read her texts. I found her social media. Everything you talked about . . . everything you didn't. And according to the time stamp on that video, you slapped her in the face, and then she went missing."

Rising up, Robin nudged Hannah behind him and started walking toward Vinnie. "I don't know what you're accusing Hannah of, but you need to leave. Now."

Outwardly calm, Vinnie shrugged a little and reached for the doorknob. "I'm happy to. But you have to know that my next stop is the sheriff's office. And speaking as somebody who used to be a cop? Avery's phone is going to indict your daughter.

"The two guys working this case . . . they *don't care*. They don't care *if* it goes down. They don't care *who* goes down for it. The only thing they care about is getting to their pensions and fucking off to Florida when they retire."

Now Robin's temper flared. He shoved past Vinnie and threw open the door. "Get out. Stay out. And stay away from my daughter."

Chapter 44

Hannah threw herself between Robin and Vinnie.

She looked incredibly small; a ring of mascara stained her eyes, but she drove the tears back. Her face was a contrast between scarlet splotches and grey bloodlessness. Words tumbled out of her, reversing and backtracking, looping with a stammer until she got her head straight.

Finally, she took a deep breath and said, "You're right. I lied, but not about the important things! The fight in history was stupid; I was being stupid. She kept ghosting me, and she wouldn't tell me why. Then I kept seeing her alone with Tyler, like close. Really close, and I'm like, What the hell are you doing?"

"Because you were getting back together with him."

"No," Hannah said, then wavered. "Maybe. I don't know. But as soon as he texted me from Avery's phone, I blocked him. Everywhere. I was stupid about him, and it looked like Avery was being stupid about him, and I just wanted to fix it. But instead of fixing it, I made it worse. I slapped her, it was a whole thing, but look at her phone, Vinnie, we were talking *after* that. Look in Guba!"

"Excuse me?"

"Guba," Hannah said desperately. Her eyes darted toward her

father, and then she sighed. It was the sound of surrender; Hannah didn't want to give up her secrets in front of her dad, but she seemed to realize she had no choice. "It looks like a game, but it's actually a messenger. That's where we talk about . . . like . . . personal stuff."

Goddammit, how many apps did one person need? Vinnie had never even heard of this one, and she had always been one of the detectives who understood the internet fairly well. This was yet another reason to miss the evidence geeks. She was too old to keep track of every goddamn app in the world. Patiently, Vinnie said, "Okay, so if you were still—"

Robin cut in. "Hannah, enough."

"I was trying to get her to stay here," Hannah said, swearing with religious conviction. "I begged her not to go with Red. She told me she was running errands with him, and I know what that would usually mean. And like once, offhandedly, she said she had a friend in Ellicott City who owed her money. I put those together the wrong way, okay?"

"What *friend*?" Vinnie asked sharply.

"I don't know! Some guy she met online; she wouldn't tell me about him. Everything was a secret, in the end. Why she was talking to Tyler alone, and who she was talking to online, and how he was going to help her when she graduated, I don't know. I really don't know, Vinnie. But I didn't hurt her! I didn't make her go missing! I left stuff out, but I never *lie* lied to you."

It was perfect teenage logic—the kind that made sense when your brain was still developing, when your whole life was otherwise charmed. Kids, as a whole, walked around with a cranium full of barely set pudding. It allowed them to be fearless in a way adults never could be, but sometimes fear was *good*. It was *necessary*.

The personal fury that had driven Vinnie to this confrontation drained away. Now she just wanted to drag as much of the truth out of Hannah while she could—with a parent there. That evened the playing field, even if they didn't realize it. Without anger, Vinnie said, "Either you lied or you didn't, kid. And you did. A lot. I can't even believe what you just told me."

"Then get ou—" Robin started, then turned when Hannah dashed down the hall abruptly. She came back with her phone, already opening it with her face and baring its innards before coming to stand next to Vinnie. An app with a purple speech bubble opened. Sprites darted across the screen. As they ran, a score scrolled steadily upward. When Hannah flicked the screen, the sprites jumped in unison. Guba really did look like a game until Hannah touched the Load Saved button. Suddenly, a chat transcript appeared, obliterating the game.

"Proof," Hannah said. "Look at the date. I'm Ines August, and Devonica Crush is Avery."

Although Vinnie now knew she couldn't trust body language with this kid, not when it came to lies, she still studied her as she asked, "You knew about Crush Baby?"

Hannah shook her head, something like shame coloring her cheeks. "I just found out today. I would have talked her out of it, if I'd known that's what she was doing. But look."

> **Ines August:** I'm really really really really sorry some more. I'm like crazy psychotic hormonal bitch right now and I don't know why.

> **Devonica Crush:** :P you didn't even leave a mark.

> **Ines August:** I still feel bad.

Devonica Crush: At least Mr. Demers was cool about it, right?

Ines August: I guess.

Thoughts rearranged themselves in Vinnie's head. Timelines, moments, statements—all parts of a machine that sat still and cold until the last, right piece fell into place. That piece knocked away the rust, and the machine roared to life. Suddenly, the case wasn't a mystery. The motion, the purpose, filled her.

It felt like a reckoning. No, an awakening, where everything that used to be a dream was suddenly stark, and clear, and real.

She'd clocked him wrong, the teacher. His soft accent, his soft hands—the way he wore his clothes, his car, his bleached hair and retro glasses. Gaydar existed; queer people in conservative places had relied on their instincts for decades. Centuries, probably. But instincts weren't perfect, and a straight guy who pinged as a twink might have some secret rage in him, especially these days.

Vinnie's thoughts tumbled in quick succession. He was the teacher Kassadee Swain had mentioned by name, the one adult at the school who was especially close to her daughter. He'd been involved in Avery and Hannah's slap fight, the cool teacher, the one who gets you out of trouble . . . And now, Vinnie had to ask Hannah—

"Who's Avery's homeroom teacher?"

"Mr. Demers. Why?"

Son of a bitch. It was *him*. *He'd* erased Hannah and Avery's fight from the school record. *He'd* marked Avery present to throw off the timeline. If Avery thought she was meeting a client and her fucking teacher showed up, she'd recoil just like she did in the McDonald's video. Fuck, fuck, *fuck*!

"I'm keeping your phone."

"Absolutely n—" Robin said, even as Hannah gave it up.

"I'd buy another one, because this one is gonna end up in evidence," Vinnie advised. This way, nobody would have a chance to delete half the contents. Vinnie let herself out. She had to go.

Robin blustered, following her, "That is my property! I'm calling the police myself!"

Vinnie kept walking and said nothing. This time, she had to keep her mouth shut. Even though Hannah followed her to the car, begging for more, Vinnie added nothing. She had a stealth creep history teacher to confront, and she didn't need a kid getting in the way. Once behind the wheel, she rolled the window down and threw Hannah one tiny bone.

"You helped, okay?" Vinnie told her as she popped it into reverse. "Now stay out of it."

Chapter 45

Looking at Christopher Demers, the history teacher, the text said.

All the pieces were coming together, everything finally pointing in the same direction. If this were last year, she'd know exactly what to do next, but Vinnie didn't have one of the most useful tools in her kit. She couldn't haul Demers into an interrogation room and make him pick apart his own story, minute by minute.

She had to find a way around, and that started with figuring out where he was. She drove past the school, just on the off chance he was there after hours with a club or something. No such luck.

Rather than driving aimlessly, she parked and looked up his address. People didn't realize how much information they left lying around the internet, which was great for cops and investigators . . . pretty good for stalkers and malcontents too. Searching by his school email address, she found Demers' LinkedIn profile, and ta-da, his résumé floated to the top.

Since Rosier had promised to share information, she texted him the address and asked, can you confirm this for the home address?

A long moment passed, then Rosier replied, matches mva records.

Good. She plugged the address into her GPS and headed that way. According to the app, she had a fifteen-minute drive, and that gave her time to think. There were still knots and tangles in her theory; they needed to be carded gently.

If Demers truly was alphatonic, if he was the one who went to meet Avery in Howard County, then *something* happened next; something undefined. Vinnie was certain he was involved, but certainty was not clarity. If it turned out that Avery's favorite teacher was secretly one of her customers, how would that have played out when she realized the truth? Could he have talked her into his car anyway?

After an abrupt turn, Vinnie found herself driving through a dark, dense community of condominiums. The whole place was shrouded by mature pines and firs, the uniform grey buildings dotted in precise increments down a hill until the community terminated in a swimming pool that overlooked the Severn River.

She wasn't sure how a teacher could afford a place like this, but she turned into an alcove, and there was his car. The unmistakable beater sat in front of the most isolated unit. It sat in a narrow court, the trees pushing in around it, on all sides but the face.

Vinnie looped the complex and parked on the street leading toward his unit. She could see his car and his front door, and since she'd slid in behind an SUV, he shouldn't be able to see her back. Not that he would know to look, she hoped.

After all, Camila had thrown Tyler Purnell to the wolves. With a suspect ready-made on the front page, Demers was probably having a pretty good day.

Settling in, Vinnie kept one eye on Demers' front door and the other eye on her phone. Her stomach turned a little as she rewatched the footage she'd recorded from McDonald's. Her hands hadn't been as steady as she'd hoped. It was all a little *Blair Witch*, and no matter how many times she watched it, it ended too soon.

She thumbed backward and forward, searching the footage for his face. If it was Demers, Avery's reaction made sense, but she just couldn't prove it. And there was no telling if a warrant for the rest of the footage was imminent or not; Rosier didn't share *that* much. Besides, he was going to have to construct an entire parallel case before taking it to a judge; that took time.

She wished she could reach into the past and just—flick herself in the ear. Nudge her past self into fast-forwarding past the outside cameras, to catch just three more seconds inside. Just one second, one frame. So close that it felt like wanting it, needing it, badly enough would somehow make it appear. If only.

The air in the car crisped at the edges, slowly turning stale. Vinnie rolled her window down an inch or so before grabbing a notepad from her glove box. She found a tiny golf pencil in her console; that's all she needed to organize her thoughts. She stilled when a woman with a massive dog walked by. The good boy swerved toward the car, but the owner kept on walking.

In short order, Vinnie saw four more breeds (in her head: big, massive, tiny, tiny) but she saw nothing from Demers' address. Not a curtain flick, not a trash removal, not a single light came on to chase away the woods' shadows. Switching back and forth from her notes to her phone to his front door, Vinnie pulled up Demers' résumé again.

He'd been working at Liberty High for three years—the way he'd talked about teaching the Adairs had made it seem much longer. Not a lie, exactly, but massaging the truth didn't look great for him. The only other school he'd worked for was in Pennsylvania, the same place alphatonic listed on his F4U profile. Circumstantial, but significant. There was also a gap. Two years there, one year off.

Pursing her lips, Vinnie wrote missing time on her notepad. A gap like that could mean a couple of things. But what it meant definitively was that Christopher Demers had an entire life in Pennsylvania—all of his family, schooling, all of his jobs, his clubs and associations . . . then a blip and he turns up in tiny little Wills Harbor, Maryland.

One thing Vinnie had learned the hard way was that nobody upped and moved an entire life without a damned good reason. She suspected he'd been fired. Spent that year searching for jobs closer to home. When nobody bit, he widened his job search just a little bit, just enough that he landed two hours south of Philadelphia, in a coastal town most people had never heard of.

The light shifted, lighter shadows chased off the hood of her car, exchanged for longer, darker ones. Even though Demers' car was still outside his house, the house remained dark and still. Where the hell was he? She put her phone aside and rubbed her eyes. This was the worst part of an investigation. Staring at screens, reading records, watching surveillance footage, and yes, sitting in a car for hours. Her coffee was cold and her ass ached from sitting.

Her phone buzzed in her lap; she put her pencil behind her ear as she glanced at the screen. Text from Camila.

I assume you've seen the article.

"Yeah, I saw the article," Vinnie muttered to herself. She could admit she did a shitty thing, showing up at Camila's house, then bailing on her for the case. There was a reason the divorce rate for detectives sat around ninety-five percent most of the time. Then again, Vinnie thought they had a deal. So she focused on that as she hit the talk-to-text button. "Yeah. It was very thorough."

Little dots hovered on the screen for a moment, then resolved into a reply. "You want to talk about it?"

"I don't know what there is to talk about. It's done. It's out there. You did what you did."

"I did my job," Camila replied. Three dots hovered on the screen. Seconds ticked by; the dots disappeared.

Finally, Vinnie followed up with "And I'm busy doing mine, atm."

Then she tossed the phone onto the dashboard. Pulling on her seat belt, she watched as the phone lit up with a reply. Lead weights hung in her chest, the weight pulling her heart toward the earth. Part of her wanted to look at the text, maybe call Camila, maybe have coffee. Another part just wanted to shut it all down. It was stupid to get involved in this case; stupid to think about dating anybody at this point in her life, let alone a reporter. It was all stupid, and so was she.

Glancing into the rearview, Vinnie froze. There was Demers, striding up with two monstrous dogs. He'd come out of nowhere—certainly hadn't left his address from the front door. Could have taken a back door straight into the woods and circled around, but either way, there he was.

Vinnie snatched her phone off the dash and ducked her head. She looked away, darkening the screen. Intensely aware of her surroundings, she listened for his footsteps. For the dogs' panting breath and jingling collars. She hadn't done anything to draw his attention, but there was also no reason for her to be there. It felt like hours, waiting for him to pass and go on his way.

Her screen lit up again just as he passed the driver's-side door. Shit.

Vinnie stole a look over the steering wheel. Demers hadn't

noticed her. His brisk steps never faltered, even when the dogs looped back for attention. They glided on, crossing the street and then heading right toward his front door. He didn't stop. Didn't look back. Didn't even hesitate as he let himself in at home.

The front porch light came on, and Vinnie sagged in relief. Now she had a choice. Keep sitting in the dark, watching a house that now definitely had a man in it . . . or fall back into research to try to connect the dots. She sat there with her hand on the ignition for a long moment, then dropped back against the seat. He probably hadn't made her, she decided. And even if he had, it was a rental. She could get a new one in the morning.

Once she was certain she was alone again, Vinnie finally read Camila's message.

Is that a good thing or a bad thing?

The only answer Vinnie had for her, one that curved her shoulders and left her heart heavier, was a classic, noncommittal, I-can't-make-any-promises-about-anything-babe kind of answer: It just is.

She hit Send, and started to settle back for the night. When the phone lit up again, she almost didn't look. Finally, curiosity gnawing at her brain, she did.

Unknown Number: Would you like to come in, Ms. Taylor?

Chapter 46

She was running out of new ways to say fuck, but fuck!

Fine, she was made. Pressing her tongue into her cheek, she accepted his offer and rolled out of the car.

If he was trying to shame her into leaving, he was shit out of luck. She wanted to get a look inside, and now she had an invitation. Practically an engraved invitation: the door was open before she hit the first step of his front walk. Then the monsters bounded out to greet her.

Friendly monsters, it turned out. They were big hunks of brown-and-black fur, boasting heads the size of early summer watermelons. They didn't jump on her; she was grateful. She had a feeling they might be taller than she was if they were fully unfurled.

Taking her time, she gave each dog a good scritching, taking steps toward the door but baby-talking the whole way. She was surprised these guys hadn't had their tails or their ears docked; that said something good about Demers, actually. Although the way he let them out seemed a little tactical. Dogs were good judges of character. Vinnie remembered a woman from her patrol days who kept a retired K9 unit for just that reason. "If Finch thinks they're hinky, they're hinky," she used to say.

That's what this was, Vinnie was sure of it. The dogs *looked* scary, but they were just a slobbery, cheerful gauntlet to run, to give Demers a chance to size her up. After all, *she* was the one he'd caught sitting outside his house in the dark.

When she finally reached the door, she straightened with a broad smile. "Big babies!"

Demers' smile was fainter. "They don't know a stranger. Please, come in."

It wasn't dark inside, exactly, but the few lights he had burning created a dusky, edge-of-twilight atmosphere. He had a sectional that looked barely used, just a shade under beige. An accent wall foreshortened the space, painted rust to complement the cream everywhere else. Someone had chosen the art carefully; impressionist prints of dusty pale ballerinas and flowers on water melted into the décor.

Rubbing the dog off her hands, Vinnie picked up the scent of vanilla. She traced that to a reed diffuser on an immaculate end table, nestled next to a stack of hardcover books. Her gaydar flared: this didn't feel like the house of a straight man.

She said, "Sorry for creeping up on you. I went by the school on the off chance you were there, then I figured I could try you at home. Nice place. Just you here?"

Demers' gaze fell on the sea of dogs at his feet as he said, "Mom owns it, but she only comes to town for the boat show. The rest of the time, it's just me, Hadrian, and Septimius Severus."

"That's a mouthful."

"I usually call him Sev," Demers said, still reserved with just a hint of twitchy. Most people were, when somebody showed up unexpectedly to ask a bunch of questions.

She said, "I wanted to follow up with you about Avery."

"Of course." Demers dropped his head as if in mourning. He moved gently in his own space, opening a baby gate and corralling the dogs in the kitchen. Then he stood there, awkward and lanky, pushing a hand into his hair like a teenager. He glanced into the kitchen, then back at her. "Would you like something to drink?"

"No, thank you," she said, trying to puzzle him out. He didn't make sense; her gut said he felt good for this, but her brain disagreed. Letting her gaze skim lightly around the room, Vinnie took in Demers' details as they talked. "I know this is delicate, but did you have any idea she was—"

"Absolutely not," Demers said instantly. "If I had known, I would have stepped in. There are resources out there, if she needed money, if she needed food . . . I could have helped her."

"You had the Purnell kid pegged, though," Vinnie said, leading softly.

Demers' jaw hardened. He straightened against the wall, his hand stilling. "When will they arrest him?"

"Probably not as soon as we'd like. They're going to have to look at the evidence I gave them and verify it independently—"

"That you gave them?" Demers asked. His soft features furrowed with curiosity.

Vinnie nodded. "Everything I find for Avery goes right to the department. I didn't want to say it outright at the time, but I was never looking at anybody but this kid. I was just hoping I would find *her*, and not . . . well, this."

"What about the . . . what about the girl they found during the search?"

"Not her; not Avery."

He let out a breath and slumped. He even closed his eyes. A

moment later they opened again, and he hardened as he asked, "Has Tyler said anything about her yet?"

Relief. Anger. It was all there. Vinnie tried to remind herself that Demers had marked Avery present for a week. That the F4U profile matched to his home state. Except Pennsylvania was a big fucking state, and sometimes computers just did weird shit. Failing to mark one kid absent was probably the least of it.

She never used to second-guess herself like this; maybe she should have. How was she different, right now, from those cops who got tunnel vision and put innocent people away? After all, she'd gotten played by a teenager, and a grown-ass reporter, in the same week.

Without moving, Vinnie said, "Not to me, but I'm sure Kerry County is working on him. I just wonder if there's something you're holding on to . . . maybe something you're scared to tell me. When we talked last time—we were on school grounds. You were *Mr. Demers*, the teacher, at work. And you were professional. You didn't want to bad-mouth the kid, and I respect that."

"But . . ." He looked miserable, slumping under an invisible weight.

"But right now, he's around to tell his side of the story, and she's not—do you mind if I take notes?" Vinnie said, flicking her phone open. "I want to make sure somebody's speaking for Avery. So if I'm not wrong, if you *were* holding back . . ."

"I had to separate them," Demers volunteered instantly. "I don't generally . . . my classroom is supposed to be a safe space. I don't assign seats. They don't have to ask to go to the bathroom. They're almost adults, so that's how I treat them. But this semester, Tyler refused to leave her alone. He started showing up early to class so he could sit next to her. He was juvenile. He stole her pencils, tried to grab her papers from her desk," he spat.

This was anger. Real anger, and while she pretended to take notes, Vinnie made sure she was recording. Motives tasted better to juries when they were served with a dollop of audio or video, preferably both. Her head and her instincts could continue their cold war. She was going to keep gathering evidence. She prodded him to keep going, saying, "He was harassing her."

"Harassing her! Exactly! She wanted nothing to do with him, and he couldn't take a hint. In fact, he couldn't even take a direct, explicit command to leave her alone." Demers' oatmeal complexion darkened, along with his eyes.

"You told him to leave her alone?"

Demers dragged a hand down his mouth. "Of course I did. Now that I know why . . . dammit. I should have followed up more. I should have gotten *more* involved."

"You can only do so much," Vinnie told him. "Hey, I don't know what procedure would be. But did you talk to his parents? Or to the principal?"

Rolling his eyes, Demers said, "I tried. But he's on the football team. The sun rises and sets from his ass, as far as they're concerned. I'm sorry. I'm sorry, that's out of line."

"I'll keep that part to myself," Vinnie lied. "So if I ask you, do you think Tyler Purnell could have killed Avery—"

"One hundred percent."

"You sound pretty sure."

Nostrils flaring slightly, Demers lifted his chin. He dripped with disdain, a sneer touching the curve of his lips. "Because guys like that think they own everything, and Avery was the only one who didn't buy into his bullshit."

Even though Demers was bristling to say more, and she was dying to hear it, it wasn't safe to push. Not on his territory, not without a good mental map of what his answers *should* be. So Vinnie turned off her screen and tucked her still-recording phone into her pocket. "I appreciate your honesty. I'll keep that between us."

Relaxing ever so slightly, Demers pushed up his glasses and nodded. "Thanks. It's hard; we're supposed to care, but not too much. How do you measure that?"

"You have my sympathy. I know I couldn't do it." Vinnie opened the door behind herself. Instead of turning her back to him, she stepped backward onto the low porch, stopping beneath the globe light that illuminated it. "One last thing . . . I'm still trying to pinpoint exactly when she went missing. Her mom says the school never called to say she was absent. There's a system for that, right?"

Faint concern crept across Demers' face as he held out an arm to hold open the door. "Yeah. I don't even call names; I just leave the Chromebook out and kids check themselves in. Ms. Swain's sure she didn't get the calls?"

"Yeah, she's positive," Vinnie said. She wanted to see the look in his eyes, to see if he quailed when she got a little closer to the one big thing she was holding against him.

"Sometimes spam blockers blacklist them; we warn parents about it at the beginning of the year," he said, almost questioningly. He gave the impression that he'd run into this before. Truth, or a convenient fact to shore up a lie? Whatever it was, Demers' expression never changed. He didn't smell like flop sweat; his face wasn't flushed. "Can I help with anything else, Ms. Taylor?"

"You've done more than enough. Thank you, Mr. Demers."

She shook his hand (not damp, not clammy), then headed out. She walked lightly back to her car, casual in the cooling air but hyperaware of the space behind her. A man jogged past, earbuds plugged in, gaze tuned out. It put distance between her and Demers, so she barely even marveled at how easily a man could move through the world—the dark, dangerous world, allowed to listen to music without interruption and pay no attention to his surroundings.

But she did marvel when she drove past Demers' condo and for the first time saw a light come on in an upstairs window.

The curtain shifted faintly, as if touched by a ghost.

Chapter 47

Jets roared overhead as Vinnie waited to trade in her rental.

The closest office open after dark was at BWI Thurgood Marshall Airport, and now that she had a bead on Demers, she wanted to make sure he didn't have a bead on her. A fluorescent light flickered anemically in the waiting room. Motor oil and gasoline hung heavy in the air, and a crack in her plastic chair nipped at her ass as she mulled over her conversation with the history teacher.

He'd asked her all the right questions, *Who did they find in the woods? What did Tyler say about her?* He was concerned; he was helpful. Hell, he knew she was talking to the police and he still let himself get angry and unprofessional about Tyler. He even saw the line, the big, white, bright line between caring about a student and caring too much about one.

Frustration crept in with exhaustion as she waited. Slumped with her elbows on her knees, and her phone loosely held in her hands, Vinnie wondered what the fuck she was doing. Twenty dollars from a teenager had landed her here; she couldn't even tell if she was in over her head anymore.

Some cops, the better ones, usually ended like this. They got into their heads and couldn't get out; couldn't trust their instincts anymore and eventually stopped trusting themselves altogether. PTSD rode the rails between insomnia and nightmares, and even perfectly quiet days let the ghosts in. Broken rag-doll bodies, the peculiar smell of someone's insides on the outside, the dry itch of an upper lip desiccated by too much Noxzema to block out the forever perfume of decomposition . . .

Swallowing at the knot in her throat, Vinnie took a deep breath and watched the last few minutes of McDonald's footage again. Maybe if she stared long enough, she'd find something. One more clue. One new lead.

She didn't find it.

It wasn't there; it was never gonna be there. Planes droned on; her chair rumbled and for a brief moment all she wanted was a cigarette and a yearlong nap. She didn't miss smoking; most days, she never thought about it. Sometimes, though, the desire resurrected itself. It hit hard; it gnawed and had to be shoved away with intent. The burn in her lungs, the menthol clarity in her head, those were memories anchored in working, in *solving* cases.

Very deliberately, she took a deep swallow from her bottle of water, then pulled up the website for the National Center for Missing and Exploited Children. Founded in the '80s, NCMEC stood sentinel; it held the records of kids missing in America, going back more than fifty years—but only the cases reported to the FBI, with the parents' permission to post. Avery was on it, and the girl in the box would be on it soon.

It was the best way to search for, or identify, the missing and unknown across jurisdictions. Rosier had mentioned looking in Virginia, Maryland, and Delaware. He hadn't mentioned Pennsylvania, though, the single thread between alphatonic and Demers; the one scrap of evidence she couldn't let go. Into the search form she plugged in white girls, twelve to eighteen years old, five years ago, Lindau, Pennsylvania.

The website chugged, then spit out the response.

Nothing.

God, she was a dog on a dry bone, but she just couldn't stop. With slow thumbs, she navigated back to the search and tried Pennsylvania in general white girls, all time, to broaden the search. Two pages of results, but no one fitting Jane Doe's description. The listings were in reverse chronological order, newest first, oldest last. The older cases echoed like the night, years rolling back, girls who probably, at this point, would never come home. At the bottom of the second page was little Marjorie West, missing since 1938. Her hand-tinted photo was a reminder that some families never stopped looking.

But some families never started.

The Adairs were searching like it was their job, but what if they weren't? Vinnie switched to social media. Hannah Candlewood wasn't the first concerned best friend to get involved, and sometimes the best friend was the *only* one concerned.

Vinnie had had a case her first year as a detective, an unidentified teenage boy, dragged out of Eagle Creek Reservoir. No foul play, but no driver's license either. He needed a name.

Vinnie had tracked him down in a canvass, when she found homemade Missing posters taped to light poles in a nearby neighborhood. The phone number on the pull tabs led to a doe-eyed fourteen-year-old, trying his best to find his buddy. He made the initial ID; the investigation confirmed it.

The body belonged to Jesse Miller, a poor student who liked

breaking into empty houses, and shoplifting. His parents—Dad and stepmom; Mom was out of the picture—had kicked him out of the house for smoking pot. They had been defiant, defending that decision furiously. They had small children together; they didn't want Jesse around them.

It turned Vinnie's stomach. Maybe Jesse wasn't a good kid, but he was still a kid. There should have been more than one kid trying to find him, but it was proof that one was enough.

That's why Vinnie took a shot and searched social media for calls for help. She started with the last year Christopher Demers worked at Moravian High School in Lindau, Pennsylvania. Even though he'd asked the right questions. Even though her hindbrain swore he was a gay man, with no use for a teenage girl, except as her teacher.

#Missing, she typed into the search engines. *#MissingTeen*, *#MissingGirl*. Pictures flashed past her, teens missing for a day, teens who'd gone on impromptu camping trips with their boyfriends and come home to families worried sick. Teens who'd run away long enough to go to a concert; teens who'd never been truly missing, just hiding from one parent with the other. A teen who had gone to meet an unknown online boyfriend only to return, disillusioned but unharmed.

There was yet another. Sixteen, from Saucon Park, Pennsylvania. Ashy-brown hair, hazy-blue eyes. She was missing and fit Avery's general description. Holding her breath, Vinnie dug for Nevaeh Parsons, for a sign that she had come home safe.

Instead, she found the teen chugging beers on Instagram and blowing smoke rings on TikTok. All the way up until the day that her best friend wrote a single, plaintive message on six different platforms, a plea answered with resounding silence:

Please please help find my best friend, Nevaeh Parsons!
Nobody else cares, but I do! #FindNevaehParsons #MissingGirl
#MissingTeen #MissingPerson #Missing

Lightning raced through Vinnie. In one of the pictures, Nevaeh wore a T-shirt with a red-and-gold cougar logo. Exactly one reverse image search later, Vinnie landed on the site for Moravian High School—Home of the Fighting Cougars. Home of Christopher goddamn Demers' first job.

She knew it. She fucking knew it!

Out of her seat, Vinnie threw herself against the counter. She rang the bell a couple of times, trying to catch sight of the clerk.

When he appeared with the keys, she all but snatched them from him. Then she declined the walkaround and hurried into the cavernous parking garage. Everything took too long, getting in the car—a Charger, thank God—and getting it adjusted. Getting her phone linked into the onboard system. But once she did, she hauled ass back to the highway.

An old part of herself awoke when she put her hands on the wheel and hit the gas. The roads still weren't familiar, but the ride was. She wasn't afraid of traffic in this thing; breaking the speed limit felt just fine. Heart pounding, and skin tingling with the rush, she ordered the car to call Rosier. When it connected, she didn't wait for hello.

"I think I found our Jane Doe," she told him, speeding back toward Wills Harbor. "Nevaeh Parsons, sixteen, went to Moravian High School in Lindau, Pennsylvania."

"Where the hell is that?"

"Forty minutes north, right up 83! You gotta catch up to me, because it's Demers. It's fucking Demers. He taught at her school,

She was from the wrong side of the tracks, just like Avery. And get this. Right after she disappeared? He left, in the middle of the school year."

"Wait a minute, wait a minute," Rosier said. Sounded like he was scrambling for something to take notes on. "Where are you getting this?"

Adrenaline burst through her, that special kind that came with breaking a case. It was sweet, old-fashioned; the best kind of drug. Better than nicotine; better than sex. It burned away the pain, the exhaustion, the doubt. It was pure and uncut and she was mainlining it. She glanced at her GPS, trying to decide what next. Back to Demers' place? Back home? Her head spun with too many possibilities.

"My keen-ass investigative skills, Rosier, keep up!"

Chapter 48

Everything rushed from her in a torrent.

"The first place he worked out of college, a girl just like Avery disappears. He's got a gap in his résumé; he ups and moves his entire life to a new town for what? For why? And I'll give you this, he talks a good game, but he's running from something. I dunno how deep into the phone you got yet—"

"Not far."

"Well, take a look at the chat logs for the Crush Baby account. Because one of her regulars convinced her to meet in person, and that regular? From Pennsylvania. I'm telling you, this Parsons kid, she could be Avery's cousin. He has a head start on us. You need to get into his condo before he scrubs it!"

Rosier huffed into the phone. "How am I supposed to get a warrant on that?"

"It's all in the fucking phone, I'm telling you," Vinnie said. "Probable cause galore. Don't tell me you don't have a favorite midnight judge."

A midnight judge was never a hardass; they relished being hauled out of bed at all hours, just because they'd get to sign off on a warrant that could lead to interesting legal places. Vinnie didn't know if the system worked the same in Maryland as it did in Indiana, but it felt like something that would be true everywhere.

Rosier made a noncommittal sound. "Why don't we have breakfast tomorrow morning, and you can walk me through it."

"Because I shook the hornet's nest. He caught me watching his place; he's already ahead of us, and the longer we wait—"

Frustration weighed Rosier's voice. "Vinnie, I can't bust in there without a warrant. Without a *good* warrant. I believe you, but there's a right way to do this. If he's the guy, I don't want to hand his lawyers a case for throwing out our evidence."

Vinnie wanted to throw elbows, to kick the shit out of the air and flail until she collapsed in exhaustion. Rosier was *right*. He was exactly right; there were laws and rules, and good justice was most often slow justice. Cases well considered, approached with clarity and consideration. Maybe she hadn't changed at all.

Actually, she had.

She hadn't quit because all the cops were like Rosier. She'd quit because not enough of them were. She'd quit because she couldn't fix a broken system alone. But she'd never quit giving a shit, and it suddenly occurred to her. She'd spent all this time worrying about how to do this job like a cop without the badge, but *she wasn't a cop.*

She had new rules. Prosecuting this case wasn't the endgame. *She* succeeded when she brought Avery home, one way or the other. She had no power over Demers; she couldn't arrest him, she couldn't make him talk, she couldn't lean on him with a long sentence. She didn't have to ignore her gut because if she turned out to be wrong, *his life wouldn't change.*

Her thoughts shifted, blocks moving into place. They created

new shapes, new patterns to follow. New job, new life, new Vinnie. She breathed deep, like it was the first time.

Then she said, "Okay. I'll let you know what I find out."

And hung up on Rosier. The horse had the water; if he had to
take weeks before he got a sip, that was his problem. Vinnie knew
exactly where she was going now. And now that she was driving
something that didn't leave her quaking like a kid, she got there
faster than expected.

When she pulled up to Demers' condo, she frowned. There
were lights on all over the house, but this time, his car was gone.
She glanced at her dash clock. She'd been gone for an hour and
a half, not a lot of time, but obviously, enough. She didn't try for
stealth this time. She walked to the front door and knocked on
it, keys in hand.

No response. Just silence.

The dogs had barked their way to the door the last time, so she
rang the bell to see if she got a different result. Again, nothing.
If Demers had cleared out minutes after she departed, he could
be anywhere by now. Baltimore, D.C., Delaware, Virginia—or
Pennsylvania, home sweet home.

Experimentally, she tried the door. Locked.

Well, it was dark as hell out here, fir trees pressing in at all
sides, and streetlights watery and thin to preserve the view of the
night sky. So she rang the bell one more time, then started around
the back. The lights glowed from the inside, still hidden behind
curtains. She doubted anyone could see her—he had no neighbors facing the back or side of his condo. Just trees, cool, light-
swallowing trees, bless them.

Selecting her house key, she ran it along the sealed edge of the glass door. Stowed that, then reached into her pockets for a pair of gloves. She used to carry a blob of latex gloves wherever she went. Now it was just a plain pair of leather Isotoners in case it got too cold. The important part was the pads on the fingertips. Designed so people could still use touchscreens while wearing them, they added just enough friction.

She pressed her hands to the half of the sliding glass door that wasn't supposed to move. Heavy on the *wasn't supposed to*. She dipped her knee and came up, pushing the glass upwards. She felt the pull in the small of her back; teeth gritted, she pushed harder. Finally, a pop. With the rubbery seal broken, she slid the glass to the side.

Before she stepped inside, she listened. No footsteps. No voices. And definitely no dogs. She made out the fridge's hum and nothing else. Another ten seconds, just in case. Then she pushed the curtain aside and stepped in.

The kitchen was almost antiseptically neat and decorated like a Tuscan vineyard. Shades of beige, accents of burgundy, with grapes and wine-bottle motifs on every surface. She wondered what his wine mom would think about Demers' extracurricular activities.

And then she saw it. Tucked in a nook by the washer and dryer: a chest freezer, faintly yellowed with age. Unlike the rest of the appliances, it showed its age. Dents and dings and nicks pocked the body; the red switch on the front flickered erratically.

All but coming out of her skin, Vinnie hurried over to it. Her brain sang in high-pitched nonsense, celebrating her first piece of hard, physical evidence. She took a handful of pictures, then carefully hooked a gloved finger beneath the freezer's lid.

It opened without protest, to reveal nothing inside. It was room temperature, and dry. It was also beaten to hell, with scratches in the thin metal shell, and dark stains on the floor of it. She'd only seen stills from the crime scene, but this freezer was exactly the right size for the body in the woods. Pulse pounding in her ears, Vinnie hated that she couldn't swab the stains. All she could do was take pictures—a lot of them.

After reluctantly closing the freezer lid, she expanded her search to the kitchen. The pantry was full of dry goods: beans and flour, canned vegetables and meal-prep boxes. Based on the fine layer of dust, he wasn't cooking for himself. He didn't have bachelor's kitchen, either, characterized by paper plates, boxes of old takeout, condiments, and invariably, half a bottle of vodka.

He had *nothing*, not a half gallon of milk, not a crust of bread . . . and no dog food. Where was the dog food? And now that she thought about it, where were the dog toys? She didn't see any in the living room as she passed through; none in the basement either. The half bath off the living room was unused: citrus-shaped soaps sat in a pristine dish, embroidered towels centered perfectly on the rack. The floor around the toilet was dusty but clean.

That left the upstairs, lights blazing, but still leading her into the unknown.

The bedroom at the top of the stairs looked like an expensive hotel room. Plush white duvet, delicately stitched with white thistles, matching white pillowcases, and a bedside table with one lamp. The curtains matched the generic seaside art on the walls—stormy blues, beachy tans.

It struck her as odd that the room didn't *smell* like anything. In her experience, bedrooms always had a scent to them. Pleasant or unpleasant, strong or faint, it was always there—the invisible signature of the human who lived and dreamed there. There was no scent here at all, no clothes in the closet either.

She shoved the attic access open and hoisted herself up for a quick look. The attic didn't have a true floor, just bare joists. Pink fiberglass made Vinnie's nose twitch, and she lowered herself to the floor. Her pulse couldn't decide whether to race or not. All the adrenaline she'd had fueling her on the way in had faded.

As she left the first bedroom, she took two steps down a passage that could barely be called a hall. She finally found signs of life in the master bedroom. Her nostrils flared; it smelled musky, male—no designer scents or air freshener to sweeten it. The room was split in two, half commanded by a desk and bookshelves, the other with an unmade bed and dingy sheets.

Travel posters decorated the walls, protected by cheap plastic frames. They were for places she mostly didn't recognize. Carthage. Teotihuacán. Skara Brae. The one that said Pompeii, that one she knew. That meant the rest were probably historical too. Demers definitely had a hard-on for the past, she decided.

Dust left a blank space on the desk where a computer should have been. A black metal frame sprawled behind it—she recognized a monitor rack when she saw one. Papers whispered as she moved, stirred out of place. She riffled through them; they were mostly flyers for historical events. Reenactments of Revolutionary War battles, an announcement for a free lecture series at St. John's College down in Annapolis.

She was about to put the papers aside when she caught sight of handwriting: the big, looping kind boys rarely used. In her head, she'd always mentally called that style Michelle, after one of her cousins. *There's Michelle all over this notebook; Michelle definitely wrote this.* Vinnie pulled that sheet from the pile.

Avery's name at the top of the page stung a little. Evidence of her; proof that she had a life that crossed paths with Demers' but nothing more. She skimmed through a comparison of the suffrage movement to the temperance movement, then flipped the page over. Three sketchy rowhouses decorated the margin, in the same ink as the essay. Otherwise, it was blank. No red pen, no penciled-in comments. It had never been processed or graded. Just kept, like a souvenir.

Captured in a moment of hesitation, Vinnie swallowed at the sour taste that rose in the back of her throat. She didn't want to put it back; if she was right about him, Demers didn't deserve souvenirs. But protecting a scrap of paper wasn't going to find Avery. She forced herself to put it down and turned her attention to the drawers.

They were relatively empty; she fished out some paper clips, a pack of playing cards, and a faintly ominous sticker that read THOSE WHO DON'T KNOW HISTORY ARE DESTINED TO REPEAT IT. On the back, a few smudged and battered Post-its clung together. A different handwriting, narrow and scratchy, in barely visible pencil: cdemers/rp!-1223, cdemers/rp!0173?, redpilledpa/rprp!889. Login and password combinations. She took a picture, even though they were useless without a list of matching websites. Well, mostly useless; she recognized the word *redpill*.

It's what short-dicked assholes online called themselves, the ones that frequented pickup-artist sites and hated women because they could say no. It wouldn't be the first time that an incel had found the motivation online to convert rage into action offline.

Vinnie's face went hot as she recalled Demers' anger over Tyler; the way he talked about him. He hadn't used any incel jargon, but he'd definitely echoed their sentiments. What had sounded vaguely feminist in the moment—*because guys like that think they own everything*—took on a darker tone now. In the redpill hierarchy, Tyler was an alpha male, and Demers? Well, Vinnie had a feeling she wasn't the first person to read him as gay.

There had to be more. Hands trembling slightly with anticipation, she pulled the drawer out to search behind it. *C'mon*, she thought desperately. *One more Post-it, one more login, c'mon, c'mon!* It felt so possible that she dumped the other drawer, too, but found nothing. No alphatonic. Dammit.

With quick, efficient scoops, she returned his belongings to the drawers, and the drawers back into the desk. She wanted to leave as little a trace behind as she could. She was tuned so tight, she felt like she might snap. So far, she'd only found confirmation that Demers was Avery's teacher, that his mommy was his landlord, and he owned a glitchy freezer. All of the online connections, the reach back to Nevaeh Parsons—it wasn't enough, not for a warrant, not for an arrest. It also wasn't enough to point her to a new direction, one that would bring her closer to finding Avery.

Hope flagging, Vinnie opened the closet without fanfare. A bare bulb glared from the ceiling, so bright it chased away the shadows. It was a walk-in, bigger than her kitchen at the cottage. Turtlenecks and slacks swung limply from the rod on one side, but the other side was empty. Something tickled her senses; something off that she couldn't quite place.

Rising onto her toes, Vinnie inspected the tops of the shelves. No dust here. He must have been living out of this room in particular, and now he was in the middle of disappearing—again. Defeated, she sank back on her heels and started to back out. Her body blotted out the light for a moment. That's how she caught sight of it. The carpet in the back corner of the closet, curled up. It rested against the wall instead of lying flush.

It's probably nothing, she thought, before leaning over to pull on the rug. And then she gasped.

THE SIDE OF GODS

Chapter 49

A coil of chain. Leg irons. Blood.

Demers had cut through the subfloor in the closet, down past the plywood, to reveal the joists. There was a bracket bolted into the side of one joist, boasting a thick loop of stainless steel. Chain ran through the loop, heavy, the kind people usually used for large dogs.

Instead of a leash, it terminated in a pair of Smith & Wesson leg irons. Vinnie recognized them instantly. They were identical to the irons used to control inmates when they were transported from lockup to court. The edges bore rusty stains, with matching smears on the bare wood and drywall beneath the carpet. She didn't have a kit to test it, but she was sure it was blood. She could smell it.

"Jesus Christ," Vinnie said. Not because of what she saw but because of what it meant:

Demers had kept someone *alive* in here.

She dug her hands into the rug, rolling it all the way back to the door. Sweat rose on her skin as she stomped the rug down to keep it from rolling. Dust and God knew what else puffed into the air, along with that soft, perfumeish scent touched with copper.

Beneath the carpet, beneath its padding, was more blood;

smears, not spatters. Three connected rectangles with triangles on top; blots made up the windows and doors. Then, a cross—like a grave, and another smear that looked like an attempt to write a word. The monstrous ink ran out after *he*. Help? He did this? It all looked rushed and ragged, tantalizingly close to complete, just like everything else on this case.

Something caught at the edge of Vinnie's thoughts. She stared at the drawing, racking her brain. Was it familiar because it was on the essay? Was that it? It couldn't be it . . . too easy, too direct. This felt like the edge of an epiphany. Vinnie reached out, her fingers tracing the air above the drawing, three rectangles, three rowhouses . . .

Suddenly, the dam broke. The pictures! The pictures from Avery and Hannah's Instagram, the bonfire in the woods in front of three stone rowhouses.

Maybe he'd taken her there, in the beginning. It would definitely be safer to hold her in the middle of nowhere until he was convinced he could control her. The condo he lived in was separate from the other units, but they were still close enough to hear screams. And now that it looked like he was in the middle of leaving, stashing her in a familiar place made a certain amount of sense.

On the other hand, if he planned to kill her, well . . . An isolated ruin would be a great place to get rid of a living victim. It would keep the evidence out of his home, and given what the paper had revealed about Avery, it would even confirm the public's worst thoughts about her. The story wrote itself: sex-working teen found dead at party spot after "date" gone wrong.

Chess pieces moved across the board; one for Avery's side, one for Demers'. Tyler was the only one in the hot seat; nobody had looked Demers' way until now. It would be the perfect escape, the mild, milky history teacher moving on long before the cops ever got to unearthing him in the digital evidence.

Shit, but how to find it? She couldn't text Hannah; *her* phone was in Vinnie's glove box. Fuck it, she chose Rosier and Camila. Attaching a picture of the drawing, she sent it to both with the question, *Where is this?*

Moments later, Camila responded with a link. It led to a website full of abandoned places, to a page titled "Cowes' Mill and Company Town." It wasn't that far from Wills Harbor, just a county over, actually. And there was history to it, all right. The pictures on the website told the tale.

Moldering brick ruins succumbing to trees and brambles— sometimes in daylight, some at night—many in moody black-and-white. Some of the building still stood; it had no windows, just gaping holes and crumbling walls. The inside wore a coat of graffiti and garbage. A lone lawn chair rotted away in the debris, obviously a more recent addition.

In a couple of shots, the ruins revealed three rowhouses standing in the near distance. They were made of stone, and still had rooves. It was impossible to tell if the doors were intact; the windows weren't—but four walls and a roof provided plenty of privacy.

Vinnie had seen places like this before in Indiana. Sometimes they became unofficial town centers for the displaced, or party spots for industrious teenagers. Almost always they were full of syringes and broken glass, squatters with nowhere else to go, and a surprisingly wide variety of wildlife.

And it looked like Vinnie was going exploring in the middle of the night, because she now knew two very important things: Avery hadn't died the day she went missing, and Demers was about to run, again.

In fact, from what Vinnie could infer, the last time something went wrong, he'd calmly packed up a teenager's dismembered body and moved it with him. Actually, she wondered how long he'd kept Nevaeh Parsons with him; the autopsy placed the body's age between sixteen and twenty-four. That gap in his résumé, had she been alive that whole time? Had she been alive long enough to *meet* Avery?

Vinnie brushed those questions aside. Those answers would matter later. Right now, she had to focus on finding Avery before Demers extinguished her. As Vinnie descended the stairs, she fired off pictures to Rosier: the freezer, the chains, the papers, the blood—all of it.

He's on the move, she warned him, escaping outside. He needed a record of what *was*, he needed the tools to build his parallel case. Demers could come back at any time, start shedding evidence before law enforcement had the chance to follow up.

Her phone flashed, message from Rosier. What the hell are you doing?

What does it look like? Finding Avery Adair.

She hopped into the car, then plugged the latitude and longitude into Maps. Soft, green light filled the whole cabin as the dash screen illuminated. The app choked for a minute, then finally decided it knew where it was. Directions spilled out, and she threw it in gear. North again, out of Kerry County.

A text from Rosier popped up on the dash and Vinnie let the car read it for her.

Where are you? I'm coming.

"Then you better hurry up," Vinnie muttered to herself, then dropped him the pin to Cowes' Mill. She couldn't risk waiting for him—she couldn't risk Avery's life. If there was any chance at all to rescue her, she had to try. She'd untied her own hands; warrants, subpoenas, laws, she'd done what she could, but they weren't her problem anymore. Knowing that, feeling it roaring through her—Vinnie drove too fast, and took the curves, and it all suddenly felt right.

At this hour, traffic on the highways had thinned. She raced through the dark, almost breathless when her exit was a tree-lined, three-hundred-sixty-degree loop that spat her into hills and woods, and a darkness so thick the air felt like velvet. The coordinates led to a scenic overlook—mostly, a gravel parking lot just off the road.

When she rolled out of the car, she stole a glance. The moon lit the scene with silver edges, a river flowing peacefully through mostly nude trees. If she'd found this spot last week, it would have been a riot of fall color. Now it was like a phantom, a ghost of itself until spring came.

Vinnie opened her first responder's kit and quickly armed herself with a Maglite flashlight and a pair of handcuffs. She checked her Glock, then the phone. GPS wanted her to walk due north, so she steeled herself and started up the hill. A silent approach was impossible. Boulders and brambles forced her to walk through dead leaves. Each step swished and crackled; answered by other movement in the dark. Hopefully wildlife. *Please be a raccoon*, she thought, her throat tight and mouth bone-dry.

She fought her way up the hill, though she had to stop a couple of times to catch her breath. The punctured lung had long healed, but it was still temperamental. A sharp, constant pressure needled between her ribs. She broke out in a sweat, gathering humidity on her skin that fought against the coolness pressing in from all sides.

That's when something grabbed her ankle.

Chapter 50

She slammed face-first into the undergrowth before she regis-tered what happened.

A root, hidden—she'd stepped right into it and tripped herself. Old pain sparked bright, all along her torso. It was like the alley still lived in her skin. Like it would always live there, an infection without a cure.

When her heart beat, it felt like it was tearing free. Each pound wrenched inside her, and it stole her breath. Her nose twitched at the low, earthy musk of the forest floor. All around her, the forest groaned. It ticked. She heard birds take flight, their wings beating against the wind, but she never saw them.

"Oh, to hell with this," Vinnie said under her breath. Gather-ing herself, she pushed up—then stilled. An arc of light reeled wildly in the distance. A phone or a flashlight. It swung in great loops, then suddenly went dark. There was no guarantee that was Demers or Avery . . . but it was somebody, for sure. Vinnie finally stood but kept it low.

Now she crept her way toward the light. One hand skimmed the ground. Her eyes darted everywhere, sweeping in front of her, beside. A knot in her throat beat time with her pulse. Blood pounded in her ears. Her nostrils flared with each breath. Her body tuned itself, tight and focused. Pain was fuel, a hot spur to drive her forward.

The light swung one more time, then went dark. Vinnie ducked. Now she heard footsteps—but not through the underbrush. They sounded soft, like pressed earth. A path. And moving water. Far enough away that it was a whisper, but she listened until the steps faded to silence. That's when she pushed through the last few feet, to get to the top of the ridge.

Cowes' Mill was more dilapidated than the pictures promised. The main building had mostly tumbled apart since Hannah's last party picture. One brick corner still stood, but the rest was rubble. Soon it would be nothing but a stone imprint in the forest floor. Just a memory, swallowed by willow oaks and ambitious pokeweed. Trying to orient herself, Vinnie kept to a crouch, edging toward the ruins. Black rings dotted the foundation, fire pits that lay cold, at least for tonight.

Vinnie shook out her hands, moving at a crawl, searching for the rowhouses. She didn't know who'd walked away, but she had a guess. Somebody who'd chained a teenager in a walk-in closet was unlikely to let her roam free in the middle of an escape attempt. Time shot past; minutes felt like seconds. It took too long to circle the ruin, too long to finally catch a glimpse of the rowhouses.

They jutted up in the darkness, outlined only because of a single light that flashed on, then off again, in the middle house. Shoving her phone in her pocket, and the Maglite through the loop of her jeans, Vinnie crept that way. There was too much everything to look everywhere at once. She chose to keep her eyes on the path—she knew for certain someone had walked that way.

Coming in low, beneath the gaping window, Vinnie stole a

peek inside. Too dark. Then a scratch, and a spark of light that died instantly. Like a strobe light it lit the room for a millisecond. Another bracket screwed into a wall, a length of chain. Bottles of water, a bag of fast food. And a figure huddled on the floor. A scratch and the flash came again. A lighter at the end of its days.

Vinnie whispered in the dark, pressed against the outside wall. "Avery. Hey, can you hear me?"

Something scrabbled inside. A chain clinked, and a face popped up in the window. Vinnie's heart stuttered to a stop. It was the face on the Missing poster. The face in Hannah's Instagram. The face Vinnie'd been searching for, Avery Adair, alive. Stringy, dirty hair shaped her face; her eyes were wild and wide. "I can hear you! I can—it's me. It's me! Who's out there? Who are you?"

"Shhh, shhh," Vinnie said, backing toward the doorway. "I'm coming in. Are you alone?"

"Yes. Please hurry, please!"

The chain rattled again and when Vinnie pushed the half-rotten door out of the way, she gasped. Avery grabbed her with both hands. Her fingers twisted the skin on Vinnie's arms, and she crashed right into her, face-to-face. Avery's voice trembled with panic, and she nearly dragged Vinnie off her feet. She clung like she was drowning, begging, "Please, please help me, please, he's coming back."

Vinnie caught her hands and squeezed them, tight. The kid was in shock, in fear for her life. "I know. You gotta hold still for me, I'm gonna get those irons off."

Avery burst into tears. She shoved a hand in her mouth, teeth digging into her own knuckles to keep the sound in. Vinnie pulled out her handcuff key—except for supermax situations, the keys were all interchangeable. With a quick twist, Vinnie freed her and Avery collapsed.

Catching her in her arms, Vinnie didn't have time to soothe. No time to feel. It was all ruthless efficiency right now. Emotions could come later, when they were safe. She gave Avery a squeeze, then dipped to look directly in her eyes. "I parked at the overlook. Do you know how to get there from here?"

Teeth chattering, Avery nodded. She was going into shock, medical shock. Even as tears streamed down her face, the shivering overtook her. She wrapped her arms around herself, so small and breakable. She was safe now, and alive, but she would never be the same. The Avery who came home would be another girl for the rest of her life.

But that's what therapists were for. There was no time to think about the enormity of the crime. Vinnie had to get Avery out of there while she was still on her own two feet. Vinnie glanced outside, saw nothing, and then moved. Linking her hand with Avery's, she pulled her out of the stone rowhouse, then stopped. She pointed down the path, then across it. *We're going this way.*

Avery simply nodded. She scrubbed at her face with her sleeve, then dropped into the same crouch Vinnie did. They zipped across the path, venturing into brambles to circle around the ruin. It was too dangerous to walk through in the dark. One light would illuminate the whole place and expose them.

"Over here," Avery said. She pulled Vinnie's hand with her, leading her toward a gentler slope. The kid knew these woods far better than Vinnie ever could, so she followed. It felt like flying, bursting into the thick of the forest. Vinnie's thoughts raced along with her body. They weren't quiet. They couldn't have been quiet if they had tried.

Hope sprang up. They had to be almost there. Branches snatched at their hair as they ran. Vinnie batted at them, numb to the strands wrenched out at the roots. It was pure survival instinct. Neither of them slowed until Avery veered hard. Under her breath, she murmured, "Hurry, hurry, hurry, hurry."

"Where was he going?" Vinnie asked. The answer wasn't important. She just didn't want Avery to lose herself in her head before they reached safety.

"To get the dogs," Avery said as the first baying howl rent the air.

Chapter 51

Sev and Hadrian were big, dumb babies, Vinnie thought.

Or maybe she prayed. She didn't have a particular god in mind. She just needed it to be true. With a firm hand on Avery's shoulder, Vinnie said, "Keep going." She didn't hear the river anymore. Just the dogs. Their keens rolled down the hill. Yelps and husky barks echoed through the forest. It sounded like they were everywhere and getting closer.

A roar broke through their din. Something human and inhuman all at once, screaming Avery's name. Demers had made it back to the rowhouse. Vinnie pushed Avery gently, urging her, "Keep going."

"I'm lost," Avery said, panicked. She stopped dead, absorbing the crash when Vinnie stopped against her. The shock was catching up with Avery. She trembled furiously, her voice quavered. Her skin had turned to chalk, and her hand was clammy in Vinnie's. If she passed out, they were fucked.

Vinnie dragged her to the ground. They huddled against the side of the hill as Vinnie unearthed her phone. The screen came on, blinding. Vinnie cursed, turning the brightness down, the sound off. She still had the coordinates in her phone. Simple, she would pull up the map, zoom in to get oriented and—

"No signal." Avery's voice sounded so young in the dark; so bereft.

Reloading the app, Vinnie cursed under her breath when it refused to connect. The goddamn thing had worked fine on the way here!

Frustrated, Vinnie shoved the phone back in her pocket. She didn't have a lot of choices here. Retrieving her Maglite, Vinnie covered the front with her hand and turned it on.

A red glow surrounded them, high-powered LED light filtered by flesh and blood. Quietly, she told Avery, "I'm going to uncover this. You're going to look around and see if you recognize anything. Then I'm covering it back up again. Got it?"

Avery nodded. An acrid scent clung to her skin, the unmistakable scent of fear. She startled when Vinnie uncovered the flashlight. She popped up, craned around. When Vinnie doused the light, Avery said, "Okay. This way. I think it's this way."

Unfolding from their knot, Vinnie let Avery take the lead. It was a hill, she reasoned, it had a bottom. She knew a road and a river flowed near here. In the daylight, they'd probably be visible—that's how close they were. All they had to do was find one or the other.

Years of search-and-rescue training howled chaotically in Vinnie's head. *When lost in the woods, stay put! Let rescuers find you!*

Except the one-man search party up there with his dogs wasn't looking to save anybody. So they kept moving. Suddenly, a white light filled the woods from above. It was shocking how close to daylight it was; so much lit at once. *That fucker has a poaching lamp*, Vinnie thought. Light spilled across the hillside, bright enough to cast a shadow. Bright enough to reveal them as they ran.

Instantly, the ground exploded. Paws thundered through the underbrush. Untroubled by the terrain, the dogs raced down the hill, running straight for them. They didn't sound like big, dumb babies anymore. They sounded like hounds on the hunt. There was no way to outrun them. No way to hide either.

So Vinnie pulled out her Glock and fired twice into the sky. The pops startled a cry from Avery, but the dogs tumbled, twisting to run away from the noise. Something white-hot buzzed Vinnie's cheek. Fuck! As Vinnie touched her face, she realized Demers had a gun too. He had all the advantages. Higher ground. Light. Everything to lose.

Crack! Another shot from Demers. Vinnie drug Avery to the ground. When Demers raised the lamp, Vinnie searched the hillside. Down a hundred yards or so, there was a dark, flat curve. It was the road, or the water. Either one worked. Shoving the Maglite and her car keys into Avery's hands, Vinnie told her, "Don't stop running until you're safe."

"You're bleeding," Avery warbled.

"I'm fine. It's a black car, parked at the overlook. Get in and get out."

"I can't go alone, I can—"

"If you don't want to die tonight, you have to."

Avery shook her head, tears starting to flow again, but Vinnie nodded at her firmly. Then she pulled away from the kid and started back up the hill. Covering them both, she fired into the air again and scrambled up the slope.

A fire roared beneath her skin, exertion and hormones sparking a blaze at the same time. Her cheek burned, blood sleek down her face. Head down, she charged. She burned away the cold. Spindly branches snatched at her; she slapped them away. As she ran, she fell into a strange Zen place of being completely in a moment, of a moment.

As Vinnie reached the top, Sev and Hadrian rushed her. She fired, scattering them. A thin ribbon of thought unspooled as she shouted toward the light. "Don't make me hurt your dogs!"

Another bullet ripped past in response.

She had nothing. No Kevlar, no helmet, nothing. Just jeans and a leather jacket, and hopefully the universe on her side. He was a black, gangly shape behind the lantern. The light blotted out the forest. Flashes of trees in negative danced before her eyes when she blinked.

Making sure to keep his focus on her, she fired above Demers' head. Then she bolted toward him. The dogs looped in a tighter circle, growing bolder. They had figured out the sound wasn't going to hurt them. Demers took off down the dirt path. Taking literal shots in the dark, he hid behind the poaching lamp's glare. Bullets rang out, a ricochet off the stones, impacts deadened by wood.

It was like chasing the will-o'-the-wisp, a creepy childhood story come to life. Trees twisted, throwing shadows from their clawed branches. There was heavy panting, and pounding footsteps, a bobbing light racing through the night. Vinnie gasped for breath. Her blood beat in her ears and it honest-to-fuck felt like her lungs might come apart.

He knew where he was going. *He* had the advantage. And he had twenty years on her. She was never going to catch him. He was going to slip from her grasp. Flee to another state, find a whole new name. Invent a whole new life. Start the cycle over again with another victim. Avery was free, but what about the next Avery?

Dammit, there wasn't gonna be a next Avery.

Leaning into the pain, Vinnie refused to slow. Gravity helped, putting a feral wildness into her sprint. Skidding in the dirt, she whipped around a bend just as the bobbing light disappeared. Where was he? Where the fuck was he? A blinding red glow lit up the trees. He'd made it to the car! She couldn't outrun a car, not at twenty and not at fifty. So she stopped, planting herself hard. She tried to catch time on a breath. He threw the car into drive and lurched forward. Slow, soft finger on the trigger, and POP! POP POP POP!

In the dark, she couldn't tell where the shots landed. His tires spun in the dirt. Then caught purchase. A plume of dust sprayed everywhere. Throwing up an arm to cover her mouth, Vinnie tried to take position again. She kept her aim low; the goal wasn't to kill him. He just needed to fucking stop.

She got off a single shot before a hundred pounds of solid muscle leapt onto her back.

Chapter 52

The dog snarled against her head.

Spittle spattered her skin. Vinnie threw an arm around the back of her neck. Paws dug into her stomach; the dog shoved his head against her, trying to roll her over. She covered her face at the last second. The dog leapt on her, over her. Its teeth flashed. Growls rolled from its maw.

Coughing, she tried to roll again. The second dog caught up. He bit her shoulder, twice, three times, crushing through the leather and grinding into her flesh.

Suddenly, gravel bit her cheek. Silken dirt filled her nose. It caked in there; every breath was thick and painful. The dog dragged her with ease. She flailed; she might have screamed. After a hard shake, the dog let go. It jounced in front of her, low on its front paws . . .

And damned if it wasn't wagging its tail.

Vinnie couldn't tell Hadrian apart from Sev. All she knew was this one nearly flipped with joy when the other bounded over. They were blurs in the dark. They jumped and tussled with each other, then darted back to Vinnie as she dragged herself out of the dirt. They jounced around her, leaping up, until she fired into the air again.

They cowered, just long enough for her to break away. A red glow appeared again, lighting the woods bloody. She heard Demers' engine. From the sounds of it, he was having trouble. Taking a chance, Vinnie yelled, "Stay!" at the dogs, then took off down the dirt path.

Around a sharp turn, Demers had veered into the ditch. His tires finally caught. The Mini rocketed backward toward Vinnie. She leapt out of the way.

"Just stop!" she yelled, grabbing the door handle. She swung the butt of her gun at the passenger window. Glass cubes fell like rain, then a flash filled the cabin. A crack so loud it hurt. The dumbass was shooting from *inside* the car. Ears ringing, Vinnie ducked low. She tried to open the door again. He hit the gas—the car shot forward.

Tumbling away from the tires, Vinnie scrabbled to her feet. It wasn't a plan. It was pure instinct and drive. Her brain focused on that door handle, that open window. If she could just get in there. If she just got one good jump . . .

Just then, headlamps raced toward them. Plan aborted; Vinnie hauled ass into the trees for protection. She just cleared the road when a black Charger plowed straight into Demers' car. Chrome and glass blasted everywhere. The impact came so swiftly, at such an angle, that the Mini flipped sideward into the ditch.

Demers suddenly appeared, crawling out the passenger window. With the last of her strength, Vinnie dove toward him. Demers fired wild. His final, improbable shot tore through her forearm. She screamed, throat ragged, head pounding. Icy pain bloomed into a blaze.

Somehow she managed to plow into him. They struggled, each trying to land a blow. A jab to the cheek lit up her whole face. It felt like time twisted around her. The sky strobed. She was back in the alley, blue light cascading down the buildings. Strobed again, back in the forest, trees holding up the sky. Something senseless and animal in her rose up. Not again. This would not happen again.

A crack exploded; Demers dropped like lead. He hit the dirt face-first, and Vinnie staggered. Wind whistled around her; then a branch. Another crack! A third!

Avery had armed herself with a branch as big as a baseball bat, and her eyes were wild. She raised the branch again, trembling with rage. She'd earned that rage, but she didn't deserve the trauma that came from killing somebody. Staggering, Vinnie pinned her against the car, gentle. She held her there with her own weight and whispered to her.

"He's down, Avery, you can let go. It's okay. You're okay now."

Avery hesitated. Her gaze was savage, her knuckles white around the branch. Then one by one, she freed her fingers and let the wood fall to the ground. It fell across Demers' body with a *thunk*.

For a few moments, Vinnie held Avery. They stood there in the dark, Avery's desperate breath hot on her collar, and Vinnie soothed her with a low voice. The shock was going to come back, but it was on hold for now. Once Vinnie was certain Avery could stand on her own, she stepped away to deal with Demers.

Awkward with her left hand, she pulled out her cuffs. Right arm tucked tight against her body, Vinnie put a knee low in the small of Demers' back. She checked his pulse—strong and steady. Good. It took some wrangling, but she managed to cuff his wrists to the rear loop in his jeans.

Distant sirens rent the air. It was about damned time; Rosier had managed to catch up and it sounded like he was bringing the whole force and fire department with him. Exhaling, all the strength drained from Vinnie's body. She rolled away from Demers and sprawled against the Charger's back bumper.

Still catching her breath, she looked up. Then she offered her good hand and said, "It's nice to finally meet you, Avery Adair."

Chapter 53

A rm in a sling, Vinnie stood at the one-way mirror.
Interrogation rooms looked pretty much the same all over. Painted cinder blocks, a table bolted to the floor, camera in the ceiling corner . . . they even smelled the same. Old sweat, stale air, and burnt coffee. This one probably smelled like onion rings too. That's the one thing Demers requested when the Howard County detective asked.

Vinnie watched as Detective Choi finished a Snapple, and sarcastically asked Demers, "So you've been living your best life lately, huh?"

That was one way to put it. Rosier had sent her a thirty-page PDF file while she sat in the emergency room, copies of posts Demers had been making online as recently as yesterday. Rosier's IT team had been working through the phone and connected Demers to accounts he'd only accessed on his laptop. It wasn't everything, not by a long shot, but it was enough to turn Vinnie's stomach.

She'd seen men hate women this much before—his thoughts weren't new; they weren't even original. There were late-night lamentations about nice guys finishing last, early-morning screeds about sluts and their body counts. The afternoon rants about teenage hos in particular dripped with venom.

In one post, he fantasized about going "ER" on them—murdering them all in a spree shooting, like Elliot Rodger's 2014 massacre in California. The dates and time stamps proved Demers wrote those posts *at school*. While watching Avery and Hannah; while teaching them, while *responsible* for them.

The IT team had recovered a short story, a post where Demers spelled out his "fantasy" to capture and train up a woman for his own use. *She needs to be ripe and fresh*, he wrote. *I deserve a virgin.* Almost as bad as a beloved high school teacher writing this shit were all the men who replied with enthusiastic thumbs-up . . . or suggestions. There were so many suggestions, layered on top of requests to be included.

Demers wasn't just an incel; he was a slow-burning sociopath seeking fuel online, and hundreds were anxious to give it. Vinnie wasn't surprised to find out that he hated women this much. It was just sobering to see how many men agreed with him.

On the other side of the glass, Demers kept his gaze low, and crowded his mouth with another onion ring, just to keep from talking. He hadn't asked for a lawyer yet, but Vinnie had a feeling it was coming. If his mom could afford a holiday house in Maryland, she no doubt had the cash for a retainer. Choi wasn't pressing him, because the jurisdictional slap fight had already begun.

Howard County claimed Demers because the abduction happened there. Kerry County claimed him because he'd transported the victim *and* held her there. Both were waiting for the FBI to step in because Nevaeh Parsons had disappeared over state lines. They'd already reached out to the Parsons family to get DNA for an official ID.

Vinnie was quietly thrilled that this wasn't her headache. Oh, she had one—the parts of her face that weren't bruised were bandaged. The bullet that grazed her cheek had left a shallow channel behind. The ER docs decided to cover it instead of suture it.

They had been more concerned with her arm initially. It ached like a bitch, even with a dose of fentanyl in her, but it was fine. (And a nice little bonus, she felt no anxiety riding over here with a police, or sitting in this station. It was there, waiting in some fuzzy distance in her mind, but everything pumped into her tonight kept it at bay.)

As for her arm, it was a through-and-through shot, which had miraculously missed both bones and all the major nerves. She had a sling, she had some prescriptions to fill, an appointment with a physical therapist, but she would be fine.

Stepping back from the glass, Vinnie swayed, then sank into a metal chair, its orange upholstered seat rubbed almost smooth with age. She was in no state to drive, and she couldn't have even if she wanted to. The rented Charger was now in police custody. She didn't know if it was running after Avery had used it as a battering ram. A patrol officer had driven Vinnie back to the Howard County Police Station after the hospital. They'd needed her statement.

Avery's statement would wait. The hospital had decided to hold her for observation—but Vinnie had personally called Kassadee to let her know her child was safe; her child was alive. Out of a sense of self-preservation, Vinnie decided to let Kassadee call Keith. No point in reminding him that she existed, just in case.

Now there was a question of getting home. She had no friends here, no family. Rosier was probably up to his ass in red tape, she was on Camila's shit list, and Vinnie didn't feel safe being half-drugged and alone in a car with a cop for the half-hour drive back to the cottage, especially since she lived in the middle of nowhere.

Eh, eventually the narcotics would wear off, and she'd get the rental company to bring her something new.

Eyes drifting closed, Vinnie slept. Little, dark flashes of dreams came, broken by the sounds of a busy office still hard at work around her. Finding herself slumped, she sat up a little straighter and took another sip of coffee. Big mistake. It hit her wrong, and she wheezed, then coughed. Looking for a trash can, she wobbled to her feet.

The cubicle farm created a maze for her. It took a few turns before she found somewhere to throw away the cup. After she dumped it, she turned to reorient herself and found herself face-to-face with Camila. It took Vinnie a second to register that it was her. Her hair was twisted up, and she wore a crimson slash of lipstick. That was the only nod to softness; she wore a sharp, pencil-legged suit and carried her phone and a digital recorder in one hand.

"Hey," Vinnie said, catching her balance.

Camila was a mystery. Her neutral expression hid everything that usually leapt from her brown eyes. "Hey."

"What are you doing here?" Vinnie asked, instantly aware it was a stupid question. Camila was a journalist, she was standing there with a tape recorder, and there was a big story locked in that interrogation room. Vinnie was impressed that Camila'd made it past the front desk, though.

"What do you think?"

Vinnie nodded. "Right."

"Because it's my job," she continued.

Frost brittled between them. On a universal scale, they'd both fucked up—fucked each other up—over their jobs. They weren't soft, silly teenagers anymore. They'd both lived decades before setting eyes on each other, and they'd both chosen career over most everything else.

Their hands fit together like they were made for it, but their minds, their ambitions, didn't melt away because of that. And they'd spent fewer than twenty-four total hours in each other's company. They were allowed to be hurt, but they weren't allowed to feel *betrayed*.

"We just have different jobs," Vinnie said, stating the obvious.

With a slight nod, Camila accepted that, then asked, "Do you want a ride home?"

"I mean . . ."

Without quite turning, Camila started for the front of the building. She'd taken only a few steps when she turned back, her expression expectant. When Vinnie just stood there in her dopey haze, Camila rolled her eyes and said, "Don't forget. You have to feed your cat."

Vinnie nodded and shuffled after her. Was shit complicated? Absolutely, yes, it was. She was part of a story that Camila wanted to keep covering, for certain. But there was no way for her to know if she was part of a relationship Camila wanted to keep having. They could be friends. They could be lovers. Or when this was all over, they could be nothing at all.

But Camila had answered when she called in the middle of the night, and now she was the one taking her home. It felt like *something*.

And for now, that was enough.

Chapter 54

Two days later, instead of flowers or balloons, Vinnie carried a steaming caramel latte into Avery's hospital room.

Kassadee Swain sat there, in a hard plastic chair, pressed against the side of the bed. She fussed over Avery, stroking her lank hair and brushing her knuckles against her cheek. Neither looked like they'd slept, though Avery seemed on the verge of dozing. She kept her face turned toward the window, soaking up the sunlight.

As soon as Vinnie knocked on the door, Kassadee flung herself at Vinnie, a whirlwind of explosive joy and gratitude. Guarding her sling, Vinnie absorbed Kassadee's exuberant hug against her left side. Behind Kassadee's back, Vinnie held the cup aloft to keep from bathing them both in scalding caffeine.

It was uncomfortable for a lot of reasons; there wasn't a lot of hugging in Vinnie's life, and Kassadee's wide-open vulnerability made her squirm. However, breaking away felt like it would be a dick move, so Vinnie leaned in until Kassadee let go. Her perfume smelled like Creamsicles.

After the embrace, Vinnie stepped back and took a quick look around. "Where's Paisley?"

Avery tended a wry smile. "At the baby daddy's."

"You hush," Kassadee said affectionately. She gestured at her chair beside the bed, urging Vinnie to take it.

Against the sheets, Avery looked pale. Whatever rest she'd managed to get in the hospital wouldn't be enough to erase almost a month of captivity. There was a haunting in her eyes, and a sort of soft trembling in her hands. She didn't look thin, but she didn't look well. Vinnie wasn't even sure she'd had a chance to shower.

Setting the coffee on Avery's tray table, Vinnie said, "I heard this was your favorite."

"Thanks," Avery said softly, but made no move to pick it up.

"Do you want me to get you some ice for it, baby?" Kassadee asked.

Avery sank back into her pillows and nodded. Her voice sounded tiny, almost childlike, when she said, "Thank you, Mommy." Then she waited for her mother to clear the door before looking at Vinnie. Shadows clung to her and pulled her voice into steady depths. "I don't know what I'm supposed to say to you. You saved my life."

"I—" Vinnie started.

Avery kept talking. "But you ruined it too. I hear all my shit is in the newspaper. Thanks for that."

A guilty weight wrapped itself around Vinnie's heart. She took Kassadee's empty chair and pulled a hand down her face. Everything Avery said was true. Vinnie sat uncomfortably, probably quiet for too long. She had excuses, explanations, but what good were they? Telling Avery *how* every inch of her personal life had become oil for the true-crime machine didn't change the fact that it *had*.

Vinnie offered what she could. "I'm so sorry, Avery. I should have protected you better."

"You probably wanna know what happened," Avery said, instantly sharp.

"Only if you want to tell me."

Avery picked up the coffee cup with both hands. Holding it just under her chin, she stared past Vinnie and said, "I was trying to get to ten thousand. So I could get a car and a place of my own. And this guy, alphatonic, was so *nice*. Super normal all the time. I mean, I knew he was into crush because obviously. But when we went private, he just wanted to talk. And a lot of times, he'd pay me *not* to go live, and I'm like, Free money? Great."

She sounded distant, like she was reporting from some faraway place contained in her own mind. Her body was out of danger, but her mind would feel like a battlefield for a long, long time. Therapy could help, if that was within her family's means. If not, maybe Victims Assistance could step in and help. Vinnie made a mental note to talk to Kassadee about that later.

For now, Vinnie asked, "You had no idea who he really was?"

Coughing up a mirthless laugh, Avery said, "Nope. I thought he was some rando, like the rest of them. He kept saying, *Let's meet, let's meet*, but I blew him off. And finally, he was like, I'll give you two thousand just to take in some history together. Two *thousand* dollars. And that's around the time Tyler started fucking with me. So like a dumbass I said yes."

"You're not dumb," Vinnie said, sliding a little closer. "You're decent. And you expect other people to be decent too. It's not your fault he wasn't."

Finally, Avery took a sip of the drink. She seemed to melt into it, moments ticking by as machines quietly whirred to take her blood pressure. Then, she took a deep breath and looked vaguely in Vinnie's direction. "I almost didn't go with him. When he showed up, you know. Like, I wanted to throw up . . . I wanted to unalive myself; it was so *embarrassing*. He just comes in, acting all shy, and says, 'Surprise!' I was like, What the fuck?! But he talked me down, right? Like, how it's not really a big deal that it's him. And it would be between us; what he really cared about was me."

Vinnie's frown deepened. "That's not how that works."

"Right? I almost left, but two thousand dollars is so much money. So much money."

"And you thought you knew him," Vinnie said.

With a bitter laugh, Avery looked away. "Yeah, I thought a lot of things. So, anyway, I got in his car—I kind of had to. How else was I getting home? My mom was at work, and I made Red go home. Spend two hundred on a Lyft? Hell no.

"So we drove by the Patapsco Female Institute, but it was closed. It was a school for women, back in the day, when we weren't allowed to go to college. Mr. D thought it would be inspirational for me. We drove past a log cabin, and the Waverly Mansion, and it was starting to get dark. So I asked him to take me home."

"How did he take that?"

"It seemed like fine. He said he had the money back at his place. So I was like, yeah, definitely, let's go get that. I met his dogs, he gave me some lemonade. He was like, I'll get it, I have a safe upstairs. The next thing I know, I'm waking up in a closet with chains on my ankles. He kept giving me lemonade, even with breakfast. One time he made me call the police and tell them I was with family out of state. I was so out of it; I just did what he said."

The enormity of the crime made Vinnie's head hurt. Demers had been planning this abduction for a while, obviously. He didn't have a sudden break from reality and act on impulse. Somehow, he found her online, where she was most vulnerable. He knew he'd have to catch her, and chain her to keep her.

This was no accidental invasion of Avery's private life; he sought it out. Cultivated her. He went to work, acting like the cool teacher, the one who knew what it was like when things got tough . . . then went home and wrote sick Internet fantasies about capturing girls and keeping them in boxes.

He graded papers and planned to mark Avery present, just to get ahead of the police. He moved around that high school, writing up Tyler, covering for Hannah, the whole time knowing what he was going to do to his favorite.

The coffee stopper became a welcome distraction for Avery. She picked it up, flicking it as she spoke. "After the call, he turned into somebody different. He wasn't nice. He was talking all this incel shit, about how girls like me don't notice guys like him. That we don't know our place. And he was gonna teach me, because I had potential. And boy, did he teach me."

Avery shuddered, her gaze trailed toward the window again. It looked out onto a parking lot, carpeted with yellow pine needles. Her eyes stayed fixed there with an all-too-familiar thousand-yard stare. She didn't fill in the details, but she didn't have to. Vinnie knew that stare; she'd sat across from it hundreds of times. There were worse things than murder in the world.

"You want to know the fucked-uppest thing, though? He lectured me about being on Fans4U. It ruins my value, apparently. Makes people think I'm a slut. 'You're lucky I still want you. Most guys wouldn't.' He said that."

"Are you serious?"

"Dead serious."

Carefully, Vinnie asked, "Was it just the two of you, all this time?"

Avery's hazy gaze narrowed; she pressed her lips together. Then, she flicked the coffee stopper off the tray table, and said, "It was just us. He freaked out when his freezer died. He was up all that night, doing—I don't know what he was doing. I heard things, but I don't know what it was, and I don't want to. My mom told me about the body, but I never saw anybody else."

They fell quiet, tension threading the air. Avery didn't owe her anything; it wasn't a companionable conversation. The details of her abduction belonged to her, at least for now. This poor kid was going to have to talk to a forensic interrogator, any number of cops, probably a phalanx of prosecutors, and ultimately a jury. And all that was besides the press and podcast crew clamoring for details.

The terrible thing had happened to Avery, and in some ways, it would never stop happening. She'd probably have to talk about this, off and on, for the rest of her life—whether she ever wanted to or not. It was time to leave her in peace. God knew she wasn't going to get much of it for a while.

It felt weak and almost insulting, but Vinnie repeated, "I'm so sorry, Avery."

"I really fucking hate you," Avery said abruptly, then burst into tears.

Chapter 55

Goofus greeted Vinnie in the driveway.

He held his tail high in the air and yowled at her as if she were some errant teenager out past curfew. For some reason, the fact that he was waiting on her cracked her shell, just a little.

She scooped him up, cuddling him against her good shoulder like a baby. His fur was warm from the sun; his claws sharp as he tried to find his balance. But once he did, he swerved and butted his head against her cheek.

Burying her fingers in his fur, Vinnie bumped back against him. She'd forgotten about the comedown after a big case. It always happened. There were no truly happy endings as a detective, with or without a badge. There could be relief, there could be justice. But a case like this, a case like myriad cases she had worked for decades, always ended in grief. And before now, in total isolation.

She used to go home to an empty apartment. She used to treat her post-case insomnia with cans of Pringles and whatever dumb shit she could find on the internet at three a.m. Neither of those things made it better, but they filled the time and the empty spaces inside her.

Part of her felt foolish for clinging to a stray cat. Burying her face in his fur and letting him nip at her cheek. Goofus purred, alive and warm, a safe harbor in her arms.

He closed his tricky green eyes, and Vinnie felt a shift around her. Things weren't all right, but they could get better. When nightfall came, and she couldn't sleep—she wouldn't be alone in the cottage in the woods.

Most important, the cat wouldn't think she was weak if she cried. He wouldn't point out the ways she could have done better, or help crowd her heart into the smallest spot possible, compress it into coal. He might knock something off the counter, but so what? She was allowed to feel around Goofus.

Sniffling, Vinnie struggled to hold on to him and fish her keys out at the same time. It was a fight to open the door with one arm and full of cat, but she managed.

The cottage still smelled like plywood—the windows were a custom size, Rich Watts had explained. They'd have to be ordered, and that never happened quickly. The boards eclipsed the cottage, throwing shadows in unexpected places, devouring the fullness of the afternoon sun.

With the venue change, Goofus tried to climb her chest to her shoulder—the same shoulder decorated with perfectly round bruises, exactly the size and shape of a dog's teeth.

Bright sparks of new pain trailed beneath Goofus' claws and that was enough. She leaned over awkwardly to let him jump on the couch. Now he was back to being the entitled asshole who'd invited himself to stay . . . and Vinnie smiled, just a little.

He strolled across the couch, knocked the throw pillow onto the floor, then planted himself under one of the intact windows. Light filtered through and revealed the sneaky, smoky tabby pattern in his black fur. A warm, buzzing calm filled Vinnie; it was something like fondness and exasperation, but like any good drug, it took the edge off.

Turning slowly, Vinnie considered a snack, or trying out that soaking tub in the bathroom. A bone-tired ache overcame her just thinking about how much work it would be to make a sandwich one-handed, or to strip off for a soak. She wasn't hungry or grungy enough to work for either, so she dropped onto the couch and retrieved the throw pillow.

Propping her arm on it, she lay her head back and closed her eyes for a moment. When she opened them again, the sun had set. The wind had picked up, pushing cold into the cottage from all eight angles, but especially through the boarded-up windows. For the first time, she made a fire in the fat, blackened stove in the living room.

The kitchen provided a sleeve of crackers, but she couldn't figure out how to use the can-opener one-handed. At least Goofus would get dinner; his cans had a pull-tab and she wasn't above brute force. She served the beast while he screamed at her feet. Then she retrieved her phone, because it was a DoorDash kind of night.

When the screen came on, it revealed a voicemail message waiting for her. She also had new texts, so she checked those first. They were all from Hannah, begging for news about Avery. Vinnie wondered if she'd tried contacting Avery herself. Then she weighed whether to respond.

She was an adult; Hannah was a child, and there never should have been a relationship between them. Vinnie *was* the adult, and that meant acting like one. It felt wrong to ghost a kid who had, in the end, only wanted to find her best friend. Abandoning her crackers, Vinnie texted Hannah and asked, "Are you and your father free for dinner?"

The restaurant called itself a café.

It was stuffed into a strip mall, and horror-movie memorabilia plastered the walls. Though it appeared the café was a spooky fan's dream year-round, they had really splashed out for Halloween. Poly-fil cobwebs hung everywhere; plastic spiders dangled from the ceiling.

An animatronic ghost went off every time the door opened, shouting electronic doom as its red eyes flashed. In the window, flyers for a Pumpkin Spice Crawl covered the spots where Missing posters had recently hung.

To make sure everybody knew he didn't want to be there, Robin Candlewood ordered a Diet Coke and nothing else. He kept his arms folded across his chest. He was so wooden, he practically breathed splinters. Hannah barely raised her head, her fingers fretting against a cup of coffee painted white with cream.

"I called her mom, and she said I shouldn't come to the hospital," Hannah finally said. "And I thought maybe you could see if—"

Vinnie cut her off. "If she doesn't want visitors right now, you should respect that."

"Yeah, but I don't know if that's *Kassadee* talking, or Avery, and I—"

"What she went through is hard. And it's going to keep being hard. She might not want you to see her this way."

Brows wavering, Hannah's expression shifted like the sea. "Are you mad at me?"

"Hannah," her father said. It sounded like a warning; a callback to a conversation Vinnie hadn't been around to hear. She understood his displeasure; she also understood Hannah needed reassurance.

Smoothing her napkin, Vinnie said, "I'm not mad at you. But I also need you to know that we're not friends. We can't *be* friends. It has nothing to do with you as a person. But I'm an adult. I have a responsibility to keep space between us. And honestly, I haven't done a very good job of that."

Robin muttered, "No kidding."

A mercurial flash darkened Hannah's eyes. "I mean, we're not *friends*, but—"

"But that's a whole sentence," Vinnie said. She leaned back when the server brought their plates: a hamburger and thick-cut fries for Hannah, a bowl of soup and a BLT for Vinnie. Robin nursed his drink with a glower.

Hannah frowned at the table. "You wouldn't have found her without me."

"You're absolutely right," Vinnie said. "But if anything comes out of this, I really hope you understand that adults have no business spending time with teenagers. They have experiences you don't; they shouldn't expect you to keep secrets from your family. They shouldn't *help* you do it either.

"I'm glad you hired me. You were looking out for your friend when nobody else was. But I crossed lines I shouldn't have, and you were way more involved than you should have been.

"*I* knew I only had good intentions, but you didn't. And you know what? Mr. Demers fooled a lot of people into thinking he only had good intentions too. You can't tell by looking at us, who's safe and who's not."

Color darkened Hannah's cheeks. "Yeah, I get it, stranger danger. But I'm not a little kid."

"You don't have to be a little kid."

"No, you don't." Robin didn't unfold his arms, but he said that aloud. There was softness in it, love for a baby girl who'd grown up in moments. Worry, anxiety, that was there too—this was a big reminder that, in the end, he couldn't do anything to protect her from the world. Gently, he said, "You think Avery's pretty smart, right?"

"I don't think it; she is."

"Look what happened to her, Hanny-bee. It's not about smart. It's about safe."

Vinnie nodded, gesturing at Robin for Hannah's benefit. Hannah didn't appreciate it, of course. But Vinnie didn't expect her to. It was a good reminder that smart, capable, curious kids were *kids*. She was also keenly aware that her détente with Robin wouldn't last long. She motioned for their vampire waitress— the woman wore a short cape, and fake blood dribbled down her chin.

"Everything okay?" she asked brightly.

"Just fine," Vinnie said, handing off her credit card. "Could I cover this and get a box, please?"

Princess Dracula bounded off, leaving them alone again. Vinnie stared at the side of Hannah's face, the deep-etched hurt in the turndown of her lips, the glossy wetness of her eyes where she caged her angry tears.

Vinnie felt a different kind of guilt in this moment, one that coiled around her throat like a garotte. She'd saved Avery's life, but at the price of her secrets. With Hannah, she'd made her life a hell of a lot less innocent. Studying her tone, Vinnie spoke. "Is there anything you want to ask me before I head out?"

"Yes, is she okay?!" Hannah burst out, pressing her fingers under her eyes. She was trying so hard to hold it all back, and Vinnie didn't know if it was because of her or because of her father. It didn't matter; eventually, that dam would break.

Vinnie patted the table between them. "No. She's not. But don't give up on her. Sooner or later, and I'm gonna guess sooner, she's gonna need a friend. She's gonna need the friend who never gave up, never doubted, never hesitated to break the rules to bring her home. That's always going to be you, Hannah. Always."

Squeaking, Hannah tried to compose herself. "Thank you for that."

Robin said nothing, but he unfolded one arm to wrap around his daughter's shoulder. Within their huddle, he caught Hannah's eye. Said something low that made her laugh in spite of herself. Then he stole one of her fries, crunching into it shamelessly. He distracted Hannah until Vinnie got the check and got out the door. It was just the two of them again, a unit—a family unit. Exactly how it always should have been.

And Goofus was gallant enough to share Vinnie's cold BLT with her by the lit living-room stove.

Chapter 56

The cottage rattled as something crashed into the front door.

Pulse already racing, but head muddled, Vinnie rolled off the couch where she'd dozed off. The wound in her arm screamed bloody murder, and her face throbbed. Joints crystallized, her knees and shoulders protesting as she slowly raised her head to look around. She'd slept through the most recent dose of her pain meds, and everything, fucking *everything*, hurt.

The pounding came again, and this time, with a voice. "Taylor! Taylor, open up!"

Rosier.

Straggling to her feet, Vinnie righted her sling, then opened the front door. "Jesus Christ, are you trying to wake the dead?"

He looked oddly relieved. "Yeah, I guess you could say that. Can I come in?"

Vinnie pushed the door the rest of the way open and stepped out of his way. "Be my guest."

His presence filled the room. Taking off his hat, he looked for somewhere to put it. Finally, he chose the bookshelf. It looked odd, sitting there. Too familiar, because if she were anyone else, he'd never put the hat down at all. It was just protocol, professionalism. So this little breach of it tickled in the hollow of Vinnie's belly.

Closing the door, Vinnie leaned against it, sizing him up. He was acting squirrely, and she didn't like it. "Do you have to arrest me?"

It was a reasonable question. Technically, by the absolute book, she had assaulted Christopher Demers—a charge she could probably beat because it was in Avery's defense. But she'd also committed a shameless B&E at his condo and had unloaded most of her magazine into the air, which was illegal pretty much everywhere. Oh, not to mention letting a teenager drive her rental car . . . who subsequently used it as a battering ram. There were all kinds of charges that she could catch, but Rosier shook his head.

"No, actually, this is a wellness check."

Vinnie literally gaped. Mouth open, catching flies, jaw dropped, the works. Incredulous, she asked, "The fuck?"

"Your mother called the station. She said she hasn't been able to reach you, and she was afraid you'd hurt yourself."

"Are you fucking kidding me?"

"I absolutely am not." Shifting his weight from foot to foot, Rosier met her gaze with his own. It was dark and steady, almost intimate. Strange currents ran between them. The clock ticked, and the air burned to breathe. Then, abruptly, he shut off the power and glanced away. "So I'm glad you're all right."

"I apologize," Vinnie said, the embarrassment creeping in. "Look, if she ever pulls this shit again, feel free to charge her with making a false report. I blocked her because she was driving me crazy, and I was too busy to deal with it."

Relief softened him. Taking a deep breath, he said, "Yeah, I had no way of knowing, so I came myself."

Vinnie *almost* asked, *Were you worried about me?* But she let the question die; she didn't want the answer. She didn't need the answer. It was complicated enough to be friendly with Rosier. Getting any closer than arm's reach away couldn't happen. Wouldn't happen.

First of all, there was the maybe-thing with Camila. But just as important, Rosier was still a cop. A good one—Vinnie was prepared to give him some grace—but part of the system. No matter how easy it was to work with him, how trustworthy he felt in spite of everything, she'd made a choice to step away. The lines had to be drawn, deep, and the walls built high. Whatever this connection was, it needed to stay within certain, very strict, boundaries for her.

Pushing off the door, Vinnie said, "Again, I apologize for my mother. She hasn't taken this move well."

A little humor floated back to the surface. Rosier smiled, and said, "Well, you might want to call her. Or at least unblock her."

"Yeah, I'll get right on that," she said, then nodded toward the kitchen. "You want some coffee to go?"

"No, no, don't." The tilt to Rosier's brows returned. "If anything, I should be making you coffee. How's the arm?"

"Hurts like a bitch," she said, still heading for the kitchen. He could stand there if he wanted to; she needed to take her meds. They lived in the cabinet above the stove, so Goofus didn't get any funny ideas about batting them into the hinterlands. Pouring herself a glass of water, she glanced back at him. "It's fine. I got lucky."

With a sigh, Rosier said, "That reminds me." He reached into his jacket pocket and produced a sheaf of papers. He offered them to her, explaining, "It's the paperwork for incorporating a private detective agency, and for getting your license to practice. I already ran the background check for you. You just need to get finger-printed and get some pictures taken."

Those deep lines shallowed a little. She took the papers, glancing over them and tending the unwelcome warmth that flooded through her. Her face felt hot, but hey, at least it was covered with bruises and bandages. That made it easy to box everything up and file it under *shit I am not going to think about.* Swallowing the knot in her throat, she said, "What makes you think I wanna keep doing this?"

Rosier shook his head. "Want to? Eh. Have to . . . well."

For as little as they knew each other, Rosier sure knew how to hit a target. Vinnie flicked through the papers again. Then, for show, she slapped them on the fridge with a magnet, like it was a picture drawn by a kindergartener. Proof, then, that she appreciated the gesture and yeah . . . evidence that he was right. "We'll see."

Shuffling in place, Rosier hesitated, then picked his hat back up. "All right, well, now that I know you're in one piece, I'll get out of your hair."

"Hold on a second." Vinnie took her pills, the cold water soothing all the way down. Then she retrieved her phone and shook it at him. "You should be here for this." She unblocked Bev, then called her. She didn't care that it was two in the morning. After all, she'd been awake to call in the wellness check, so . . .

The phone rang three times, and Vinnie said, "If she doesn't answer, so help me God . . ."

Then, the line opened. "Vanetta? Is that you?!"

Shaking her head, Vinnie said, "Yes, Mom, of course it's me. Who else would call you from my phone?"

"I don't know! I called the police to check on you!"

"Yeah, about that," Vinnie said with a frown, gesturing at the phone for Rosier's benefit. As if to say, *You see what I mean?* Bev said something that Vinnie couldn't make out, so she asked her, "Are you talking to me?"

When Bev replied, she spoke to Vinnie like she was a child. "No. There's someone here you need to talk to. I'm giving him the phone."

Rosier leaned his head back, his frown matching Vinnie's. Vinnie tried to ward off whatever batshittery this was, calling for her mother several times. But Bev didn't come back. Instead, an old, familiar voice came through the line with a tentative, "Hello?"

As soon as the sound hit, Vinnie sagged, then sat heavily on the edge of the couch. A razor-edged numbness started to crawl her spine as he spoke. If there had been anything in her stomach, it would have turned itself inside out, right there on the floor.

"I got nothing to say, Kyle. Tell my mother I'll call her later."

"Vin, wait!" He sounded urgent, almost panicked.

The nickname struck hard, piercing right through the chest. A mixture of fury and fear rose up in her—he wasn't allowed to call her Vin anymore. They weren't friends. They weren't partners. She was the one who took a beating, and he was the one who watched—she didn't even know what the fuck that made them. But it wasn't good, whatever it was.

Rosier gestured at her, a pretend phone in his hand, asking who it was.

She mouthed, *My old partner*, and his brows flew up. He knew enough of the story—not all of it, but enough—to know that this wasn't a friendly chinwag in the middle of the fucking night.

Nostrils narrowing, Vinnie sucked in a deep breath and said, "Spit it out."

"Blaese's out on appeal and he jumped bail. We don't know where he is. Based on what his cellmates said, he could be coming for you."

The words felt like a slap. Vinnie looked up at Rosier, and she knew he could see her fear. He had solidified, forming himself back into a great wall of cop. He asked softly, prompting her, "How long has he been gone?"

She repeated the question, numb and floating outside of herself. She was supposed to be safe now. All of that was supposed to be over. She barely heard the answer, but it didn't matter. He'd been gone long enough. The nine hours between Wills Harbor and Indianapolis felt like minutes now. She should have kept running. She should have crossed the sea, found a cave, buried herself in a forest . . .

Hanging up, without a thank-you or a goodbye, Vinnie sat in stunned silence.

The phone dangled from her hand, on the verge of slipping from her fingers. What was she going to do? Where the hell was she going to go? Under her skin, she was both detached and panicking, a bad combination.

Then Rosier crouched down in front of her. He dipped his head so he could meet her eye to eye. He reached out, but only to push the phone back into her palm. It was a subtle gesture, a thoughtful one, and it brought Vinnie back to the surface. She was there, fully there, when he said: "I think you need to tell me everything."

Acknowledgments

Writing is solitary, but it's never lonely. I've wanted to write Vinnie's story for more than twenty years. Many people remember the first versions of Vinnie Taylor—Jo, Bethy, Maura, Kathie, and Lucy knew this character by a different name, but they greeted her like an old friend. Wendi Finch, my best friend, knows Vinnie as well as I do; the character developed and solidified as we wrote our stories together.

My dear friend Eden Royce insisted that I contend with this (mostly) final version of the character; my wife, Jayne, has patiently read every single iteration without complaint. My fearless editor, Laura Schreiber, has finally given her a voice.

I owe gratitude to my mother, Sheryl, my aunt Melody, and my Grandma Williams, who told me stories before I could read, and plied me with books after. My favorite summer memory is hot and sticky, hitting every garage sale in a five-mile radius with Grandma, to pick them clean of nickel paperbacks and ten-cent hardcovers.

Then there's Mom Bettis, my mentor who always said, "When you write a book," not "if," and Mrs. Redman, my high school English teacher—a great lover of words who made me one as well. This book wouldn't exist without this extraordinary collection of women; I would not be the writer I am without them, either. They deserve so much more credit than I can give in an author's note.

I owe thanks to Jim McCarthy, my agent of fifteen years, in incomprehensible amounts. His support comes in the shape of snappy comebacks and heartfelt soliloquies, text messages and emails, phone calls and memes. I've given up on myself countless times, but he's never wavered. He's also nudged me for years to finally write a novel for adults, and here it is. I have the courage to try new, hard things because I know Jim has the endless enthusiasm to try them with me.

Thank you so much to Julie Maggio, who answered my questions about boats and Maryland waterways; Lori Boone from the Howard County Police Department Office of Public Affairs, who answered my questions about rank and responsibilities; Robert J. Koester, whose lectures on Lost Person Behavior and search party organization were invaluable during my research; and Dr. Ashley H. McKeown for her help trying to find Ms. Laura Beth Wagster, MA, whose thesis, "Decomposition and the Freeze-Thaw Process in Northwestern Montana: A Preliminary Study," provided me much needed information while drafting. Any and all mistakes that remain in this novel are mine alone.

Finally, I want to thank the 2009 Debs. We all shared our first published novels together, when we were new and knew nothing, but at least we knew enough to stick together. We've all gone in different directions since then, but I still feel the connection every time I hit a publishing first, and I celebrate each time I see one of your books in the wild. How about a reunion in 2029? I'll bring the candy.

About the Author

Saundra Mitchell (she/they) has been a phone psychic, a car salesperson, a denture-deliverer, and a layout waxer. She's dodged trains, endured basic training, and hitchhiked from Montana to California. Mitchell has authored fourteen books for tweens and teens, including Edgar Award nominee *Shadowed Summer* and Indiana Author Award winner and Lambda nominee *All the Things We Do in the Dark*. She's also the editor of four anthologies for teens: *Defy the Dark*, *All Out*, *Out Now*, and *Out There*. *This Side of Gone* is her first novel for adults. She lives in Maryland with her wife, daughter, and two awful, wonderful cats.